I0822305

Wayward Magic

Wayward Magic

A.D. Reece

Font used: Bell MT, Pirata One, UnifrakturCook, Steam Charms
Published by Plush & Regal Press
www.plushandregal.press
1st edition 2026

979-8-9882096-4-5 (Hardcover) 979-8-9882096-7-6 (Paperback)
979-8-9882096-5-2 (Digital)

Book cover designed by Stephanie Hulsebus

for my wife

Thank you for loving me every day it took to write this fairytale and promising to love me every day after

1

Once upon this morning, my life was absolutely perfect. I had simple, achievable goals that were well within my grasp. I had a home, a good job, and enough people to rub elbows with day in and day out that I never truly felt alone. Gods, I've lost my only living parent in what started as an insignificant strike of midnight.

Blinking around myself at the mess, the pink glitter that sticks to my clothes and blasts through holes in the tavern, I try to rack my mind to find where it all went wrong.

Sometime before midnight. Before even the sun began to set. With a man in a wheelchair holding an illegal book.

Definitely that and the insane excuse for a fairy godmother that barged into my small corner of the kingdom.

Once upon this morning, life was exactly how I expected it to be, how it has played out nearly every day for my almost thirty years of existence, and then it all went terribly wrong.

❦

Pulling myself up onto one of the main, exposed beams that hang over the dining area of the tavern, I shimmy away from the ladder and towards the nuisance that is blue webs left by moon spiders. I don't mind the spiders in general. Smaller than my palm with eight legs and too many eyes, they sparkle in a silver sheen that adds to their namesake. Some nights, I lie out on the floor and watch them move from one spot to another like resting stars using our tavern as a temporary home. They make up for the mess they leave by eating otherwise problematic pests, so I don't lecture them as I wave them away from my indoor plants and maneuver from one side of the tavern to the other to wash away their discarded webs before the busiest night of the year.

"Slow down, we have all afternoon," my father chides from behind the bar, wiping out glasses between organizing ingredients for the drink menu this evening.

I tuck the bottle of cleaning solution into a loop on my pants and then sit back with my feet dangling towards the floor; I already swept and mopped and polished this morning. "We have a list of things left to do."

He shakes his head at me, trim, gray beard wobbling with the movement as it makes up for the thinning at his crown. "The same people come every year, Eli. They're the same people who come most evenings. They know what it looks like in here."

"Well, mom would have liked it cleaned up."

The statement hangs in the air between us, lingering like the dust motes catching the day's sun through the open windows. He doesn't immediately argue, giving me time to water the thirsty, leafy plant that lives up here, where it can always turn towards the light filtering in through glass panels in the roof. I stand, walking around the plant and towards the next spider web, hoping I can manage to bat it down without losing my balance and having to admit that my father was right about something in the middle of this little argument.

Sticky, blue and gray pieces of web come back on my rag. They glimmer. It's the most beautiful mess I've had to deal with all day.

I don't know much about my mother beyond the fairytales my father told me growing up. He did his best to raise me, softening her loss with fiction since I was far too young to understand the convoluted lines of fate that led her to leave us early to ferry across to what he describes as a peaceful afterlife. Stories are good. They keep us alive. If anything, I know she would have wanted her home presentable for guests and the counters to be filled with enough food that nobody leaves hungry, so I ignore the ache that has gathered in my shoulders and continue to scrub away at months of accrued dust in less-than-advantageous parts of the tavern.

Awkward air stiffens between us while I finish the current rafter and then crawl back down the ladder, slipping once and tossing my rags to the ground to save myself from the drop. My father is by me in an instant, tripping around tables and sending a chair toppling to its side in his urgent need to settle the ladder. Old hurt flares in his bright eyes from the reminder of all we've lost, and the idea that he still has plenty to lose should I break my neck doing reckless chores.

One more step. Two. I find my way to the floor and let out a sigh. "Thanks. I'm sorry. I-."

He pats my shoulder. "No. No need for that. You were right. I know your birthday is still a few months off, but I wanted to give you this since she means as much to you as she has to me all these years."

With that, he undoes the clasp of the silver chain at his neck and clips it behind my own nape, fingers trembling where they meet the shaved end of my hairline. The heart-shaped locket dangles down at my chest. I know what's inside. A portrait of my mom, the only remaining image of her, and a pressed flower she once sent him in a love letter.

"This is way too much. You don't have to…"

He quiets me with a wave of his hand, taking the ladder before I have a chance to do so myself and walking off to the back of the tavern. "There will come a time when you won't have me there to catch you and I hope she's enough of a reminder that your life is important, it's meant to be filled with good things despite the bad. Besides, I'm supposed to be retired soon, so I'll have plenty of time to work on perfecting my drawing skills until we have a portrait for the living room."

Right. Our agreement. My thirtieth birthday is coming sooner rather than later. With the coming of spring, so, too, will be my maturing as the full owner of this family business. I've spent the best parts of my life here, curled under the counter with a book when I was younger, doing the odd cleaning jobs best saved for nimble fingers for the promise of sweets and a modest allowance, and then learning to deal with customers and make drinks and run our little staff as though my life fully depended on it.

No. More than that. Like this place is my only purpose in life, and its success is the only way to satisfy an ache that is lodged between my fifth and sixth ribs.

My father figured out how to raise me and keep us fed and safe in the years after our loss. It's only right I give back. There's nothing I can do to change the state of the world. I can't make the King take back his execution of a woman I wish I had real memories of rather than the stories my father concocted. I can't make society be kinder to people who are like her, people who carry a little bit of magic in their bones. Nothing will bring her back or change the rampant hatred that has festered in the Kingdom of Briargild for as long as the history books have covered, but we do try to do the best we can with what we have. It wasn't the plan to build a rebellious establishment. It shouldn't be a revolutionary act to welcome everyone despite their race, species, or magical ability. Most of our clientele don't dare to touch the magic living latently in their blood, even within the walls of our tavern, but it's a show of resistance to allow it nonetheless.

I clutch the silver heart in my hand for a moment before tucking it into my shirt to sit as close to my own beating organ. Throat tighter than I realized possible, any response I would have for my father is whisked away by memory and mutual melancholy. The winter solstice isn't when we lost her, but it is when we realize her absence the most, and I don't want to have to spend the best day of the year riddled with the grief we've shared my entire life.

"Is there anything else I can help with?"

Without the ladder he is securely putting away, I won't be dusting the chandeliers or trekking up to the roof to scrub at the tiles people can see from the ground. I need something else to occupy my time. I need to feel busy or I'll drown in emotions I'm trying to ignore.

"Harold should be here before long with the decorations. You can be in charge of getting the place outfitted for the festivities."

Well, there's no point in waiting for that to happen. The satyr that runs the nearest tailor shop regularly runs late. I clap my father on the shoulder, make sure he and our head chef are prepared to carry out our holiday menu, and then hurry out the door into the fading light of day. Briargild meets me halfway. Comprised of sloping streets that lead up towards the castle, I take in the gold that mars most surfaces here. It's in the paint. There are gold flecks in the paved road. It's a color used in every sign, on every doorframe, and winks from every household that has its wash hanging on the line as though the citizens of Briargild are trying their hardest to shine brighter than the falling sun. I've heard rumors that the gold isn't just paint in the noble areas closer to the castle, that it's the real thing, and nobody steals it for fear of the King's guards catching them.

Rumors often aren't true.

They're fun, though.

I'm not beyond eavesdropping or nodding along to whispered conversations about the conspiratorial truths of the kingdom. Some say the reason we've never seen the crown prince in the last thirty years is because he died the same day the last witch was burned. Others say he's a disgrace. An ugly beast, the King cannot present as his heir to the people. I don't really care if any of it is true. It's just easy to talk about those who would never deign to step foot in our less-than-luxurious part of the kingdom.

Already, there are decorations lining the fronts of the nearby buildings. The apartments are crushed together between family-owned businesses ranging from butchers to tea shops to the occasional clothing store that's truly a front for books the crown would rather we not read. Gold streamers dangle from shop windows. There are paper stars hung from bits of twine off of gutters and window frames. Children have taken chalk to the edges of the street, marking it in spats of color that clash and collide in a vehement display of unauthorized decor, I'm sure would never be acceptable in the prim and proper parts of the upper city, but only make this place feel more like home. It's quiet out here, the general populace running errands closer to the border of the middle city or getting their outfits ready or making all the food for tonight's festivities. I don't mind being on my own as I walk further still, glancing at the golden squashes set on every stoop, an old tradition suggesting those who keep the rare vegetable nearby are more likely to have their midnight wish granted.

Wishes run the kingdom.

Doled out by fairy godmothers who work directly for the King, they rarely come true for people around here.

I haven't made one all of my life. Not since my father warned against falling into a trap of wording it wrong or getting something worse than what we already have. Our lives are simple, but they're good, and all I could ever wish for is more time to enjoy exactly what we have, which is beyond the typically scripted kind of wish people make. Most want money, resources, a chance at finding a better career, or a person meant to be more than a friend. It's normal then for the regular crowds to gather at the stroke of midnight to squeeze their eyes tight and hope with all of their hearts that this is the year their wish comes true.

Two streets over, my feet on firm dirt since our taxes never seem to pay for more pavement in these areas while the King's guards are constantly outfitted in more ostentatious outfits, I walk towards the tailor shop to find a line running from the door to the place I need to turn. Some of them are strangers. Most are familiar faces I've seen around the tavern. Many are women with their hair done up in special styles for the holiday. A few are men in hole-ridden clothes and likely stopping in to borrow something a little more festive for the night's parties. I nod to anyone who meets my eyes, gently excusing myself to walk through the door on the promise I'm not cutting the line but instead here for supplies to dress up my father's tavern.

Harold catches sight of me as soon as I get inside the dim shop, his mouth full of pins, so he gives me a nod instead of his typical, hearty hello. It seems this year's late alterations are in full swing. He's too kind to turn anyone away. Every season, he puts up signs to dictate when the last day for orders will be allowed, and every season, he goes against his word, desperately trying to dress the entire lower city on his own. Which is hardly different than my father and me running our tavern into the latest hours of the morning in order to give our clientele a safe space regardless of our own exhaustion or needs.

It's the right thing to do. To give. To help. To hold out a hand and provide someone with enough hope to get them through a few more days while the world continues to be a hard place to live in.

Finished pinning the hem of the young woman standing by his sewing station, he jerks his head towards the sales counter. "Your old man asked for some things, and I put them all in a box there. If you want to get started without me, I should be around in a few hours." I shoot him a sarcastic salute, a gesture we've been giving to each other ever since he gifted me a series on pirates in my early teens.

"Whatever you say, Captain."

Crossing the store, I pass the row of mirrors my father helped Harold install along one wall of the small shop. There are rows of fabric lined up on the other side, creating a backdrop of a textured rainbow against my figure. The yellow section is near my head, highlighting the dark skin at my brow. There are blue cobwebs stuck in my short hair, which I choose to leave before I get it stuck on my fingers and then accidentally ruin any of the gorgeous garments in here. I look terribly out of place with my rugged and worn attire, the patches I've done over and over again on my knees, and the snug fit of my shirt on my shoulders since I've grown out of it a few years ago and refused to spend money on replacing my closet until the articles are scraps of fabric made lewd by my continued use of them.

Harold pats the woman, promising she's done and can leave her payment at the counter before he calls in the next customer. Her crumpled bills are set next to the box I need while the man I fondly see as my uncle by choice, if not blood, lurches to his hooves and grabs a package off of a nearby shelf to hold out to me.

"Did you two plan this?" I demand, knowing full well this is a gift and none of us are fortunate enough to be handing out presents left and right as he and my father seem to be doing today.

He shrugs, the motion rumpling his green flannel around his shoulders. "Your father may have mentioned his intentions. I thought you might want to look good for the occasion, though. You can't be ensnaring beauties with your charms alone, Eli."

"If my charms aren't enough, I don't want to waste my time."

Laughing, he sets the finely wrapped package on top of the very full box and pats it twice. "You know, John worries all the time that he didn't make sure to raise you with a good head, but you have one. I cannot wait to meet the girl who is brave enough to rein you in."

I duck my head at that. My father knows that my inclinations sway to men far more than women, but it's not been a conversation I've felt the need to broadcast to the rest of the kingdom. The King and his men are out to punish people for differences. I don't have magic, but I do have rebellion pumping in my blood every time I let another man make me blush, and that's enough to be thrown in the dungeons if I'm not careful. Besides, it's not like I'm ever going to find someone willing to spend their entire life tied to the tavern with me, so it's a useless conversation anyway.

I'm happy with my occasional midnight trysts. I like my life of endless chores and new menus and hearing the same stories from the same tired customers at the end of each day that looks so much like the day that came before it. Cinderfella's Cup has become a pinnacle of the community in the lower city. If all the legacy I ever carry on is making sure my father's life's work is cared for even without either of us running it, then I'll have surely done enough.

Hoisting the box off the counter, I thank Harold for the gift and the decorations and remind him he is still expected to celebrate with us later if he ever finds a moment away from his work. He chuckles and strokes his beard at that, brows raised towards his small, fuzzy horns as if to challenge me on the ridiculous amount of work I do, too. It's a good moment, and I would linger if the two of us didn't have pressing matters pulling us away.

There's no telling what my father and our head cook have done to my carefully crafted recipe cards without me there to supervise them. The last time I left them alone, they tried to replace all mentions of paprika with orange-tinged salt I'd been saving for a festive fall dish rather than the soup they were supposed to make. Plus, we're running out of daylight as the last few hours of the day tick by. I need to get the tavern outfitted for the festivities before our first customers arrive.

Outside once more, I shimmy past the line and then a few more steps past a centaur with grass stains on her sleeves who wishes me a happy solstice. As the only place in the lower city inclined to outfit all types of people, Harold is going to be more than a little busy. Already, the sun is touching the tops of the buildings, peeking out at the landscape like a small child trying to glimpse presents before they're wrapped and hidden under the festive tree. It blushes pink and turns the gray clouds that have been hanging around all day into marshmallow puffs of streaked orange. For one beautiful moment, the weather is the most interesting part of my world.

I let my gaze stay above the rooftops as a swirl of gentle music falls from an open window, just loud enough to tangle itself with the gentle murmuring of the crowd at my back. Something upbeat and played in halting blows of the unknown wind instrument. A person practicing for their show tonight. I'm nearly lost to its staggered, upbeat tune, my steps following it up the street.

We're here. We're alive. We're making music and spending a holiday together.

Perhaps the world is not a terrible place.

Then, there's a yell.

It's not even a word. Rather, it's a piercing call against the calm of the world. It's a demand that is choked out and left to die like a weed cut off at the base of its stem.

I don't remember choosing to respond. I'm not even conscious of setting down the box, but I did. At least, it's no longer in my hands as I sprint to the edge of the street to see to whoever is in distress.

The man in question is in a wheelchair and surrounded by three larger men on foot. Long hair tousled, one eye covered by a black patch, his knuckles are pale on the wheels of his chair. A brown book has been torn to shreds and is now mere litter on the ground, the ripped pages tugged by the wind.

This isn't my fight. Yet, I can't walk away, either.

Hands curled into fists at my sides, I stride into the tense situation, putting myself between the biggest of the three men and the gentleman in the wheelchair. "Come on, fellas. This isn't how we deal with things out here."

"Yeah? How should we be dealing with things then?"

Upon closer inspection, I am incredibly aware of the fact that the three men are not the usual upper-class bullies. Each has a gold pin secured to his lapel of a rose, the center smoothed out to depict a dragon with a sword piercing its heart. It's the official insignia of Briargild.

I didn't just step into a regular scuffle. No. I've gone and put myself in the view of the guardsmen.

Which is not great.

Most of the community would be able to point them in my general direction if they were forced to find me. I've been serving drinks for over a decade with a wide grin and an affectionate attention to detail. Anyone could find the dark-skinned man who sticks his nose where it doesn't belong.

Obviously, I don't want to draw trouble back to the tavern, especially on a day like today, so I carefully unclench my fists and clear my throat, attempting to take on the calm tone my father uses every time we have a particularly belligerent drunk in our midst. I need to be confident. I need to not show fear. More than anything, I need them to stop what they're doing, so I can go back to my own tasks.

"With our words, good sirs," is my not-so-clever reply.

The one to my left with hair sticking out of his scalp like straw dried in the summer puffs a scoff. "You should step aside before you're an accomplice to crimes. That was a book on magic." As if I don't understand what he's saying, he taps the side of his nose and leans in towards me with a sarcastic, hushed tone. "Which is illegal."

My hands are already fisted at my side again. Briefly, I send a prayer out to whoever may be listening from the skies above to have some of the levelheadedness my father wants to prevail, but I'm warm and irritable and not entirely my father's son. The locket at my throat hangs heavier than it did at first. My mom went down fighting. She wouldn't have stood for the blatant abuse of another being.

So, I won't, either.

"You've already ruined the book. There's no need to hurt him, too. I'm sure the lower city is safe now due to your brave work."

To my right, the guard with a red bandana wrapped around his throat gives a growl of his own arrogant anger. "He's getting away!"

The fight that I was sure was coming arrives more suddenly than I could have anticipated. The man directly in front of me knees me in the stomach, pushing me over to lie in the rumpled pages of the ruined book while I gasp for air that refuses to fill my lungs. Together, the three guards take off after the other man.

I roll onto my back and stare up at the first stars blinking against the fading daylight, early for their own party and twinkling down at me with curious flares of light. A wheeze escapes me. Air crushes itself to my lips, scraping the sides of my throat with icy talons. I suck in another breath anyway. Then, again. Until I can breathe without pain, and then I push myself to a sitting position, glad I could lose a fight far from an audience and on a street likely left alone until after chores begin tomorrow.

I absently grab the nearest piece of aged paper and hold it up to my eyes to see what I just risked my health for. An inked drawing lives there. Not of herbs or magic casting. Not a rune or the speckled act of spells done by fairy godmothers. Instead, staring out at me from its paper prison is the depiction of a dragon.

Cursing under my breath, I toss it back onto the ground and then push to my feet. It wouldn't have mattered to the guards that this book was mere fantasy. Dragons aren't real. They're the things of stories fathers tell their sons when they refuse to settle in for the night. It's enough that magic existed in fiction, and that is something the king wants squashed in all ways possible if they don't directly benefit him or his cruel kingdom.

Dirtier than I was on the way here, I retrieve my box and then start the trek back to the tavern, looking carefully at every crossroad to make sure I don't run into any more guards. It's really a night for fun more than trouble. I should be appreciative that any bruises left by that altercation will be buried in my clothes and not on view for my father to fret over. I, however, rarely appreciate the guards and don't intend to start tonight.

We aren't all born heroes, but I hope, if she's watching from the other side, my mom is proud I haven't bent to the outstretched fingers of tyranny. It doesn't even matter that I didn't know the man in the wheeled chair. I gave him the time to escape, and that's more than anyone else would have done. Reaching into my collar, I pull out the silver heart and let the warm metal rest in my palm for the final steps home.

2

On one hand, I picked the right day to get into a scuffle with the King's guard since my father doesn't ask me what took so long for a simple errand, and I wouldn't have made a reasonable cover story. On the other hand, I can't help glancing out the windows and over my shoulder, even after I make it to the tavern; sure, trouble is padding along behind me like a stray dog in search of a vulnerable meal. I have no regrets, but I do have plenty of concerns.

I hope the man in the wheelchair got away. I hope everyone out on the streets tonight is left alone. I hope. I hope. I really, really hope.

Letting out a steady breath, I return to the box of decorations on the counter as the first customers flit to the tavern. The festivities won't start until well after the moon is in the sky, but the early-comers know to get here early to mark their tables and hold space for the friends they intend to celebrate with at the welcoming strike of midnight. We'll be crammed in here like sardines by the time all the clocks go off together. It's the absolute best night of the year.

My father is busy behind the counter, directing the staff with a comfortable air of authority riddled with jokes in between every instruction. He's met with laughter and teasing back from the cook and our two waitresses. An easy rhythm has taken over the back half of the tavern, the kitchen awake now and in full swing as vegetables are chopped, poultry is sliced, and stocks for soup are poured. Savory scents fill the space, the beginnings of it creeping into the front half of the tavern to mingle with the sprigs of mint my father has been readying as the garnish to the night's signature cocktail. He notes me watching and shoos me to hurry with the decor.

I'm elbow-deep in gold tinsel a moment later. We haven't completely turned our backs on the traditions of the kingdom. Gold, though, is not the only color we incorporate.

While gold tinsel frames the windows we've shut and locked against both the cooling weather and prying eyes, we have stars in other shades. Blue for the fairies that flit in the rafters, where it's safe for them to lounge without fear of being trampled. The winged people are kind enough to supply us with cups and seating for their own purposes. Green for the nymphs that were the first to bless us with their presence, peeking in through the windows after telling my father that the lumber used for the walls was from a very special place, and then making our family business a second home away from their rivers and trees. Red for the centaurs and satyrs, the folks that carry the brunt of physical labor in the kingdom, but were known for their ability to shape fire into beautiful works of blown glass or ornate weaponry before Briargild took that pleasure away. Finally, purple that dangles from the chandeliers and I tack to the walls with the rest of the decor to signify the witches.

Those people like my mother.

Gifted with innate magic that King Anerald Charming never learned to control, and so he chose to exterminate them instead. Witches were the first to fall in the making of Briargild. The last one, supposedly my mother.

And so, my father has thanked Gods I don't believe in every day since losing her that she left him with a son. Men in our lineage wouldn't be affected by the cloying touch of magic. He wouldn't have to face a pyre and loss like that ever again. I touch the locket at my throat and then swallow down the nauseating roll of grief that hasn't faded after almost three decades.

I lost her to discrimination and hatred. To fear. To a man who thinks he's above the empathy and compassion of regular people.

A gentle hand grazes my shoulder. I sniff and look over at familiar faces. Two nymphs, women who have been in my life since I was just able to peek above the bar and ask us to only refer to them as Maple and Oaklyn as their chosen names rather than the basic nomenclature the crown stamped onto their identification paperwork when they crossed the threshold of golden pillars that line the boundaries of Briargild from the forest beyond. Maple pulls me into a hug before I can say anything. She's a summer breeze in the middle of winter, a happy moment tucked within a season of grief.

I sniff again, clear my throat, and force a smile onto my face for their sake as well as my sanity. "It's not a party without a little emotion, right?"

Oaklyn pats my hand, her skin always a little sharp from the brittle bark she refuses to shed. "We miss people the most on the good days."

They insist on helping me then, each taking handfuls of gold confetti to toss around the place. It's on the tables and sparkling on chairs. Most of it ends up on the floor, shimmering in the candles that took me the better part of the afternoon to fully light. It's a mess, a truly delightful mess that I'll be cleaning later and I smile even wider. We're together. Those of us still standing resilient in the current state of the world. We're together, celebrating a holiday, and everything bad gets to wait until tomorrow morning.

Tonight is ours.

"Eli?" My father is beside me, his hands on his hips as he admires the space.

We watch people filter into the tavern, old friends and acquaintances with a few new faces. They admire the new decor and fingers stray to touch the leaves of plants that my father once told me should stay outside, before I proved that they liven the place with their green fronds in all shapes and sizes. Everyone is smiling, chatting, and directing their attention to the waitresses to put in food orders as the night and its festivities begin.

"You should go get ready," he reminds me, pointing to the package I'd laid on the bar when I first got back.

"I can just stay down here and keep helping," I argue, feeling more self-conscious than I would like to admit.

It's not every day I'm showered with heartfelt gifts, and I don't exactly know how to accept it. My life has never been about stepping into the metaphorical center stage. I'm okay living on the edges, handing out drinks and advice from a safe distance away. New clothes will only have more people noticing me than I'm prepared to deal with.

He shakes his head against my argument, steering me behind the bar and towards the stairs that lead to our upper apartments. “Go on. The owner of this place needs to look his absolute best, Eli.” Before I can even try to string together another protest, my feet are on the base of the steps, and he’s continuing on. “It would bring Harold joy. He’s been asking me ceaselessly what styles you favor when you’re not wrapped in rags.”

“For Harold, then,” I tease, taking my package and turning around halfway up to stare down at him, at the man who gave me a solid sense of humor and the dimple to the left of my smile, even though we lack many other physical similarities. “Happy Solstice, Dad. I hope it’s the best one yet.”

“I know it will be.”

With that hanging in the air, he turns to go back to the already growing crowd, and I lock myself behind the door to our home to finally peel away the wrapping on the package. The paper falls to the floor as I unveil the clothing underneath. I’m glad I’m alone for this. My throat is unbearably tight, and I pass a sleeve under my nose to stifle the sniffle that tries to escape me.

This is far too extravagant for a mere tavern keep.

Harold has strayed from the beloved colors of red and gold that signify the kingdom of Briargild. Instead, he’s dressing me in silver and green. Not the emerald shade of riches I’ll never see in this line of business. This is the green of forests stretching out in spring. An abrupt juxtaposition to everything I’ve seen and known growing up, it’s a color combination daring me to be only myself in this treacherous world.

I bite back a happy cry at the embroidery done on the pocket of the green vest. My initials curl together in a beautiful script within a square of silver leaves.

Donning dark pants and the gray, long-sleeved undershirt threaded with silver striping, I put the vest on top and button myself into the softest garments I’ve ever owned. Once I’m tucked and buttoned and I’ve wiped sweaty palms on a wash rag rather than my pants like I normally would, I take a moment to stare at myself in the sliver of a mirror we keep beside the bathroom.

I look…well, the most I've ever felt like myself.

Rolling the sleeves back to my elbows, I stare at the person in the mirror. My hair is still shaved close to my scalp, the curly mess of it too much to deal with when I already have plenty of other responsibilities. Dark skin. Darker eyes, twin orbs of unrelenting curiosity. I clutch the silver locket and give it a gentle squeeze. I have my mother's eyes, her wide nose, the strong jut of her chin.

This is the man my father sees. It's who Harold claps on the back and wishes to spoil with reckless abandon, the man without children of his own, and insisting I'm better than anything he could have made anyway. For the first time in twenty-nine years, I look like I have figured out how to deal with life, and I'm so incredibly excited to embrace everything that is to come.

Love stories are beautiful, but I don't think that's where my own path belongs. My heart is already taken by the tavern. It is full from taking care of my community and offering resilience in the face of consequences. I am decidedly happy right here.

Settling into that fact, I rush downstairs as giddy as a kid and grab a tray of drinks before anyone can slow me down. The party has started. It's time to jump right in.

Chaos has overtaken the last fifteen minutes of my life as the midnight hour slips closer to the present moment. We're far beyond standard capacities for the tavern with all manner of magical folk filling the place from wall to glitter-studded wall. Sweat cakes the back of my neck as I elbow through the crowd and weave between furred hindquarters to hand out more glasses of the sparkling blue tonic to every reaching hand.

This is our tradition. I double-check the curtains are tightly drawn to obscure the crowd as more orders are shouted for, and the rest of the people without drinks hurry to get them for the celebratory sip at the strike of twelve.

Small bits of magic are adding to the warmth and chaos of the space. To my right, a farmer snaps his fingers and extinguishes the flame of the candle on the table to his company's surprise. Somewhere in the center of the room, there's a group of satyrs playing wind instruments with a player who has magicked several pipes to play all on their own while he directs them. Cards are tossed expertly at a table in the back, and one could argue that the woman dealing is crafty with a sleight of hand technique, but I'm convinced she's making them disappear and reappear at will, her thin fingers moving too quickly to tell if she's drawing invisible runes in the air or simply being flashy for the crowd.

Witches are not a common occurrence. If they still exist, even in hiding, it makes sense one would find a safe seat here for the night.

Not that I'm making any accusations.

All in all, it's nice to see people relaxed enough to let their secrets seep into the friendly atmosphere.

Right now, just for tonight, it's safe to be exactly as we are.

The seconds are scurrying by even faster as though time itself is also giddy to announce midnight. I pass out drinks as quickly as possible to snatching hands and clawed fingers and the occasional paw from laborers who, like me, will never know the ornate inside of the castle. This, though, seems like a plenty good party. We have no needs and the best company. What we lack in riches and freedoms the rest of the year, we forget on the winter solstice in favor of relishing in this precious moment together.

Gathering my last orders at the bar, I delve back into the ruckus and revelry as a loud clearing of a throat, accompanied by the tapping of fork tines on glasses, tears through the space. "We've only a couple minutes left, folks. I wanted to say a little something if you'll give me your time and lend me your ears."

Oh. Oh no. My father is always one for speeches. He usually keeps to only doing them once a year, deliberately on my birthday. I duck my head as people politely clap and then loudly encourage him to go for it. It's seconds later than he has every single person in the tavern turn to look at me.

Me. In my finest clothes. The man meant to take over the family business.

"I'm proud to share this moment with all of you," my father goes on, "and to announce that this is the last solstice I'll be in charge of providing your pleasantries as my son will be taking over as owner and leader of this fine establishment."

My heart thumps erratically until its beat is the only sound processing in my narrowed experience of the world. Distantly, I note people clapping for me while those closest squeeze my shoulder and cheer boisterous syllables I can't seem to comprehend. I knew this was a real goal I was working towards, but I had honestly expected my father to be more reticent in giving me full control of the tavern. Sparking heat ignites behind my eyes. It alights on my shoulders and shivers down to my toes until I am too warm and confined and…

Happy.

Far happier than I've ever been, I think.

It's quickly accompanied by mild terror at failing now that he has openly announced me as his successor of this place.

Pride. Creeping confidence. My life is unfolding as I always imagined it would, and I can't possibly see it going wrong.

Coming out of my shocked stupor, I raise one of the glasses off my tray to toast my father as he leads a cheer in my honor. I thank those near me, nearly glowing with the open praise and excitement from the community that has watched me grow from a nervous child constantly dropping things and cleaning messes to the man in charge of fixing problems all on his own.

This is truly my night.

And so, midnight arrives.

Surrounded by those I care about, those I've served as long as I've been alive, and those I hope to see well into my life as I turn gray and jovial like my father, we hold our sparkling, blue drinks together as the clocks begin to chime. Midnight is marked by every clock in every noble household. It rings out from the clock towers spread through the main parts of the kingdom that serve as the undeniable line marking the different tiers of upper, middle, and lower cities. The tiny noises strike together to create a bodiless scream. Everyone in the tavern shifts and then freezes, the lot of us standing just a bit taller together. Time is passing, and it demands we listen.

Somewhere in the center of Briargild, noblemen and gentlewomen are parading around rooms filled with more expensive artifacts than anything I'll ever see or dare to hope to own. They'll be dancing with each other when not working to ensconce one another in political schemes that those of us out here could never be bothered to try to understand. Those less fortunate stand out under the full moon with melted nubs of candles in cracked teacups in order to give their wishes the freedom of open air and a better chance of being graced by an answer. Winter solstice is for everyone, regardless of age or status, a communal holiday marking the longest night of the year as well as a true chance for change. It's commonly believed that whispering a wish at the right moment with pure intent will spark the interest of a fairy godmother. Birthday wishes pale in comparison to this special hour, the hopeful and hopeless drawn in equal groupings to this grand event as they cast their chances into the dark fold of Fate.

And for those who don't believe?

They're here in Cinderfella's Cup already tossing back the bubbly, blue tonic and demanding another round with raucous laughter. It's not always for one's benefit to rely on wishes. Instead, we hoist our cocktails to the roof and let out a cheer certainly heard beyond the walls of this joyous place to celebrate the simple truths. We've made it one more year alive. We have one more year to fight. Not everybody is a soldier, but to live and to stay proud of one's heritage has become as revolutionary as the rumored assassination attempts on the crown prince as of late.

The tolling of the clocks fades out, but the cheery atmosphere remains. I use my tray to collect glasses from needy hands while the celebrations take on a new volume. Usually, we try to quiet the guests and keep our tavern from being noticed by an odd guard passing by. Tonight isn't for micromanaging the joy and folly of others, though. At this point, everyone should be dropping into the bottom of their glasses and huddling into warm places with the people they care the most about.

Even the guards.

Instead, the festivities draw on past the midnight hour. More rounds are poured. I work alongside the rest of the staff to feed and quench the thirst of our rowdy patrons. All around me, people of every walk of life take to a shared moment of unfettered joy. Peering out, I see satyrs whittling in one corner across from a group of women I believe to be shapeshifters, marked only by their loose clothing and sharpened smiles. A hawk perches on top of one of the chandeliers, seemingly impervious to the smoldering candles, several of which have sputtered out altogether from the late hour. Centaurs huff hearty laughs. A calvacade of dwarves toss small, copper coins to me and shout for faster service, their teasing and prodding probably seeming rude from an outward view, but a small comfort to me. I'd like to think this is what my life will always look like, that I'll always be immersed in the pure chaos of happy moments.

Collecting drink orders and stray glassware alike, I make my way back towards the bar. Cash is pressed into my hands, stuffed into my pockets, and waved frantically as I get near. A young woman I haven't been able to place as a forest nymph or wayward witch for the past three weeks steps into my path and slips money into the front of my shirt.

"You still haven't given me your name," she pouts, proudly standing in my way with mischief, adding an edge to her amber gaze.

The heavy perfume of flowers in the heat washes over me, and I take a shallow breath in order to keep from sneezing. "It'll cost you more than that for such information," I tease back, more than capable of moving through this interaction with her.

She rolls her eyes. She isn't really looking for my name. Every other patron here knows it. My father practically yelled it just before midnight. Besides, the group gathered here is loyal to a fault, but they're liquored up and likely to gossip between themselves. I've overheard several conversations talking about conspiracies of rebels meeting in the woods and two separate mentions of a supposed ball the King is going to throw. If she asked the right questions, she could know my entire life story between gulps of golden beer. Realistically, the tavern keep's son isn't the kind of title people typically yearn after, but it has bought me a popularity I wouldn't have experienced had my father been a farmer or a quiet tradesman. All she really wants is my attention, and I, unfortunately for her, have an entire tavern full of patrons with the same expectation of my time.

"My offer still stands. If you want to meet me at the edge of the forest, I could show you a world you've never imagined."

Women and their promises. I shake my head. This is a dutiful dance I politely move through as I sidestep her and insist that my responsibilities here keep me far too busy for trysts in the woods.

Her bottom lip jutting out, she doesn't stop me. She never does. Rarely do people try to follow up on a soft rejection. I probably could fend her off quicker if I announced that I would much prefer if she had a brother to offer me, but that just seems lewd and likely to cause more of a scene than I ever intend. Instead, we go through this conversation a couple of times a week, and I'll continue to do it until she's found someone else pretty enough to steal her haunting gaze from me.

I make it back around the bar and start mixing drinks only to reunite with the only other person in the establishment, desperately trying to make sure I don't spend my nights alone. "You know, she looks very nice. Are you sure you don't want to give it a try?"

My father tilts his face away from me, but I catch a snippet of his grin as he passes out drinks to the group standing near the bar. "I'm not looking for nice."

"And what was it you're looking for again, Eli?"

"To send you to retirement, old man."

He hums, chuckling at my answer before quieting Harold's guffaw, and then takes up a towel to wipe the outside of a glass before passing the blue mixture to yet another groping hand in need of liquid betterment. "I've given my blessing, but there has to be something more than just this, son." Shoulder brushing mine, he drops his voice low. "What about the fellow over there?"

While I wouldn't normally pay any attention to my father's matchmaking attempts, I can't stop myself from looking up. A hooded man leans against the wall next to the door. He doesn't have a drink in either of his gloved hands. In all honesty, he doesn't look particularly dressed for or interested in being in a tavern, but his gaze, the only noteworthy part of him since he wears a loose mask over the bottom of his face, latches onto mine.

One brown eye. One silver.

My breath freezes in mid-exhale. I fumble the drink I'm pouring, sloshing sticky blue alcohol over my knuckles and the top of the bar. Cursing under my breath, I pull myself together, averting my own eyes before I can forget where I am and what I'm supposed to be doing.

"I've never seen him around before," I offer my father, who has taken my hesitation as a sign that he's finally figured out just who I'm attracted to when it comes to my quiet affairs. "I don't hook up with strangers."

"Not even on the holidays?"

I roll my eyes, making sure most people are turned away from us before giving my retort. "What kind of person are you trying to raise? Harold said you wanted me to have a good head, and I'm smart enough to not chase men in dark clothing out into the night. Isn't that good?"

"You won't tell me who else you've snuck off with. How am I supposed to know any better, Eli?"

The words come out like a whispered reprimand, but there's no fire to them. He's joking with me. We're just joking about my love life as if I'll ever have time for one.

"It's not my place to give out other people's secrets, Dad. Are you going to actually make drinks, or am I supposed to do this all myself? I'm not technically in charge yet."

Huffing a deep laugh, he shoos me away from the bar with my full tray. When I think he's not looking, I do chance a glance back towards the door to see if I can catch another glimpse of the strange man attending our holiday get together, but there's no trace of him. Perhaps he was a friend of someone already deep in their cups here. Maybe he was stood up by a lover or grieving a lost one and trying to stay near people to remind himself that there's more to the world than lost relations. Whatever his story, he's gone now, and I have other priorities besides sorting out unknown men in a tavern that blatantly calls strangers to its painted, red door.

Midnight becomes one, and that hour is pulled long and thin like taffy until it's closer to two when we start to wave off our holiday clientele. I stretch my neck and shoulders and start to move tables back to their regular positions as my father grabs a broom to sweep up anything and everything besides the worn floorboards. The stragglers, tipsy and slow to leave, help me with the chairs in a cheerful reluctance to return to their homes and the eventual routine that tomorrow brings. We fall into the relaxed rhythm that we've repeated most nights for the last decade.

As the last of them trail out, the door is locked to any more stubborn drunkards or curfew-free party goers. It's time to buckle down and get the place clean, and then go collapse with a slice of that pie I saw waiting in the back of the tavern. As such, it's quite a surprise when there's not just a knock, but a thundering pound at the door.

"Sorry, guys. We're truly done for the night. You'll have to see us tomorrow," I call out, knelt behind the bar for a moment to get a particularly sticky situation resolved.

The door must not have latched behind the last people. It pushes open with a resolute squeak as though it already knows that it has betrayed us.

"That's him," a stranger murmurs.

I whip my head up to see what's going on, only to find the plain-clothes guards from the street by Harold's shop standing in the tavern. There's a curse pressed to my tongue, but I don't have a chance to release it before my father rounds the corner and sees that we have company.

"Morning, gents. Sorry to say we're closed. I hope you'll be kind enough to grace us tomorrow," he says, a jovial script he's been perfecting ever since opening the doors here.

The man in the middle, the one who attacked me in the street, never looks at my father. His bright gaze is glued to me. Gesturing for his friends to block the exits, he carefully walks towards me.

I match him step for step, putting myself between him and my father. "Look, whatever you need to talk about, we can do it tomorrow."

I'm desperately trying to cut this off before it becomes an altercation. It's been years since I've thrown myself into a fight that didn't involve me. The last time I was bloodied and bruised for two weeks and had to have my left arm reset in a cast. It was the only time I came home to the full force of my father's worry and following disappointment. He'd threatened to never give me ownership of the tavern if I let it happen again.

And I've been so good.

I've bowed my head and groveled to every castle goon that has decided to try out our little spot. I even knelt like a good citizen the last time the King's carriage pulled through the lower city, regardless of the sour taste it left in my mouth and the ways my hands shook just knowing my mother's murderer was so damn close. I've gone out of my way to be a responsible and decent person, someone my father could be proud of, and these guys, these bullies dressed as guards, are doing everything they can to ruin it.

"This afternoon was the closest we've ever gotten to capturing the person slipping magical contraband into the kingdom. You," he's close enough now to press a thick finger against my chest, "got in the way of that. So, without your little ally to take the fall, I guess the repercussions are going to go to you."

My father sputters behind me. I hold my hands up beside my head, aware that any action on my part will be noted as resistance to the crown. Talking isn't exactly my strong suit. I'm plenty capable of carrying on a conversation while pouring drinks, but I'm much more a man of action. The guards have me pressed into a tough spot with this ridiculous proposition.

Too preoccupied with the inevitability of my demise, I'm not even grateful they waited for everyone to leave before coming in here.

They…

They waited for everyone to leave.

This is a scare tactic.

Okay. Alright. I'm thinking. I know what I'm doing. I can talk my way out of this, and my father and I can go back to finishing out our holiday as we always do.

Of course, I've spent too long trying to weigh my options, and the rest of the room has been moving on without me. My father has his wallet in hand. I didn't even see him move. He's trying to bribe the wretches who have come to ruin our good day on the merit that I stopped them from doing their jobs earlier this afternoon.

There's no proof that they were doing any duty to the crown.

I slap my father's wallet out of his hand before he can manage to barter off the entirety of our lives' savings to these men. He's already been going out of his way to pay the King's men off earlier and earlier, the taxes always seeming to be higher than we agreed to in the first place. Money isn't going to solve this problem.

Bullies respond to one thing and only one thing: someone being brave enough to stand up to them.

Maybe he didn't like the way I slapped away my father's attempt to pay them, or maybe he realized where my mind would be after all of the craziness of the last couple of minutes, but the leader of the three, the average height, curly-haired man with a penchant for striking out at unsuspecting victims, steps up to attack me. I see it coming. I've been expecting it after all. Sidestepping the sloppy punch, I knee him in the stomach and push him back, satisfied by his gasping cough that I've at least given back what he doled out earlier this afternoon. I'm ready to fall on top of him and not stop fighting until we're pulled away from each other like feral cats caught in the alley, but I'm slowed by the sound of shattering glass.

My father croaks behind me, choking on a sob I wish he never expressed.

A second bottle of alcohol tumbles off the top shelf with the helpful push from the taller guard's hand and breaks into a thousand pieces that slosh in the expensive amber fluid it takes us months to make.

"Stop that!"

Three more bottles are examined and then smashed in quick succession as their leader clambers back to his feet. That'll probably cost us nearly as much as the cash my father was trying to pawn off before I started this fight. I could throw up. My hands shake. Shame mixes with guilt, my chest burning with the weight of my inaction and the consequences now unfolding in front of me. I brought this trouble home because I couldn't keep my business and my broken family to myself.

Another two bottles are plucked from the top shelf, fine liquors that are brought over on boats we see once every couple of years. They're irreplaceable. Fortunately, I suppose, they don't meet the same fate on the floor. Instead, each of the cronies behind the bar takes one into their possession as the leader tells them to grab another for him.

"Now, I think we can consider this penance for everything else you cost us today if you'll just grant us the decency of an apology to go with it," the leader then snorts, his voice a booming blow to my ears as I stare hard at the bar, at a chip in the front of it I've been meaning to patch but hadn't gotten to lately.

Maybe if I were here taking care of the tavern better than I was this afternoon, I wouldn't have been anywhere near that stupid altercation. Why did I choose today of all days to go play hero? That's not the kind of man I am, anyway. I'm here to be a good member of the community, but I'm not the person leading a revolution or doing more than handing out food and drink during hard times.

The tavern is supposed to be my entire world, and I screwed that up by trying to be a decent person.

"Eli."

I jump from the reminder that my father is watching all of this happen. He doesn't reach out to console me. Not that I think he should. It's just the first time in my entire life he hasn't rushed to cover up for me.

The alcohol seeping into the floorboards is a pretty good metaphor for the way the blood is leaving my heart. I wish I could be shattered and lost to time, too. It would be less painful than standing here and forcing myself to give in to the demands of men who don't deserve anything from me.

"I'm sorry for my son, gentlemen," my father continues, always the best citizen, always too damn scared to infuriate men loyal to the King in case he got second thoughts about finishing off the family line of a supposed witch.

Well, I'm not scared.

The tremor in my hands has much more to do with my fury at the entirety of the situation.

Distantly, my father says something else, but it's lost to the ringing in my ears. My name graces his lips with the same reverence as a spat curse. The prodigal son, the favorite son, the only son. None of that matters anymore. I can't disappoint him any more than I already have.

I think I mentioned that talking wasn't my strongest skill.

When I move to attack the leader once more, prepared to put all of the hurt and emotional agony of the last several minutes into the single strike, he responds with a huffing laugh. "You just don't get it, do you?"

I hear a crunch in the side of my face more than I feel the bottle connect with my cheek. Blood pools in my mouth. It bursts from my nose. The floorboards catch me as though they heard my silent plea to be allowed to seep into them, an unforgiving grip that may bruise just as much as my throbbing face.

The leader bends over, his thick lips nearly brushing my ear as his hot breath cascades over what has to be more blood on the side of my face, a disgusting sensation that will follow me into my nightmares. "You're nobody and nothing. You will never be anything. Learn to stay down when you have the choice because you will never win this battle."

Any other time, I would respond. I would spit and snarl and snap and revert to something akin to the beast they see me as. It has been years since I last dealt with the stereotypes and cruelties of the guardsmen. I thought I was above feeling such shame at the hands of these pompous bastards who sink their teeth into my community for the satisfaction of making us bleed for fun. I'd forgotten all the good and kindness that my father had sown here in this community, in our home, that my existence in the lower city alone made me a target, and then I went and kicked a metaphorical wasp nest and brought hate to our stoop.

Right eye swelling shut, my world narrows to the steady thump of their boots leaving our tavern, every vibration from their movements aggravating the pain in my face as it throbs in my cheek and seeps into my jaw. I try to find the will to peel myself off of the floor as the door slams. It isn't there. My father crosses the room to shut it fully and make sure it's locked. His knees then give out, and he slumps against the wood that honestly wouldn't save us if those brutes came back.

"Eli," my name is broken, the two syllables seeming to take all his strength to utter. "How could you do this?"

I would understand rage if it coiled its head like the snakes I've feared since being bitten in my youth. Anger makes sense. I've been attacked and I should want to retaliate.

Anger, though, doesn't come.

I curl in on myself. My face aches, but my chest hurts more. He's right. I know he's right, and that is impossible to accept.

"I'm sorry," I choke on the blood pooled in my mouth and dripping to the floorboards.

Finding the strength to push myself up before I let myself drown in my pity and the unwavering red leaking from me, I look across the room at my father, his face in his hands and his gray hair seeming to reflect his bleakness as it hangs limply around his fingers. My apology falls flat between us. It doesn't make anything better.

The world tips precariously around me as I find my way to my knees. "I'll clean this. I'll fix it."

The words are a clogged whisper. I'm not sure they even reach him. My father, though, a man who lost his wife and learned to walk again, finds his way to his feet faster than I can. He walks past me again without pausing to glance my way. A moment later, he has a mug filled with ice, and he holds it out to me.

It's not a peace offering.

I barely have it in my weak grasp before he clears his throat. "You're not in any condition to take care of this. I will do it myself. I believe I spoke too early on thinking you were ready to take on the business, and I will pay the price of that mistake today."

No. No, no, no. Not that. Anything but that.

I would cry if I had any spare fluid left in my body. Head throbbing, world spinning, I push to my feet with a muffled groan.

He steps back before I can reach him, and so I lean on the fervency of my plea. "Dad. It's my mistake. I didn't mean for all of this, but I can fix it. Please…"

My words don't matter. There's nothing I can say to undo the damage my actions have wrought. His mind is made up, the truth there in his twisted grimace, and the swell of disappointment making a home in his tormented gaze. It's my blood on the floor, but his dreams were shattered along with the wasted alcohol behind the bar.

This is supposed to be a safe space. Our home. Trouble infiltrated it nonetheless. After almost three decades of avoiding the cruel gaze of the guards, they came in and reminded him how quickly they can ruin things.

Just as he was ready to relinquish his careful hold of everything here, just as he was about to trust that he raised someone as careful and promising as he always hoped, I let the hatred of the kingdom walk through the front door. If they had tracked me down a mere hour earlier, our customers and friends and community members would have been found out, possibly arrested for their frivolous displays of magic on a holiday when too much liquor swam through the place, and we let our guards down. This night could have gone so much worse. Rationally, even with the ungoverned pounding in my skull, I understand that, and yet, I don't feel better because of it.

This was my dream, too.

"Just," his bottom lip quivers, and he huffs a hard breath as though irritated with his own ability to maneuver through this emotionally heavy moment without showing his own aches to me. "Go. Please. To your room. To anywhere. Just not here right now."

I stagger to the bar before I can give in to the desire to crumple back to the floor, holding myself up with that mug full of ice pressed to my face. "I'm not leaving. I'll help," I beg, throwing myself on the pities of his mercy, on the fact that he's never cast me out before today.

He didn't turn his back on me the first time I came home bloodied and bruised as a mere teen, having wandered into the market in the middle city and too full of fairytales to understand that speaking out when nobility literally kicked the lower class, that I was not a hero, but another person to be beaten down. My father didn't reprimand me when he caught me in the storage area with my fingers tangled in the hair of a man I couldn't be seen with publicly. Just a kiss that could be a death sentence, if not a long stay in the castle dungeons. Every time I stepped out of society's carefully curated box, he sat me down with a drink or a bag of ice and told me a story.

He has always told me stories. Little ones. Large ones that took more than one night to cover, chiding me to sleep or else he wouldn't relinquish the next lines of fiction to me, all of it cemented in his memory and not in a book I could simply slip from the shelves. Tales of knights who swore to follow ethical codes and princes who made hard decisions for the betterment of their kingdoms. He told me about a witch who fell in love with a regular man and still did not escape the ties of fate that would put her in front of a wicked king, a witch who did not waver in her attempt to do the right thing with her magic and who loved her son even though she was forced to leave him.

There has always been a story to cover the way I've acted or how I'm feeling, and a lesson to learn. More than once, he promised all of life's answers lay waiting in stories. I just had to figure out how to find it.

Rebellion, he whispered one night after I became an adult and couldn't bear the cruelty around us, is sometimes a story persevering. To survive is to allow the next generation to hear our stories. To garner hope. To give us a chance for something better than what we were handed today.

My lip wobbles as he shakes his head and cuts off anything else I might say for my own case, my mind aflame with all of the typical routes that he once used to console me, as I know full well he won't go down any of those tonight. "So often," he says softly, "I am proud to call you my son. I see so much of myself in you, in your hard work and the heart you pour into everything. Today," he is sure not to look at me, his gaze cast harshly over my shoulder instead, "all I see is your mother."

Carefree. Dangerous. A magic wielder who chose not to hide. She was pure imagination, a force to be reckoned with, and a woman who had grown too powerful for the desires of the men who ran this kingdom.

Now, I see the truth is that he couldn't accept me if I grew up to be her son. Not after all the work he's done to carefully shape me in his own image. Community first. Others' needs before my own. Never foolish enough to make these grand gestures of rebellion.

Different is fine. My taste in romance and relationships is skewed from what's approved and normal, but that's okay by him. Growing up to have an unshakeable backbone and moral code is where he draws the line.

The anger I had lacked moments ago sears me now like a brand on the very core of my soul. "Well, mom wouldn't have sat around and accepted that life is unfair. She did something about it and made a sacrifice despite everything in order to try to make the world a better place. I'd rather be her than you every single gods damned day."

Those last words are a snarl. They're garbled from the blood pooling in my mouth and seem detached from me, my right ear struggling to hear anything besides my heartbeat thudding along like a clock already aware its demise is nearing.

The fight leaves my father, his shoulders slouched even more. "What do you want, Eli?" His voice cracks, and it's almost enough to make me back down on what I've said, but my free hand is clenched, and the pain is making it difficult to be rational right now. "I'm keeping us alive. That's the best I can do."

Finally, he looks me in the eye, his face a contorted grimace of anguish and disgust, but I'm not sure if it's for himself or for what he's seeing right now. It doesn't matter either way. I'm upset and hurt and disgusted and struggling, too. We're not going to reach a common ground or forget the things we've said. More than anything, I want to get to bed sooner rather than later, so I wave off his question and spit the only thing that comes to mind.

"I just wish everything were different."

My father says something. It's probably a warning about my words and that we don't make wishes in this family. One more disappointment for him, then. I don't stick around to hear anything else. There are dishes to be washed and a tavern to finish closing up. This is a big enough place for the two of us to sulk in, so I plan to do just that.

Leaving him in the front to right the chairs and wipe the tables and mop up my blood from the floorboards, I make my way to the storage area. The cook leaves a couple of hours before we stop selling drinks, his station clean enough for an orc that spends too much time outside on a smoke break. There's nobody else in the outer city who makes chili and roasts birds on a budget the way he does, so we let some things slide, and I pick up the slack. Tonight, each extra dirty dish feels like an additional ten-pound weight added to my arms, the stack threatening to tip me over as the events of the day and the emotions of the last few minutes leave me outright exhausted.

I can do another hour, I tell myself, blinking past dark spots muddying my vision. I just need to clean up. I need to show my father I'm still responsible, and I'll give him the plate of food I set aside for us to share earlier in the shift, and we'll go upstairs, and things will go back to something akin to normal after I've slept through tomorrow's afternoon.

There has to be a way for things to go back to normal.

It's the only line of hope I allow myself to cling to as I waver above the sink, dipping my hands into the lukewarm water and dragging out mugs to scrub.

I've almost figured out a way to believe it to be true when a knock sounds at the back door.

3

Honestly, I don't think another soul should be allowed to knock at our door after the scuffle with the guards and the trouble it has caused in my life. Door knocking should be for honorable people. Everyone else should at least wait until I'm foolish enough to walk outside before they accost me. The world rarely waits for my approval, though. I hesitate next to the sink, lukewarm water dripping from my elbows to my fingertips as I wait for it to just go away.

Of course, it doesn't.

It's not an average knock like that of a drunkard who has misplaced their keys and lost their way home, rapping on doors that seem familiar yet are ultimately not their destination. This is louder than that of the men who came to ruin my life simply because I stopped them from bullying a man in the streets. Almost inhuman with its urgency, it's a pounding that demands not to be ignored. This is a knock suggesting that I've avoided a reckoning, and it's now come to collect me for grander consequences.

Which is just not fair.

Every slamming sound of fist on wood makes my jaw throb as I clench my teeth, which in turn makes the whole rest of my face hurt. Today has truly been more than enough. Perhaps it's a good time to admit I've lived a fairly good life. Sure, there was tragedy and discrimination comes for us all, but this is the worst day of my life, and I just want it to end.

Instead, the knocking persists.

When shutting my eyes and hoping the problem will resolve itself without my intervention doesn't work, I let out a ragged sigh and shuffle around the wall that separates the dry storage from the sink area. Everything is as it should be back here. The shelves are emptier than usual from the busy night. There are crates of potatoes shoved along the bottom and baskets of onions interspersed by smaller bushels of ingredients we use in our brewing, and an entire area dedicated to spices, most of which my father restocks in loving memory of the flavors my mother loved. The floor is scuffed, and the shelves could have another layer of paint to cover the rust that has developed along the feet, but it's functional and loved, and a good spot in the tavern.

It is clearly not the reason there's a heathen at the door.

Wiping blood from my nose onto the back of my hand and then into the opposite sleeve of my ruined shirt, I stare at the offensive door. I've been telling my father for years that we should have a window cut into this wooden barrier. Maybe I'd felt a premonition of this very moment. That rattling knock comes again, the wood groaning under the assault, and I stare at it as apprehension hooks claws into my spinal column.

It can't be the guards who already assaulted and robbed us, can it?

As hot-headed as I can be, I'm not stupid enough to think I'll survive another fight tonight.

The knock comes in a reckless swing of three and four against the sturdy door. Whoever is out there isn't about to be deterred by my inaction. I will myself to step forward. It's best I deal with this before they decide to wander towards the front door and include my father, who has remained blissfully unaware up until this point of yet another thing that must be my fault.

"Eli Cinderfella!"

Well, that cements the fact that this is definitely my problem. My name is muffled, but it's definitely my name that's shouted through the thick wood. I blink once, twice, three times to clear my good eye as though that will help me deal with this situation. The person on the other side of the door isn't who I thought it would.

That's not one of the guards out there.

It's not even a man.

I creep closer without thinking about it as the woman screeches my name once more against the coming of morning's first light. Never has a woman needed to see me in the darkness of early hours. The lock is under my fingers. I fumble, the discolored metal we should have repaired or replaced years ago catches on the latch. Finally, it scrapes open, and I push the door out.

Commotion follows my simple action. There's a curse and a flurry of motion. All the arm waving in the world couldn't have saved the woman on the other side of the door. Her thick skirt is knocked asunder, the garment far too fancy for anyone to be wearing around these parts. She wavers on thin heels and then falls backwards, letting out an oomph of air along with another expletive that I wasn't aware women even knew existed.

An apology is on my swollen lip as I reach down to find her in the puddle of fabrics. There's too much here for any one person. I think she's wearing more in this one dress than I have in my entire closet. Swatting the hoop skirt out of the way, I plunge my arms into the yellow fabric until I find her wrists and then tug backwards. It takes the two of us huffing and puffing and pulling and pushing to get her on her feet and wriggling through the back doorway.

The woman scrambles to right herself, slapping her dress back into position and pinching bunches of fabric that have been knocked off their proper places. It's a dazzling display of artistry. Harold has probably never made anything so grand and loud. There's no need to waste so much of a finite source of materials out here. While she likely fit in just fine at the parties in the upper city, she's a blazing star falling into the tavern now, blinding me as she catches her breath and holds me in suspense for why this is now a part of my day.

I swallow the urge to groan as she brushes her curly, blonde hair back from her face to reveal blue eyes and a thin patch of freckles across her nose. "You're Eli Cinderfella?"

"As far as I know," I grit out, trying not to be affected by the way her eyes widen as she takes in the brutalized condition of my face.

"Great," she mutters back, reaching into her skirts to pull a wand from a secret pocket, and then clears her throat. "By decree of the kingdom of Briargild, I'm your assigned fairy godmother, and I'm here to make your wish come true."

People wait their entire lives for this kind of opportunity. They blow out candles every birthday and float paper boats on the river at the change of the seasons and gather outside at midnight to whisper their wishes to the sky. I'm not dense enough to miss the importance of this moment, but, perhaps because of the head trauma, I can't seem to recall what I wished for.

I wasn't outside with anyone at midnight. I wasn't in here kissing my beloved and sending up a wish that we'll have a good year. I took people's drink orders and used glasses and lived in the moment until those guards came to ruin my night.

This is quite literally the night that won't end.

I don't have enough patience for any of this. "You must be confused. I didn't place a wish this year."

She shakes her head, waving her wand in a complicated pattern in front of herself. "The council doesn't make mistakes. This is your wish, Mr. Cinderfella. I hope all your dreams come true."

Even as she tries to put a cheerful inflection on the words, it comes off as a tired script. She sounds far older than she looks. I have no idea how many wishes she's been granting tonight. It's likely the busiest night of the year for anyone appointed to the Guild of Fairy Godmothers.

As interesting as that may be, it doesn't change the fact that I have no idea what wish she thinks she's granting.

I'm captivated for a moment while her wand continues to whip through the air between us. One moment it's a polished piece of finely crafted wood with a gold handle that spirals up towards the tip, the next it's glowing in her tight grasp, and golden glitter begins to pour out of it. While I would never admit it out loud, it is something special to behold. Magic isn't flaunted out here besides the small bits done in the tavern on special nights like tonight and even then people are usually pretty coy about their talents. Nothing like this. Alive with it. The air naturally expands around her in a gentle warning that something extraordinary is about to happen.

I've never been this close to anything so impressive.

Mesmerized, I note the way her eyes have glazed over. This isn't an act she's consciously committing. She's become a conduit for the kingdom's will. Magic is tightly leashed in Briargild and brandished only by fairy godmothers, mostly as a way for King Anerald to control people and occasionally get his followers to fawn over him for access to eccentric wishes they'd no longer have if he lost his control over the entirety of the magic system.

If it had been up to him, magic would have been abolished the moment King Anerald took over, but it's too embedded in our day-to-day life. Rather, the lives of the nobility. I've heard whole houses don't have any candles because magic lights their sconces the moment the sun leans beneath the horizon. It does other things, I'm sure, things people can't see with their bare eyes like cleaning our water sources in the golden pipes that wind all through the city and helps the harvests every season produce unfathomably large vegetables. I'd like to see the magic lights, though.

Like the glittering tendril of it amassing in front of the young woman who named herself my fairy godmother.

Almost directly in response to my spiraling thoughts, the golden glitter skitters away from her wand. It bounces across the ground and starts to reach for the storage shelves. I don't pay attention to where else it spreads as I watch holes begin to form in the floor.

Is there a way I could have been given the wrong wish?

Because I definitely didn't wish for that.

Watching the glitter, I see a sparkling cluster collide with the cleaning supplies we keep propped against an empty corner. The brooms jump away from the wall, quickly joined by the mop in desperate need of a cleaning itself. The instruments brush and twirl and scrub away at the floor, widening the holes that the glitter had already begun to eat away in the tiles.

This isn't happening.

My tongue trapped in my mouth, my good eye not believing that this is real, and my brain on the fritz from the stress of it all, I watch the gold glitter spread further outwards. When it touches the supplies on the shelves, potatoes shrink and onions shrivel. The seasoning bottles wriggle and jiggle and pop into non-existence. None of it seems to deter the insidious spread of glitter.

It makes its way to the sink, and the whole thing rattles with the new substance, old metal creaking and wailing from the golden touch. There's a groan. A screw is launched out from somewhere beneath it, the tiny thing thundering out a disgruntled click of announcement from wherever it's thrown, and then another follows, the whole sink tipping away from the wall. Inside the sink, mugs I was in the process of cleaning soared out of the sudsy water, scooping up as much liquid as possible in the motion. Moving like a trained group of performers, they flit and dance through the air, sloshing dirty water left and right with every dip and twirl and impossible maneuver. This is a scene from a dream. It would be comical if it were happening in a story and not in the back of our tavern. I'm almost too focused on the mugs to watch what happens when the water makes contact with the tavern surfaces.

Almost.

More holes appear. The sink disappears, a flood of water washes across the floor that used to be a combination of floorboards and hand-pressed tiles, and is now merely dirt. Actually, mud. I'm sinking into the floor that is no longer a floor. The foundation of the tavern is vanishing.

Holes bloom in the walls. The prep tables are disintegrating under the greedy attention of the gold glitter. Magic is alive, and it is tearing down everything I've ever hoped and dreamed about.

This isn't my wish.

I choke on the thought, propelling myself out of my confused stupor to turn on the fairy godmother still standing entranced by her magical employ. She doesn't look up from her wand when I yell. There's no way to even tell that she can hear me in this state.

All around, the back areas of the tavern are vanishing as though they were never built. Glitter hangs in the air. It's an imminent threat to everything in my life.

My father cannot know I've failed him yet again.

Since yelling doesn't seem to work, I take a step towards the fairy godmother. The broom swishes into my path, trying to sweep me back from her. Staggering, I swat it out of my way only to be drowned by a mug of dishwater that pummels me from above. I wait an awful half a breath to see if I'm affected by the magic the same way the tavern seems to be, my chest aflame and face burning, but nothing happens to me. I'm just wet and pissed off.

"Come on. Knock it off!"

I trip on the mop and smash a different mug on the ground, the glass glimmering momentarily before disappearing like everything else around me. The fairy godmother still hasn't responded. At this rate, I'm running out of time before the magic makes it to the front of the tavern. This needs to stop right now before we lose absolutely everything.

I'm out of options.

Except…

I won't watch my home, my father's whole life beyond his care for me, just get washed away in a cloud of glitter.

There has to be something I can do. I blink drops of water from my gaze as the clattering of magically enhanced cleaning supplies continues to develop behind me and step towards the fairy godmother again. It's not a good plan, but I think I can wake her up from this wish business.

Lurching forward, I grab the wand right above her fist and try to yank it out of her grasp. She doesn't wake. Not to ask me what I'm doing or demand I unhand her. Nothing. If not the magic working through her, then she's stronger than her short, full frame would have suggested. Neither the wand nor my fairy godmother budges. Wrapping my other hand around my wrist to stabilize myself, I tug again, tipping back on my heels to give myself more leverage.

The fairy godmother shifts, her grip loosening the slightest bit. Consciousness bleeds back into her flustered gaze. Her mouth forms a helpless 'o', and then she rallies her own grip on the wand with a cry for me to back off.

"No," I snarl back. "This isn't my wish. Make it stop!"

"Wishes can't be stopped," she snaps, shrieking as I adjust my grip to hold the wand on either side of her hands, giving myself even more of a chance to overpower her.

If we can just stop the spell or whatever she cast, we can talk about this. Obviously, she has to see that this is a bad outcome. Nobody wants their home eaten by glitter that may as well be locusts with how quickly it devours everything in its path.

No amount of trying to shout that over our wrestling match is working. She is still holding on. I'm still tugging and jerking and trying to pry it out of her hands as glitter spills over the both of us in a dazzling display to mark the futility of my actions.

Beyond our scuffle, the tavern continues to deteriorate. I'll be able to see straight through the walls and into the front of the building in a few moments, and then I'll have to explain to my father that I didn't just get into another fight, but I decided to fight a woman. I'll never live down the disgrace and disappointment. I also don't stand a chance of fixing any of this if the tavern is completely gone, so I double down, wrenching on the damned harbinger of my demise with a huff of frustration.

The wand snaps.

In two clean, wooden halves. The spiraling gold handle falls to the floor with a broken ting. Everything else is now in my hands. My fairy godmother claps her own fingers over her mouth in a dramatic expression of her horror, the two separated ends of the wand still spewing unreasonable amounts of the golden glitter.

How is this possible?

The force of my winning the altercation had me staggering back. Now, I let my knees give out and crumple to the floor. Gold leaks from the pieces of the wand I'm holding tight against my palms. It coats the front of my shirt and stains my pants as I sit in a seemingly never-ending stream of glitter.

This isn't supposed to happen.

What else can I do?

I yell at the damn thing. Nonsense mostly. Demands for it to stop. Pleas for it to give me back my life. This is magic, and I have no idea how it works. Nobody else in the history of Briargild has stolen a wand. That has to mean something, right?

Apparently not. This is officially the worst night of my life.

Sensing my distress or simply running out of ammunition for its desire to rip apart the tavern, the wand sputters and stops creating buckets of glitter. I'm left sitting on the ground looking at the wooden halves as my fairy godmother hyperventilates in the corner. Just as I'm prepared to relax into finding a solution now that the glitter has stopped, the unthinkable happens.

The glitter returns full force. This time, though, it's pink. Even more ravenous in this shade, it consumes the wand. I move to throw the pieces away and get out of the new color of devastation it's creating, but I can't. They're stuck to my palms. I shake my hands and curse to no avail. There isn't time to ask the fairy godmother what's happening before the two halves sink into my palms.

The wand is in my hands.

It's under my skin.

I absorbed it.

Before I can ask my very unwanted fairy godmother what's happening or for her to do something to fix it, the brooms are back with a vengeance. They catch her skirts and sweep her off her feet. Groaning as she's likely going to have some matching bruises to mine from all of this falling, the fairy godmother is once more a turtle flipped back on her shell and unable to come to my aid.

Which is fine.

I didn't truly need her help. She's the one who showed up to make everything so much worse than it already was.

Half hoping this is all some hallucination from my throbbing head wound, I scramble to my feet, glitter and mud coating me in equal measure as water continues to drip from my hair. I walk the war zone that used to be the sink and prep area, ducking away from mugs in search of more water and sidestepping the mop aggressively scrubbing at the naked floor. The tavern is still disappearing around me, even with the wand broken.

It's time to admit that this problem is beyond my control.

I hurry up front, my throat tight as I try to figure out just how I'm going to explain all of this to my father, so close to the festering moments of our last fight. There's no right way to explain a random fairy godmother showed up to grant a wish I don't recall wishing. Plus, I have no idea why this wish is hellbent on tearing down the tavern.

I spot the bar, the broken glass from the guards has vanished. The liquid has evaporated or been whisked away by magic. The shelves behind the bar are filled with holes like some giant version of Swiss cheese. Most of our drink supplies are simply not there anymore.

I turn the corner, sure my father has to be out here fending off flying chairs or purely confused by things that shouldn't be happening, but that's not what I find. The scene in front of me takes the already dwindling strength out of my legs. I stagger. I kneel on the ground, the bare dirt ground.

The entirety of the tavern is gone. There's no tables or chairs or chandeliers. I'm kneeling alone in a place that looks like it has been deserted for no less than a hundred years. Blue cobwebs shimmer in places where the moon sneaks a peek through gnawed holes in the roof.

All of our cleaning. All of our lives' work. Gone in a terrible moment.

My father isn't here.

That's the only thought that gets me back on my feet. If he's not here, then he must have gone upstairs after our fight. That's probably why he didn't hear the fairy godmother pounding away at the back door.

By the time I retrace my steps towards the stairs that lead to our apartment, the fairy godmother has managed to get back to her feet and is barreling my way. "Eli Cinderfella, you need to come here this instant."

Fairy tales always talk about people fearing dragons. They're bigger than anything else and breathe fire. I think more people should be worried about fearing women like my fairy godmother, though. Her ringlet curls whipped back with the ferocity of her speed, teeth bared, and hands reaching out for me; I know I've never seen anything quite so disturbing.

That feels like a problem I can avoid for just a little bit longer.

Outpacing her, I take the steps two at a time up to our apartment, being careful not to step through the quickly deteriorating wood. I know she's right behind me as I scramble up the stairs, but I don't turn back to look at her or slow down. I have to find my father. I have to apologize and figure out a way to fix this before we lose absolutely everything that has ever mattered in one night.

I stumble through the door. It's not latched. Hanging crooked from its frame, I don't think it would close even if I put all my strength into it, so I leave it open behind me as I move into the main living area.

"Dad..."

My voice is an instrument cracked beyond repair. I can't get anything else past my teeth. I barely get my feet to move forward a few more steps.

I found him. Alive. Here. My eyes stick to my father like honey on the outside of a jar. Gold glitter covers him from the toes of his work shoes to his neck. It's climbing further. Soon enough, it's in his hair and woven into his mustache and eyebrows. When he opens his mouth to call back to me, there's gold on his tongue.

No noise passes between us.

Fear sparkles in his gaze.

I reach out a hand to him. The pink glitter firmly associated with whatever I've done wrong when I broke this wand spurts between us. Pink and gold dance. They mingle. Then, the glitter begins to fall. It's no longer held up by his wide form. It drips to the ground like wet paint, splattering in gooey globs.

It falls and falls and falls until there's nothing left beneath it.

My father isn't here.

My father…

"Dad!"

My knees crack against the creaking floor. My own pain doesn't matter. I plunge my hands into that gold glitter and sift through it to find any pieces left of him, but there's nothing. I try to press it back together into a shape that could hold a person. It sloughs off to the side as sobs wrack my contorted form.

"This isn't my wish!" I scream at the mess.

A terrible groan comes from the building. "Eli."

I almost jump at the reminder that someone is watching my life fall to glittering pieces, but I don't answer her. This is more important than some fancy fairy godmother. This is my life. It's my only living parent reduced to thin air and magic dust. I couldn't care less about what she wants right now.

My stomach claws its way past my lungs to lodge itself closer to my throat as the building gives a nauseating sway. Her hands are on my shoulders, pulling me backwards. "We have to get out now!"

As much as I would prefer to lie down in the gold glitter piled in our living room and submit to the same fate as my father, I know there's no way to fix any of this if I give up now. Death isn't my next step. I have to try to undo the damage I've brought on the tavern today.

By her sheer force more than my own, I find my way back to my feet as the building lurches again. Then, we're back on the stairs. She's cursing as her dress snags on broken pieces of wood and scattered glass from the mugs that have fallen to the ground in a graveyard of my hopes and dreams. Her hand flings back to grab my wrist, and she pulls me through the front of the tavern, past the bar that looks like it has become the home for a wild nest of termites, and beyond the space I was just toasting the new year at a few hours ago. She runs and drags us through the front door, the frame broken and warped wide enough for her to slip through, even with her enormous skirts. Breathless, we make it out onto the single, paved road as the building gives a final shudder and collapses in on itself.

Gold glitter shimmers in the air above the destruction, vying for more attention than the stars in the sky. They twinkle and shimmer and shine and fall back down on top of the carcass of the tavern. Dirt clogs my throat and sticks to the blood I never washed from my face. Everything else on the street remains eerily silent and fully intact, the buildings otherwise unbothered by the loss of their neighbor.

It's all gone.

My fairy godmother is still holding my wrist, and I pull away from her more sharply than necessary. "I would never have wished this."

The words are a whisper that's deafening in the quiet settled over the street. Exhausted and overworked and spinning from the sheer speed at which my life crumbled, I try to pick through what I could have done to bring this terrible fate down on myself.

No. Not what I did. What I said.

The answer hits me harder than any punch I've taken in my life.

Different. I wished for everything to be different hours after the strike of midnight.

This isn't anything like what I wanted.

In no version of my story would I have wanted to lose the tavern or my father or any chance to fix the mess I had already made. Yes, the world should be different. It should be kinder and gentler to those in need of a rest from tragedy. This wish has gone too far, though, stealing from me everything I care about, everything that matters, everything that makes me strive to be a better person.

The urge to yell, to scream, to kick the rubble and riot against the magic that has cut my world down to the bleeding marrow is nearly all-consuming. Instead, I turn on the woman who introduced herself as my fairy godmother. She's dirt-smeared and wide-eyed.

"You have to fix this."

It's not a command, and it doesn't come out as the demand I feel fluttering against my ribcage like a thousand shadowy moths caught in a too-small jar. It's a plea. I'm begging as the words wobble from my lips to be on their own in the still dusty air left by the tavern's collapse.

Her bottom lip wobbles when she meets my gaze, and she wipes a hand over her face, a line of dirt smearing with the motion over her freckled nose. "There's nothing I can do."

At this point, I don't care who hears me. I'm coming apart at the seams. My day has been ruined. My life is practically over. There's no one here besides this self-appointed fairy godmother, and I am determined to make sure she knows that I blame her entirely for this disaster.

It may have been my words, but it was her who cast the magic on the tavern.

She staggers back from my accusations with tears in her eyes that have more to do with me than the state of the air pollution from the tavern's demise. "I'm serious. Even if I had my wand," she pointedly gestures to my palms, "I can't just do magic. It's commissioned by the kingdom's magistrate. There's no granting wishes that aren't previously approved. Fairy godmothers are just conduits."

My head is throbbing too much to deal with the specifics of magic in our world. "I have lost everything. It's the middle of the night. What am I supposed to do?"

"That's not exactly my problem. I just show up, do the magic, and leave. Don't you think I want tonight to end, too?"

"So, you get to go home and I'm, what, supposed to sleep on the street?"

My fairy godmother shifts uncomfortably from one foot to the other. She chews the corner of her pink lip. It's a long moment before she reaches into yet another hidden pocket in her ridiculous, tattered skirt and pulls out a small box.

"Here. Sit down. Let me patch you up and we'll talk about what to do next."

It's best to blame my tired and frayed state. As much as I want to yell at her some more or punch a wall, I sink to the street in a heap of limbs that feel too heavy and detached to be my own. I don't flinch away when she kneels in front of me with her box, and I accept the petals she holds out towards me.

"Come on. The pink ones will help dull the pain, and the yellow will help with being tired. We have a lot more to do tonight."

I chew the petals without complaint. Floral and fruity and a little dense, I eventually swallow them as she cleans my face with wet towelettes and then applies a salve to my cheek that's meant to bring down the swelling. I've never been able to afford magical healing before now. It's immediately obvious why people go out of their way for these services, though. By the time she has me cleaned up, announced by her staggering back and clapping her hands in a gleeful show of pride in her work, I can see out of my right eye again, and I feel a bit more myself, even though the sense of devastation has made a home at the base of my heart.

She stands over me, cleaning off her hands and packing up her magical medical kit while I carefully figure out how to function once more. "Thank you for…" I gesture at my face as I curl my knees to my chest and then glance off at the sky.

The moon is heading towards the horizon once more, her face also turned away from the shameful state of my life. Behind me, the tavern is just a pile of rubble, and my father is gone. My chest is heavier from the responsibility of holding onto the broken pieces of my heart. I stare up at the sky like it'll have some kind of answer for me, but my hopes are dashed like a drink dropped from a table.

"Don't you have a friend you can stay with until this is better?"

I shake my head. Customers aren't exactly friends, and I can't imagine turning up on Harold's stoop to admit what I've done. I don't deserve kindness after this mess. Gods, he wouldn't be able to meet my gaze if I told him I magicked away his best friend because of an errant wish.

"You have to help me make it better."

My fairy godmother lets out a frustrated sigh and stomps her heeled foot on the ground. "What do you expect me to do? You broke and absorbed my wand. Even if I wanted to do more, I'm stuck here with you, and if the council finds out I misplaced yet another wand, they're going to fire me, so looks like we're both in a bit of trouble, friend."

"We're not friends," I say into the unforgiving night.

Nor should I consider being friends with fairy godmothers. She's literally from the part of the kingdom that thinks it's better than all of us out here on the edges. This isn't all her fault, though. I also should have listened to my father and kept my head down instead of playing hero for some guy who ran off before I could even introduce myself.

Chivalry should be dead.

Right now, I wish I were. At least, I wish I were the one taken away from this and not my father. He didn't deserve any of it.

"What happened to my father?" I ask, chin cupped in my hands with my elbows propped on my knees.

She shrugs, her shoulder bare where her sleeve has torn. "He must not exist in this version of the world according to your wish."

My first instinct is to argue. I want to spit and curse up at her, but that hasn't gotten us anywhere. Instead, I latch onto our conversation and try to puzzle this out myself. If I'm going to have a chance to rescue my father and rebuild the tavern and fix everything I've broken, I'm going to have to accept help even from unlikely sources.

"You're telling the truth?"

Her blue eyes are so wide as she rolls them at me. "What good would it do me to lie to you right now?"

So, she didn't intentionally break everything with magic. She just happened upon me in the line of work. Wrong place, wrong time. All of that.

My mind snags on the one morsel of hope she offered up in this bleak moment.

"Where do you get a new wand?"

She picks at loose glitter stuck to her top, clearly thinking about whether or not she should tell me anything about new wands. There are probably rules about talking about magic with outsiders. It's not exactly easy for one to become a part of the Guild of Fairy Godmothers, and I know there's a huge ceremony with a bunch of oaths they go through before getting appointed to the job. I do expect her to lie or give me some kind of non-answer.

Instead, her fingers moving to fiddle with her hair, she leans down and whispers an inch from my nose. "There's a witch in the woods who has helped me a few times."

"You've lost your wand a few times?"

"Hey! This is the first time someone absorbed it," she hisses, reaching her hands down to quiet me as if there's someone eavesdropping from the wreckage of the tavern. "We can't all be perfect at our jobs."

The fairy godmother takes a couple of steps away from me once she's sure I'm not about to scream into the night. I swallow my ire. I'm not going to get anywhere if I chase off the one person who can help me.

"Okay. Fine. I'm part of the problem," I concede, my hands held out in a way that I hope looks to be placating. "Obviously, this wish wasn't something I really wanted. If I agree to help you get a new wand and not tattle on you for losing it in the first place, will you help me undo all of this?"

"Technically, any wishes people want to repute have to be taken straight to the King. There's paperwork to go through with the magistrate. It's a long process. There's nothing I can do about that."

It has come to my attention that spikes in my emotions are now causing pink glitter to fall from my fingertips. I hold up my hands to her. "Is this something you want the King to see?"

My fairy godmother doesn't need to know there's no way I would ever step in front of that man to ask for my life back. Besides the mess I've created tonight, he's caused every other major source of misery in my world. I can't even conceive of a scenario in which I would kneel in front of him and grovel. That would be the ultimate betrayal to both my parents.

Luckily, I don't have to pressure her any harder. The fairy godmother curses under her breath, kicks her glass heel on the concrete, and then sets her hands firmly on her hips. This is the kind of woman who gets things done. She's not going to sit here and pout with me. We're going to fix this.

"What do you want me to do?"

"Take me to see the witch," I respond, jumping off the floor with more energy than I've had all night, thanks to that magical pick-me-up she fed me.

Her eyes are so wide. "I can't exactly lead some guy to her front door."

I wave my hands again, pink glitter sporadically dropping in the air between us. "If she can help you get the wand out of me, then there will be no more problems for you. I won't have proof anything ever went wrong tonight. You'll have your wand back, and then you can help me with my wish. Just take me and let's see what we can do about fixing both of our problems."

Her shoulder slumped in a silent defeat. "I'm not promising that I can undo your wish, Eli Cinderfella."

I hold out my hand to her, determined to strike this deal. "Tonight, my life was magicked away. I've lost my father and our tavern and my home. I'm now incredibly desperate, and I've got nothing but time and a new access to magic on my hands." As if to accentuate this point, more glitter pours out of me, the rosy specks scratching beneath my fingernails and making my joints ache in a way I won't admit to just yet. "I vow not to stop being a problem for you if you don't agree to help me. Please, just promise to agree to try to help me with this, Miss Fairy Godmother."

"You drive an irritating bargain," she starts, her palm soft as she reaches out to me, "but, fine, yes, I'll try to help you." We shake on it, the pink glitter a dazzling connection between the two of us as it flickers and falls to the ground. "Also, you can call me Gemma."

Dropping my hand, she scoops up what's left of her bedraggled skirts and gives me a stern tilt of her chin. "Let's go do this thing."

This is what I asked for. So, with the desolate state of my life left piled behind me, I walk through the dust motes and lingering glitter of a thousand small choices that led to my downfall in hopes I can find a way to fix it.

4

Gemma promptly drops her skirts and turns back to face me, our journey stalled after only three steps. "We need a carriage."

I wave my arms out from myself to gesture at the entirety of the street, the rubble that represents my life up until this point, and the lack of a vehicle. "I don't know if you can tell, but we aren't really carriage people. Is it really too far to walk?"

She flutters a hand to her chest. "Walk? In this?" Her hands flap above her incredibly tattered ensemble and those glass heels that most definitely won't be getting us far. "You must have hit your head very hard if you think that's a good idea."

While I have some comments about who the crazy one is here, I suppress them to snap my next question; Gemma's general presence is enough to get my blood pressure somewhere close to boiling, whether or not we're allies now. "What do you suggest we do then? There isn't exactly luxury transportation just waiting to be used out here."

She blinks twice, her lips quirked into an odd expression that I'm not entirely comfortable having fixed on me. She's watching the glitter on my hands. Pink and disorderly. I'm fizzing with magic, and it's creating a mess.

"We're going to make one," she announces, pointing down the street to a pile of squashes left out for the holiday. "Grab one of those and come back here."

I have more arguments, but, apparently, all I'm good for is collecting vegetables. Walking up the street, I glance at the pumpkins and various squash set out. There are bugs on a few. Soft spots on others. I try to pick the best of the bunch, a plump acorn squash with taut green skin and an orange spot near the corded vine. It's a sturdy squash. I'm sure it'll be fun to watch my fairy godmother try to turn it into more than that.

"Come on now, we don't have all night," she grumbles as I amble back towards her.

I stick my tongue at her and then plant the squash in the middle of the street. "There. Vegetable acquired. How are you going to make a carriage?"

Her eyes glimmer with mischief. "I'm not. You are, Eli."

Right. I stare down at my glitter-ridden palms. I'm in possession of Gemma's wand. Magic is illegal. It's outlawed in several parts of the kingdom unless otherwise ordained by the crown, the lower city being more heavily policed than those close to the castle. I'm not sure what we've done is a good enough loophole to talk our way out of being sent to the dungeons for wielding magic. Accidents happen, but I'm not in any position to talk my way out of or pay to get out of trouble.

Instead of outright disagreeing with the headstrong fairy godmother, I try to pull from her own earlier statement in order to keep myself from becoming an outlaw on a magical basis. "You said you couldn't just do magic. It had to be approved by your superiors or whatever. How do you expect me to make this squash into a carriage?"

Her eyes roll up towards the still peeking moon, the only entity aware of our shenanigans at this odd hour. She's going to hurt herself if she keeps being so aggressive about her disappointment in me. As is, she returns her gaze to me, crosses her arms over her chest, and nods towards the squash again.

"Eli, it's not granting a wish. Fairy godmothers can wield small magics. It's basically the only perk to the job." When I don't jump to just believing her, she lets out a sigh that blooms in front of her in a frosted cloud. "The wand comes with an innate amount of magic. We use it for day-to-day activities."

Her shoulders slump. This is the posture of someone exasperated by my general existence. Which is fine. I feel the same way about her.

Although this is never how I imagined a fairy godmother would be. In most stories and the gossip that spreads through the tavern faster than any plague, they're always described as such polite women with soft voices who want nothing more than to grant wishes. Older. Wiser. Caring and creative in equal doses. Doling out magical fixes and fancy clothes and making life better for those blessed to share their space. Fairy godmothers always seemed whimsical. It was a position granted by a mixture of talent and rich connections along with sheer magical inclination, at least that is what's repeated in the speech given at every bi-yearly celebration of promoted godmothers. I've never heard of it as just a job.

"Did you not want to be a fairy godmother?"

She snaps her fingers at me, cheeks rosy from the cold weather as her brows pinch in towards her nose. "Do not change the subject right now, Eli Cinderfella. Make us a carriage."

It seems I'm not getting out of this. After everything else I've done tonight, casting some magic can't be my worst crime, can it?

I glance up and down the street. Out here, everything besides the tavern is untouched by my fairy godmother's cruel attempt to grant my wish. It seems everyone has gone home to sleep through the rest of the winter solstice and won't be bothered until the adamant fingers of the sun shove through their thin curtains. If I wanted to try to cast magic, now is as good a time as any, since there won't be wandering eyes to catch me in the act.

What else do I really have to lose?

I rub my hands together and then look between Gemma and the acorn squash as pink glitter rains down on my weathered boots. "Any tips?"

Her expression lights up at my acquiescence. "Just imagine a carriage. The way it looks and smells and feels. Focus all of that on the squash and then push the magic onto it."

Right. That sounds simple. I've never been in a carriage. There's not really anywhere I need to go that isn't within a reasonable walking distance.

I stretch my neck and roll my shoulders. This isn't the time for complaints and nitpicking or rubbing it in my fairy godmother's face that we've obviously lived very different lives. I know what a carriage is. I can do this.

Recalling a few models I've seen over the years, from the ostentatious carriages that pull visiting nobility to the simpler carts that farmers use to bring their products to market, I shape it in my mind like Gemma instructed. I hold my hands out towards the acorn squash as I solidify the concept in my mind. A boxy area for the body. Four wheels of similar size. A place to hitch to an animal.

Magic buzzes in my arms. It starts in my palms. Vibrations like a hive of bees that has been shaken up and left to fester. The incessant hum builds just under the surface of my palms, wriggling all the way up to my elbows. I grit my teeth against it. It itches. I want to run my hands over the harsh gravel until I bleed and the sensation stops. Of course, I can't. I'm in charge of building our carriage.

"You're doing good. Now, push," Gemma coaches from next to me, her hands gently adjusting my wrists to a better position above the acorn squash.

Letting out an excited breath, I will the magic to do whatever it is that magic does, and the pink glitter doesn't wait for a second chance. It bursts from my palms like water out of a collapsed dam. Piling onto the cracked pavement, I struggle to hold my arms steady as the magic pours out of me.

Gemma braces my elbows. "Don't let go of your image. It needs to be a carriage, okay?"

Yes. Yeah. Carriage.

My arms are so heavy, the constant vibration working my muscles in a way that lugging around barrels and dishes never has before now. I ignore it. That and the way my spine is wavering like a building on soft foundations in a storm. I try to tense and hold firm in this onslaught of released magic from a wand that shouldn't be stuffed into my palms but remains resolutely there like an extra punishment on top of all my other issues tonight. Finally, the pink glitter, almost hip high, a shape begins to form from the gathered mess.

Round wheels. Thicker than what's usually screwed onto the side of an average carriage. It's awkward and clumsy like a rendition by a young artist unsure of the materials he's using, but capturing the essence anyway. Magic climbs up itself, overlapping and stretching and forming the bottom of the carriage.

It's happening. I'm actually doing magic.

Knees weak, arms shaking, I try to hold steady while Gemma

moves to cradle me from behind, her hands firm on my biceps lest I have any inclination to sway away from my project. The magic wand may have all the power we need, but it's taking a toll on me in the process. There's no time to ask her about the effects on myself. Pink glitter falls from me, and she holds me up, and together we cast magic.

Sweat gathers at my neck as Gemma's voice breaks through my desperate concentration. "Just breathe. Focus. Magic is alive and more than willing to flit to a different project if you don't keep it motivated."

Tavern life has made me a quick learner, but I am not prepared for the rules that come with wielding magic. I should have been handed a guidebook before she demanded magic out of me. My fairy godmother is trying to do her best, but already, the glitter is spreading, escaping my carriage and skipping away before wriggling into cracks in the pavement. My attention is torn. I need to make a carriage and figure out how we're going to drive it and...

Did more of my glitter just get away from me?

Work on my carriage pauses as I watch the pavement. A yellow glow emanates from the cracks.

Yellow. Not pink. It's not gold like all of Briargild gleams to be, but something festering there beneath a healing bruise.

"What's it doing?"

Gemma scoffs, her chin poking into my arm as she leans over to look around me. "How should I know?"

"You're the one who does magic!"

"Not like this," she groans, trapped with me as we watch the magic glow and then begin to grow out of the cracks.

Golden vines take shape. They stretch upwards towards the fading stars of the coming morning sky. I read a book once with illustrations of sea creatures on the edges. These vines look almost like the arms of an octopus and are far more deadly.

My fairy godmother shrieks as one snaps out of its upward reverie and towards us. It tries to wrap around her ankle. The rest of the vines aim only for my carriage. With a creak and squeal, the vines smash my progress on the carriage, crushing the wheels and dragging the carcass of my vehicle towards the widening pavements, a streak of pink glitter left behind like blood seeping from a wound.

It gives another tug. The ground shakes violently. A hole opens big enough for my carriage pieces to be pulled into the street.

Whatever is under the pavement is consuming my carriage.

It's growing stronger. It's getting bigger. It's draining the magic from my amateur spell and using it to better itself.

"Eli, make it stop!"

Great freaking plan, Gemma.

I try to yell at her that she wasn't very successful when I asked her to stop doing magic in the tavern, but I'm no longer safe from my own creation. One of the golden vines is wrapped around my wrist. It's pulling and tugging, dragging me closer to the same fate as my partially built carriage.

Today is not the day I get eaten by magic.

Digging my heels into the ground, I grab for some of the crushed pieces of my carriage, anything to give myself an anchor against this monster that was once a vegetable. I catch the curved edge of a wheel. It's a fruitless action. The wheel bursts into glittering dust that wafts over my arms in splashes of pink. I suck in an itching handful of it as I fall forward, the vines strong enough to overpower me.

Coughing and wheezing and falling is a terrible combination.

Gemma isn't much better off. Both of her hands are now entangled as well as her ankle. Her skin glows where the vines connect. It's searching for magic that she doesn't currently have, winding her tighter in its grip as she yelps and whines and not-so-nicely declares that we're even when it comes to destroying each other's lives.

The ground rumbles again, and the creature pokes up out of the pavement. A wrinkled, golden mess of fleshy substance with a mouth. Sharpened teeth the length of my hand sprout from its lips. It has no eyes, but seems to latch its entire focus on me anyway.

"Eli!"

The carnivorous creature pulls us closer. "What do I do?"

"Anything! Just don't let it eat us!"

Not exactly going down without a fight, I thrash. I yell profanities. I try to not visualize my demise here in the middle of the street, where people headed to this area for early morning errands will find my remains and shake their heads at the failure of a taven keep's son. That is, if they remember who I was before the travesty of my wish gone wrong. I'll be pieces and glitter and a pile of disappointment.

The words 'stop' and 'no' seem to only encourage it. Every inch I manage to step backwards motivates it to pull me harder. I stagger forward, the road coming up fast under me. Balance lost with my quickly withering hope to survive this encounter, I'm dragged across the road towards the squirming, golden creature. It pulls me even closer, the gaping hole in the pavement coming up sooner than I expected. Mushy vegetable body pulses as it widens its mouth.

No. Nope. Not today.

I cling to the edge of the pavement with scraped palms. Glittery, gold drool drips from the upper jaw of the beast. Its teeth are so sharp. A purple tongue flicks out to run along its puffy, bottom lip.

Maybe I should take it as a compliment that I look delicious.

Maybe I should spend more time being upset that my first attempt at magic created a catastrophic monster.

Off to my side, Gemma screeches at me once more as the vines tear at her dress. Sweat coating my back, dirt and grime and an exorbitant amount of glitter chafing along with the squash tendrils on my limbs, I wrack my mind for a semblance of a solution. This isn't exactly a normal circumstance. Monsters shouldn't rise up from cracks in the road. That behavior is reserved for persistent weeds and the occasional daisy.

Which gives me an idea for an absolutely horrible plan.

While I would like to consider my options for just a moment longer, my elected fairy godmother lets out a scream that could wake up the guards all the way at the castle, and I have no choice but to move.

This had better work.

The magical concoction of malcontent doesn't prevent me from moving towards it, and that's all the wiggle room I need. I plunge my hand into its mouth and grab that purple tongue. Flower. I want to see a normal flower. I pull the image to the forefront of my mind and push it outwards in a quick flash that leaves my arms singed from the sudden surge of magic.

White petals, green leaves, a little yellow center.

I stay focused on my idea, on the almost childlike aspects of what makes a flower a real thing, as the magical being under me thrashes and groans and tries to gnaw on me. Its teeth prickle along my forearm, but they don't pierce my skin. For now, the magical properties of the wand embedded in my palm seem to be keeping me safe. The gelatinous tongue wriggles in my hold. Drool splashes onto my cheek. The monster writhes.

"Be a flower, dammit!"

Whether it's a matter of wills or simply the wand being more powerful than the creature it created, I win this particular war. The tongue stills. It turns gray and then dissolves into ash in my hand as the magic is drained from it. The rest of the creature pulses, glowing brighter, so bright that my fairy godmother gasps, and I have to fling a hand over my eyes to keep from being blinded. Once thick vines shrivel into dusty fragments and then release us with a thud and a mixed pair of groans.

Simultaneously, Gemma and I scramble backwards over the ground as it resettles into its normal position atop the dying creature. The places that were yellow begin to glow a soft pink. Leaves sprout from the crack, lying in the middle of the road as if it doesn't matter how much space it takes up or care that it'll impede traffic come morning. Jutting from the middle, my flower bud stretches towards the sky and then blooms, a dazzling pink light that threatens the brilliance of the stars. Nearly as thin as a butterfly's wing, the petals rustle in the breeze. The plant sways on its thick stem as Gemma and I try to catch our breath, but otherwise, it seems to no longer have an appetite for everything in its vicinity.

It's not what I was picturing in my mind, but it's beautiful and far less violent, so I'm happy with the results until I turn to stare into the dazed expression etched onto my fairy godmother's features. "What's wrong?"

Mouth agape, she rubs her hands over her face. "What's not wrong tonight?"

On that, we agree. I give her a moment to gather her thoughts. A lot has happened since she barged into the back of our tavern. My whole life has been turned upside down. A small voice at the back of my mind reminds me that I've lost my father, but I push it away. He's not gone. Not the way my mother was taken far too soon with the kind of finality only death provides. He's missing. Magicked somewhere I don't know or understand. I'm going to get him back.

I fervently repeat that twice more and then turn my attention back on my bewildered fairy godmother. She looks the way I feel. Frazzled, her hair sticking out in odd clumps around her face with all sorts of dirt, leaves, and sparkly glitter tangled in it. Her hands are shaking. For the first time since meeting her, I see her as a person rather than an obstinate being in charge of my life's destruction. As upset as I've been about the results of my misplaced wish, she has to be despaired over losing her wand and access to magic before being more or less blackmailed into helping me instead of continuing on to her immediate future.

We're both having a bad night.

She's the first to feel ready to talk. "Magic doesn't work like that."

It's a broad statement. I stare at her, both of us now standing in the middle of the road with our attention divided between each other and the glowing plant as we come to terms with a shared reality. "I mean, apparently it does."

"But it doesn't," she snaps, swiping her fingers through her messy curls and growling when her hand gets stuck, but continuing to speak with it raised next to her head rather than slow down and deal with the inconvenience. "It never does. I've seen a thousand wishes. I've been called to bestow plenty myself since getting my wand and status as a fairy godmother. This is not how any of it works."

I have questions about the making of a fairy godmother since regular folks aren't typically privy to that information, but I hold them in as I think over her statement. Magic is supposed to be controlled. She's already told me there are rules and regulations and an expected, consistent process. Wishes don't go awry. People don't steal wands and get them embedded in their skin. They don't stagger into the street and conjure up monsters with wild abandon of every societal expectation ever laid out in the history of pretty much forever.

"What are you?" She blurts, her own thought process cutting quicker to the core of our problem than my own.

"Why are you assuming I'm the problem?"

I try to keep my voice even, but I can hear from the inflection of my own voice that this is just a half-hearted attempt to throw the conversation off of myself. Gemma has experience on her side. I'm the only difference in her standard, magical equation. While there's an obvious answer connected to my heritage, I can't just announce that I think my mother was really a witch, supposedly the last free witch in the history of Briargild, and made to be an example for future generations. My father buried the details of his wife in stories, not just because I was young and impressionable, but because it's dangerous to go around claiming family ties to someone so wildly apart from our modern world. Even with the current state of things, I'm not about to out myself to a fairy godmother who works for the King of Briargild.

I glance over at the flower I made with my hands and sheer will and a heavy helping of desperation. Pink and beaming. A fluttering symbol of hope. Plants have always been a passion of mine. A magical flower seems like the universe's way of tying me back to my mother and the heritage I was never allowed to learn.

But this is all new.

I might be wrong. There could be a hundred other reasons that magic went awry at the tavern and out here. I've never been magical before today.

"How often do people break your wand? This is all some weird accident," I manage to come up with before she can argue with me too much.

Her expression scrunches into a glare as she finally manages to disentangle herself from her own hair. "You're becoming quite a problem, Eli Cinderfella."

"I could say the same to you, Gemma."

With all the stress and magical insanity of the last few moments, I'm glad she doesn't just yell at me. She shakes her head. She huffs at my comment. Then, she laughs. It's a desperate, choking gust of lost air, but a laugh nonetheless.

I chuckle, too. It's better than sinking into crying. I won't be getting to the bottom of my problems if I give in to the need to despair now, so I release hysterical giggles at our situation and then step forward with my hand extended to brush Gemma's stubborn curls into their proper places.

A blush blossoming on her cheeks, Gemma kicks the ground. "Thanks. You're not all that bad. You did make this after all."

She brushes glitter from my shoulders and glances at the hip-high, pink creation fit to be in a fairytale. For a moment, we're a team. Two people in an impossible circumstance, and merely doing our best. I let out a gentle sigh.

"So, you're still going to help me fix this?"

"Well, I have no intention of letting you do any more magic," she announces quickly. "But I guess you win. We'll just have to deal with walking to the witch's hut."

Waving her on to lead the way, I check our surroundings with my heart pounding in my throat. My home a wreckage. My neighbors oblivious. Magic a real thing in the glowing petals of the flower I created.

There's nothing left for me to do here.

I whisper an apology for my father, one I hope transcends space and time to reach him wherever he is right now.

I'm going to fix this.

I'm going to fix all of it.

With those words as a mantra in my mind, I follow Gemma to the woods.

5

Gemma's insensible shoes send twinkling echoes through the outermost streets of Briargild. She curses more than once about her aching feet and asks me if we're a similar shoe size before looking over at my worn and fraying boots. Once brown, they're peeling around the toe in several shades that are almost gray, with laces I've replaced with twine after the third time they broke. I only notice the holes in the soles when I step in a puddle. These are the shoes of the working class, and my fairy godmother does not seem to approve.

In relatively disgruntled silence, we pass through the lower city. Crumpled bits of yellow paper that used to be stars litter the dirt roads. This far away from the tavern, everything seems undisturbed by my misplaced magic. Evidence of partying lingers on gold-stained stoops and confetti-specked gutters. For months after the solstice every year, it's common to see gold paper stuffed into bird nests and gathered in trash piles or used as kindling for fire in the lingering cold months.

Buildings with crumbled facades and broken windows covered with cheap wood are the ones nearest the forest. Gemma sniffs, but doesn't say anything out loud about it. I'm sure it's quite different from what she's used to in the noble living areas. She does her best not to wrinkle her nose at the smell of pigs and cattle out here on the perimeter, the last few meters of community before the golden guard towers that mark the end of Briargild's control.

Due more to the amount of liquor consumed and partying done for the celebration of the solstice than our stealth, we manage to exit the lower city without a single soul seeing us. There are no guards posted on the outermost watch towers. There rarely is anymore. The original kings conquered and colonized all of the smaller communities that once lived out here. On every map available, there's only Briargild and lush forests hiding more magic than even Anerald can dream of controlling. The next kingdom is across the sea, leaving our large island at the mercy of Briargildian royalty. A shiver works its way over my shoulders and trickles down my spine as we pass the golden spires and the slight golden sheen that marks the shield separating the kingdom from the forest. Magic woven centuries ago that we're not supposed to walk through. Out here, we won't be protected by the barriers, but we will be free to make some magical mishap and maybe retrieve the wand in my palms, so it's a fair trade.

Besides, it's just me and my mercurial fairy godmother and our trek towards the forest. There can't be anything more dangerous than her and the magic living in my hands.

"What's the chance we'll see a bear?" I muse aloud, aware of the way my fairy godmother doesn't seem to be jittery and unsettled by the walk through the barrier.

Like she's done this before.

Not just in dire need of replacing her wand. She seems almost relaxed out here. Gold hair bobbing amongst the background of evergreen pines and wintery white, Gemma never slows in her steady pace ever forward.

"Bears belong in storybooks just as much as dragons," she mutters back from ahead of me, kicking her shoes off with a huff when they stick in the mud.

Dragons. That's the second time in a day I've seen them referenced outside of fairytales. I pass Gemma's glass heels, the smooth material glinting in the moonlight that manages to peek through wispy clouds. Then, we're in the trees.

There's no clear path here. Gemma romps forward without reconsidering our movements. She isn't in the mood to talk, keeping a steady six or seven steps ahead of me at all times while her golden locks bounce in the shadows of the looming trees.

Which leaves me alone with my thoughts and observations.

I note a few areas of the dirt that're riddled with footsteps not left by my fairy godmother or myself. Footsteps probably of some poor fool convinced to come dance out here in the rain while supposed witches lured him to his fate. At least, that's the rumor that flits through the tavern. Witches still exist in hiding and prey upon those who have misplaced their common sense. Some say these dalliances are a kiss and fuzzy memories that haunt the victims for years to come. Others whisper that bargains are made in the darkest moments of the evening and shadowy fingers claw at those who stepped out of the forest, hungry to pull them back and devour those who don't complete their ends of oddly worded contracts. It's not kind to stereotype any being based on their magical background, but I think it's best we remain cautious as we traipse straight into unknown territory in search of a witch my fairy godmother supposedly knows.

My fingers find the locket around my throat. The last witch. The last woman burned and executed for being a witch. I doubt I'll be marked safe from magical shenanigans or odd deals due to my ties to my mother, so I brace myself against the eerie quiet of the forest and call out to my fairy godmother.

"Gemma? Maybe we should slow down?"

My concerns fall on deafened ears. She's either too busy keeping focused on picking up the right trail to the witch's home or doing a damn good job of pretending that she can't hear me as we move along the dirt walkways carved by perilous travelers and the occasional weather event—wilted grasses in shades of green and yellow tickle our ankles. Long branches hang down to pluck at our collars and pull at our hair, the evergreen bristles itching and tickling as they fall from above. The needles litter our clothes and then thud to the cold ground in a resounding echo that chases us along our unplanned path.

It's too quiet. I'm too jumpy, but I know the falling needles shouldn't be audible. Breath held hostage in my lungs, I try to listen for anything else: the near-silent flutter of a bird, the impatient scurry of a rodent, even the nervous tip-tapping of insects going about their nightly routines despite our presence.

Yet, there's absolutely nothing out here.

"Gemma?" I try again, all too sure that a quiet forest is a dangerous forest and that we need to figure out what's going on before we become yet another set of victims swallowed by the bark and greenery.

"Would you grow a backbone?" She snaps over her shoulder, her voice a shock in the otherwise silent forest that has me staggering. "We're out here because of you. Just be quiet and let's get this over with."

Her outburst is louder than fireworks set off for the holidays. I wait for a few seconds to see if now is the time for a rampant bear or some kind of supernatural creature to spring from the trees and nab us. When it doesn't, I return to following Gemma. An apology immediately leaps to my cold lips, and I force myself to swallow it. She's as much a part of this problem as I am. I just have more of a desire to survive the night than she seems to.

Unimpressed with the offerings of the forest, Gemma continues in her irate walk forward, huffing and puffing as she kicks her feet through the underbrush. She's so busy trying to put space between us and gather all eighteen ripped and fraying layers of her ridiculously fancy dress that she doesn't see the trap. She's in front of me one moment, and then a gust of wind steals her scream. Branches snap and groan. The pile of leaves and dead grass she had been tromping through give out.

Forgetting my fears of the forest, I run to catch up, peering into the enormous hole in the ground. Gemma is at the bottom. Her curly hair is even more full of crushed leaves. She wheezes out a breath, patting her arms and side where stray branches bit into her, and then curses for all the world to hear.

"You alright?" I say when she's better equipped to answer me with a word longer than four letters.

"Do I look alright?"

She waves her arms at me from her packed-dirt enclosure, her sleeves torn and stripes of blood trickling towards her elbows. I roll my eyes without thinking. She responds with a gesture that's not very ladylike. We're at a standstill until she lets out a shaky breath and tells me to help her.

"I can't reach you," I confirm, lying on my stomach and reaching my arm into the deep hole in the ground as she staggers to her feet. "I could try magic."

"DO NOT DO THAT!"

An exasperated sigh tears itself from my throat. What's even the point of having access to magic if I don't get to use it? Pink sparkles coat my palms as though to agree. I push back to my feet and curl my hands into fists before I can give in to the notion to just try something spontaneous.

"I made that flower, isn't that proof I can do this?"

Gemma looks prepared to pull out her hair. "Fixing one of your mistakes is far from enough, Eli Cinderfella. The fact that you even conjured a plant in Briargild is a bad sign."

"What do you want me to do then?" I grumble. My plant was beautiful. She shouldn't take her frustration out on it.

"Go find help," Gemma nearly screeches, her hands tucked into her armpits as she curls in on herself.

I'm too far away and it's too dark to tell if those are tears on her cheek, but I lower my voice anyway. "Okay. Hey. Don't stress. I'll get you out of there, and everything will be okay."

She slumps backwards, sliding down the dirt wall and coming to a stop in a ball on the ground. "Nothing will ever be okay again," she moans, her words slurred and muffled as she pulls up an edge of her dress and then blows her nose on it.

Keeping my opinions on that particular action to myself, I clear my throat to get her attention back on me. "Look, if someone set a trap, then they have to be nearby to check it. I'm sure they weren't trying to catch fairy godmothers, so we'll explain the situation and they'll help me get you out of there."

It's a solid plan. I feel very good about the logic I plucked from thin air. Gemma, though, doesn't respond. Her shoulders shake and shudder. I don't dare say anything else as she gives in to the tears and then the sobs that follow.

This is up to me.

My chest tight, I move away from the edge of the hole and hope she believes that I can fix this. It's just one more thing on the list I've compiled. My father. The collapsed tavern. Now, my fairy godmother. With hours left until the full flush of morning and only the stars peering through the trees to guide me, I start walking.

This was supposed to be the best night. It was going to be perfect. I should be sleeping in my chair by the fire right now, exhausted from the day and left sharing the dregs of freshly brewed ale for the winter season with my father. He would snore. I'd eventually wake and drag us both to bed. If it weren't for those guards and the man with magical contraband, I would have never broken my father's trust, I wouldn't have made a bad wish, and Gemma wouldn't now be at the bottom of a hole.

It's terrible how connected everything seems to be.

I shiver, rub my hands together to fend off the chill, and then try to focus on my surroundings rather than my guilt and despair over the rest of the night. Everything looks the same. It's just looming trees and the constant threat of my imminent demise. I have no idea how she expected to drive a carriage through here. Moving slower than necessary, I make sure to double-check every leafy patch I step in on the chance it's one more trap. As bad as a fairy godmother in a hole is, we certainly won't survive both of us spending the night that way. I count my steps, moving in a straight line away from Gemma's spot so as not to lose her in my search for help.

I can do this. Cinderfella's don't back down from a challenge.

If I can save her, then I can still believe in my ability to fix everything else, right?

There has to be someone around here. An outsider banished from the city and forced to live here at the outskirts of the lower city. Maybe a nymph trying to sleep through the night. At this point, I would love to stumble upon a witch, regardless of whether it's the one we were trying to find or not. Anyone would be a great help to our current problem.

After several long moments spent counting my steps and finding absolutely nothing, I kick at the dirt and let out a frustrated sigh. A long rope could solve my problem.

Of course, the forest offers no solutions. I step through the underbrush that overtakes the slim path extending away from Gemma's trapped position and pray that I can find help before some kind of snake can make me its dinner every time my ankle plunges somewhere I can't quite see it. I'd forgotten about normal problems with so much magic on my mind. Now, every tremble of tree bristles from the soft, winter wind sets me on edge as I keep an eye out for dangerous fauna.

Fortunately, there are a lot of trees and not a whole lot of anything else. The branches I swat out of my way are frostbitten and too brittle to use as a makeshift ladder for my fairy godmother. There are no vines or other long and flexible organic materials to work with in this particular circumstance. It's just me, in the dark, with no clue as to whether I'm getting closer to another living person as the forest remains unnaturally silent.

Wait.

There.

I pause in my forward motion, my feet frozen in my shoes as I stop on chilled dirt.

I heard something.

"Hello?"

There's no answer. I didn't really expect one, but I try again, anyway, trying to get back to Gemma as quickly as possible and open to shouting into the forest like a fool if it gets us closer to that objective. "Hey. I could really use some help."

About to give up and return to counting steps forward, I hear a rustle off to my left. "I don't suppose you have an invitation?"

I watch the woman from the tavern, the one with amber eyes I've been trying to avoid, materialize out of what seems to be thin air. Startled, I instinctively step back. My palms prickle. There's definitely magic at play here.

She smiles, a thin curve of lips that are stained dark with what I hope is makeup and not the blood of an innocent victim. "Come on, tavern keep. Why are you out here if you don't have an invitation?"

I open my mouth and then shut it. I have no idea what invitation she's talking about. That doesn't seem to matter, though. Her eyes catch on my palms, on the trail of pink glitter that seems to be following me because I cannot figure out how to stay calm in any of these new and tense situations. She's speaking again before I can reiterate that I need help.

"I need a date to this party. Come with me, and then I'll help you."

I don't really have time for a party, but she holds her hand out and snatches one of mine from my side. Her grip is more calloused than I would have imagined; she keeps a tight hold on me and then tugs me back towards where she came from. I expect her to turn invisible once more. The woman in a plain, black top, only a few shades darker than her skin, winks at me and paces forward four more steps until we're standing on the outside of a shimmering, golden door just hanging in the middle of the forest.

I want to tell her she doesn't look dressed for a party, but she's already speaking. "Touch that, will you?"

I may not have expected the hole that Gemma fell into, but I know a trap when I see one. I try to jerk away from her, only until she sinks sharp nails into the back of my hand. This is it. I'm the fool who got taken under the last light of a full moon and lost his soul to a witch.

"Come on. Your magic will activate it. Just touch the door, tavern boy."

Tavern keep was a much more respectable name. "Where does it go?"

She rolls her eyes. "To the party. Just touch it."

I'm not usually one for giving in to peer pressure, but I'm on a time limit until Gemma really starts to think I won't be back to save her, and this woman has already agreed to help me, so I let out a frustrated breath and reach forward. Warmth grazes my skin. The door shines brighter, and I feel a hot brush of power search my palm. It must find what it's looking for because there's a rumble.

"Now, say this: When dragons return."

I do, the words a leaden weight on my tongue of promises I don't understand. Dragons again. This isn't a coincidence anymore.

Of course, there isn't time to question anything as a loud click resounds and the door swings inward. Releasing a victorious hiss, the woman with me steps in first and then looks back over her shoulder when I hesitate, her fingers still a tight cuff around my hand.

"Come on. The party won't wait all night for you."

And so, my fairy godmother left in a hole and a woman I shouldn't trust leading me along, I step through the door.

6

One moment, I'm mostly alone in a barren wasteland of slushy spots where snow settled during the storm last week, and the next I'm in a meadow that looks to be preserved in the finest grip of Spring. Flowers in shades of blue and yellow speckle an expanse of the brightest green grass I've ever seen. Warmth replaces the cold touch of winter lingering on my skin. My limbs tingle from the sudden change in temperature. The air is clean and fresh, and I stand firmly in a place that belongs in a fairytale, completely dazed.

Behind us, the door vanishes, and I'm left looking up at the same night sky, interrupted only by floating glass orbs holding fireflies. I step closer to peer up at the pesky bugs known for their domain over fire magic and their ability to burn down whole crops in a fit of rage, almost too large for their tiny stature. Yellow bodies with nearly invisible wings and a glowing bit of orange in their abdomen, they're almost cute like this. Almost. I have no intention of ever getting more familiar with the bugs. They tap their walls every so often, but otherwise, hover quietly in their respective containers, floating on magic alone.

"What is this place?"

The woman doesn't respond, and I'm too invested in this particular venture that I don't really mind. There is so much to see, and I'm reveling in the warmth that has more pink glitter gathering at my palms. She gently tugs me as she moves forward, pulling me away from the captured fireflies without any comments about my glittery disposition. Overtaken by curiosity, I toss a silent apology to Gemma for taking a detour from my goal to save her and then plunge forward into the unknown.

The meadow is a perfect circle within a ring of trees. Across the spring lawn, there's a table set up with food and drinks. Everywhere I look, there seem to be magical beings. Pixies flit between tree branches, swooping down to pull at the hair of people below them and then snickering as they take off, their wings blending into the leaves for a perfect camouflage act. There are several normal-looking individuals off to the side of the heavily laden table. Dressed in bright blues, they designate themselves with silver pins on their lapels as shifters. Human-presenting creatures with an ability to blend with the animals of the known universe and a bloodlust said to rise and fall with the phases of the moon, there are more of them around Briargild than any of the other species of beings, and still, I know the briefest synopsis on them. There was an entire group of shifters in the tavern only a few hours ago, and I didn't have the courage to ask them personal questions then, either. It's probably best for my sake that I steer clear of that group.

Several satyrs sit on the edge of the lawn, winding together floral crowns. There are five centaurs in total, standing in two separate groups. It's the most of them I've ever seen at one time, and they seem to understand the intimidation large groups of them can cause, talking in calm, low murmurs as they cross their arms over their broad chests and leave the weapons at their waists alone.

Weapons. Swords. It's an illegal practice to have magic in one's veins, but it's easier to hide that. Bows and arrows and unconcealed daggers aren't something I see walking through the streets of Briargild. Why are they sporting them now?

Questions trapped on my tongue like flies in a moon spider's web, I let the woman at my side continue to lead me along. Nobody here is dressed in the finery that I met Gemma in. These are people more like myself than any of the nobility in Briargild's highest ranks. I have no idea why they're all here in the early morning hours of a holiday instead of resting off the hangovers that should stifle them through tomorrow as regular life is reinstated.

"What is happening out here?" I try to ask my presumed date for the magical event when I manage to unstick my tongue from the roof of my mouth.

Instead of offering me an answer, she leads me towards the food table and plucks two drinks off of the edge. Mischief makes a home in her amber gaze as she holds one out to me. It feels like a dare, a challenge, a metaphorical gauntlet thrown at my feet. I'm not one for backing down, so I accept it, trying not to be too interested in the literal flower preserved and used as a cup, the petals still soft to the touch, and the yellow center shining through the pale drink.

"What is this?"

She tips her head back and sips her own cup with a helpful shrug. I may be stubborn, but I'm not entirely stupid. I refuse to follow her action until she sighs and answers me.

"It isn't going to hurt you, tavern boy. Just try it."

Probably too easily goaded, I follow her lead. The drink explodes across my palate. A hint of florals. Something sweet, sweeter than honey. A burst of bubbliness. Lemon to finish. It's good. Really good. I take another drink as the woman with me laughs.

"Easy there. You're only human."

Not sure what that means, I let my glass hang from my fingertips, empty besides a few lingering drops. "What was it? You just said it wouldn't hurt me."

"Fairy wine," she answers half-heartedly as though explaining anything to me is a chore she didn't realize she signed up for when she convinced me to sneak into this party with her.

My father made alcohol his entire livelihood. We dreamt of the stuff, spending our free hours adjusting recipes to make the best products we could and always coming up with new flavor blends with the changing seasons. Our fresh-brewed ale and cocktails are something nobody has ever been able to compete with, but we don't have anything like this.

"What haven't I heard of this before?"

She sets my empty glass with a stack of others and then crosses her slender arms over her chest, our equal height making it almost too easy for her to tilt her chin in such a way that it feels like she's looking down at me in the haughtiest manner. "We may be forced to live in close proximity these days, but there's plenty we don't wish to share with humans, Cinderfella."

"You do know my name!"

People glance over at my outburst, and she grabs my wrist, pulling me behind the food table for some semblance of privacy in this very open space. "Keep it down. You're not supposed to be in here. We don't want people to start asking questions."

"Tell me your name."

Much like the fairy godmother I left in a hole in the forest, she is very good at rolling her eyes at me. "The less you know about me, the better. Just calm down."

I tug my arm out of her hold. "Why did you drag me into this then? I told you I needed help."

We're standing close to each other, almost too close for my own comfort, but I dare not step away as other people and beings of magic circle the table. Her jaw tenses. Absently, she pushes her braids off of her left shoulder and waits as a centaur trods by with a refreshed glass of fairy wine in his hold.

"To be honest," she grumbles, realizing we're not going to get anywhere until she answers, and I hold the power to get very loud and obnoxious. "You caught my eye. I was going to use you for my own needs, but you made yourself interesting when you had enough magic to get in here, so I want to see where the night takes us."

The night isn't going to take us anywhere. My personal tastes skew towards people far less magical, much less dangerous, and typically presenting as the same gender as myself. Besides, I'm on a mission. I have to get back to Gemma sooner rather than later, and I'm willing to look into getting someone else to help me if they'll do so without bartering for a literal arm and leg in return.

Clearing my throat, I change the subject instead of answering her directly. "You know I'm human. Would you be willing to tell me what you are?"

She smiles. Paired with her amber eyes, those sharpened canines are more than mildly threatening. She takes her sweet time thinking up a reply, sipping her fairy wine and letting it swish from one cheek to the other before settling on her answer.

"No, I don't think I will. It's not really the thing you ask a lady about, you know?"

Coy doesn't work for her as well as she wants. "I don't think gender should stop us from being honest with each other."

Her laugh is a barking cough. "You're quick, Mr. Cinderfella. That might be enough to save your life tonight."

Woah. Hold on. Danger wasn't something we previously discussed.

"I know I look like the only human here, but why does that put me in danger?"

Her fingers graze my shoulder as she keeps me in place beside her. "You're not yet. Relax. While most of the beings here are more than capable of doing away with you with half a thought, you're only in trouble if the Necromancer chooses you for his show."

Oh. Well, that's great. I'm surrounded by more magic than I've seen in my entire life besides the fiasco at the tavern, and still, there's something supposedly more dangerous. I'm not even going to get started on the moniker of the unknown being. I really have no plan to stick around long enough to know what someone is doing with dead bodies that has everyone at this party standing on edge.

"Look," I pull away from her again, earning a frown that tugs her lips and creases her brow. "If that's the case, I should just leave. I have someone waiting on me."

"The door closed behind us, tavern boy. You're stuck until he lets us leave."

If I make it out of this, I will not be telling Gemma that I, too, walked right into a trap. I should have walked away from this woman who's been stalking me for weeks. It was too good to be true that she was waiting in the woods to offer help. Of course, her end of the bargain would be more than getting through a floating door and attending a party. There's more for me to say and grumble about and maybe even yell, but I notice the chatter of the party around us sputtering and then stopping completely as their attention turns as one to something behind me.

"Avert your eyes and don't act surprised," my impromptu date instructs.

I'm done following her lead, though. I turn around with the crowd and look for all that I'm worth at the dazzling, golden door that reappears and then opens to allow a figure to step through. To be completely honest, I'm expecting to see a monster. Something half alive and dripping gooey things for dramatic effect. Maybe a humanoid shape of a dead thing that crawled out of a grave and has a smell to match, or a stooped figure wrapped in gauze, too terrifying to behold in the direct light.

The man cloaked in darkness is the opposite of all of that. Standing a few inches taller than myself, he moves with a stiff gait as though his knees aren't quite willing to cooperate, or perhaps he's struggling from the cold, but is otherwise vibrant and alive like everyone else in this clearing. He steps over the edge of the door and treads carefully towards the middle of the gathering. Hands in the deep pockets of his trenchcoat, he swivels his gaze over the collected creatures, and I get a clear view of his face. A loose, black mask covers his nose and mouth and obscures the curve of his jaw, leaving his eyes as the only thing to focus on.

His eyes that I've seen before now.

One brown. One silver.

This man was at the tavern earlier. I wouldn't have guessed that he had played with magic, but it makes sense now as burly shifters dip their head in submission. The silver must be a consequence of his attempt to control the natural world, marking him as someone to be wary of for all future enemies.

There's a tug at my wrist, but I can't take my eyes off the newcomer long enough to pay attention to my date. This must be the so-called Necromancer. He's the man of the mid-morning hour and, if we're being quite honest, he could play as a stand-in for my late-night dreams. My father had unknowingly nailed the kind of person I'm attracted to on his first attempt to set me up. Gods, the things I might allow this man to do to me from semi-visible looks alone.

The woman tugs me harder, but I'm entranced as the man walks around the wide circle. Everywhere he moves, people touch their chests and bow their heads. He stops here and there, presumably asking after his gathered followers, and they answer diligently with idolizing awe sparkling in their gazes. There are almost forty people here of different magical backgrounds, and every single one of them treats him with more respect than the actual king of Briargild. The pixies hover lower, showering his black hood with glitter from their fluttering wings. Centaurs kneel on furry forelegs and repeat the phrase my date had me say on the way in.

"When dragons return."

Over and over. It's a chorus repeated in waves more consistent than those of the oceans. A promise. A plea. A hope registered on every face here.

Dragons.

Like they're even a possibility.

It's certainly not anything King Anerald and his guards would be repeating. Nobody in Briargild would dare say things about the very creatures that Anerald's ancestors exterminated. Dragons were the first to fall. Witches the next. Everyone else forced to kneel in the face of tyranny or be squashed themselves.

The Necromancer steadily paces the inside of the circle. His eyes move around the space, impassive and impenetrable, but stick on me more than once with an interest that makes my heart stumble over itself. This is the kind of man who is used to being heard and followed and bowed down to, and I'm standing here like a fool.

The thought bats at my mind like a moth trying to touch a flame under a glass cover. I should be kneeling for this man. It is exactly what everyone else is doing, including my date, who has now abandoned me to my fate as the Necromancer makes his way towards us.

He stops in front of me. An inch taller. His gaze to my right.

"I believe you had your invitation revoked."

Shoulders curling inward in the first sign of wavering confidence I've seen from her, she answers with her eyes still on the swaying strands of grass beside her knees as her thin braids curtain around the sides of her face. "I'm aware you didn't approve of our last conversation, but-."

He doesn't let her finish. Stepping closer, grass and flowers doing nothing to hinder him, the Necromancer stops mere inches from me. "I certainly didn't extend an invitation to you."

I've spent years sidestepping the ambitious claws of the upper class. I've had practice talking back to my superiors. It is an inelegant skill set I've developed to understand when I'm being talked about, to realize the power imbalance when I'm approached, and to know when I have to do more than bristle at that observation.

"Are you suggesting your security let the wrong person in? You would think a random spot in the forest in the middle of the night was private enough for someone like you."

"Someone like me?" He repeats, his voice dropped to an octave too personal for this setting.

I've had a long night. Even with Gemma's magical pick-me-up,

I'm tired and emotionally drained and thoroughly in need of a bath as well as a full day of sleep. Magic has invaded my life, and I've lost more than I can hope to verbalize anytime soon. All of that working in combination is enough to make my logic faulty. It must certainly be the reason my brain and my body have ceased communicating. The way I feel warm under his gaze is inappropriate for this moment, yet I embrace the feeling, so different from my despair.

"I saw you before," I announce rather lamely.

His left eyebrow ticks upwards. It's the only indication that he understands what I'm saying and recognizes me, too. I almost don't catch the small mannerism since my attention has flitted to his shoulders and the way they're wider than my own.

Turning on his heel, he faces the rest of the crowd, most of them having put as much space between themselves and me while I was acting as the center of the Necromancer's attention, apparently freed from their obligations to kneel while he was focused on me. "It would seem today we have a volunteer."

A soft, simultaneous sigh passes through the crowd like a wave moving down a coastline. Their relief spikes my own emotions. Anxiety needles the back of my neck as I curl my hands into fists at my side to keep them from shaking. I'm supposed to be saving Gemma, not getting myself mixed up with mysterious men.

"What am I volunteering for?"

Those multi-colored eyes are back on me, and he tilts his head one way and then the other as though weighing the options of answering me. "Well, intruder, this group of people are meeting to overthrow the tyranny of our government and lending their magic to a cause for greater good. Are you still interested in sneaking into affairs that don't concern you?"

Until just a few hours ago, I wasn't actually a part of the magical society besides my close association with our indiscriminate clientele at the tavern. That doesn't mean I lack the means to hate the king. Magic isn't the only thing he's put laws against or sought to fully control. Under King Anerald Charming's care, the economy has more or less collapsed as trade routes between other kingdoms were cut off, leaving those of us living within the lower city to struggle even more than we should have had to. Poverty and social status are just as unifying as magical ability.

"Fuck the crown."

It could be my imagination, but I swear his mask pulls a little tighter over his lips as he smiles. "What kind of experience do you have in magical combat?"

The separate pieces of this party start to fall into place in my mind. A wide open space with plenty of room left in the middle as the tables and groups are pressed to the outer limits— people dressed in clothes that are loose or easy to remove. Different factions of magical people coming together for a single idea. This isn't just a place for talking out disgruntled opinions about the state of the world. It's a class for standing up to those powers and doing it well enough so no one remains to fight back.

In my attempt to find help for Gemma, I've stumbled into a call for the revolution.

"None."

He turns his back to me, steadily walking to the far side of the clearing while the other members of the group press further to the edges, a few ducking behind the food table while others already have their hands raised to guard their faces with mixed expressions of trepidation and excitement. "Well, you got in here somehow. How are you at thinking fast?"

The Necromancer throws out his right hand. Something white flies my way. I hit the ground without thinking, looking up just in time to make out the curved shape of the bone he cast my way.

Bones.

Right. He is called the Necromancer. It's better than fleshy dead pieces, I guess.

I don't have time to yell or complain. He's controlling our battlefield with another flick of his wrist. The ground rumbles and then bursts upwards with a spray of gold sparks. An entire graveyard's worth of bones enter the clearing, dangling in the air between us, their sharpened points jutting towards me as he holds his palm flat in my direction.

Nobody and nothing moves as he speaks. "Now, would be a good time to throw up a shield."

He's serious about me doing magic. Right here. Out in the middle of the forest with a live audience watching me, and the cloying scent of upturned graves settled in the back of my throat. My palms tingle in response, pink sparking at the corner of my vision.

It's not like anyone here is going to run off and rat me out to the king, right?

I have magic at my disposal, and now is as good a time as any to learn to use it.

He snaps his fingers, clearly done waiting for me to come to terms with this development. The first bones launch towards me faster than flaming pumpkins from a trebuchet. I skip backwards out of the way, losing ground as grass tears under my feet and the scent of dying plants overtakes the danger-laden air.

This began with a clue. He told me to put on a shield. Since no one here came equipped with the round, metal pieces the guards carry in times of possible siege, I assume that means I need to make one from the power trapped in my palms.

I can do this. Gemma taught me the basics when we tried to conjure a carriage. I just need to think of it, focus on it, and will it into existence.

Easy peasy, even a tavern keep can handle it.

What is a shield besides a big hunk of metal between a man and an oncoming sword? Round. Heavy. It doesn't have to be pretty. I just need it to stop the projectiles from being shot continuously in my direction; the bones always close, but never quite hit me as I move. A large piece of what must be a human rib zips through the air. Move or magic. The Necromancer keeps pulling more bones from the ground, extending his arsenal while I struggle with my choices. If I don't do something now, I'm going to be trapped here all night, a fool in yet another circumstance I cannot control or change.

This is it.

I can do magic. I'm going to put up a shield. When I rescue my fairy godmother from that hole in the ground, I'm going to make her proud with how well I control the magic I stole from her.

Or she'll yell at me.

I'll fight that battle after I survive this one.

The bone lunges for me. It becomes my sole focus, and everything else is only extraneous noise buzzing at the back of my mind. There's no crowd, no woman who stalked me and then used me to break into this meeting of the rebellion. I don't even notice the fuzziness of the fairy wine in my limbs anymore. It's just me and this thing I'm trying to stop. Hands up, thrust forward, I hold the thought of a shield in my mind and then try to push it out of my body with sheer will and a frazzled hope that I'm faster than the coming bone.

I really don't need to be impaled today.

Pink glitter drifts from my palms. It doesn't extend outward. There's no shield in front of me.

I'm not going to be able to conjure it fast enough.

Panic tips my voice into another octave as I hold my hands out and scream the only word I can seem to think. "Stop!"

The bone explodes. White and green fragments litter the area. Pink glitter splashes onto the grass. I don't have time to examine it more as the circle of the Necromancer's arsenal reforms around me this time, instead of just a wall between us. Vaguely, I hear the gathered crowd letting out yips and hurrahs for me while also ducking further away from this particular battle.

"So, you do have magic?"

The Necromancer moves like a shadow cast from the falling sun, languid and unaffected by his surroundings as he leaves no mark behind in his steady circle around me. I can't come up with a response as bones are hurled my way. I duck and spin and drop to the ground and roll out of the way. I hold out my pink-stained hands and yell for the blurred fragments to stop with further explosive results. It's not what I imagined. I didn't make a shield, and it could be said that my magic is faulty, but everyone would have to admit that it works.

I'm not entirely losing this duel.

Happy as I am about that fact, I can't stay on the defensive forever.

The ground is littered with pieces of bone. If he can use them, so can I. Besides, I don't have to depend on magic to help me.

Taking the lead, I match him step for step, stomping over disturbed mounds of dirt and plenty of bones that crack and crumble under my weight. This entire night started because I lost a fight. I'm not about to lose this one.

He realizes my plan and stops evading me. With a wry cock of his eyebrow, the Necromancer holds his ground. His mask is slightly askew, giving me a better sense of the way his lips are moving as he says something under his breath, be it a spell or a curse. Either way, it's directed towards me. I'm a little too caught up in studying him. It's too late to avoid the pulse of power that wraps around my ankle and tugs.

I hit the ground hard. All the air that supposedly filled my lungs before escapes me now. I catch the wispy tendril of a root folding back into the ground amid a pile of bones. Coughing and gasping, my ass throbbing, my spine prepared to go on its own revolution to spite my careless use of it, I lay supposedly helpless on the ground as the Necromancer looms ever nearer. He is as caught up in my theatrics as I was his.

Which is what I need.

His boots stomp closer.

I rake my right hand over the ground near me, scooping up everything I can fit into my palm: bones, small rocks, and plenty of trodden-on dirt.

Sucking in a breath my lungs aren't ready to take, I wait for one more step. He's right over me. I fling my arm up, tossing my fistful of inventive weaponry as hard as I can into his face. For the first time, the Necromancer lets out a roar, a sound that is not calm or composed or very in control.

It thrills me.

I scramble backwards, unsure how to deal with that particular emotion and more concerned with living to see the morning sun. Snarling curses chase my heels as he rubs the grit from his eyes. Unfortunately for him, he can't see the rest of my plan falling into place.

Back on my feet, my hands in front of me and the battlefield at my disposal, I concentrate on making the bones come together. Sweat clings to my neck. My arms shake. Heat gathers in my armpits and elbows and swarms to my hands with reckless abandon.

Cuts mar my fingers, giving the pink glitter that signifies my magic more places to squeeze out of me. It itches. It hurts. It is the least of my concerns. There isn't time to care about anything besides my plans for the battle. The bones rattle and then slink a bit closer to each other.

More.

I need them to be something so much more.

If we're really serious, I need a gods damned hero, and I might have to be one myself since no one else is prepared to intervene.

In a blast of pink light, the bones slam together, cobbling themselves into the form of a human skeleton, albeit with a few extra pieces. Sharpened bones stick up from the shoulders. The arms definitely don't look quite right, but they're functional. I think one of the ribs is on backwards. It doesn't matter, though. I'm not a scientist or doctor. It looks close enough. The skeleton leans over to pick up a vicious shard of bone and holds it like a dagger in its fist.

This is it. My winning maneuver.

I spare a glance at my opponent. His hands are at his sides. Eyes cleared, he gazes at my magical concoction of cobbled body parts. There's no fight, no murmuring, no anything. He stands unfazed as he lets me finish my foolhardy attempt at magic.

Cocky bastard.

The ground firm beneath me, I inch away from the skeleton I intend to send after the Necromancer, as I'm not entirely sure with my current track record that the magic will actually do as I want. I'm desperate to give myself some space, should I need to conjure up an escape plan. "I'm sure you're not used to people standing up to you, but now would be a good time to call all of this off if you want to maintain your intimidating image."

It's never too late to try to bluff one's way out of a fight, is it?

As if remembering the crowd of cowering individuals around us, he surveys the scene with a shrug. "That was a neat trick. Were you done? I've been waiting to demonstrate some real magic."

A murmur skitters through the gathering. I have the decency to shudder in my boots. I was excited that the skeleton didn't turn into a carnivorous plant like my carriage attempt, and I may have overexerted my confidence— a fact the Necromancer can't fully know as he casually holds his place across from me.

I still have time. Before I can give way to the apprehension winding through my muscles like a millipede making its home, I point a finger to my skeleton, the creature scratching the top of its stained skull with the makeshift dagger while awaiting my direction. "Attack!"

Nothing happens. Of course, nothing freaking happens. The skeleton uses a bony finger to pluck grass out of its misshapen eye socket. It's bored, rather unconcerned, and altogether useless. My attempt at a surprise attack thwarted by my own creation, I huff and snap my command again.

The Necromancer is kind enough to cut me off before I can embarrass myself for a third time. "Magic needs exact direction. There can't be room for misinterpretation, or it'll be lost to do as it pleases rather than what you want." His gloved hands are held out in front of himself, and his chest puffs with his loud command. "Collapse."

And my skeleton listens.

Fuck.

No. Nope. Not today. I've lost enough. He's not going to take this from me.

"Rebuild!"

Pink bursts through the gold of the other man's magic as the bones rattle and then clamber up each other to return to my disjointed depiction of a human skeleton. "Is this really the game you want to play, outsider?"

The Necromancer and I are standing on opposite sides of the field, both breathing a little hard from our magic fight. I tilt my chin up in earnest and not because he's definitely taller. "It's the game I'm going to win."

I shout my next command. There's no room for misinterpretation. The skeleton races forward, its vicious bone dagger held over its shoulder as it lunges towards the Necromancer. The other man doesn't move. Anxiety splashes through my system, sweeping through me faster than the rapids that drown wandering livestock to the east of the main city. Perhaps I went too extreme. Maybe I should stop this before it makes it all the way across the field. Trembling fingers cup my mouth as I forget words and merely watch.

I shouldn't have commanded it to cut out his heart.

All of my worry is wasted. The dagger never makes it close to the Necromancer or what I can only assume is his well-defined chest under those layers of black clothing. His hands held out, the skeleton freezes in place with only a murmured command on his part. He lets the crowd lean in as he returns to our conversation with a devilish glint to his gaze, the flickering light of the overhead fireflies doing things to his features that should be more irritating than alluring in this moment.

"That was cute."

I don't shrink from his backhanded compliment. If we're honest, I don't do much of anything. The next seconds pass too quickly. He swirls his hands in front of himself, conjuring some magic well about my current experience level and projecting it onto the space between us. The battlefield erupts. Hundreds of bones are purged from the softened soil. They move towards my still frozen skeleton, bouncing over one another in an urgent demand to be close to my creation. The bones stack and grow and assemble in mind-boggling efficiency until my cobbled depiction of a skeleton is standing several meters above me.

It's not a human anymore.

Sharpened bones jam themselves together to create wings that nearly stretch from one end of the clearing to the other. The creature drops down onto four legs, sending a tremor through the field. Its neck forms like that of a horse and then continues, growing longer and longer as I gasp into my palm.

I'm not going to be okay if this thing turns into a giant snake.

As if sensing my discomfort, the bones continue to assemble with a general leaning in that direction. It still has legs and wings. This isn't like any animal I've ever seen in my life. It's something out of a storybook from my childhood.

Dragons aren't real, right?

I want to pinch myself, unable to believe my eyes. This is still real life, right?

The face finishes forming, far too reptilian for my own tastes. A shiver rakes nails down my back. Terror opens a pit in my stomach as I back up and lose my footing.

He couldn't pick anything else, could he? It had to look like a freaking snake.

Hands shaking, I manage to suck in one, two, and a half breaths before staggering back to my feet as the jaws of the beast open. Bone shards stick down, impossibly sharp and ready to impale me as easily as the teeth of any predator. It is a predator. My magic attempts have literally been consumed and turned against me in the most horrifying way.

Murmurs and shrieks speckle the crowd, most more excited than fearful, but the skeletal creature never wavers in its direct stare at me. Nobody else is its target. This dragon is only going to eat me.

Mouth agape, knobby wings extended to remind me of its giant stature, the creature stills as a voice booms from behind it. "Still feel like you're going to win?"

Anger warring with outright panic, I aim an inappropriate hand gesture at him as I carefully get back to my feet and put a few steps between me and that dragon. "It's not over yet," I snarl, eyes never leaving the beast stationed like a statue in the midst of a storm, unbelievably still until unthinkable action overtakes it.

The dragon digs claws into the ground, readying itself into a crouch that'll give it the push it needs to jump to my position; it's the only hint I have that it's getting ready to move as my gaze is momentarily torn between those claws that are prepared to shred me and its open chest where a ball of pink glitter pulses like a heart. "Last chance to back down, outsider."

Fuck him. Fuck this. Fuck every gods damned magical incident that brought me here.

I don't care about my honor, my image, or trying to come out the bigger man in a fight I was designed to lose. I care about living. There's no way to rescue my father and undo my bad wish if I'm no more than meat in a dragon's mouth.

As much as I enjoy throwing a punch, survival isn't always winning a fight. Running is a valid option. Perhaps my only option.

Letting him have the last word, I take off in the opposite direction, sprinting very much as if my life depends on it. Breath curled in my lungs like a caterpillar trapped in its chrysalis, I stumble and stagger and altogether run down towards the tree line, sending up a silent plea that my date was wrong when she implied we wouldn't be able to leave.

I didn't mean to be a part of the revolution. Clearly, I wasn't ready to go up against their supposed leader. Maybe there will come a day when I don't feel the need to fight every single authoritative figure that stumbles into my path. Today, though, I pay the consequences. I have to stay out of the snapping maw of the bone dragon if I want any chance to become a different man.

And so, I run.

7

One foot in front of the other is about as far as my plan has taken me. Off the battlefield, through the line of gasping revolutionaries turned morbid audience for my demise, I launch myself towards the supposed safety of the trees. No boundary line tries to stop me. I don't even register the buzz of golden magic on my skin. No tingle. No jolt. Nobody says anything, either, but I hear glass break and a firefly catches up to me to scorch my cheek with a burning kiss.

Whether or not the woman who got me into the revolutionary meeting was lying, I stepped out without needing another golden door. One step, I'm wrapped in warmth and the secrets of Spring, and then next, winter envelopes me once more in a freezing embrace. Beneath my boots, branches snap. I slip with a mouthful of curses on mud turned sludge from the settled patches of snow. Every part of the scenery seems to be against me as low-hanging branches catch my shoulders and shrubs wrap crisp, crunching tendrils around my ankles that trip me.

Is it not enough that I have a dragon on my heels?

Slipping, sliding, scrambling, I make more noise than the beast. I can only assume the lithe combination of bones makes it silent since I'm not brave enough to look over my shoulder and confirm it's really still there. Instead, I gather my dwindling stores of courage and let my panic lead me deeper into the forest.

The trees look the same every way I turn. It's just evergreen bristles and my breath pluming in front of my face while the last sliver of the moon turns away from me altogether. Darkness consumes my immediate surroundings— that and the pink hue falling from my fingertips and leaving a glittering trail behind me.

I'm leading this creature back to Gemma. Maybe. I'm not altogether sure if this is the way I came in the first place. Not good. Very bad. I'm probably lost, and I don't need to put my fairy godmother in even more danger than she already is.

So, I veer left.

My knees ache and threaten to give out, but I hear a resounding crash behind me, a lot like a clattering of bones against a tree. Snapping teeth, clicking in the dark. Scrambling and a vibrating dissonance that might be the growl of a creature without vocal cords. A pulsing, pink glow that may be the heart of the dragon and way too close for comfort. There's no slowing down to check on any of that, so I keep moving forward as my muscles seize, and the fact that all I've put in my stomach in the last twelve hours is alcohol starts to have an impact.

If I survive this, I'm going to puke.

Rustling overtakes the forest off to my left. Not the dragon still scrambling behind me. A fresh horror to complicate my night. I'm turned around. I have no idea if it's someone from the rebel meeting or simply a person wandering through the forest on the one night in the year they're least likely to be caught leaving the boundaries of Briargild. Maybe it's the bear I mentioned to Gemma.

A dark shape lunges out of the forest and into me. Arms and legs askew, the two of us roll before I have any idea who my new attacker is. Off of the narrow trail I'd been following and through crunching brush that relishes in pawing at my clothes and naked forearms and dusts scratches over my brow, I spit a curse that is covered by an inconvenient and glove-covered palm.

"Shh. Let it pass."

I'm not taking commands from someone who calls themself the Necromancer. Honestly, I'm not open to taking commands from anyone right now. The forest is teeming with people who have their own agendas, and I'm tired of being pulled around by my naivety.

There's a woman in a hole I'm supposed to be rescuing, and instead I'm trapped under a fairly heavy man.

Distantly, the rumble of the dragon passes us, and then I tear his hand off my mouth. "Get off of me."

"Do you even understand what just happened?" He asks rather than doing what I said, eyes wide as the coming morning fog settles around us.

"You sent a fucking dragon after me!"

His hand is back on my mouth. He's hushing and holding me down, and I'm tired of it all. I push him. Pink handprints mar his perfectly black attire. Evidence of my hands is left on his chest, his shoulders, his waist as I try to twist out from under him. It isn't until I try to claw at his mask that he relents and gives me a modicum of personal space, both of us panting and sitting in the forest with only lingering frost between us. I make a point to not think about all the places I begin to go cold from his sudden departure, and swallow any comments about the lasting touch of him on me.

"I didn't create the dragon. I was just going to send your skeleton back to you, but the magic changed."

I wish I had slipped that mask off his face. It's impossible to tell if he's truly bewildered by the situation when I can't see his lips. As is, his pupils are dilated, and his attention remains completely ensnared on me as I wipe blood from my forehead, one of the branches having gotten in a damaging shot in my run here.

In the words of my fairy godmother, I scoff, "That's not how magic works."

His brow lowers. Those strange mismatched eyes roam my face with an emotion I can't quite place. Disapproval. A reluctance to be told he's wrong. I'm not sure, but I do enjoy the effect I seem to have on him, our chests rising in unison as we spar for the greater quantity of fresh air after all the running that brought us here.

"You didn't pick a dragon on purpose, then?"

I roll my eyes at him. One of us is being rather obtuse right now, and it isn't me. "I couldn't do magic until very recently, so, no, I did not choose to create a meadow-sized dragon. Especially," I huff, finding my bearings long enough to push up onto my feet to stand over him, "not one with teeth that can chase me through the forest."

From this angle, I can see the bushes leaning in around the Necromancer, how the winter-thinned branches seem to caress his collar and try to whisper in his ear. It's an odd thing to see life clinging to a man who has made death his title and personality. He sits in a puddle of shadow, the darkness having a firmer grasp on him than any life lingering here in the cold season. Head tilted up to me, the Necromancer's eyes shine in the dim light of the stars blinking out with morning's approach.

"I've been waiting my whole life for you, and you really have no clue about any of this, do you?"

The implication that I'm a stupid, lower-class man has glitter running from my fingertips. I cross my arms over my chest to stop the steady flow of magic that increases with my emotional fluctuations. His voice is low, each syllable carefully laid out between us. Noble. At least, someone who has grown up around the aristocratic class that flocks to the castle rather than the gutters of Briargild's outcasts.

I already didn't like his name. Now, I don't like that he's pretending to be some kind of revolutionary of our time when he's reaped the benefits of a broken system. Light skin. Dark eyes. A mask to hide his identity. His whole act is starting to make a lot of sense.

"Who are you?"

"Someone who believes Briargild should change whether or not the prophecy comes true."

Great. He has a weird name to conceal his identity, and he believes in made-up things. Really wonderful company for the middle of the forest. I thought being stuck out here with my fairy godmother was going to be the worst. I'll have to tell her how much I appreciate her firm grasp on reality whenever I find and pull her out of that hole.

The Necromancer starts to speak again, but I don't hear it as a crash overtakes the space behind me— pink pulses against the dry branches of nearby bushes. The color blooms out from either side of me, painting the shrubbery as well as my dueling combatant in the bright shade. It's not coming from me.

I jump out of the bushes just as those teeth snap together. Of course, the beast wastes no time following me. It couldn't be distracted for even one minute by that inconveniencing man in the underbrush. The silent forest is a percussive nightmare of rattling bones and my heavy footsteps. I run, and it follows, pushing all other concerns of the night and weird wording out of my mind.

That brief moment on the ground with my masked assailant was not enough time to rest.

All of my limbs are too heavy. My lungs already ache and sputter in discontent at the gasping breaths of air I allow them. Head swimming, I focus on just moving.

Despite the cold. Despite the leaves and brush trying desperately to trip me. Despite the fact that a dragon is chasing me, and none of this should even be possible.

All the while, it keeps pace with me. Definitely larger, definitely faster, it does nothing to close the gap as I run as fast as my legs will carry me. Somewhere in the back of my frazzled and oxygen-deprived mind, I note that such a thing shouldn't be possible. I can't realistically outrun a dragon, not one made of flesh and blood and certainly not the aerated version behind me. If it hasn't caught up to me by now, there's only one reason: it's enjoying the chase.

So, this must be it.

A dragon and I on the worst winter solstice in history.

My father certainly wouldn't be proud of that. All my life, he told stories about the extraordinary things my mother did. He made up faraway places and dangerous escapades. He kept her alive by making her the main figure in our shared narratives, but, given the choice, had I not accidentally wished him out of this world, he probably wouldn't do the same for me.

I am one bad decision after another, desperately trying to outrun my problems and failing. I'm not what a hero looks like. I'm just an ordinary person in a ridiculous, probably completely avoidable situation.

With my thoughts taking up most of my attention and the dragon behind me doing away with all the rest, I forget to watch my footing. All that mattered was moving and staying out of teeth made from the remains of a mass grave. I had forgotten about Gemma or how to get back to her.

Air meets my next step.

Perhaps the mouth of the bone dragon would have been a better demise than the tumble that takes me to the bottom of the same trap I was meant to rescue my fairy godmother from.

Wheezing, every muscle in my body screaming disgust at the way they've been treated, I stare up as the black silhouettes of the trees are interrupted by the white snout of my assailant. I was wrong.

Eli Cinderfella and the Bone Dragon would have been a cool title for the end of my life. At least, it would have been so much better than Eli Cinderfella and the Great Big Hole He Should Have Seen Coming.

Gemma is several words into a rant when she realizes I'm not listening, but, rather, staring up past her to the creation at the top of our now shared abode. "What did you do?" She screeches, crouching down behind me, my fairy godmother having no qualms with feeding me to the dragon before she perishes herself.

"I didn't do this one," I snap back, fully aware that the pink glitter falling off the creature is enough to get me caught in the lie.

Claws dug into the top of the hole, it snapped once and then twice, twisting its head one way and then the other to get a better view of us through its empty sockets. I have my hands raised in front of my face as spots distort my vision from the way my head hit the muddy wall on the way down. We're not getting out of here alive if I don't do something.

Magic got me into this problem. It's now the only hope of getting us out.

With no clue as to what the Necromancer told it to do or why he claims my magic created it, I need to come up with a command that has no room for misinterpretation. Ears ringing, I squint up at the creature as it flaps useless wings. It's only a matter of time before it comes down here with us. Pink glitter itches along my forearms.

I need something effective.

I need to save us.

The dragon's makeshift teeth gleam in the little bit of light that can reach us here. Still flat on my ass, almost lying in Gemma's lap as she quivers behind me with her hands clamped hard around my shoulders, I point a finger at the dragon as it leers down at us. "Sit!"

And it does.

Of course, it does. Why wouldn't it? Magic is real and apparently works when following simple rules.

There's a muffled thumping coming from somewhere near the hole's opening. Gemma pops up, brushing dirt off her skirts and dumping me out of her lap as she tries to get a better view of our current problem. "Eli, is it wagging its tail?"

In response, the dragon clacks its jaw together twice, but it doesn't try to come any closer. It almost seems cheerful. Taking a step past me, Gemma holds up a hand to the looming creature.

"You're actually a sweetie pie, aren't you?"

I'm on my feet in seconds, tendons whining and my heart a thunderous swell in my ears. Maybe all of the time spent down here has affected my fairy godmother's sense of self-preservation. I reach out to grab Gemma's wrist, but she's done with me, swatting me away as the dragon settles its weight further into the opening.

Rocks and dirt skitter down to us. Then, it leans in. So far in. A terrified cry builds in my throat as it comes closer, and I'm helpless to watch its approach. Gently, far too gently, that large snout presses into her fingers.

There's no biting. Not a single snap. It doesn't make noise since it lacks any vocal cords, but if it could, I imagine it would purr like some of the stray cats we get around the tavern. As is, it grinds its top and bottom jaw together to create a strained, squealing noise, which is an effective substitute.

"Come on, Gem. We can't trust it. You need to be careful."

Pushing dirty, blonde curls out of her face, she looks over her shoulder at me. "Aw, you're worried about little old me?" She waits long enough for me to roll my eyes before pressing on. "You made it, Eli. Clearly, it was just scared. It wouldn't have tried to really hurt you."

I don't correct her on who made the dragon since I don't want to get into the truth on my dishonorable end of a fight I should never have started. "Did you forget about the carnivorous plant I created instead of a carriage? It had teeth and a bad attitude, too."

Gemma shakes her head, her curls bobbing as her eyes shimmer in the bright, pink glow emanating from the dragon's chest. "This one is different. I can feel it."

My jaw opens, but I don't have any more words. We're in an impossible predicament, and she wants to befriend the thing that just tried to eat me. I'm done making wishes, but if I were to make one more, I would wish that magic didn't exist at all, as it has become the absolute bane of my existence.

Gemma doesn't need me to reply; she's perfectly capable of carrying the conversation all on her own. "Do you think he could pick us up?"

Now, she's gendering the pile of bones. "Do not give it a name. We're not keeping it."

"He'll tell us his name when he's ready." Focus back on the dragon, she tosses another question back to me, even as she phrases it to the creature. "Can you get us out of here, sweetheart?"

The bones along its back rattle. There's no cartilage or feathers to help with flight, but the shake of its shoulders and hips causes the wings to shiver and make the kind of noise most people would never hear except in some perverse nightmare. It's certainly a sound I'll never be able to get out of my head, which makes sense since this is my nightmare. Squealing and rubbing and the warning of a storm not quite hitting home, I just want it to stop.

While it seems excited by Gemma's words and continues to nuzzle her fingers, the dragon doesn't otherwise move. "Eli? Can you ask him, please?"

Right. My messed-up magic, my not-so-very-great solution to our current predicament, of course, it'll take my words to get this thing moving. As much as I would like not to participate in this scene, Gemma and the dragon are waiting for me.

"Fine. Gently," I glare up at the bone-fused abomination, "lift her out of here."

It snaps its jaw open and closed a few times and wags its tail some more, apparently so excited to be of assistance now that my magic has a leash on it. Gemma never flinches. She's head-over-heels loyal to the damned thing. Craning further down, claws still latched onto the edge of the pit, he lets her wrap her arms around the smooth bones of its neck and then drags her upwards with him.

Gemma squeals as she's lifted. She kicks her bare feet and lets out a giggle. In return, the abomination shaped like a dragon makes that purring rub of its teeth as it gently moves back. Holding my breath, I watch as she goes up, up, up along with the dragon. It steps back, taking her with it. Once more, there's one of us trapped in a hole in the middle of the forest, but Gemma cheers her delight at being released, celebrating with a wriggle of her hips that is definitely not an appropriate dance move for an upper-class woman like herself.

At least one of us is having the time of their life. My mood sours as I stare around the steep hole in the ground. They better not leave me here.

Fighting the urge to smile at her antics and sure now that the dragon isn't going to eat her, I clear my throat to get their attention back on me. Gemma leans over the edge of the hole, her cheeks flushed and one hand on the dragon as she absently pets the magical being. She looks way too smug for someone with dirt smeared on the tip of her nose.

"Not so fun being down there all by yourself, is it?"

"I got you out!"

She sticks her tongue at me. Not for the first time, I wonder about the childish behavior of my fairy godmother and me. The general rules of society have ceased to matter. Magic is so very real and unpredictable, and currently, I'm the only one who has it. For just a little while longer, there are no consequences for my actions. I stick my tongue back at her.

With a quick command to the dragon, I await my release from the hole. It doesn't offer its neck to me the way it did for Gemma, though. Instead, its bone shard teeth sink into the back of my shirt, and it tugs me upwards with a swift jerk of its head. Once more, flexible air fumbles its attempt to catch me, and I fall until the ground rises up to claim me. Gemma's laughter rings through the clearing along with the chattering clack of the dragon's jaw. Coughing and sore, I crawl to my feet and stand with my hands on my hips as I take in the gleeful pair in front of me.

I'm not actually sure what's next.

We're out of the hole.

We're now accompanied by a dragon, the magic sustaining it without any sign that it'll stop.

"Are we still trying to see the witch?"

There's a rustle behind Gemma. The woman from the tavern, the one who begged me to play as her date to a secret society of rebelling magical beings, the woman who wouldn't tell me if she was a witch or nymph or something far more nefarious just a few moments ago steps out of the nearby tree line with a smile that can only be described as absolutely devious.

"I hope so," she croons. "The Witch of the Woods is ready to see you now."

8

After her overzealous acceptance of the bone dragon that literally chased me here, I'm surprised to see Gemma step away from the other woman. I'd assumed her pleasant, carefree personality would extend to everyone around her. The odd motion staggers me. It catches my attention entirely, my weary body and possibly concussed mind incapable of taking on anything more than the subject of my fairy godmother. I suppose I have to admit I've never seen her interact with another person, the two of us entrenched in magical dilemmas together for the entirety of our relationship, but I figured her for a pretty social person. Her attire spoke to that, at the very least. She isn't exactly a wallflower.

Gemma has gone silent, though. Stiffly, her fingers continue to brush the dragon's lowered face as she does her best impression of a woman sinking into the forest floor. Odd tension beyond my ability to untangle, I adjust my sights on the woman who just introduced herself as the very witch we were looking for.

"Why lead me on at the party if you knew I was out here looking for you?"

Those amber eyes are about to be my least favorite thing I've ever looked into with the way they shimmer with secrets. "Where exactly did I lead you?"

Smack dab in to the middle of trouble. Ensnared in danger. She led me to the Necromancer, and I have no idea why.

Of course, she grins at the way I've been opening and closing my mouth without a real answer and then waves me off, silver rings glittering in the ball of dim light of the stars. "Let's not be drawn to dramatics. I made introductions you were bound to fall into anyway, and now we should go inside to discuss things properly. It's not like there's anyone else around here prepared to help with that missing wand, is there?"

"How do you even know that?" I snap, almost oblivious to the way she's been looking past me to the other woman.

Almost.

Gemma is still avoiding making eye contact with anyone, her bare feet shuffling uncomfortably on the frozen ground. "Because I'm the only fairy godmother who has managed to misplace her wand, and this isn't the first time."

"Yes, well," the witch crosses her slim arms over her chest, a defiant stance that has her bare shoulders bunching towards her ears, "it was really a matter of time before you came crawling back here anyway, wasn't it?"

Whatever that means, Gemma doesn't respond to it. Instead, she sniffs and changes the subject. "Traps aren't very nice."

"I can't be too careful right now. His Royal Highness is sending out more and more search parties to rid the country of free magic. Maybe you should take your concerns to him since you just love Briargild so damn much."

Oh man. This is not good. I should have realized sooner that I was being led into an uncomfortable situation. Fairy godmothers and witches aren't exactly friendly characters in old stories. It was the fairy godmothers who looked the other way as witches were burned and sent out of Briargild thirty years ago. Both women have an implicit control over magic, one is illegal and meant to be fully quashed by the current crown, while the other has the full support of the kingdom. Regardless of anything else, that puts Gemma and this witch on opposite sides of a harsh spectrum.

Staggering slightly away from the venom in the witch's words, I bump into the bone dragon, the creature having sidled up next to me as Gemma's hands balled into fists in the still poofy layers of her destroyed dress. It's almost sweet until I realize how close those teeth are to my shoulder. The gaping eye sockets seem to stare through me as it cranes its neck to my head level. Still very much a snake with a dragon body. My skin crawls, and I hold very still lest any sudden movements spur it back into action.

I clear my throat. "You said there was somewhere to go inside?"

With a smirk, the witch raises her arms over her head and snaps her fingers. Her magic is a lively blue. It's a stark contrast to my own pink and the gold of everything else I've seen up until this point. Less sparkling dust and more a plume of smoke that appears out of thin air, a thought given form and leashed to her command. It's beautiful, the shade tipping into shimmering layers of purple as it zips behind her and starts to seemingly eat away at the landscape of trees I've walked by twice now.

Except there aren't really trees there. It was an illusion. I wouldn't have ever slowed down and noticed it if Gemma hadn't been unfortunate enough to fall into the hole first. It doesn't take much for me to be flabbergasted by the things magic can do. Self-consciously, I wriggle my fingers at my side. That's something I theoretically could do if I took the time to understand better the power pulsing in my palms. Magic isn't my favorite thing in the world right now, but when I see displays such as this, I have to admit I'm intrigued by it.

Maybe wild magic isn't the evil the kings of Briargild have made it out to be.

Of course, with my luck, I would attempt something like this, and it would grow teeth and try to eat me. It's still best to get this witch to remove the wand— no more magic for me. My wish undone. My life my own again

That's still my priority. It's really all I want.

The tavern. My father. I'll grovel and take responsibility for all I did tonight, and we can go back to living our lives in relative contentment despite the state of the world. Not everything has to be my problem. I won't go back to rebel meetings. I won't go searching for other ways to do magic even though the zing of it in my veins makes me think it's always been meant for me, a tie to a mother I didn't get to know and yet feel close to in my current state. I will just be Eli Cinderfella, the tavern keep, and it'll be enough.

Next to me, Gemma is silent. Her hands are busy, rapidly plucking bits of dirt and debris from her hair. She rakes her fingers through her tangled curls with a curse under her breath. Aware that I must look incredibly haphazard as well after all of the running and the falling and general shenanigans of the night, I don't understand why her hair matters so much right this second. All attempts to fix her appearance stop as soon as the witch fixes her gaze back on us rather than the work of her magic.

Perhaps there's more here than I'm willing to ask about.

My hands itching from glittering magic that wants to leap out and swirl with the purple remnants of the witch's display, a dragon at my side and the firm belief that I'm a pawn in much bigger schemes, I don't wait for the magic to finish revealing the wooden boards of the cabin or unfurl away from the three steps leading down from the bright, lavender door before blurting my biggest concern. "Do you think you can fix me?"

Amber eyes scrape over me, marking me from my bruised cheek to the still bleeding cuts on my hands and finally to my feet, wet from trekking through the winter landscape in worn boots. "A woman cannot fix a man more than he'll allow."

There's no stopping the groan that escapes me. I've been fully immersed in the world of magic for less than twelve hours. I would really like people to stop talking in riddles and acting like all of this is so freaking normal. My question was simple. I just need a yes or a no. Can the wand be removed? Can I have my life back?

A smaller voice pipes up in the back of my exhausted and buzzing mind. I will beg before the answer is no. Please. Is there a way to get my father back and undo all the damage I did before Gemma showed up? I can't let that last fight be all we ever get to say to one another.

Before I can swallow my frustration and grief and pepper her with the rest of my questions, the witch cuts me off, silver bracelets tinkling on her left wrist with her motion to quiet me. "Stop wallowing. You're the one who stole a magic wand, so you have to pay the consequences."

I still don't know how she knows that. Besides the fact that she has been stalking me at the tavern and the distinct glitter that seems always to be coating my hands now, there's no way to know that's why I was out here. I wasn't even with Gemma when she found me. Those thoughts and questions swirl around a metaphorical toilet bowl, flushing from my mind before they can be thoroughly investigated. It doesn't matter anyway. I'm new to the magic scene. Everyone just seems to know more than I do. If I can get help, I'll take it and ignore the niggling inconsistencies at the back of my mind.

As is, the witch has turned away from us, her layered skirts twirling around her calves. I gaze at her back, at her odd ensemble, and the fact that she changed her top from the black one she was wearing earlier this evening. Now, she's in a lilac shirt that leaves her shoulders out in the cold, the bottom of it hacked away to hang in frayed strings over her exposed navel. She's revealing far more skin than most women do in the warmer seasons, and her gaze can't quite stay away from Gemma as she checks to make sure we're following her. Walking up those steps, her skirts sway, giving me just a handful of seconds to take in the patchwork of quilted squares stitched together with lines of flowers that speak to a love of hand sewing I've never seen up close. Confident and serene even in her haughty opinions, she embodies the spirit of spring even as that season remains months off in the undetermined future.

Staring hard at her back, I note the carefully woven braids that fall to the middle of her spine, each one thin and decorated with dried flowers or delicate pieces of silver metal that shimmer in the light of the candles adorning the space around her open doorway. Gemma is two steps behind me, reluctant to come in and shamelessly looking at the witch as well. There's something indiscernible in her gaze. A part of me wants to ask. I want to bump shoulders with her and whisper my question, a conspiratory kind of secret pressed between the two of us in the wake of the witch's direction.

I don't get the chance as the Witch of the Woods stops and looks back at us from just past the door. "Tell your pet to stay outside. There isn't room for all of us in here, and I have antiques I would like to make it to the next century."

"You know that he's not mine," I grumble back at her. "Why is it even still here? Shouldn't the magic just wear off?"

The witch waves at me, my questions not her problem, apparently. That leaves Gemma to huff a sigh when I flick my attention to her instead of raising my voice at the woman I still need to beg to help me.

Posture slumped, voice low, Gemma shakes her head, revealing even more crushed leaves and dirt in various curls in her hair; she hasn't had time to dislodge them. "How should I know, Eli?

Everything I know about magic ceases to be true when it comes to you. Things aren't supposed to come to life. Magic is a tool just like a hammer, and yet, when you do it, there's so much more happening. Just do what she said and get in there. I want to go to bed at some point tonight."

Still not entirely sure what I walked into by being here with these two women, I mutter a comment about her snippy tone under my breath and then clear my throat at the dragon. "I guess sit and stay. We'll be back."

The dragon snaps its jaws and then shakes its head, vibrating the bones from its neck to its tail before plopping onto the soft dirt. Happy it listened without me having to be overly firm, I try to ignore the rattling noise coming from it as it scratches where its ear would be if it were made of more than bones and magic. I also avert my eyes from those teeth, fangs, and bone shards carved into a deadly point. It lies like a dog settling in a cozy bed, but those reptilian features threaten to make me hyperventilate. I absolutely do not agree with Gemma's cooing about how cute it is.

Trusting my command will last, I start for the witch's cottage since it seems Gemma isn't about to be the first through the door. A thousand questions bat at my mind as I step up onto the worn stoop and duck into the doorway. It's dark. Candles burn on nearly every viable surface. They ring the doorway on little hand-carved shelves— nubs and tapers and what looks like jam jars filled with wax. The witch has a very extensive candle collection and an affinity, it seems, for burning them all at once.

Past the doorway, I squint into the flickering light of the candles to see a stove bracketed by counters full of cookbooks, knick-knacks, and an assortment of labeled glasses with ingredients I don't recognize. There are some kitchen accessories, cupboards that look too full to close properly, and a yellow rug nearly threadbare but lovingly displayed in the center of the space. Walking further, I have to duck my head to avoid bumping it on bundles of dried herbs that dangle from the ceiling. I recognize some of them: rosemary, thyme, gathered bits of wheat, and roses. Others are beyond me and likely a secret of the magical society. Something in the corner past the pantry glows with an odd, green tinge. Another unidentified specimen curls willowy tendrils towards the ground from a perch in a pot on top of a bookshelf, moving ever so slightly as if reaching out for unsuspecting prey.

The whole place carries the stench of lavender. I tug at the collar of my shirt and try not to breathe in too deeply. Hot from the flames of a hundred candles and now lightheaded from the effects of lavender exposure, I blink away the desire to sit down and let the drowsiness pull me away from my current mission.

Narrowly avoiding pricking myself on yet another dangerous-looking plant as we cross the open floor plan from the kitchen to the seating area, I check to make sure Gemma is close. She is. Her eyes don't swivel over the strange space. She doesn't once seem captivated by the star charts tacked to the wall to our left or seem curious about what lies behind a beaded curtain at the far end of the cottage. Gemma is making sure she stays equidistant from the witch with me in between them.

As such, we come to the seating area, which consists of two chairs and a wooden bench separated by a cauldron. Before I can make my own decisions, Gemma grabs my wrist and tugs me into the chair beside her, forcing the witch to take a place across from us. She stares across the gentle smoke pouring out of her cauldron and gives it a stir with a wooden spoon, clearly unconcerned with breaking certain, witchy stereotypes as the purple mixture gurgles and bubbles and then burps another cloud of smoke to add to the eerie ambience of her home.

"Now, what was it you wanted to ask of me?" I open my mouth to answer her immediately, questions about my father and the tavern and how to get my life back in order, racing to be the first to express, but she holds up a palm before I can. "Ladies first."

Gemma huffs a sigh. "Wynn," she says softly, speaking towards her lap, "I know we said last time was the last time, but I really can't get caught without my wand."

"How many times have you lost your wand?"

Neither of them spares me a glance. They don't answer my question, either. Clearly, there's a complicated history between the two of them, and I've become extraneous noise outside of it.

"What did I say last time, Gem?"

The nickname seems to jolt my fairy godmother out of her submissive, recoiled state. Her spine straightens. For the first time since the witch joined us, she raises her head and juts out her chin. I note the way her fingers curl around the edges of her chair seat, all of her knuckles a bright white.

"This is bigger than me now, Wynnifred. It sounds like you used Eli for your own ridiculous purposes, too. If you don't want to help me, then fine, but you can do something for him, and you can do it without these stupid games."

The witch is frowning. I don't enjoy being on the receiving end of it. After the display of magic outside, I firmly believe she could turn me into a frog or newt or something equally miserable if she wanted to, which makes everything even more tense and dangerous than it needs to be. Not sure if I should interject or distract or just leave the room entirely before the consequences of my proximity to Gemma catch up to me, she answers my fairy godmother.

"I told you so."

Just those four words. They're dipped in malice, though. Irritation and contempt. She utters them with the same efficiency as an assassin slipping a knife into their victim's back and, if Gemma's stifled whimper means anything, she's twisting it in an open wound.

Gemma's bottom lip wobbles. She sniffs. She doesn't back down. "I'm sorry, I don't want to hide away in a shack in the woods. I made the choices I had to make to be able to live in society to the best of my ability. I may not be the best at being a fairy godmother, and I've had more than a few mishaps, but I'm doing better than you," she snarls the last statement. "I'm helping people now instead of waiting for some magical day to come out and start doing the work to help the world be a better place."

Wynnifred, the witch with amber eyes, looks unperturbed by Gemma's outburst. "Would he say that you helped him?"

"This was out of my control!"

The bickering goes back and forth like that for several moments. Gemma bites out an argument. Wynnifred deflects, a verbal sparring partner with deadly aim for my fairy godmother's weakest points. Neither of them truly makes ground in patching up their strained relationship or helping me.

I'm a tavern keep, not a therapist. It's time to stop this before their squabble costs me every chance of getting my father back.

"I'm in the room, too," I snap after the third time Wynnifred points out that we wouldn't be here right now if Gemma hadn't messed up my wish and lost her wand, and that maybe twenty-five isn't mature enough to be a fairy godmother. "Why don't you try speaking to me instead of about me?"

"Because you look just barely capable of tying your boot laces. Hush and let the people who understand magic figure this out."

Gemma's hand moves to my knee, my fairy godmother coming to my aid against the witch. "Hey. You can rub it in my face all you want that I messed up everything, but he didn't ask for your nastiness. He's not the reason you've locked yourself away out here to be miserable."

Wynnifred's lips stay closed. They press into a firm line. The red paint of her lipstick crinkles with her ire. It seems Gemma also knows how to strike a nerve. Taking a moment to coax a handful of herbs into the bubbling cauldron, she chooses to ignore that line of conversation and turns the whole thing back on me, instead.

"What is it you think I can do for you, tavern boy?"

I hold up my palms as if it's obvious. "I've got a bad splinter and thought you could look at it."

Her left eyebrow cocks towards her brow, a thin metal piercing bobbing with the motion. "Well, I can't remove it."

I'm a brewery that has suddenly dehydrated, dried up, and been dispatched for its uselessness. All the anxiety and adrenaline I had been using to get through each moment since the tavern's total collapse rushes out of me all at once. Leaning hard against the back of the chair, I stare down at my palms and the glittery specks that have died down since my duel in the forest clearing, but are still present enough as a reminder of the magical relic stuck just below my skin.

"What can you do?" I don't try to keep the desperation out of my voice.

Her eyes are the windows to another realm, hot and judgmental as they stroke over my face in a languid press. "What are you willing to do for me, Cinderfella?"

Gods. I glare at the witch, reaching out to put my hand over Gemma's on my knee when I realize she's shaking. Perhaps we're more than just reluctant allies forced together in a bad situation. Gemma truly didn't want any of this to happen, either, and is stepping out of her comfort zone to help me. More than strangers and not yet friends, we sit on the precipice of devastation, our tangled futures now resting in the lap of a witch who seems happy to watch us struggle. This is so much more than we bargained for.

"I was under the impression you two had an understanding," I say through my teeth, trying to stay civil in the wake of so much disappointment.

Alarms are echoing in the cavernous expanse of my exhausted mind. Sharp, pinging sounds to stop, to not say another word, to not even think about the next question already lying on the back of my tongue like stones to a path that leads unwary travelers off of a steep cliff. Nobody else made this decision for me. I had one opinion of people who walked away from Briargild to meet with witches in the woods before trekking out here. They were wrong for doing it, selfish or vain or just greedy to have more than what the world allots the average person, but now I understand that some situations call for bigger sacrifices than I would have been ready to make on any night before this one.

I hate that I've run out of options and despise myself for not getting out of this particular trap, one made of quiet ensnaring so different from the hole in the witch's yard. "You're going to make me make a deal, aren't you?"

Her shrug annoys me, but I watch as she flicks a painted, black nail between herself and Gemma. "We had an understanding, but you and I do not." The witch commits to more unnecessary finger flicking towards me in case I couldn't figure out that I'm the only other person in the room before leaning towards me over her bubbling concoction, the swirling smoke distorting her features as her voice drops to a near whisper. "What is fixing this problem worth to you?"

Everything.

The word slams through me. It's not just the tavern or the bad wish or the fact that I don't think there's a cream that exists that would help with the constant itching in my palms. My father has been lost. My entire life was taken in a single moment. It would mean everything to get it back.

I'm willing to do anything for that.

"I don't have anything physical to offer," I start, patting my pockets absently as though I had forgotten gems stored in them that I could pull out at such a moment as this. Alas, I'm poor. This whole ordeal started because my family didn't have enough money to pay off taxes and bribe guards.

Her head tilts to the side as she appraises me. "I negotiate in less substantial ways. Will you do me a favor?"

While I may not have spent all of my time paying attention to the ways of magic folk or frolicking in the forest getting wrapped up in politics I can barely understand, I do know a few key things about moments like this. I should definitely not make a deal without knowing the fine details. Words are binding. Magic makes sure of that. If I overstep now, I could be ensnared in something even worse than just losing my home, life, and father. I chew the edge of my lip and consider how to avoid the worst of magical mayhem in any kind of barter between the two of us.

"What kind of favor?"

"A delivery."

That doesn't sound too bad. It's actually something within the scope of my abilities. I used to deliver everything for our tavern: casks of ale for private gatherings, boxes of food, a keg or two of spiced beer gently rolled through the city to another bar willing to sell our recipe. It was good work. Easy work. I could do this, too.

"What would I be delivering?"

Her chin dips to the cauldron between us. "A potion."

Uh-huh. Right. Just a potion.

"Would it hurt anyone?"

"It's not for consumption." Before I ask clarifying questions or demand a more straightforward response, she holds up a hand, the lavender smoke wafting through her splayed fingers. "I just need someone to take it for me, so I can stay here in the relative safety of my cottage. Witches aren't welcome in the city anymore."

That's true. Witches are more or less considered extinct. Nothing is going to change that. The rising tensions between the culture King Anerald is building with his clear distaste of magic that doesn't immediately serve his noble class and the people who simply want to live unshackled by his hatred have been growing for the better part of three decades. Nobody came to save the witches, and they're all too scared now to speak out lest their magical sect be targeted next. Wynnifred the witch cannot simply waltz into Briargild. Regardless of anything else, I believe she's telling the truth about that.

"So, if I deliver this potion, you'll remove Gemma's wand from my hands?"

She snorts. "I already told you that was impossible. I can't undo the kind of magic you're creating through your connection with that wand, but," she has me fully captivated, my heart threatening to vacate my chest entirely if she offers meaningless hope. "I can teach you how to break the wish that got you here."

"Wynn, that's dangerous," Gemma butts in.

The witch cuts her a withering glare. "Letting a regular person absorb your wand was dangerous. Let's not get up on any high horses, fairy godmother."

Gemma's title is a sneer. There's clearly no love lost between these two. I can't figure out why Gemma was so sure this was the only place we could come for help, but I'm too invested to back out now.

My deepest desire is being dangled in front of me. As much as magic is making me crazy and complicating everything, I need to take back that wish. More than that. I need to get my father back, fix the tavern, and return our lives to how they were before I uttered angry words I should've just swallowed. I'll deal with the rest of the consequences and settle for having sparkling bits of magic following me around for the rest of my days if that's the price I have to pay to fix things. I wasn't meant to be anything besides a tavern keep. I never needed to be anyone besides his son. This isn't how our story ends.

Likely sensing my desperation, the witch holds a hand out to me. I lick my lips, frozen with hesitation on the edge of change. Her hand remains between us. This is it. One shake and our deal will be tied together.

What harm could this bring when she's the answer to my other problems?

Still, I glance to Gemma, who looks fit to cry and is trying very hard to remain brave in the face of this moment. "Is there any other way?"

"She could be a good person for once."

Wynnifred snips back that she's good enough to help me as long as I'll help her, and then Gemma returns her gaze to her lap. She doesn't offer me any more words or condolences. This was the extent of her plan to fix everything we broke between the two of us. I have no idea if this agreement will get her another wand and a way back to her regular life, but it might just be the only way to get my father back, and I can't let that go.

I reach forward, trembling and desperate. The witch doesn't meet my hand, though. She grabs my forearm and plunges my hand down into the bubbling cauldron.

The purple substance laps at me like a starved dog, first with a testing nibble and then all at once. I yelp. I wriggle and pull and curse. Wynnifred's nails dig into my arm, her desperation meeting mine head-on and winning. No better off than we were in that hole outside, I'm trapped. A drop of my blood slips from under her thumb and mingles with the already frothing mixture as I struggle.

Heat brushes my knuckles. It's not hot enough to burn, but uncomfortably warm on my skin nonetheless. The scent of summer-soaked flowers overtakes me as I cling to the side of the cauldron and stare at the spot where I can no longer see my immersed hand.

There's a nip at my palm. A bug bite. Barely noticeable and then angry with a desire to be felt. The glitter was already obnoxious. This is red ants poured through a gash in my palm and left to chew on my exposed ligament. Pink glitter sparks to the surface of the roiling cauldron, a futile battle my immature magic loses before it can even begin to make a difference against the swirling, spinning, suffocating spill of purple over my hand.

Directly in front of me, somehow dry despite my attempts to yank myself free, Wynnifred's amber eyes gleam lilac, and her voice drops to the husky intonation of someone speaking in their sleep.

"The rebels always forget there's more to this than dragons and crowns. We cannot simply kill a king and hope the broken infrastructure of this kingdom manages to do better in his absence. We have to commit fully to change." Her chest heaves, she looks past me as if I'm entirely irrelevant, and the mixture scalds my palm in painful, indecipherable lines. "A hand for a heart, Eli Cinderfella. You will be the arrow I wield to save this continent."

Slumping back onto her bench, she releases me, and I rip my hand out of the purple mixture to see the damage. There are no burns on the back. My fingers are intact. My palm, though, is not the same. A gold rune rests there, interrupted only by the fine lines of my palm and the consistent pink glitter of my stolen magic. It's a mysterious symbol, something ancient; I have no hopes of recognizing it with my generalized knowledge of magic that shouldn't even exist anymore. Marked for more than I bargained for, I stare down at yet another magical piece meant to torment me and ruin my gods damned life.

"What is this?"

All of the unnatural shades have drained from her gaze. "The solution to your problems," she answers, carefully wiping her hand on her skirt and then standing from her bench. "There's an event in the center of the city tomorrow. You'll be there. Lucky for you, you don't have to do much more than stand in proximity of my client for the magic to take effect. Return here afterwards for your reward, tavern boy."

No. Nope. This wasn't the deal. Arrows and hearts. I have no idea what she was talking about, but I know I've just agreed to do something awful.

I want my father back. I want my life back, but not at the cost I think she's proposing.

Gods, my father was disappointed and angry the last time we spoke. It would break him to know I stooped to murder to bring him back. I can't do this.

Anything but this.

"I'm not your harbinger of doom," I croak, my heart relocated to my throat. "You can take it back."

Her nose scrunches with a curt laugh. "There's no take-backs, Cinderfella. The magic will happen. If your morals keep you from coming to retrieve your reward, then that's on you."

I shake my head. This isn't happening. I try to grasp at anything to find control of the situation.

"Why were you not invited to that party? Why did you need me to go with you?"

I expect her to feign ignorance or ignore me altogether, but she meets my gaze and shrugs. "The Necromancer has lost sight of winning this war. He and I disagree on how to do things anymore. Thankfully, I've already set you up as a rebel magic wielder, so nobody will think twice of the chaos you cause tomorrow, and no one will come here to blame me for it, either."

I curse then. Every bad word in my vocabulary. She tricked me. I throw everything I can verbally across the cauldron at her, sweating and panting, and only distantly aware that Gemma is holding me back from flinging myself whole bodily at the witch.

It occurs to me far too late that my chest is tight and my legs are weak from the spread of foreign magic in my veins from her potion.

"Life is far from fair. We no longer live in a world built on trust or decency. I'm doing what must be done to further the fates of my people, and you are merely doing the same for your line. Let us be done here and blame the universe for any adverse emotions on the matter."

The witch I never should have made a deal with snaps her fingers. The cauldron bubbles further. Smoke fills the room, and the stench of lavender becomes a wet garb wrapped around my face, clogging my nose and digging itself into the lines of my throat. I list forward, vaguely aware of Gemma catching me before I plunge headfirst into more of that dangerous potion. My fairy godmother swears, too. She's smaller and younger and altogether not equipped to deal with any of this, either.

Trapped by circumstance and desperation and the legacy of a crumbling kingdom, I slump into her. Her chair is knocked off balance under our combined weight. My body is no longer my own, and Gemma cradles me like I'm the only thing keeping her from breaking, too.

Magic winds through me, unbidden and nefarious. Purple and gold and pink spar in an amazing display of color behind my closed eyelids. Distantly, the ground meets me. Gemma's voice is there, but I can't understand her.

I'm wrapped in lavender folds.

I'm so very tired.

I don't remember what it was that I was fighting, and I don't try to anymore as the darkness claims me fully.

9

If I dream, I do so in lavender. The color. The smell. The brush of soft, softer petals across my aching limbs. It envelopes me until all that's left is a sense of drifting helplessness. Voices filter through every so often, marking my time floating in the purple waves of oblivion as passing even though I have no idea of how long I've been here or how long I'll remain. Most are things I've heard before. My father's last words to me. The false promises from a witch. Gemma cursing my name through gritted teeth.

There are others, too. Boys I haven't spoken to in years, but who I got to hold in the darkest hours of secret nights. A whisper here. A plea there. Always my name.

It's as though the ghosts of my subconscious have all come out to haunt me together.

Imprisoned in purple, I can do nothing to fight the final contender. The Necromancer makes his grand appearance in my dreams. He's everything I thought he could be and more, a sight for closed eyes and hearts that yearn for desperate hopes. I know nothing about him besides the fact that he dresses head to toe in black, has mismatched eyes, and is an arrogant ass on the battlefield. That's enough, though. A fire has started in my blood. Spreading like an infection, it hums along my entire form, making me dizzy with the intensity of which I want to be seen again by this man.

Not a customer. Not even an equal, some hardworking man I accidentally bumped into while running errands around town. No, this man is so much more, and he looked at me like I held the entire potential of his future.

Nobody looks at someone else like that if they aren't having their own inappropriate thoughts, are they?

The lavender waves are tugged out from under me. My mind's conjuration of the Necromancer slips away like the stars at the approach of sunlight. With me one moment and gone in the next. I don't have time to contend with the way I miss him before my world lurches to the left.

Consciousness comes back to me in receding waves, taking more than it leaves. My memory is fuzzy. My body hurts. Something smooth pokes my cheek, prompting me to leave behind the clutches of sleep sooner than I would like. I slap it away with a groan.

What in the lowest level of proposed hell happened?

Vaguely, I'm aware that I'm outside as my dreams ebb away and reality seeps back in. Daylight warms my face through the filter of thin branches and pine needles above me. Yellow in complete defiance of the purple that held me prisoner. Leaves crunched into my close-shaven hair. I tried to turn my face one way and then the other as that smooth object returned to poke at me again. I'm going to fight whoever is trying to wake me up. Sleep doesn't hold the answers for my current situation, but it feels better than waking up and dealing with any of this crap.

It takes far more strength than I want to expend to pry my eyelids fully apart and look at the person trying to wake me. Not a person. A white snout. The bone dragon grinds its teeth together when it sees me looking up at it, aware of my wakefulness even without eyes of its own. Its wings clatter as it gives them a flap or two and then wags its tail in that jarring shiver of bone shards. I have to admit it looks exciting for me to wake up.

Which makes one of us.

"Can you back up?" I grunt, hoisting myself onto my elbows to give myself a better view of everything around me.

Bones give off another irritating round of rattling with the swift shake of its head. It sits down a few hand widths from me, more or less, still blocking the entirety of the scenery with its looming form. Good enough. I didn't give it a direct command and, once again, it listened even as it continues to exist outside of the realm of normal magic. I was sure that most things gave out within an assumed time limit, and Gemma hasn't been able to tell me what's different here. I've heard so many stories of girls losing their shoes at the fateful strike of midnight or vehicles failing before they made it all the way to their destination. Still, the bone dragon looms and scratches its head and watches me with eyeless sockets. Magic has always been a wily element, only made manageable by the Briargild monarchs and associated Guild of Fairy Godmothers working to contain it in golden pipes and fixtures around the kingdom. This beast does not fit any of those stipulations.

I didn't create it alone.

That thought thunders at the forefront of my mind, but I toss it aside before I can let myself be wrapped back into musings on a man with a moniker rather than a name. He's not important right now. What's important is that we're not in the cottage, and there were other people in the forest last night. We might not be safe here.

Time to move. I have to get up. Blinking into the light of day, I groan again, far more sore than I've been in years as I push myself to a seated position. Standing seems impossible right now. It works out then that Gemma spots me from her spot several feet away tending to a fire.

"I was trying to let you rest," she informs me, wiping her hands on her thoroughly ruined gown. "Magic takes a lot of energy out of new users."

Magic.

That's the acrid aftertaste I can't place lingering at the back of my throat. It's why I'm not just sore in my knees from running and tumbling, but in every muscle in my body, the entirety of me thrumming with the invasion of power that has scorched me to my core. I didn't just use magic last night. I dueled the Necromancer. I had a large hand in creating a dragon. I made a bad deal with a witch and nearly choked on cauldron fumes.

The witch. Wynnifred. The deal. I glance at my hand to see that the rune is still very visible in the daylight, sparkling slightly and unmarked by pink glitter since it seems I wasn't casting any magic in my sleep. "So, everything was real?"

Gemma doesn't answer at first, her expression pinched as she stirs something in a pot she got from I don't know where. She seems to understand, though, that I need a moment to process my thoughts. I meant it as an off-handed remark. The realization that it truly was all real and not some sick hallucination brought on by drinking bad beer for the holiday settles like a stone in my stomach.

The tavern is really gone. My father is really gone. I really embarked on a journey into the forest because there's a magic wand in my hands.

Oh, and I made a deal that might get someone else hurt because I was selfish and stupid and living up to the man my father saw in the moments before he was whisked away from me by magic.

"We have a couple of hours before the event Wynn mentioned. You should try to eat."

Gemma scoops porridge into a wooden bowl, tops it with some dried fruits she has in a pouch next to a bag of supplies she certainly didn't have when we trekked out here, and then crosses the space to me to hold it out like the peace offering it is. An unasked question blooms in the space between us. Now, in the light of the next day, do I still want to deal with her?

She's the fairy godmother who ruined my life.

She's, by all accounts, including her own, not a very good fairy godmother.

It would be reasonable for me to sever our connection now, throw up my hands, and storm off to do the witch's bidding without looking back at her even once. I would probably never see her again if I decided to do that, the two of us moving in very different social circles, and wouldn't have to face the guilt of turning my back on someone else. I don't want to walk away, though. Not just because she knows more about magic than I do or because the dragon that hasn't fallen back into a pile of bones seems to like her. I can't leave Gemma now because she looks as lost and desperate as I feel, and she's being kind to me.

I take the bowl and cradle it in my left hand as I accept a spoon from her. "Where did you get all of this stuff? I don't believe it was all in your skirt."

Barking a laugh, Gemma shakes her head, fills her own bowl, and then settles on the edge of a fallen tree that lines the backside of what appears to be our personal campground. "I stole it from Wynn."

Right. I'm glad one of us had our shit together in the witch's cottage. I certainly wasn't in any condition to be ransacking the place. Instead, I made a bad deal and Gemma had to fend for the both of us.

"So, did you guys use to be friends?" I ask after a few bites of the still hot porridge, picking out dried berries to chew on while she stares off into the forest instead of right at me.

"I'm sorry I dragged you out here last night and things didn't go as planned," she says, ever the expert at avoiding direct questions.

The dragon is done with not being a part of the conversation. It sidles up to Gemma, almost lovingly draping its head down next to her elbow. If it had eyes, they would shimmer and widen to an impossible size. As is, the entire process of trying to quietly move a loud body to be near someone so as to beg for a bite of dried berry is pretty damn cute.

Not that I think it's cute.

It still looks like assembled bones of a snake, and snakes are terrifying.

Gemma doesn't mind the dragon's theatrics, plucking a blueberry out of her bowl and holding it out for its gaping jaw. She doesn't flinch away from its fangs. No fear winds its way through my fairy godmother as she holds out the treat while the dragon taps excited front feet on the ground and waits. The berry falls straight through its open jaw. Yet, it seems delighted in Gemma's spectacle of sharing and wags its tail in open approval.

We continue to eat our late breakfast, the bone dragon accepting and dropping tidbits out of Gemma's bowl before scratching at them with its claws. In the daylight, his teeth and claws don't seem as scary as they had last night. Honestly, this all feels relatively normal. Magic is beginning to feel like it belongs in my life.

Which is incredibly wrong.

Rather than sit in that discomfort, I scrape at the last of the porridge in my bowl and push the conversation back on Gemma. "So, you and Wynnifred?"

"An old story," she snaps, dropping her bowl on the ground with no intention of cleaning it. "Let's get going, Cinderfella."

Gemma has herself gathered, the fire snuffed out, and the dragon following at her heel before I have the sense to scramble to my feet. I drop my own bowl onto the forest floor. Dirt clings to my palms as

I push up. There's dirt over most of me. It's smeared on my pants and on my…sock.

Did I lose a shoe?

Did the witch take my shoe?

Why is every new revelation in this forest weirder than the last?

Since my shoe doesn't seem to be nearby, I scramble to my feet and grimace at the crunch of cold leaves under my mostly bare foot. I make it six or seven steps before Gemma whirls back around to face me. Still in that obnoxious ballgown from last night, albeit tattered and nearly scandalous with the damage that's come to the corseted top, Gemma looks the smallest she's ever been in our short acquaintance. Her normal fire isn't beating out of her in a yell of my name or a fairly consistent stream of profanity. Instead, her shoulders are slouched and her gaze is watery as she looks anywhere but directly at me.

"Do you know how to get out of here?"

Oh. Oh no. I'm not supposed to be the one in charge. Gemma is kicking the ground now, attempting to melt into the forest floor instead of dealing with this next part of our journey together.

I try to glance right to left to see if I recognize anything. With all the running last night, though, I can't get my bearings. The illusion in front of the witch's house is either back in place or we're far from it, dumped into another location due to whatever feud the two women were reigniting last night. The giant hole isn't around here for reference. I don't even know what direction we entered the forest from last night. In the light of day, I'm utterly lost.

This is all lovely. I'm having a perfectly great time. Hands on my hips, my sock already soaked from winter's presence in the forest, I force myself to take a deep breath instead of emitting the kind of screech my soul currently demands.

"I'm sorry about getting you involved in all of this," Gemma says before I can rationalize our way out of the forest.

Her apology knocks me back a step. She had said sorry earlier, but I'm used to people doing that reflexively. Nobody apologizes to a tavern keep. They make a mess and expect I'll have a solution for fixing it. That's the deal.

Well, I can't let her down.

We're going to get out of the forest, carry out our mission, and get both of our lives back together.

Besides, I might just have a plan.

"Come here and stay close," I warn Gemma before narrowing my gaze on the skeletal creation that has been carefully pulling strands of frosted grass out of the forest floor while we talk. "Hey. Dragon. Take us to the center of the city."

Gemma's fingers find my forearm, her grip a little too tight to be comfortable as the dragon tilts its head in my direction. It shakes, spreads its wings, and then paws at the ground as if uncomfortable with us staring at it. It doesn't come any closer.

Pink glitter doesn't even spark on my palms. I don't understand. I spoke directly to it. I gave it a direct command. It should be doing something, even if that something is going catastrophically wrong.

"Magic doesn't work on impossibilities," Gemma coaches me with a gentle squeeze of my arm. "You have to ask it to do reasonable things."

"I think it's pretty reasonable that the enormous creature is our vehicle out of the woods."

Pouting, her bottom lip pressed further out than her top, Gemma shakes her head. "We need an actual plan, Eli. We can't just expect magic to do everything for us. There's so much more to life than easy answers."

If I were back at the tavern, this would be a great moment to flip a table or smash a glass or do something equally harsh and destructive. Not necessarily to cause a scene, but to give myself a grasp of control in the middle of chaos. Most of my messes are easily cleaned with a wet rag or a broom. All of this, this magic and mayhem, is so much more than I ever bargained to deal with.

Glancing down at the golden mark on my hand, I blow out a breath. "I think I deserve to have something easy once in a while."

"The easy route is for people who will never find greatness," Gemma responds.

My father used to say something like that. It was from a book. A large tome with golden edges. He loved reading fairytales because of the way they carried the kinds of lessons he wanted to imprint on me.

"What's so great about all of this?"

Her eyes are far too wide, far too kind and sincere. "You're creating magic that has been banished from the kingdom for years and years, Eli. I know this hasn't been a great experience for either of us, but there's a reason we were brought together. You are the beginning of a lot of change the world might not be ready to accept."

The wind picks at my sleeve. I'm frozen, staring down at my fairy godmother. I think she's trying to be sweet. Gemma is usually so crass and unbearably abrasive. Her words right now are meant to be a balm to my frayed nerves. They, however, are flint against the fire already blooming in my heart.

"I'm tired of being something the world isn't ready to accept."

The bone dragon sidles closer to Gemma, spooked by my tone and leering down at me with its empty eye sockets as I run my fingers back over my head to dislodge some more leaves and stalk away from them. Gemma gives me a moment. She doesn't flinch away from me, no more afraid of me than she is of the creature in our midst. Instead, she lets out a slow breath and continues on in that honey-dipped tone.

"Yeah, I am, too." I don't ask her to expand because she's already speaking, not nervously filling the air as she has so many times since our meeting, but with a purpose that stalls my irritation. "I never wanted to be a fairy godmother. It's about the only job a woman can have without having to marry a man.

"When I met Wynnifred, I thought things were going to be better. I had a friend," pink blush paints across her cheeks. "Well, I had more than a friend, and I was happy to keep things quiet. Our private moments were more than enough reward to survive the agonizing trivialities of the real world. She made me feel more magical than any spell I ever cast."

Here, Gemma pauses. Her lips tremble. She wipes her palms on her skirts.

She hurries forward in a cracking rumble of honesty. "It wasn't enough for her. I lost her because the world is a cruel place to people like us, and I don't know that my heart will ever not be broken over it."

I'm moving before making a decision about it. My own dilemmas shoved aside, my wet sock far less of an inconvenience, I cross the space I created between the two of us and reach forward. As a friend. As someone who has been forced to make the same choices. I pull her into me, letting her lean into my chest when the words stop and the sobs begin.

My arms wrapped around Gemma, I rub a circle on her back. I never considered there were people like me in higher fields of work. Going against the grain of society seemed like the ideal of someone without much to lose. I had my father and the tavern, but that was it, so I never questioned meetings in barns with boys or late-night dinners with men who focused on their apprenticeships in art or metalwork. Those brief relations were good, great, even grand. They were fun, but they weren't ever worth losing my livelihood over or having soldiers tear through the tavern in search of evidence of criminal activities. The irony that I lost everything from a place of acting as a good civilian and not for any major gesture of standing up for love isn't lost on me.

Gemma sniffles as I find my voice. "I wanted nothing more than a quiet life."

My father's voice echoes through the back of my mind. He always wanted to chide me for working too much. There was meant to be more to life. At the time, I thought he was gently trying to get me to settle down in a meaningful relationship. Perhaps get some grandkids out of me. Maybe, though, he knew the dormant magic in my blood would eventually complicate things. He told me time and again that magic was the tipping point for ruination in my mother's story. It was dangerous to be different and outspoken and allow wildness to flourish like dandelions in cracks in the road. I was meant to cherish more than the tavern in case I ever lost it by simply being myself.

Throat tight, I give Gemma one last squeeze and then step away, trying to wipe away her tears with my fingers without smearing more dirt on her face. "Hey, we're going to be okay. We're just going to have to be a little more extraordinary than we previously planned."

Her smile wavers, but it's definitely there. "All the best people are."

The bone dragon wags its tail. I'm not sure how much it understands on its own or if it merely mirrors my emotions, but I don't hate it. I might even be growing fond of the weird sounds it makes.

"Since magic doesn't work, I suppose we could walk."

"You were a large proponent for walking last night," Gemma reminds me with a smirk, gathering her skirts and making her best guess as to which way is the one back to the city.

I laugh. It's a hoarse combination of mirth and acknowledgment of her teasing, and it feels good. Right, even. It wasn't the plan, but maybe I was meant to be in the middle of the woods with a fairy godmother and our adopted dragon.

Speaking of dragons, I clear my throat. "Do you think people are going to notice him?"

"I've gotten away with some pretty crazy things, but he might draw attention."

The dragon plods along behind us like some kind of oversized puppy that has been lost and is now more than happy to latch onto a new owner. We have no idea how long the magic will last, and I don't have the heart to abandon it here, so I stretch my neck one way and then the other as I think over my next magical plan. I need a simple command. Nothing complicated. Nothing that is vague or leaves room for misinterpretation, since this particular spell has already taken on a life of its own and remains resilient in the face of my half-thought-out ideas. I wait until we're close enough to the city to hear the braying of sheep and the rattling wheels of horse-pulled carts before turning back to the dragon.

This has to work. I'm going to be out of ideas if it doesn't.

Almost obedient, the dragon sits as I face it. The pink glow in its ribcage continues to pulse steadily like a barely contained heart. It's alive and awaiting me.

I hold out my hands as Gemma admonishes me for trying magic without her consent. Pink glitter sparks in the midday sunlight. I'm about to do magic willingly. The man I was less than twenty-four hours ago would have never agreed to this, believed it would happen, or fallen for the trap that is over-dressed fairy godmothers at his back door.

Here I am, though. Mildly confident that this might go well.

"Shrink!"

I say it loudly, clearly, suddenly, as if I can sneak up on the magic and force it to work. Whether that idea has any merit, I can't be sure, but I see the pink glitter overtake the surface of the dragon from its bony snout to the spindly tips of his wings like locusts alighting on a field. It wriggles like it tickles, and then there's a whoosh of air.

The bone dragon is gone.

Gemma squeals. I'm expecting her to yell at me for another failed attempt at magic, but instead, she leaps forward to scoop something off the ground. No longer the massive threat that it was last night, our dragon sits in the cradled cup of her hands.

It wriggles in her hold, wagging its tail and flapping its wings even though they're still not designed for flight. It bounces around her palms and then scurries up her arms to hide in the hair that sits on her shoulder. Gemma looks prepared to collapse from cuteness.

"You can hang onto it for me."

Giggling and snout petting ensues. The now mouse-sized dragon has captured all of Gemma's attention. She's completely taken away by it, cooing to it as it scrambles from her shoulder to her hands and back in tiny, rapid steps. I guide my fairy godmother forward with a hand to her elbow.

It's not too much farther until the line of trees breaks. Briargild is ahead of us once more. The golden barrier is even brighter in the day.

"Is that a problem?"

"He's perfect, Eli."

I roll my eyes. "Not the dragon. The barrier. What does it really do?"

Gemma's steps falter. She leaves the dragon frolicking on her shoulder as she crosses her arms over her chest and stares straight ahead with me. A shimmering, golden sheen separates us from our next steps. Briargild is right there, but I'm not the same person who walked away from it.

The wand in my skin was bad enough, but there's a rune now on my palm and a dragon with us, too. That's far too much magic to be sneaking through this barrier that was erected to keep Briargild separated from the wild witches it openly villainized and banished.

"Well, Wynn's magic is blue and purple, so she worked hard to disguise that spell on you. That shouldn't set off any alarms."

Great. One problem might not be a problem. "What about the pink glitter and tiny dragon that shouldn't exist?"

Gemma's expression scrunches tight in thought. Beyond the barrier, nobody seems to be out. There aren't many homes pressed close to the edge of the kingdom, but I figured we would see some farmers or guards going about their daily routines. I don't believe we're lucky enough to waltz back into Briargild without being seen.

"The wand is causing the glitter, and that came from me, so it should be okay." She tilts her head to look at the dragon nibbling on the edge of her sleeve. "And it created him, too. What could go wrong?"

That's not exactly a question that boasts confidence for me. "Maybe give me the dragon. I don't want anything to happen to you."

Gemma plucks the magical creation from her shoulder, holds him eye level with herself, and then asks a question not meant for me. "You're not inherently evil, right? That's what the original wards were for. Especially at the size you are now, you're not going to cause trouble or eat anybody. I think you'll be just fine."

And then she jumps forward through the barrier.

The golden wall ripples. I hold my breath as Gemma and the dragon pass through to the other side. With no reference as to what exactly it will do if it detects the kinds of magic it wards against, I'm waiting for a scream, a groan, an awful crunch, and a cry for help. None of that comes.

Gemma makes it to the other side and hoists the dragon up into the air for me to see it prancing around her palm. "Okay. Your turn."

Right. Me. If the dragon that belongs in some kind of rebellious poem can make it through the ward, I should be able to walk back into the place that has always been my home. Should. Pink glitter itches along my fingertips. It's embedded under my nails and waiting for a purpose to flee me altogether. There is so much magic in me now that wasn't there before, and I'm worried it will never leave.

What if I can't walk through this golden shimmer of safety protocols for a kingdom that purposefully attempted to exterminate every last witch or banish them to the forests?

Does it make me a terrible person to yearn to return home to a place that is inherently terrible?

Can it be a terrible place if good people still live on the fringes? The ones who fight through every day with a thousand obstacles in their way. The people who were my community didn't pick the king we have now. They didn't ask for bigotry and hate. If not for my wish gone wrong, would they miss me if I couldn't come home?

"Eli," Gemma says softly, her free hand reaching back through the golden barrier for me. "You're going to be okay. We can do this together."

The golden shimmer of the barrier stands between us. Her on one side and me on the other. An apt metaphor for the differences in our lives.

And yet, she's reaching back. She's staying. She's willing to do this crazy sneaking of potentially dangerous magic back into Briargild with me.

I'm not alone in this.

Hesitantly, I place my hand in hers. Gemma doesn't give me a chance to overthink. She grabs me back and tugs hard, dragging me through the barrier with her.

Before, it was a shiver that touched my shoulders and made me uneasy. Now, the golden shimmer of an ancient magic quakes at my entrance. It wobbles. Then, it falls.

Like stained glass spraying from the empty walls of abandoned churches, shimmering, golden pieces of the barrier rain down around me in soundless plops. It dissipates as it hits the patch of dead grass at my feet. Golden and vibrating one moment and simply gone in the next.

Gemma still has a hold on me, yanking me through the disaster and then stepping in front of me as though her short, round frame could possibly save me from what I've done. Again. Every time I come into contact with magic, I make everything worse.

The golden wall no longer stands between us and the forest outside of Briargild. I watch the nearest guard tower shiver. It tilts left. The entire structure surrounding Briargild is going to come crashing to the ground in an awful display of dominoes if I don't do something.

Anything.

What exactly do I think I can do?

"Eli?"

Gemma has her hand on my shoulder. She wants to run, to leave this behind us, and pretend it's not our problem.

I'm not exactly sure if it would help the people of the lower city if I let everything come toppling down. There's certainly a chance people will get hurt from the towering buildings falling into their homes or farms or in the general paths that connect us.

"Don't you dare try to do magic, Eli Cinderfella. Let's just go."

I can't just walk away. Whether or not these people remember me and the tavern and my father, who has been an upstanding member of the community for as long as the community has existed here, they don't deserve to be crushed by my mistakes. Feet planted in the dirt and shimmering dredges of the barrier, I raise my hands over my head.

One word.

A command.

No room for misinterpretation.

"Back!"

Not to the side. Not forward. I need the towering structure of brick and gold and ancient magic to fall backwards into the forest. Pink meets gray amidst the crumbled side of the building. It swells. The spot of pink becomes a thin layer on the wobbling tower, a visible wind pressing to the side of it. There's a moment in which the building wavers. I'm not sure if my magic will be enough. Then, it presses just enough, and the tower that completes the circle around Briargild tips towards the forest.

We should be far enough from any hidden witches' huts. Nothing truly seems to lurk in the forest around the golden barrier as much as rumors would insist that danger is just steps beyond the protection put in place generations ago. The nymphs should be safe. Gemma said there weren't any bears. Deers and birds and squirrels and anything else should be fast enough to escape the building, fully casting a shadow onto the trees below.

It's too late for me to come up with another plan.

Together, in the lingering sun creeping towards midday, my fairy godmother and I watch the tower topple. There's no chance for the king to send someone to fix the barrier now. At least, not without fully erecting a new tower in the place I broke this one. The Kingdom of Briargild is officially without a magical barrier.

"We really have to go now," Gemma has her fingers hooked around my elbow, tugging me away from the sight I can't unsee.

First, I brought the tavern to its muddy foundation. Then, I infiltrated a rebel meeting and helped make a dragon that is currently breaking every rule of magic. Now, I'm tampering with systems that have been in place since almost the beginning of Briargild.

I'm still busy watching the dust settle and making sure I didn't make anything worse with my basic understanding of magic when Gemma pulls me away to the ringing calls of guards. Destroying golden barriers is clearly not conducive to our stealthiness. In ragged clothes and covered head-to-toe in dirt, Gemma leads the way as we run.

10

"You have no idea where we're going. Follow me!"

Gemma is happy to give up the leading position, the two of us linked to each other by our hands as we race down familiar, dirt roads.

We're a parade of two desperate people and a hidden, tiny dragon as a procession of guards takes the streets behind us. From splintered doorways and dusted windows covered by tattered sheets in place of actual curtains, the people of the lower city watch us in our race away from trouble.

My fairy godmother lets out gasping breaths behind me. We've made it a couple of streets and only managed to gather more attention. There's no way we can keep this up for much longer.

"Can't you tell them you're a fairy godmother and get us out of this?" I call back over my shoulder, passing an intersection of two farms and a local butcher shop.

"How would I prove that?"

Right. I have her wand. We're both a mess. There's not a guard in the entire kingdom who would believe that story. Speaking of guards, how are there so many already out here? Were they investigating the wild magic that broke through the foundations of the tavern?

Whatever the reason, they're here. More guards appear ahead of us, and I have to shove Gemma back the way we came before we walk right into the obvious trap. We need a shortcut, and we need it now.

I look left and then right.

Farms that lead to the forest and an entire brigade of guards ready to arrest me for the toppled tower or the butchershop.

It's not really an option.

"Come on. Don't stop now."

I break through a side door to scrambling footsteps and yells behind us. Ahead, the butcher stands with a cleaver in hand and blood on his apron. Gemma screams. I apologize. We slip and slide and dash for the front of the shop while Gemma snaps at the dragon to stay put.

"You need to keep it hidden!" I bark back at her when the butcher demands to know what kind of rodent we just brought through his establishment, before being more distracted by the brunt force of six guards bursting through the back door after us with swords raised and more curses than should be allowed in a single room.

"Skelly is just interested. He's never seen so many things!"

Of course, she named it. The one thing I told her not to do, and she went and named it. There are too many guards bustling through the back of the butcher shop and several shouting from outside. As much as we need to make it to the city center, we need to find somewhere to hide.

I know a place.

But we can't bring the guards to Harold's door.

Magic is illegal. Performing it in front of a gratuitous crowd is not a good idea, but I've already gone and brought down the barrier around Briargild. If we're caught now, there's no way I'm surviving to see life after visiting the castle dungeons.

What's one more act of magic if it's to save Gemma and me?

"Stay close," I tell her as we make our way through the front, past bleary-eyed customers to the butcher shop, who don't look twice at our race through the front door.

When we're back on the street, I hold my hands out in front of myself and towards the onslaught of guards. It's time to make up for my duel with the Necromancer. I won't live with a legacy of failed carriage-making.

I'm Eli Cinderfella, and I can do magic.

Gemma, holding her breath behind me, our dragon cupped in her hands along with our remaining hope, I yell past the guards and the confused lower city crowd and the raucous of the last few moments. "Grow!"

My focus isn't on any of the guards. It's on the ivy vine wrapped around the butcher shop gutter. Pink glitter explodes from me and across the street to weave itself around the greenery. Pointed leaves expand instantly. The vine itself begins to grow like a magical beanstalk my father once told me about when I was younger. Not up. Out. The gutter creaks and groans, ripping away from the building. It drops a heavy, green body into the street amid cries of shock, disgust, and disapproval, firmly cutting us off from the oncoming guards.

With Gemma at my heels, we run before they have their swords out to cut through my vine.

"I've never seen anything like that!" Gemma hoots.

I shush her, running us through the streets towards the tavern that no longer exists. We won't need to go that far. Kicking up dirt we cough on in ragged breaths, we run until we see the sign of a rabbit in a vest and top hat that denotes Harold's tailor shop.

Safe. Safe enough. It's the only place I can think of to stall for a few minutes, so it has to work. I rush Gemma through the door before she can sputter any questions.

"Ruined clothes and only one shoe," a voice booms from the darkened depths of the shop as I blink away the brightness of day and corral Gemma away from the door and subsequent windows our pursuers could see us through.

Harold walks out from behind his sewing table, hooves clipping on the worn floors with his hands on his hips. For just a second, I wait for him to say more, to say my name, to recognize me despite the magic that has knocked my entire world asunder. Instead, he takes in our ragged appearances and smiles.

"Friends, it looks like you came to the right place."

Customers. Just people here for clothes. No recognition flares in his gaze, even as it remains gentle and kind.

Sorrow seeps through my intestines like pumpkin vines reaching for the stifled sight of the sun. I already lost my father. I've had less than a day to process everything since I made my bad wish, and I hadn't realized how much I needed someone to know who I was. To care that Cinderfella's Cup is no longer a real place in the lower city. Just to reach out a hand and tell me that it won't simply be okay, but things will go back to how they were.

Gemma doesn't understand all that I've lost.

She's here. She's my friend. She's not the kind of person who would have been by my side for the last almost thirty years. I just hoped Harold would...

"You got us," Gemma chimes through my thoughts, her hands suspiciously intertwined in her hair as she hides the dragon. "We're in dire need of fresh clothes and heard you were the best."

I do appreciate my fairy godmother so much for being here. My throat is too tight to get out any words. She has things under control, though, quickly pulling out a purse from her pocket to show that we have money to pay for what we need to replace.

Harold runs a hand between his horns, scratching at his curly hair. "I hope the two of you find all you need."

Taking off immediately, Gemma runs for the women's sections and the pre-made dresses awaiting her there, since we don't have time for any freshly sewn garments. I shuffle away from the door, still hearing no yells or calls or stampeding guards outside. Clothes. I'm supposed to be picking out clothes. I can do that, right?

I only make it a few moments before Harold is at my side, his fingers gingerly reaching forward to point at the curling letters on my chest. "Did you get this vest from me? This looks like my work, but..."

More evidence that he doesn't remember. I swallow hard. There's no way to explain any of this to him, not under the time constraints or magical implications of my life. When I don't find the words to answer his question, he lets his hand fall.

"Rough day, then?"

I nod, wishing he had put his hand on my shoulder and offered advice instead of leaning into his placating tone for troubled guests. "It's been a very long night."

Then, he's gone. Harold wishes that I find all I need and to let him know if I have questions or concerns, and then he plods back to his sewing station. I bite back my harsh response. Wishes are the last thing I want. I could live the rest of my life without another wish and hopefully be a happy man.

Still, the sentiment is kind, and I let it linger as I take myself to the shirts. I don't need anything too fancy. No ornate buttons or embroidered finishes. Just enough fabric to cover me. I'm holding one in midnight blue when Gemma leaps to my side.

She grabs my arms and pulls me away to the corner furthest from Harold, our steps creaking along the worn flooring, almost loud enough to cover up her question. "Did you see him?"

"It's not polite to talk about people in their own shops."

She punches me in the arm and then tries to cover my mouth when I raise my voice to ask what she thinks she's doing. "Not him," she murmurs and then points to her very empty shoulder. "Skelly?"

Oh. Oh no. No, no, no. We did not just lose a dragon in a dress shop.

"You had one job," I hiss at Gemma, dropping my gaze to the floor and trying to see if there are any hints as to where the bone dragon could have gotten off to in its excitement to explore its new surroundings.

Perhaps we would have had less trouble if I hadn't shrunk the creature down to the size of a mouse, but I refuse to take responsibility for this. Damn. I walk away from my rather useless fairy godmother and start ducking down to look under shelves in what I hope is a completely normal and discreet way.

No spare bones are sprinkled underneath the clothing. There are no tiny footsteps in the dusty spots under the shelves of spooled fabric that line one whole wall of the shop. Nothing. He's gone and vanished.

Could the magic have finally given out?

I almost feel sad about that when Harold speaks up. "Mind your feet. I seem to have misplaced my needle."

He doesn't know me anymore, but I know him, and there's no way this meticulous tailor would just lose a needle. Gemma and I make eye contact across the shop. Of course, Skelly would be attracted to the shiny tools. The dragon has to be close.

My gaze snags on a piece of red thread that's pulled under Harold's work table. Gemma sees it, too. Clearing her throat, she becomes the distraction we need. "Do you think you have something like this in yellow for me?"

My fairy godmother proceeds to ask what must be the most ridiculous line of questions in order to draw Harold away from his table, while I work my way around it and drop down onto my knees. Where is that dragon? The red string darts back the other way. A minuscule rustling of bones against one another sounds from under the stool Harold was just in. Skelly evades my attempts to grab any of his bony legs and runs by with a needle clamped in his jaw, the red thread flying behind him.

Quicker than he was at full size, the dragon avoids me as I swipe again. He outmaneuvers me and sprints out into the main area of the room. There's nowhere for him to hide, and he seems not to care. That red thread continues to fly behind him like a trail of fire, incapable of going unnoticed. Skelly is headed straight for Harold.

Magic by anyone who isn't a fairy godmother is highly illegal. Merely existing as a satyr with an affinity for gardening is dangerous in this political climate. Nymphs stay hidden in the city out of fear they'll be targeted for their magic, even as they're unable to live fully without their connection to trees and the river. Skelly's not just a magical creature. He isn't the missing point for some rebellion rhyme. He's a creature made entirely of magic with no way to hide it and a clear connection to me in every pulse of his little pink heart.

If he's caught, neither of us will survive the implications.

Gemma is thinking the same. We both lunge towards the red thread and subsequently connected dragon. With no real eyes, Skelly sees us coming and veers to the right. I'm moving too fast. My fairy godmother has never been one to watch where she's going. Our existences in this space were recipe enough for disaster. We crash into each other and crumple in a heap on the floor as the dragon returns to racing for Harold.

I don't know who yells first, but Gemma and I are making quite a ruckus. Harold doesn't check on us. He's already looking at the dragon. Slowly, the large man leans down and holds out his hand. Skelly hops right into his extended palm and preens as Harold lifts him for inspection.

"Please," I start, pushing Gemma off of me and scrambling to my feet. "I know you don't remember me, but I need you not to report us for this. He's not bad."

I can't believe my life has come to this point. I'm still dirty and missing a shoe and now avidly advocating for the rights of a creature that didn't exist until the very early hours of this morning. Still, I don't want to imagine a life without the little guy. I've lost enough. Whether I like it or not, I've become firmly attached to Skelly, the bone dragon.

Harold runs his thumb over the top of Skelly's raised head, his gaze on the dragon while he answers me. "I thought you looked familiar, but my memory has caved with age. I don't know why you're here, but we don't turn on our kind. Not even the smallest members of the community."

If my throat weren't already tight from this entire interaction, I probably would have let out a wretched sob. Harold is just being himself, and it gives me more hope than I've had in a very long time. Speechless and diligently trying to fight the emotions welling just behind my eyes, I nod to his words.

Skelly is one of us now.

We're going to keep him safe.

Harold thanks Skelly for relinquishing his needle and then carries the dragon over to his work table. Tiny bones clatter as the dragon is set onto the wooden surface. Harold sits down and pulls the red thread out of his needle, gently reaching out to tie it into a bow around the base of the dragon's neck. He clips away extra thread to keep it from tripping up the tiny creature and then holds up a hand mirror to show it off. Skelly seems elated, hopping from foot to foot and clacking his jaw as he throws his head. The flaps of his minuscule wings are like the accumulated thunder of a dropped box of toothpicks. It's good to see one of us having the time of their life.

"Take what you need, friends," Harold says then, petting the dragon with his index finger as Gemma gathers our previously discarded clothing selections and reaches into her pocket to pull out coins for our purchase, but he just shakes his head. "I've no need for payment when you're in need of help."

No amount of arguments is going to change his mind. Instead, he takes hold of the entire interaction and tells us to make use of his washroom off to the side of the changing area. He even offers to stay in charge of watching Skelly as we clean up, allowing the dragon to chew on his sleeve and bump into his horns when he raises him to his face once more.

"You can go first," I tell Gemma, sinking into an offered chair across from Harold while she disappears into the back. "I will pay you back when this is all over."

He waves me off. "If you're in luck, I may not even remember your debts."

We banter back and forth for a few moments, the pieces of my jumbled life feeling like they've come back together. This is how it should be. Bad things interrupted by good people, making everything worth it once again.

Gemma emerges from the back in her new gown. Light yellow with little blue flowers, it's so much simpler than the gown she was wearing when we met. It looks like it was made for her. All of her possessions have been added to a small clutch that matches her outfit. Her face and hands are clean of dirt, and her hair even looks brushed, the curls messy but free of foliage. My fairy godmother is ready to take on the world once more.

She sends me on the way with a flick of her wrist and a comment that my smell is going to keep us from getting anywhere if I don't wash up. I take the blue shirt, some pants, and a pair of shoes that Harold insisted on and make my way to the washroom. The door clicks shut behind me.

It's the first time I've been alone, truly alone, in what feels like forever.

I set my things down and grip the edge of the white sink, looking at myself in the mirror above it. That's me. Dark skin, hair shaved short at the sides and slightly longer at the top, where the entirety of a plant sticks out in a haphazard fashion. There's still blood under my nose. Thankfully, the swelling from my black eye has gone since Gemma gave me her medicinal, magic supplements. Still, there's lingering bruising on the side of my face, a new cut on my forehead from my wrestling match with the Necromancer, and more than my fair share of dirt spread over my features. I look as tired as I feel, worn down and struggling to continue.

This is not the visage of a hero.

I don't even think it's the reflection of a good man.

Turning on the tap, I dip my head so I can stop looking at myself and splash cold water on my face. I use the bar of soap and a spare cloth left on the side of the sink to scrub at myself. Dirt drips into the sink. Brown splotches mingle with red and crusty bits of leaf, combining with it all to make a pretty gross soup. By the time I'm done cleaning the mud out from under my nails and plucking debris from my hair and stripping out of my old clothes that I leave in a trash can with Gemma's discarded gown, I feel a little bit more like myself.

Brown pants cover me from hip to boot, and my new shoes are a blessing after the trek here. Finally, not cold from the night's uncompromising air, I roll the long sleeves of my blue shirt to my elbow. I spare a final glance at the mirror as I finish buttoning myself into it.

This guy looks like he might be able to survive the day.

Gemma's teasing tone meets me the moment I re-enter the main room of the tailor shop. "You actually clean up decently, Eli Cinderfella. I'm proud to call you my wish gone wrong."

"You look pretty good, too," I tell her, holding out my hand to help her twirl before she turns back to Harold.

"Don't I? I haven't been in something this comfortable since I was a girl. Your work is impeccable," she implores as he tips his head to her compliments. "You could be somewhere far better with this kind of talent."

The man I've seen as my mentor and family for my whole life gives a shrug. "I don't want to go somewhere besides here, my Lady. Talent is just hard work brought to fruition. Anyone can do what I've done if they have enough time."

Perfectly said. Gemma inclines her head to him, understanding shimmering in her gaze that it is a small power to be able to choose what makes us happy. I think about those words, how they're an echo to something my father said after his cocktail concoction was turned down for one of the noble house's grand parties. Winning his way into their revelry would have pushed him into far richer waters, but it wouldn't have made him any happier. Our tavern was enough. Our clients, friends, and chosen members of family were more than enough to make our lives good. Perhaps it is another act of rebellion not to allow the rich to hold all of the most talented individuals in a kingdom at their beck and call.

We're all just doing the best we can with our circumstances, aren't we?

"We need to make it to the city center by midday for some event being held there. Would you know the quickest way?" I ask, changing the course of the conversation.

"You can go out the back door so as to avoid the trouble that brought you in," Harold confides, pointing us towards it as he rattles off a quick set of directions that matched what I thought would be the best way there.

Dressed in his bow, Skelly reluctantly returns to Gemma's care as we say our repeated thanks and goodbyes to Harold. The rune on my palm warms and itches. This has been a much-needed break from reality, but my magical appointment is drawing nearer.

11

Our party restored, we take the path from Harold's back door to cut towards the center of the middle city. Trouble doesn't find us. There's no yelling, no more need to grow enormous plants, or break golden barriers. If anyone has noticed the trouble I've caused, they're not yet prepared to deal with it. Perhaps they'll all find a different tavern tonight to spread rumors and gossip.

Midday looms, an ever-present deadline coming closer as the sun beats down on us. The short buildings of the lower city offer no shade. Most people linger out in the streets, woken from their holiday stupors to get through the day's responsibilities in thin hats and long-sleeved shirts. All of the decorations for the solstice have been pulled down and stuffed away for next year's party, or lie limply in sewer drains that sluggishly take care of the winter's runoff. Gold litters the floors. It shimmers dully, the yellow leeching from paper surfaces to leave bug-nibbled paper and stained paths trodden by the same tired feet. Far from the scene of my most recent crime and dressed anew, Gemma and I only get a passing glance now and again from those around us as we slip from the lower city to the middle.

The boundary between the lower and middle city is made clear by the change in the road. It seems to be no trouble for the government to pave the streets here. The trash and clutter lining the areas closer to my home don't exist here. Plants are displayed on the edge of polished, street signs or hung from buildings, not for any real purpose besides their beauty, the buds closed but greenery starkly alive in the winter season.

Fresh paint adorns most of the places out here, on front doors and freshly rejuvenated signs for tea shops, and on murals that are dedicated to the might of the King. Bookshops are on every corner. There are advertisements for hobbies. Here, there's leeway for pastime activities for people not burnt out by hard work at the end of every day. Less than an hour's walk, and the culture of the kingdom has completely changed.

Gemma doesn't look at any of it. Skelly's safety is hidden in her hair with a threat to be put in her bag if he doesn't behave. She walks through this area as though she's done so a thousand times before. She probably has. The people here are likely the ones who get most of their wishes answered.

It would be a wish come true to be able to live in such lavish conditions.

Peddlers with carts offer us freshly baked bread and cooked meats. It smells divine; the entirety of this area not overrun with the kinds of smells attributed to farms. Gemma pays for an oversized sausage that we share, my own appetite not truly alert as my palm continues to itch and tingle from the rune resting there.

The sights and sounds would be enough to overwhelm me if we weren't also facing the crowds. I don't think running faster than a centaur would have gotten us to the city center in time. As is, we weave between people until we manage to get close enough to the event, peeking over shoulders at a stage erected in the usually empty space in the center of the collected streets from an alleyway.

The audience is mostly human, which makes sense. I never chose to come to these kinds of things before, and I can't imagine the magical folk who live as farmhands taking time out of their chores to come all the way here. If I didn't have to take care of this rune, I wouldn't be here today, either. As is, I'm ignoring looks shot my way from those around us and depending on Gemma's presence at my side for what it offers in the way of safety. She has a better understanding of this situation. It helps to have the word of a fairy godmother; should anyone give us trouble, even without her wand, she has prestige I couldn't pretend to share. The guards wouldn't be fooled, but these people will think twice about the presence of a woman claiming to be a fairy godmother, and I cling to that desperately as we're pressed tight into the alley as more people show up for this event.

I try to ignore the crowd and focus instead on the speech being given from the stage I can't quite see. It's nothing good. Bigotry has had time to grow and expand, and is now making big statements in the center of the city for anyone here to listen to as an advisor to the King reads from a scroll.

It's the same drivel that has been repeated my entire life. Magic is bad. Those caught using it without the right permits or allowances will be subject to punishment, whether that's a fine, time in the dungeons, or a public execution. Anybody holding differing opinions should silence themselves now or give themselves up as co-conspirators to the revolution against the crown. The rebellion will surely be obliterated, so there's no point in fighting back.

The crowd had already been worked into a frenzy by the time we pushed our way into this alley. Now, they shout their agreements and acceptance of the King's rule. These aren't the kind of people I serve at the tavern. Most are wearing red. Hats and scarves and brooches of roses to show their approval of Briargild's monarchy. With Gemma in yellow and me in blue, we're once again obvious outsiders in the crowd.

It's hot in the crush of bodies trying to watch the speaker. Sweat drips down the back of my neck. My skin crawls being close to so many people spitting hatred without reason. I have to bite my tongue to keep from cursing about their mob mentality. Half of the things being shouted have no real foundation in truth. Magic isn't inherently bad, and I'm saying that as someone who has spent the last day being really upset about magic as a concept in my life. I'm not completely alone in my stance. Peeking past broad shoulders in front of me, I study the crowd ringed around the stage and pick out people with frowns or tense lines on their foreheads, most dressed in basic whites and browns and lacking the red adornment of their neighbors— a quiet rebellion in plain sight. There are still people who see the danger of flocking towards a ruler who doesn't truly care for his kingdom or the people within it. They seem few and far between, but so does the rebellion, and I walked into a large meeting of them last night. Justice cannot be avoided forever. Instead of acting, even as my muscles urge me to start throwing punches at every good-for-nothing bastard crammed into this crowd in front of me, I tuck Gemma firmly behind me and watch what's happening with baited breath.

The King's advisor is done. There's a lull as he steps back from the stage and motions up the next speaker.

Nothing could have prepared me for what I see— not having to think quickly on my feet every night for the last twenty-odd years in the tavern. Not the amount of fights I have started and ended. Not even the day of magic that has overturned my life.

On the stage, rolling forward to a round of sporadic, polite applause is the man I tried to help yesterday afternoon. His previously tousled, brown hair is pulled back into a loose tail at the back of his neck. That black eye patch is in place. His hands are careful on the wheels of his chair as he guides himself up a ramp and onto the main stage.

No wonder he had made himself scarce with my distraction.

No longer in plain clothes or carrying illegal texts, he takes up space on the stage in the finest clothing I've ever seen, covered in red and gold from head to toe. The crown on his head seems like a particularly cruel addition. My entire life changed after stepping between him and those guards.

I stepped in to help the one fucking person who didn't need it.

I played a chivalrous citizen for the crown prince of Briargild.

"Thank you all for being here today," Prince Alexander Charming begins, smooth and charismatic and so far from the desperate plea for help he called out in the lower city.

Why was he even down there?

If he wanted illegal texts, couldn't he pay someone to pick them up for him?

He's not exactly inconspicuous in his chair. Of course, I hadn't guessed who he was, and likely no one else would think twice about him. King Anerald Charming has made a point of keeping his son out of the metaphorical spotlight. He didn't disown him in some sign of love for his beloved wife, but he snuffed his own son in every other way, including making him a stranger to the very people he would someday come to rule.

Now, he's sitting above a crowd that sneers and shifts uncomfortably as though standing this close to the prince will cause them also to be physically impaired. Differences are hard enough to live with and survive in quiet corners of the world. To do it now, with his chin tipped up and his voice even, is a show of courage far greater than any vestiges I may have.

I'm not happy he's the reason my life has been knocked so completely off course, but I can't fault him, either.

So, I listen. Pushed up onto my tiptoes and squinting hard against the glare of the sun, I put all of my attention on the periled man turned prince.

"We are at an important moment in time," he goes on, without a scroll to read from, and his hands carefully laid out in his lap as a magic spell from a nearby fairy godmother grants him the ability to speak loud enough for all of us to hear unhindered. "We're at an intersection for the very soul of our kingdom. My father has gained your trust and admiration and done many things in his lifetime, but I'm here today to offer a different way of life.

"One where we care for our neighbor, regardless of their species or skin color or sexuality or innate magical ability. One where we come together to thrive instead of tearing each other apart while the kingdom suffers for it. Already, the barriers are failing. It is only a matter of time before another kingdom realizes we're without that ancient protection and makes a move to reach out. Magic doesn't have to be the enemy, and we can be ready to make allies rather than start wars if we start by looking around ourselves now and taking the first steps to relinquish our tight holds on our prejudices."

Oh. He mentioned the golden barrier. Does he know that it's not merely failing but fully shattered?

Would he recognize me now if I stepped closer to that stage and tilted my chin up to look at him?

Would it matter?

I glance around the crowd again, half-heartedly allowing myself a chance to see a black hood and mismatched eyes even though I'm aware the Necromancer probably wouldn't be allowed in this kind of setting. He is irritatingly stuck on my mind in moments where his presence is unnecessary. Instead, I watch those people adorned in red and faith to the current king frown. They shuffle against one another with murmurs cupped behind hands. Some outright leave.

The crowd thins slightly, allowed Gemma and me to move into the main courtyard.

The prince is still speaking, undeterred by the disinterest of so many citizens, but I can't pay attention; my palm burns. Hot like the handle of a pan that's been left too long on the stove, it sears the top layers of skin and sinks further, boiling my blood, too. I gasp and stagger. Gemma has the back of my shirt in a fist before I can tip over from the sudden onslaught of pain.

I turn back towards her, my fairy godmother. Dressed in yellow and brimming with hope, I can't always seem to find it on my own. She started this journey with me; she introduced me to the witch, but she wasn't the one who made a bad deal. Things are about to go badly.

I can feel it in my heart, as well as I can the now constant burning on my palm.

That witch was prepared to make a deal because she was sure I wouldn't come back to collect on her end. This was always meant to be a one-way mission.

"You need to get somewhere safe," I tell her, shakily flexing my fingers as the pain ebbs away from my palm and wedges itself between the smaller bones of my wrist.

Gemma, for her part, never listens to me. I shouldn't have thought this would be the time she begins. Danger isn't her concern. My fairy godmother is on this trek with me and sticking to my side better than honey to its jar.

"I'm not leaving you, Eli," she reaches down to grab my hand, the one not festering from the golden rune. "Let's not get distracted now."

Yeah. Okay. I try not to think too much about how I appreciate Gemma not leaving me alone for this and how I'm also sure we're doomed regardless of her kind gesture. Everybody in the crowd is focused on the prince's speech. As long as we don't draw any extra attention to ourselves, it should be so easy to get through this ordeal, right?

"She didn't give me any instructions. How am I supposed to know who to deliver this spell to?"

Gemma offers me a very helpful shrug when I glance back at her. "Most body magic warms up as you get closer to its destination.

Maybe see if your hand heats up near anybody."

Great. I didn't enjoy the last time it got hot, the pain suggesting blisters beneath the surface of my skin, and now she's suggesting I push my way through this crowd and perhaps get handsy with the people here. Already, I don't feel comfortable standing on the outskirts. It's been a little less than a day that I've been an active, magic user, but I've always stood apart from this sea of better-off citizens marked by their bright clothing and the fact that most have no signs of manual labor etched into the contours of their bodies. I have no idea why Wynnifred would conspire to make potions for any of them, but we all do what we have to in order to make a little money and get by, right?

"Maybe I should wait until it's over," I try to sway Gemma away from the plan to have me blindly grope my way through the crowd, but she responds with a sharp prodding at my back.

Forward. I'm going forward. Palm out, I pass next to people who grumble about my interruption. The smell of the street carts has been beaten back by the cloying fragrances used by these people. My eyes water as I'm assaulted by the scent of florals, fake leather, and perfumes with names that likely make men feel manlier instead of actually listing the ingredients. I'm almost wishing for a heady wash of B.O. when a man shoves at my attempt to get past, cursing me for distracting from the prince.

Because people are actively listening to the prince. I should probably be doing that, too.

Tilting my head towards the man who sits above the crowd, I listen as he proudly declares that he's not conceding to the King's rule. He's asking for gentler punishments against the people under attack for simply having magic be a part of their lives. Using far more words than I have in my own vocabulary, he implores the crowd to help him make the kingdom a safer place for everyone, magic wielders and normal folk alike, declaring that this is a place that would be stronger and better off if we were unified in our talents. This could be a kingdom of uplifting and mutual compassion if we could let go of our prejudices and fear.

There's far less cheering at every punctuation of the prince's words. The crowd has thinned, but there's still a large gathering here giving him a chance to convince them or at least giving them something to talk about later when the sun has set and rumors are best tilled in the space between acquaintances. A few civilians snarl crude remarks up towards the stage. Others sidle away from the outbursts and then leave as well. None of it seems to bother the prince. Sitting straight in his wheeled chair, draped in the gold and red of his kingdom, he keeps his chin lifted, keeps speaking, and keeps insisting that his father can't continue to rule in fear if enough of us rise up to hold his actions accountable.

The prince isn't merely asking for peace. He's speaking out against the actions of his family. The current King and the two before, men of his generational line who came into power of the throne through their bloodthirsty ruthlessness and have been priding themselves on it for years. This is almost as illegal as casting magic.

Almost.

He is still a prince. He's the least likely person to be shoved into the dungeons or beheaded for speaking up. It should be the duty of him and other nobility to stand up on behalf of the people who aren't afforded such safety.

Under the assumption that none of the people leaving are the person I'm looking for, I continue to wriggle my way through the crowd with gentle apologies. My hand out, waiting for warmth, my eyes remain on the prince. I saw him as someone in need of assistance before, someone who had faced hardships and required a hero. He's not letting his appearance stop him, though. Speaking to a crowd calling for the advisor to step back up to the stage in order to silence his rational speech on the ways we could adjust the culture of our kingdom, his one, brown eye blinking into the harsh rays of the midday sun, I admire him for a half breath.

Perhaps if we had met on different terms and he wasn't the root cause of all my problems, I could find myself not disliking him for his general existence. He doesn't seem half as monstrous as his father, and that's more than one can wish when it comes to royalty. As is, I watch him stay unwavering in his attempt to communicate to the mob around the stage and feel the urge to go to him once more.

He looks like a man who could use help.

Not from me, of course. But someone. Someone with a background in political espionage and the practice of manipulating the highly moldable minds of the masses. I'm better at quick brawls and serving exquisite drinks.

Plus, I'm incredibly busy.

I still have a potion to deliver and a wish to undo. Turning back to the crowd, I curse to myself again about the witch's unclear instructions. A brief description of her client would have really come in handy. I have no idea how I'm supposed to stumble onto anybody of importance in this crowd.

Gemma, her fingers holding onto the back of my shirt to keep the two of us from getting separated, nudges me. I step closer to the stage, the crowd thinning slightly up here where nobody wants to stand too close to the armed guards surrounding it. My palm tingles. It itches. I'm holding a fire that only I can feel the heat of. I pass another pair of tense shoulders, glancing widely around for the person who must be my victim.

Client.

The witch's client.

Could it be a guard?

The advisor pacing behind the stage?

It makes sense that someone attached to the castle would have the means to make deals with witches and feel like they wouldn't be caught.

I step another row closer to the stage, separated from the prince's speech by only a handful of people in the front row and the sparse guards standing at bored intervals around the platform. The spell is definitely working. My hand burns hotter. I'm headed in the right direction. Gemma keeps pushing me as I falter, a steady presence at my back as I grit my teeth against the effects of the potion in my palm.

Gods, it hurts.

The pain radiates from my palm to my wrist and rattles the bones at my elbow. All of the fire and despair I had anticipated when the witch dunked my hand into the cauldron is catching up to me now. My fingers are locked, half-curled towards my palm in a fist that won't close. I won't be able to stop myself from spreading the spell if I happen to find the person who's meant to accept it.

This isn't how I meant to go about delivering the spell. I wanted to see the person who had paid for a spell from a witch in the woods. Had it been one of the guards who had harassed me yesterday evening and followed Gemma and me today, I might have released the acidic potion on them without hesitation. Even with the knowledge that people can never be their best under the constant duress from a fractured and cruel government, I would have been glad to unleash the ire of the witch on them as her words pound through the front of my mind like a separate heartbeat.

A hand for a heart.

Now, though, pressing close to the stage with any number of victims around me from those who are excited by the prince's gentle call to action to those who look angrier than the gods that once rested in the hills to the west, I can't determine morality or the justness of the spell. I probably never could have. I'm merely a pawn in the grand scheme of things. My left hand clutching my right bicep, I gasp out ragged breaths around the pain overtaking that side of my body.

A horrible thought occurs somewhere in the fragmented realm of my logic. If I don't deliver this potion, this insidious rune etched into the flesh of my palm, I very well could be losing my hand. Wynnifred had said a hand for a heart. Everything hurts enough for that to be an option.

Is it selfish of me to want to keep my hand if it means someone else loses their heart?

Maybe I should lie down and let the magic have its way with me.

Gemma keeps that from being an option, her hands steadying me every time I waver. Ahead, the prince is finishing his speech. I'm running out of time to find whoever needs this gods damned delivery.

Sweat drips from my brow as the sun ruthlessly shines down on this area, yet another all-powerful being perfectly happy to watch me commit crimes of magic. I stop as we shoulder our way to the front row, near the center of the stage, and slowly turn my palm up to look at it. Blood speckles the raised lines of the golden rune. It's stealing my energy to work its magic, and I absolutely hate it.

Whether it's my mental unease or my position, the rune pulses; it jars my whole hand, likely leaving an impression of itself in the makeup of my bones. Gold flashes brighter than the overhanging sun, and I turn my hand away from my face to keep from going blind.

I blink away bright spots from my vision as the rune does what it was always going to do. There's a sharp tug at my palm. The pain stops. I don't have time to appreciate that, though, before the screaming begins.

It's everywhere all at once. Hoarse shouts from the men closest to me. Frightened gasps from a handful of women off to my left, their heels clicking on the paved floor as they rush back from me. Distantly, I hear Gemma curse as she grabs me by my shirt collar and drags me backwards.

I stagger three or four steps before my vision finally clears. The stage is still in front of me. Nobody is at my side as the crowd takes my interruption as a reason to leave early. I'm looking up at the stage and not fully processing what's right there in front of me.

The spell created a physical arrow. One carved out of a golden shaft with glittering feathers. It's a real arrow that's plunged through the chest of the crown prince of Briargild.

He was already dressed in red. The arrow could almost be a part of his attire, shining like the crown on his head and the filigree lining his suit jacket. A darker, wet patch spread from the wound to his chest. It seeps and drips and keeps expanding.

Of all the nefarious advisors and noblemen vying for power over the throne, why would the witch target him? Did she know this is where her spell would lead me? Did he make the purchase of the potion in some odd desire for death?

Gemma is pulling me, but I'm reaching up towards the man who is casting confused, pained looks between me and that arrow. I don't understand, either. This is far from a typical story, and I seem to have found myself playing both the roles of the hero and villain.

"I'm sorry," I manage, sputtering over the syllables as my previous relief to be done with the rune turns into stifling guilt.

If I had known, I would have held onto it longer. I would have kept him from experiencing this pain. He didn't deserve this.

Gemma pulls me again, harder than before, as panic offers her strength. She's three steps ahead of me as realization blooms like hot honey across toast. I didn't just shoot the crown prince. I did it in a crowd, and there are a lot of guards coming towards us now. By accidentally delivering that arrow to the prince, I've signed our death warrants.

Guards in shimmering, gold-plated armor line the crowd. They block any exits via the alleys or connected streets. With more efficiency than I could pull off, they've created a trap for me and the hundred other crowd goers. Swords drawn, shields lifted, they create an unbreakable wall as those that were near the stage zero in on me.

I did this. It was only me. I shouldn't have been playing with magic I didn't understand in the first place, even if the purpose was to get my father back and return to my life before my terrible wish. If it's bloodshed and execution they'll demand, I'll surrender, but Gemma shouldn't pay for my crimes.

Whipping my head away from the oncoming guards, I look at my fairy godmother. Her mouth is open. She's yelling at me to get a move on. I don't, though. Instead, I stare at her for the first time since our meeting, and I realize how young she is. Stripped of her gaudy noble clothes, her blonde locks shining a brilliant yellow that refuses to cave into the golden desire of the kingdom, Gemma is just a person like me with hopes and dreams, and she doesn't deserve to have a couple of mistakes define her entire life, or, in this case, end it.

I think if we had been together longer, we would have been best friends.

"I need you to put Skelly on the ground."

Gemma's bottom lip quivers, her blue eyes dart around the thinning crowd as the guards separate civilians from the likes of me. "You can't do magic, Eli."

Gently, I pull her hand off my shirt and release her with a squeeze. "We're past the point of not breaking the law. Please, put Skelly on the ground."

"I'm not leaving you."

I ignore the single tear that streaks down her cheek. "We don't have a choice."

All around me, the guards are yelling commands back and forth. My display of magic has made them cautious about approaching, but they're getting pretty close with their swords extended in my direction. Someone grabbed the prince and rolled him off of the stage. Briefly, I pray he lives. There isn't any more time than that to spend on men I barely know and desperately wish I could have done more for.

"Drop him, Gemma!" A sob shakes her shoulders. I don't wait for the tiny dragon to hit the ground before I hold out my palm and shout the only word that can cause more chaos than my assassination attempt. "Enlarge!"

Skelly is midair when the magic hits. Pink glitter overtakes the city center, blowing back at me and painting the nearest buildings with a residue that I hope lasts long after my head is no longer attached to my shoulders. The bone dragon lands, and the city street quivers under his weight. A glorious defiance of everything Briargild is, Skelly takes up the courtyard. He opens his mouth, snapping and stepping between me and the guards as the men scramble back from the beast in their midst. Restored to his full glory, sharpened teeth hanging from his jaw and wings extended, Skelly is just as terrifying as he was last night.

I'm going to miss him.

Gemma is next to me, her hands fluttering to cover her mouth as she watches our dragon display his most fearsome tactics for the guards without actually chasing any of them away. We only have the element of surprise. As much as I want to comfort her or make false promises that everything is going to be okay, I have to move. Nearly invisible now that everyone is focused on the bone dragon, I grab the bow around Skelly's neck, the thread having grown with the magic, and thrust the ends into Gemma's hands.

"Have you ever ridden a horse?"

"This is not a horse, Eli Cinderfella!"

It's the best I could do on short notice. Kneeling down, I instruct her to step onto my leg and then hoist her up onto the back of the bone dragon. His ribs are slim enough to make riding accessible and strong enough to hold far more than her weight. Beneath her skirts, the fabric bunched up to her thighs, his pink heart beats a steady rhythm.

I wish I had time to ask the Necromancer about the specifics of this magic, how it has lasted, and made something so sturdy. Something amazing. I rub Skelly's back for just a moment, appreciating the skeletal creature more than I have up until this point.

The guards start yelling after I have Gemma settled. She's up and away from the imminent danger, a martyr raised above the crowd, as I stay behind as the true sacrifice.

"Skelly, get her somewhere safe. Get out of the city."

I don't use magic in my command. There's no way for me to find the right, incapable of being misinterpreted word at a moment like this. I'm tiptoeing on the edge of full-blown panic. I just need him to work with me. Instead of magic, I tap his rump and hope he's as smart as he looks.

For once, things go my way. Gemma lets out a sound that can only be described as a war cry. She screams, and Skelly clacks his oversized jaw, and the two of them take off at a sprint right for the guards blocking the alley we came through. Less courageous than they started, the guards cry and jump out of the way, their armor clanking in an earsplitting chorus of metal.

I catch sight of Skelly's tail flicking side to side as they disappear down the next street. It's likely the last I'll ever see of them. I swallow past a lump in my throat.

Now, it's time to face the consequences of delivering the witch's rune.

The guards pull themselves together fast enough. They come closer. I let my hands dangle at my sides. Raised next to my head, they'll see me as even more of a threat as the lingering dusting of pink glitter continues to fall from my palms. There's no pleas for me to verbalize, no magic to call to my aid, no last ditch efforts to save myself.

I surrender.

Three guards circle me, their swords raised and at the ready— one more steps directly in front of me. The visor of his helmet is pushed back. His eyes are a pale green. I would probably call him handsome if he weren't about to be my murderer.

Green will have to do. Here, standing in a place that will likely be my last in the face of my crimes, I can admit to myself that I'd rather stare into shades of brown and gray. The Necromancer has figured out how to haunt me since our quick romp in the forest, and I regret not having another chance to best him.

The guards are so close. I don't move. I think this is what my mother must have faced. An immigrant turned on by the society she had claimed as her home, her magic a weapon of change and destruction that left higher powers feeling threatened, I'm sure she also felt cornered like this and held up her chin regardless.

I'm going to do the same.

Hopefully, I can meet her on the other side of a glinting blade.

Maybe we'll find my father, too. I'd still like a chance to apologize for all the mistakes I've made since our fight. This isn't the end I wanted, but it's the one I'll accept.

"Halt!"

The voice rings out across the noisy square, silencing the grumbles and gossip of the crowd being held back by a circle of guards. I take my eyes off my potential executioner long enough to look towards the stage. A thick towel held to his chest, Prince Alexander Charming kneels with his fiery gaze directed at me.

They must have tried to detain him in his chair. He fought to get away. To crawl. To yell now for me.

I wish I had time to say thank you. I've seen enough violence in my day to know that I won't survive this altercation. Someone like me, someone not noble, not pale, not with assets to his name, is never going to be allowed to live beyond the scope of my rebellion. Allowing me to do so would be a mistake on the King's part. People would start to think he was getting lax in his laws. No. Anyone who is different is meant to be exterminated. Typically, in a public fashion, to keep the masses in fear of possible repercussions.

I appreciate the prince anyway. I can only imagine the consequences for a man of his status to be seen struggling across the stage now for a peasant like me.

All of that being said, I don't believe that even a prince could save me now.

"Just make it quick, alright?" I tell the green-eyed guard.

A quiver tightens his jaw and runs through to his sword hand. Maybe he's tempted. The King would likely offer him a promotion for striking down the man who attempted to assassinate the prince. To my surprise, he doesn't move.

Perhaps the crown prince of Briargild has more power than I realized.

I let out a shuddering breath as my neck has not yet been severed, and let my attention drift back to the man kneeling on the stage. There are so many questions I have for him. First and foremost, why he would stay the act of my execution?

Did he forget that I shot him with a magical arrow?

Doesn't he realize that I deserve to be beheaded and left as a lesson to the people of this kingdom?

His father wouldn't hesitate to deal out my punishment.

Besides, I've lived long enough to know I was never meant to be someone special. I'm just a tavern keep. Yet, the prince is looking at me as though he's never truly seen another person before this point.

Like we're connected. Even only briefly. I wish it could have happened without magic and bloodshed, but I, definitely in a foolish stroke of logic, wouldn't ask to stop being the center of his world even for an instant.

I've never felt more seen, more noted, more wanted.

Out of all the men I've ever shared my time with, ever risked kissing, none of them have looked at me the way Prince Alexander Charming is doing now.

Well, maybe nobody besides him and the Necromancer.

Not breaking eye contact with me, that one dark eye scorching my features, he directs his words to the waiting guards. "We need him as a prisoner. He will be kept until I can interrogate him for this crime," he grits out around the pain that is the arrow lodged to the side of his heart.

Reality shatters around me. Right. I'm over here with my head in the clouds, and the prince, well, the prince is bleeding out and treating this situation with the rationality it requires.

Of course, he wouldn't want me dead.

I'm obviously not a trained mercenary.

He's going to want to know how, why, and who enlisted me for this assassination attempt.

I don't fight back when the soldiers surge forward. Two have my hands immediately, clapping shackles onto my wrists that are far heavier than necessary. The too-cold metal bites into my skin as my heart slows.

That's not right.

It's not just metal.

Magic.

The magic that lives in my palms.

I can't feel it anymore.

My mouth falls open, and all I taste is sweat and desperation and the lingering dirt kicked up by Skelly's retreat. Briefly, I note the wind on my face, caressing me as if it too knows that this will be my last chance outside in the sun as a free man. I'm cold and hopeless as the guards lead me away.

12

The walk to the castle is everything that I expect: humiliating, grueling, and far too long. I grit my teeth against it all, watching the pavement under my feet as shivers overtake my body, nearly dependent on the guards at my sides to keep me from falling to my knees. All the while, my gaze sticks on the cuffs hanging heavy from my wrists. Gold is inset into the metal in the shape of a rose, and it grins up at me as the most prominent symbol of Briargild. It's a flower that means downfall as the manacles bleed the magic out of me. Cold clings to my bones, my wrists numb from the constant, chilling contact that even the sun cannot combat.

With all of the chaos of our procession, the same two guards manage to keep pace with me, each with a hand on my shoulder and the other resting on their swords as though I'm in any position to show resistance. They pretend they don't see anything when the crowd fills the sidewalks and vegetables are thrown. I don't even know why these people have access to so many rotten tomatoes in their plush abodes of pampered living, but the juice sticks to my chin from an expert toss by a man with a pinch-lipped wife at his side, their clothes a bright red to show their support of the kingdom.

The guards are not oblivious to the curses spat. Some take part in the name-calling and jeering, and the overall act of watching a rebellious prisoner being walked to the castle. They don't bawk when vegetables become rocks. I feel bruises start to form with the impacts, the upper city community coming together to punish me for my impudence as we step onto cobblestone roads inlaid with golden grout.

Maybe some rumors are true. The ground truly sparkles here. I think it might be real gold that I walk over as a trickle of blood traces the edge of my jaw before jumping down to join the shining grout.

Still, we press onwards. A mob forms around us. The rest of the guards in our immediate party aren't any better than their civilian counterparts. I feel them prod at my back with sharpened weapons, not enough to draw blood, but plenty to ruin yet another outfit from Harold. I'm pushed and pulled. Someone trips me, barking out a laugh when I fall to my knees. The gold in the ground attempts to lodge itself into my shins. Slowing down gives them a reason to attack, so there isn't time to catch my breath or rest before I'm pushing back up to continue the treacherous march to meet my fate.

Blood drips from a nick on my ear. All of the healing herbs in Gemma's pouch couldn't save me now. My left eye is puffy and sore, getting more and more difficult to blink. Each of my steps is the full concern of my attention; I try to block it out, let the cries of admonishment blend together to the same kind of racket that is a storm in the forest. I am the trees, and the sky cannot bother me. I am here. Here, but not a part of the thundering wails outside of my own bubble.

I don't put up a fight. I can't. I simply bear the brunt of a kingdom turned into merciless wolves against a single deer as I'm paraded through the city.

Nearly to the castle, the houses of the richest nobility circling it like vultures prepared to pick it clean, I catch sight of more people called to the sidewalks to see my dishonorable march. Servants stand three steps behind their masters. My heart clenches as I make eye contact with a girl who looks like me. Her skin darkened. Her hair cut short to her scalp. Her eyes wide.

Shame curdles my blood at the watery emotion in her gaze.

I'm not a lesson to magic wielders. These people have little to no clue that I cast a spell the guards neither suspected nor could stop. They only know that I look different from the upper-class men of this area, that I look like someone who would commit a crime, and that I've been stopped to the joyous contentment of the white nobility. I'm one more sentence in the story of a colonized people, not one of hope, but one of the stark reality that we may never escape this plotline.

How could we?

We're so spread out from one another. The streets are lined with red and gold, and people who sneer at me with feathers in ostentatious hats and dresses that drag on the floor. It takes me several steps at a time and a dutiful search of the crowd to break through the barrier of nobility to catch sight of others like myself. Some are servants in old, ill-fitting clothes, several shades removed from beige. Some are working-class men and women who travel up here to fix the nobility's homes or gowns or otherwise use their talents to get them a pittance in this life, marked by gold pins on their lapels and no other nod to the general kingdom. Crouched low, I spot satyrs behind bushes, their plant magic a resource needed to keep this area beautiful, and yet a dangerous occupation should their employers decide to punish them for simply being themselves. Finally, a centaur I saw at the rebel meeting, his broad chest covered in a red flannel shirt cut by green and gold lines.

He raises a hand up to me, his voice a boom above the hisses and curses of the noble class. "When dragons return!"

My throat tightens, and I stagger a step. We lock eyes. Earnest blue makes a clear path over the heads of the noble class to reach me in this moment.

These people might not know what I've done, but everyone here who matters will have heard that odd, prophetic term. Heads snapped up from where they had been focused on the grass and pavement. Like the ocean coming to meet the land, a swell of that phrase reaches me where the guards are struggling to get me to move again.

The crown will fall when dragons return.

I think Skelly counts. Clearly, the centaur in the crowd saw Skelly and believed in him. If nothing else, my dragon is filling these people with a hope they haven't felt in the last three decades.

I wish I could reach up and grab the locket around my throat, but I don't want to draw attention to one more thing that could be taken from me. Even with every bad decision that brought me here, I feel closer to my mother than ever before. I know now why she held up her chin for her execution. Before she was a mother and a wife, she was a witch who cared about her people. She was making a statement and becoming a symbol that simmers in the embers of the falling sun.

I wouldn't be her son if I didn't carry on that legacy.

I pick up my chin. I stare out at the people. Those who sneer, those who look at me with renewed understanding and borderline awe, and some who try to hide the fear that tightens like a noose in the muscles of their jaw, I see it all. Before, I was merely a lower city citizen. I was a tavern keep. I was a man with little ambition beyond the walls of our family business.

Now, I let them see me.

Ensnared by the kingdom's guard, but not cowering.

I brought dragons back.

"The crown will fall," I shout back to the repeated phrase that has turned to a murmur as nobles attempt to hush and stifle the lower-class people nearest them.

The guard on my left kicks me in the back of the leg, and I fall to my knees as the thunderous reply comes. "When dragons return! The crown will fall!"

Over and over again. The crowd continues to yell at me as I'm dragged forward until I can find my footing once more. I might not be able to physically fight back or pull magic from my palms in my current state, but I can make a scene. Nobody is going to forget today for a long, long time.

The echoing chants follow me like a stray dog long after I'm off the main road to the castle. No punches are thrown by the protestors. They do not break windows or stop the traffic in the streets. They merely hold their ground and use their voices to unsettle those made comfortable by the current state of the kingdom. It's not enough to change anything, but it's the first step towards demanding a different way of life. It's a message that can no longer be ignored.

Guards file past us with instructions to stop the riots that don't exist as we continue our journey forward. Roses mark the grounds nearest the castle. Full, blooms in the darkest shades of red luxuriate in the midday sun despite the chill season. Magic again used for aesthetics rather than a necessity and always saved for the noble class. Red and green and far, too sharp, the flowers are crammed in every space possible, a message to those walking these steps that they have gone too far to be saved. It seems to be an unmanaged maze, our own path memorized by the people at my side. More than once, the guards have to squeeze in close to me to avoid the trailing, thorny vines that threaten to pull them in, the roses acting as sentries of the very foundation of Briargild's fortress and more than happy to bury dissenters near their roots.

I do not walk through the front doors. Instead, the guards at my side make a direct turn down a path that leads to a smaller door on the side of the building. Muted, red bricks of the castle glare down at me as we move together. They're granted entry after a brief knock, and I'm dragged more than led down a staircase.

Shut within the lower bowels of the castle, I rack my mind for anything I know about this area. I've heard a number of things about the dungeon from rumors and ghost stories. It's cold and dark, and most people don't return from a stay down here. Supposedly, there are screams at all hours of the night. Inhumane punishments are carried out, and there isn't a person up here who would risk their own life to save a rotten soul stuffed down below the soil. Perhaps all prisoners merely become rose mulch.

We only go down one flight, even though the stairs continue down into a dark nothingness squinting can't pierce. There's no argument from me. My knees hardly want to take another step. I keep my head up, my eyes taking in the dirt that has accumulated in the edges of the gray halls and the cracks in the walls that have long since gone unpatched.

The guard with green eyes uses a key to open a door, and then they shove me inside, slamming it shut again without joining me. The lock clicks back into place. Isolation doesn't feel like the worst punishment after everything that just happened outside. I wait for their receding footsteps to stop echoing down the hall before I take in my new space.

There are no windows besides the one on the door I came through, a closed thing that looks like it opens from the outside to give a viewer an idea of what I'm up to without having to fully open the door. The entire room is a concrete box. There's a table in the middle with one chair. No bed. No cushions. No sign of simple comforts besides a chamber pot in the corner that looks like it hasn't been cleaned out since the last person to enter this interrogation room. I appreciate that the side of my face is swollen, and I've been breathing out of my mouth for the last several moments, sure the smell is also permeating this room.

I wonder how many people have sat here, how many waited for a trial that never came, or how many desperately fought to be released only to be struck down in this room. The stains on the floor don't give me any comfort that I'm leaving here without injury. Dark splotches can be seen at several intervals, the largest a small lake by the door I came through.

I truly question whether or not I should sit down in the chair and await my fate.

My body is tired, though. I'm still bleeding from some of my wounds. As much as I would like a bath and a bed, I settle myself into the chair that faces the door like a good prisoner.

A phrase is written in a language I can't read above the doorway. Maybe it's old spell work from a time before magic was very nearly outlawed. Of course, King Anerald would keep a few pieces of vicious magic for himself. It's probably triggered by someone trying to escape. Maybe it's to stop someone from wielding their own magic, and it is now a moot point with these muffling shackles on my wrists.

Advancements in technology are sometimes terrible things, aren't they?

I don't know how long I sit alone. Long enough for the blood to stop dripping from my ear and the wound to become crusty. Longer still for the shivers wracking my shoulders to give way as my body, now addicted to magic, learns to forget the exotic taste long enough that my head is curled on my arms and sleep beckons when the door finally bangs open.

I sit up with a start, a guard entering and holding the door open for the prince, who, without access to a wheelchair ramp, has found himself crutches that he uses to drag his lower half into view before sitting once more in his chair, being carried down by a second guard. Once the prince is all the way into the room, his clothes changed and a white bandage peeking out from under the collar of his loose shirt, the first guard approaches the table, securing my shackles to a lock underneath that I hadn't seen before now.

Bound and vulnerable, I say nothing as the prince bids the two guards to wait outside. He sits across from me with his hands on the wheels of his chair, his crutches left propped next to the door. There's no longer a crown on his head, I note, looking above him rather than straight at him as I feel more than see his own gaze travel over me.

When he doesn't speak, I find my own voice, desperate to escape my thoughts and the intensity of his undivided attention. "How's your shoulder?"

"I've been through worse. You're a terrible shot."

I nod. I'm glad. I really don't need to add murder to my already disappointing list of mistakes from the past twenty-four hours.

The prince taps his fingers on his wheel. "You don't seem upset to see me alive."

It's not a question. This is an interrogation, though. I shrug, the motion pulling at the multitude of cuts on my back from the assault outside, all of them having attempted to adhere to the fabric of my shirt and reopening with any attempt at motion.

"If you don't want me dead, that means you were working for someone. I can help you if you'll give me answers."

His voice is soft. Honey dripping into warm tea. I want to tell him everything.

But I can't. More than my own life hangs in the balance. While I owe no real loyalties to Wynnifred, Gemma still cares for the witch. I won't sign someone else's life away to save my own.

So, I shake my head and keep my gaze on a cobweb in the corner of the room, curious to know whether or not the spider died down here, too.

I've had more than enough time to accept my fate. Maybe I'll live to see a different room in this castle— the real dungeons. Maybe I'll be tried and executed in a private setting; the king more than prepared to do away with people like me. Either way, I have no hope of talking my way out of this circumstance, and I'm not going to try. I made a spectacle on my way here, and I hope it's enough to spark the revolution the Necromancer was already building out in the forest.

Briargild is in need of change, and I'm okay with my death being the beginning of the end for King Anerald Charming.

"Did the witch tell you I was your target?"

My head whips to meet him before I can still myself. I don't know how to hide information. The entire point of my occupation before was to make genuine contact with people, remember their quirks and needs, and make myself accessible to them. It was not a good skill set for evading questions in an interrogation. The prince knows immediately he's guessed correctly.

So, I give in and ask my own question. "How could you know that?"

His gaze should be cruel. He should be angry. If anything, having to stare into the leather covering one of his eyes should be enough to remind me that this man has seen difficult circumstances and survived. He should terrify me.

He doesn't, though.

My throat is dry when he answers. "I'm fond of your fairy godmother. I know she wouldn't have let you come if she knew what was going to happen, so I assume you've made a bad deal and ended up here."

Gemma. He knows Gemma. My pulse is deafening. It's probably loud enough for him to hear across the table.

"Please, she didn't have anything to do with this. Please, don't hurt her."

For the first time since meeting him, his lips downturn into a frown. "I wouldn't."

Maybe I'm comfortable being a prisoner because I've been trapped by rules my entire life. I laugh in his face. Not a happy sound. A sniffling, biting burst of nervous air.

"Of course you would," I snap. "That's all you people do."

The prince jerks back like I hit him, like I shot him again with a golden arrow, like I'm the dangerous person in this gods damned room. I don't move from my spot, trussed up under the table as I am. Still, there's a wariness in his single eye as he watches me.

"If I guarantee her safety, will you answer my questions?"

It seems he's found a weakness in my heart that I should have hidden. Even so, I shake my head. I put her on a dragon and told them to leave. There's no way the guards caught them, and my fairy godmother is smart enough to get herself out of trouble. Even without magic, she's resourceful.

I have to believe Gemma will be okay.

The prince hisses annoyance and spreads his hands on the table in front of me, leaving them there for me to see the scars that line the space between his fingers and across the back of them, curling around his wrist while he makes his next gamble. "What can I give you to get you to work with me?"

Nothing.

The truth plunges into my stomach like a rock through the surface of a frozen lake. This prince can't give me anything that would make it worth my speaking out against Gemma or Wynnifred or the things I saw in the forest last night. He survived the arrow attempt and should be happy about it. I'm a dead end. There's nothing I can offer him besides reluctance now.

"You're not very good at interrogations, are you?"

The prince bites his lip and leans back in his chair. "Nobody out there seems to know who you are. Not a name. Not a motivation for this attack. If you work with me, I can set you up with some land and a life worth living."

"With your father's money?" I bare my teeth. "I'd rather rot here."

His eye widens. I watch him swallow hard. Hands returned to his lap, he fiddles with a button on his shirt. It's a long moment of staring at each other before he leans forward with his voice low and intimate, meant just for me.

"The guards can hear us. Nod if you're part of the rebellion."

I don't move. Of course, I believe in a lot of the objectives they stand for, but my only experience with the group is getting into a hopeless duel with their leader and then sparking the cheering riot outside. I'm not about to tell the prince about any of that.

In return for my continued resistance, he frowns. "What was the point in making a deal with a witch if you won't make a better deal with someone else?"

I would cross my arms over my chest if I could. Silence spreads between us, long-fingered and shameless. I'm not giving up any more information. I made a bad deal that brought me here, but I'm not stupid enough to make another one.

Outside the interrogation room, a thundering parade of footsteps sounds. We're about to have a crowd. The prince's eye goes even wider than before.

"I'm part of the rebellion," he blurts in a rushed whisper. "Do not trust anyone else here. Nod if you understand."

Shock sits me back in my chair. The welts and cuts on my back shriek from the sudden contact with the metal, but it's not enough to take my attention off the man pushing a hand back through his hair. It had been a mess when he came in. Now, it's completely unbound and falling around his clean-shaven jaw.

"You can't trust me," I murmur, my gaze torn between watching for visitors at the door and the shellshocked expression on the prince's face.

He just shakes his head, gathering himself with a chuckling breath. "I don't have a choice." His hands pressed to the table, revealing those vicious scars raking over his fingers once more. "I'm running out of time to help the people here. My father is making plans for the upcoming ball. If I don't figure out how to stop him, it'll be too late to do anything else, so I need to collect all the help I can.

"Do not speak to anyone else. I will find a way to get you out of the dungeon, okay?"

Prince Alexander Charming doesn't wait for my response. His hands are on his chair. A cool mask of indifference slips over his features as the door opens. Three guards flank King Anerald Charming.

My heart leaves me like a sparrow heading to warmer climates, swiftly and without looking back. I sit in resigned silence, appreciating that my hands are tied under the table so he can't see how they shake. King Anerald looks down at me. Red cape touching the floor. Red at his throat. Red covering every part of him. Next to the prince in white, he looks like a visage of Death come to claim me.

His fingers are weighed down by gold rings that glint in the bit of magic light caught in a golden orb in this room as he runs a hand over his beard. "This is the person who tried to start a coup?"

I would be lying if I said I kept my chin up. Mouth dry, head full of all the ways this could go wrong, I stare at the table and wait for my execution to be announced.

I'm the one who shot the prince with a magic arrow.

If he wants consequences, he only has me in his hold. There's no way he could get Wynnifred or Gemma, no matter my connections to them. At least, I try to believe that as he snorts and murmurs a command to his guards.

"He's not the sort worth our time. Put him in the belly and throw away the damned key."

The prince clears his throat. "He deserves a trial. You can't just pretend this will all go away. Did you not hear the people outside?"

Prince Alexander is calm, composed, and leveling his one good eye on his father. An obvious power struggle ensues. The king has been so full of power for so long that he must be finding it a mistake to finally allow his son out of the castle. In an effort to appease the questions of his citizens, he named an heir he found to be an unlikely candidate to steal his crown. Different, yes. Incapable. I would never describe the prince in such terms. As is, Prince Alexander Charming has learned to be seen and heard and is an expert in the act of shifting his voice in such a way to direct all attention to him, winning the initial, wary respect of the kingdom in his first outing. I wish I hadn't cut it short by setting off that sordid spellwork.

The guards hanging around the doorway step from one foot to the other. They, too, feel like they're standing far too close to what looks like an altercation about to come to blows. Prince Alexander doesn't shudder away from his father, even if his jaw tenses and the fingers of his left hand move to fiddle with his shirt buttons once more. He's truly putting himself between me and a man who hates all beings of difference and magic. The prince is once more exposing his throat to the people, truly giving them every reason to see him as the rebellious oaf he just admitted to being to me.

I don't know how he's survived this long without someone to watch his back.

Maybe he does have someone to watch his back.

Briefly, I let a fantasy overtake me in which the prince in front of me knows the Necromancer from the forest. The two most interesting men I've ever had the experience of sparring, verbally and physically. It would knock my world asunder to deal with the both of them at once.

I would probably be too flustered to do much more than sputter and look between them.

Much like right now. I'm not flustered for reasons of the errant heart. My pulse is unsteady because the man who killed my mother and started a siege on the magical people of this kingdom is only a table length away. He hasn't spared me a glance since walking in. Fully focused on the prince, his hands on his hips as his cape flutters just above the floor, he grits out an irritated response.

"A trial is what those bastards want. They need the spectacle to turn the masses in their favor. I won't be playing into their little games, and you should learn to think more than one step ahead if you have any hope of ruling your own kingdom."

The prince's hand clenches for just a second. He is rigid as though he were struck, while the two men have yet to move. The guards pass worried looks between the three of them. This must be a common occurrence that has been getting worse in the months since the rebels began acting out.

The rebels.

Like the one in his chair with his chin tilted up against blatant tyranny.

He gave me the ability to buy my freedom by ratting him out. Nobody should trust me that much. I wouldn't trust myself that much. Unsure of how I keep running into good people now that Gemma isn't the only one, I stare ahead at the father and son and remind myself that silence is as potent a weapon as speaking out if used correctly. I dare not speak as the two of them continue their bickering back and forth before the king declares his response.

"Isolation, then. We will discuss a trial with the castle generals and administration. I want a constant guard in the hall and nobody near his cell. Is all of that clear?"

The trio of guards gives a unified salute, and the king whips his cape behind him in a dramatic flourish as he exits without another word to his son. The prince doesn't look at me. He doesn't apologize or act any way but diplomatic as my cuffs are untied from the bottom of the table and I'm led out of the room.

I may not understand everything that's happening right now, but I know one thing. The prince is playing a very dangerous game and has gambled his one secret to gain my trust. There's no telling what he'll ask of me when he comes to get me released.

13

Days pass in the steel and brick-walled cell. The cuffs remain on my wrists, making it uncomfortable to eat the gruel slipped through the smaller door cut into the bottom of my room and locked tight every time it's done being used. Nobody enters the room to take away my used dishes or clean out the chamber pot in the corner. I'm not even given a blanket. I lay on the floor and stare up at the ceiling, and curse the prince for making this happen.

The dungeon is as disgusting as I've heard whispered over tankards of ale. The walls are worn by the cold and moist, warping in certain places where smudges of past prisoners' fingers have been left and never wiped. Shivering, I curl in on myself, trying to shield my face with my bound arms as I lie on a floor that has never seen a mop. If my counting is correct, the last guard of the day has come down, and I'll be thoroughly alone for the night since they only visit once in the morning and once in the evening, my stack of dishes a makeshift clock for keeping my misery.

I'm almost tempted to eat the gray slop tonight. Almost. Instead, I lay on my side and watch the flicker of the orange light from the dim orb in the center of the ceiling glisten over the slimy top of it. Magic is right above me, a convenient capture of light that makes it so I have no access to fire, and yet there's no magic in my veins.

My wrists have been rubbed sore from the shackles. I lay on my side to avoid getting more debris in the festering wounds on my back. There's a good chance the gash on my ear is infected from the way it throbs and oozes. At this rate, there won't need to be a trial. I'll probably pass from natural causes.

I huff a breath of air, my lungs quaking from the effort. Any kind of trial would be a sham anyway. I've broken plenty of laws and injured the prince with magic. There's no way I'm going to survive this ordeal, not even if a man with one brown eye promises that he'll help me.

I've had a lot of time to think about the prince down here. It's hard to keep track of time between sleeping and meals, but when I do get restful pockets of dreams, I find myself across from the prince once more. He is kind. His fingers are soft on my wrists where he removes the shackles.

I melt for him as pink glitter returns to my palms.

And then I wake up here, frozen and aching.

Who needs a prince anyway? I had my focus set on a Necromancer before all of that business in the city center. I'm not too cowardly to admit that I think about him, too. It's not like there's anything else for me to do besides fantasize about all the things I could have had and will never know.

In my dreams, the Necromancer is not soft or kind. His different colored eyes haunt me as I'm chased through the woods. Sometimes, when the dream is prolonged, I let him catch me. I try to imagine what he would look like if I pulled down that face mask. Would there be stubble to rub my thumbs over? I want to know how he would taste, panting above me with his hands fisted in the green grass of a meadow kept out of season. Gods, I would strip him of all those black clothes and...

Heavy footsteps pull me out of my thoughts. There are never footsteps after the last guard. A few times in the first day, different administrators were led down here to gaze through the bars on the door and allowed to determine that I was a real threat. I was real, at least, and that seemed like more than enough.

None of them stomped like this.

It sounds like a giant is working its way down the stone steps. This is someone not truly worried about stealth. Perhaps the king has come down here to do away with me in the dark and secret depths of the castle.

I wouldn't blame him. I've been a huge problem.

My only regret is not having the time to save my father. I would have liked a chance to see Harold one last time and thank him for helping me, even though he had forgotten me in the throes of a bad wish. Gemma should be safe, though. And her witch. There's nobody else out there who even knows about me besides a handful of rebels and men who stare at me in awe but give me no true solutions to my life's quest.

There's no hesitation in the steps. I know a flight of stairs separates me from the entry door above. It's not too far, and yet it seems to take an eternity for the steps to get closer as I squint up at the ceiling with more questions than answers. I would sit up if I had the energy to do so. Instead, I stay on the floor, fully prepared to just wait for doom and gloom to come to my door. I hold my breath and peek past the edge of my arm to watch for the boots that should be stopping at my door soon enough. Hoping for the mended and worn boot of a guard more so than the new and polished shoe of nobility, I'm left staring into the dim, orange-hued edge of the hall.

The steps are here. They've stopped in the same place every guard has come to pass me the food I refuse to eat and the water I've been hoarding in case they decide to stop showing up. Echoes of the final step resound through the cold, decrepit hall of the isolation ward, but nobody is there.

Nothing is in front of my cell.

That's not possible.

Tempting my body's current tendency to nausea, I force myself to sit up and rub my eyes as bursts of white overtake my vision. I have aches and a wavering tension in limp muscles. I'm staggering breaths and denial. When my vision clears, I stare into the hall to meet the same, impossible sight. It's just me and the dim passageway.

Maybe I've gone and lost my mind.

Before I can allow myself to consider whether or not the existence of magic in my life leaves me open to believing in ghosts, a voice calls out to me. "Cinderfella. Get off the floor."

What. The. Fuck.

I scrub my hands over my face again, the shackles clanking with my movements. Again, I blink at empty space. Nothing is there. This has to be in my head. Nobody knows my name anyway. I've gone and conjured up a hallucination.

That's it.

All in my head.

There's a huff and a grunt, and then a body flashes into view. The Necromancer yanks off his second boot and chucks it into the cell at me. "I'm here to break you out," he snaps.

All of the energy I thought I was lacking surges into my frozen bones, it seeps into my muscles left in withdrawals without access to magic, and heats my blood as my heart stammers back to life. I push to my feet. It's a process. Slower than I would like, difficult in my current predicament, but I make it to my full height and stagger towards the barred door.

Emotion clogs my throat. I stare directly into the mismatched gaze of a man who was just a presence in my fantasies and shouldn't be here. I don't know if I should be relieved that I'm not losing my mind, or excited that he's really here, or angry and offended that he's throwing shoes at me. All three seem to be fair.

When I finally have control over my vocal cords once more, my voice cracks from the lack of use and shuffles past the bars in a wobbling wince. "Why?"

His face, mostly covered by the mask over his nose and mouth, is lit by the flickering magic orb, the orange light giving him an ethereal air as it presses into the creases of his dark clothes. Compounded with the fact that he's dangerous with magic, I stare up at him in utter disbelief. This man could be a god with his skill alone. There's no reason he needed to risk capture to come get me out of here. He's not someone I would consider to be a friend or ally. He chased me out of a field of revolutionaries with a freakin dragon and then tackled me in the forest, spurring on my less-than-appropriate thoughts but really doing nothing good for me.

It's fun to imagine that I'm a damsel in distress and someone might actually save me, but I can't comprehend why he would really do it.

Why the Necromancer when Prince Alexander Charming promised to get me out of here?

My thoughts are cut off by his adamant reply. "Nobody wants to end this way. I heard what Wynn did. I'm here to undo some of the damage."

Oh. Right. She must have gone to her leader and admitted to her plan. This was the whole reason she wasn't allowed into that rebel meeting. Wynnifred the witch was done waiting for someone to save the day and concocted a plan that was more direct and aggressive than anything the Necromancer was probably telling them to do. My heart aches as I imagine the witch didn't fess up to this because I didn't show up, but, instead, because my fairy godmother raged at her to do the right thing. Gemma would have done anything for me. She hadn't wanted to leave me, and she must have heard I was taken as a prisoner even after I sent her out of the city.

Maybe.

I don't voice any of that.

Instead, I lean harder against the bars of the cell that has become my final resting place and try to reach through. My shackles clank on the metal. Cold shoots from my wrists to my elbows.

"You have no idea how I want to end," I grit out through clenched teeth when I realize I can't reach him.

It's been days. I've had time to come to terms with all of this. There have been so many listless hours lying here to give me time to make amends with the finality of my tale. It isn't the life my father wanted and far from what I envisioned for myself, but I do think it's okay. I stood up for the right things, tried to help where I had the chance, and accepted when my actions caused problems that deserved consequences. My only regret would be not listening to his stories for the warnings they were, but I'm my mother's son. All I've had for years were stories and snippets of rumors about her, and I still grew up to resemble everything she was to this kingdom. Headstrong with a desire to be free, to be spirited, to be compassionate in the face of tyranny, it's a generational curse that has finally caught up to me.

My story has been written in red ink since I came into this world. I'm one more name meant to be wiped from history. If the people outside of this castle can remember me long enough to rally and make some change, then it all has to be enough, doesn't it?

"Really?" The Necromancer snarls back from behind that black mask, his gloved hand reaching through the bars in a way I can't in my bound position. "The same guy who thought he could best me in a magical battle now wants to throw up his hands in defeat. The man I heard tamed that skeletal dragon by making up his own rules.

That man wants to die here and now?"

He's warm where his fingers touch my hand. Momentarily, I forget why I'm upset. What exactly was the point I was trying to make? Does it matter if he's right here, reaching out to me, and so much closer than even in my dreams?

I don't pull away when I gather the threads of my argument once more, like a sweater unraveling around my waist, holding onto my indignation and frustration and days' worth of upset tighter than necessary. "What right do you have to come drag me out of here? You're the revered Necromancer. Shouldn't you just wait until my head is separated from my body and then make use of my leftovers?"

The Necromancer's breath plumes in front of his face as he lets out an emotionally charged sigh. That cloud hangs between us. It tries and fails to obscure him from my view. Brown and gray reach me anyway. My own breath hitches in my throat. There isn't a power in this universe that could keep me from looking at him right now.

"Come on, Cinderfella. Cut the dramatics. The both of us have to realize I'm not really a necromancer."

If I had been standing without the entirety of my weight already on the cell door, I would have stumbled. My world has shifted several centimeters to the left. The witch introduced him under that title. He only used magically charged bones to attack me. This man dug up a mass grave and helped me build the dragon that would become Skelly. It only made sense to believe him at his word.

I shake my head. I babble something incomprehensible. I'm tired and starved and in over my head when it comes to meeting with darkly clad gentlemen in dungeon halls. Before I can get an actual question to leave my chest and this cell and berate him in the way I wish I could if all of this metal wasn't between us, the door slams open at the top of the stairs.

"What are you?" I whisper in a hurry as he shoves his free hand into his pocket and then thrusts it into the cell to join his first.

"Come find out," he replies, a cool object leaving his fingers as he presses it into my palm.

A call to action. A dare. A bet that he thinks he can't lose.

I hold the key tight, hope filtering through my misery in bright stripes that could combat the full fury of the sun. Today might not be the day I die. I won't have to leave my corpse here to gather dust.

I had accepted my end would be this place of dirt and grime and walls dripping with enough moisture to allow algae to congeal in the corners. I was willing to settle into this ending if it meant Gemma was allowed to go free, to run from our accidental attack on the prince, and survive to keep the people of Briargild hoping to fight back against a system meant to break us. Acceptance is easily shoved off, though, as I cling to the key and a second option.

Off to the left, up those stairs I barely remember coming down, there's an urgent yell for more guards. Somebody thinks I've already escaped, and they're bringing a full battalion down here to stop me.

"Guess you're not very sneaky."

The Necromancer curses and brushes a hand over the top of his hood. "Undo the cuffs. Put the shoes on. Be ready to move when they open the door, Eli."

He's talking, but I'm not processing any of it. I think he just provided a list. There are guards imminently approaching. All of the hope I had been floating on starts to evaporate.

I'm not getting out of this cell.

"I can't get caught here, Eli," he reaches back into the cell and grabs the key from my trembling hand, unlocking my first shackle when I don't immediately follow his directions. "You have to start moving."

He repeats the list. I can't stop staring into his stormy eyes. It wouldn't be the worst thing if he were the last thing I saw, would it?

"Cuffs. Shoes. Be ready to move," the Necromancer snaps again as dozens of steps ricochet down the hall.

He pulls away. A step. Two. I grab his hand before he can fully escape.

I don't know what to say. Danger is jogging down the hall that has never felt so short. It's usually several minutes of walking before they deliver my meals. I wet my lips and desperately stare across the metal bars towards the man who came to save me. I don't want to be alone to face the unknown.

"Please stay."

He squeezes my fingertips. "I'm so sorry, Eli, but I can't. You're going to get out of here. You're going to come find me. I'll be in the gardens at midnight. You do that and I'll answer every question you have."

Every movement he makes is stiff and hesitant, like he can't be the one to break the connection between us. For the first time in my life, someone else is as enraptured in me as I am in them. It's terrible that I have to have such a revelation in a dingy dungeon. The Necromancer is waiting until the last second to leave me to my fate, though, and I swallow hard. Heavy pressure swirls through my chest. Responsibility sits on my shoulders. If I die tonight, the rebellion could still live through him.

I let go of his hand and stagger backwards. "I'm going to hold you to that, whatever your name is."

If this were a traditional fairytale, his mask would slip down enough for me to see him smile. He'd let me in on his secret, and we'd have something to fight for in my attempt out of this cold prison. Instead, he remains a mystery as we quickly run out of time. His coat flutters behind him as he takes off at a sprint away from the entrance to this area, flapping in such a way that for a moment I swear there's a flash of white underneath. It's gone before I can put much thought into his break in monochromatic outerwear. I have no idea what lies that way into the deeper bowels of this castle, but he clearly has a plan for escape, and I only have the time to worry about one of us.

The steps are getting closer as I shove the key into the lock on my other wrist. My fingers are stiff and frozen, the Necromancer having stolen back all the warmth he'd given me. Panic has me dropping it twice. On the third try, amidst the yells from a general to get down here even faster, I hold the key in my mouth and manage to get it into the lock, turning my head to the side until I hear the sharp click of release.

The shackles fall from my wrists in an incredibly satisfying rattle. Cursing from the sweet relief, I drop the key and start for the boots. I need to be faster. I don't want this prison break attempt to be wasted on the Necromancer's part, and I also can't have him thinking I lose every battle between the two of us. I promise myself that this will be the last time I listen to the advice of an arrogant, good-for-nothing man with haunting, mismatched eyes, and then start to shove my feet into the boots.

Free from the shackles, warmth creeps through my arms and over my shoulders and wraps a hug over my ribs. Magic. It's coming back to me in tingling pulses. I have to stifle a gasp at the way it prickles like a limb that's fallen asleep and then abruptly been shoved into an obstacle. I hadn't realized how comfortable I'd become with its existence, and I try not to think about the fact that the point of my magical abilities seems to have left my palms to settle somewhere just below my heart. I don't know the technicalities or anatomical possibilities of magical transference. Honestly, the wand can live wherever it wants as long as it doesn't give me any further problems.

The guards are on the move. I need to get these boots on.

I try to keep from being distracted by the way it seems the Necromancer and I share a shoe size, the dyed-blue leather wrapping neatly around my frozen feet. Slimmer and far less heavy than the work boots I wore around the tavern, the top ends at my ankle in a firm line against the ruined pants I haven't been able to change since my so-called assassination attempt. They don't shimmer or sparkle or otherwise seem to be marked by anything special besides a rune etched on the inner sole. One set of laces tied in a messy knot, I shove my other foot into the second boot, my knee cracking as my heel hits the bottom of the shoe.

Nothing feels immediately different. I'm still stiff and sore and dizzy, and I can see my hand in front of myself. I swear, I'd better be invisible. The Necromancer was completely invisible when he walked in here, but I will find a different way out of this dungeon to berate him for giving me faulty shoes if these end up not working.

Spite is a very good motivator.

Amid the thunder of oncoming guards, I push myself into the corner of the cell and take quick, sharp breaths. It was all of my lingering strength to unbind myself and get shoes on, the second boot not even fully tied. I lean on the bars of the cell as my vision swims and my head pounds. While I appreciate the supposedly magic shoes, I could really have used a tonic for pain or nausea or something to speed the return of my magic, my body under attack from the bone-deep exhaustion I already felt and the sudden spur of energy from the pink sparkles returning to me. Gemma had treated me that first night after the tavern. There has to be a potion for quick recovery or something that could melt these bars, so I could have left with the guy who understands how to wield magic instead of being left to my own miserable devices. If the shoes are the least of my issues, I'm going to compile a list of ways he could have made this rescue attempt better and throw it at the Necromancer when I see him next.

If I see him…

The boots are on my feet. That's what matters. I need to focus.

Woozy and clutching the cell bars as hard as I can, I listen to the gathered guards finally make their way down here amid a chorus of complaints and hesitations that they shouldn't be dealing with a magical rebel without one of the court-appointed mages nearby. They're almost as scared as I am exhausted, and I wonder what it was the Necromancer did to show these people he's truly dangerous. Whether or not they want to be, though, the guards are here.

Flinching back from the stampede of golden armor, I wait for the inevitable heckling that is sure to come with so many of them down here to see me. Instead, the first guard lets out a curse and taps the shoulder of the next. It takes four or five of them gathered together in front of the cell, pressing their faces to the bars, for them to come to the same conclusion.

The Necromancer didn't let me down. I am really, truly invisible.

Now, I just need to escape.

The guards pull a portable magic light from a pocket and flash it close to the bars of the cell. It's blinding after however long I've been down here. I have to bite down my hiss of surprise at the sudden, yellow-tinged glow waved an inch from my nose, the beam so much harsher than the waver of a candle. Thankfully, he can't see me. I don't leave so much as a shadow in the unnatural light.

Come on. Open the door. Make sure I'm not in here.

I breathe slowly through my mouth, standing as still as I can while I wait for them to come to the same consensus. Clearly, I'm not here. They're going to have to come in and make sure, right?

The general in charge of chasing down the Necromancer is shouting commands from up the hall, sending men past my cell as he nears and takes his own peek. "You. Back upstairs. Tell them we have an issue."

He pulls a key ring from his hip. The missing component to the Necromancer's scheme to get me out of here. They must not have duplicates of that key. Anticipation and apprehension wrestle each other in my stomach to be the dominant emotion overtaking me, but I'm just focused on watching him handle his key ring.

Yes. That's it. Open this freaking door and let me out of here.

It doesn't matter that he'll still be close or that there are now two guards scampering back upstairs to warn the others of my escape. That'll complicate my next steps, but it's okay. The Necromancer laid out the grand scheme, and I'm already through two parts. Cuffs. Boots. Move. If I can get out of here, I have the best chance in days of being a free man once more.

Who needs a prince to save them anyway? I have a Necromancer who admitted to lying to me about his identity and provided the better half an escape plan. I'm doing about as well as I was leaving the ruins of the tavern to enter the forest, and I survived that, so I'll get through this, too.

Finally, slowly, the door swings open. The general is marked by his gleaming armor and no helmet, so I get a clear view of the mustache he must have spent a very long time curling into such a symmetrical shape this morning. He leans in. He's taking up the entirety of the doorframe, swinging the magic light one way and then the other in a way that allows the orange strip to touch every crevice of this cell. For him, there's nothing here besides the key in the shackles and the single set of footprints pressed into the dust from the Necromancer's quick exit.

He curses. Low and fast. He doesn't come further into the cell. Instead, he starts to close the door.

Damn.

I wanted an easier escape. Life, though, is rarely easy, and I have a tendency towards violence anyway. Throwing caution to the stale remains of my cell, I grab the door and yank it open. The general has no chance to question the odd movement before I tackle him with my head down and my shoulder immediately bruising from the abrupt impact.

His armor clangs. We're trapped in the doorway. A tangle of limbs and expletives, the general manages to grab the back of my shirt even as I try to use invisibility to my full advantage. I elbow him in the naked joints of his armor until he bellows with rage. The rest of the guards scatter backwards. They must be surprised to see their leader downed by nothing more substantial than the wind.

I don't want to have to fight several people to get out of here, but I've already started, and I won't accept losing now. It doesn't matter that my head is pounding or the injury on my ear has reopened, dripping hot liquid down the side of my neck. I don't care that I'm dizzy or sore or a hundred other small inconveniences. Adrenaline courses through me. It's a river that has overcome its dam, and I'm swept away with it. Between that and my renewed attachment to magic and the hope the Necromancer planted in me like wild flower seeds, I feel invincible.

I manage a clear strike to the general's chin, my bones ringing with the impact. He loses his grip on my shirt as I groan about the pain in my elbow. Scrambling over him with the grace of a newly born calf, I crawl as my vision flares with the bursting light of ancient stars. At my best health, this would have been a hard fight. Using everything I have at my disposal now, I barely slink away from the general.

Free.

At least more free than I had been a minute ago.

Momentarily, I gasp into the floor a few feet from him and let the invisibility do its job as I celebrate my small success. I have a limited range of options. Up or down. As much as I want to chase after the Necromancer and see what's waiting at the edge of the dungeon, the guards have gathered around their general and blocked that path. Besides, it's where they would expect me to go, the general demonstrating that as he flings his arms around him in a blind attempt to find me.

Back up it is, then.

The castle is about to be on lockdown. I can stay invisible and wait until there's an unguarded door for me to sneak out through. Midnight has to be a few hours off, and I have a date in the gardens I'm determined to make.

I'm a meager two steps away from the cell before my attempt at a rational plan is literally yanked out from under me. The general, still on his back, manages to find me. He hooks his fingers into my right boot, the one I didn't manage to tie, and tugs it off my foot. Everyone in the dungeon hall gasps. I'm no longer invisible.

Gods freaking damn it.

Why can't I have one good thing?

I'm well past the point of begging to be heard out. Nobody here would have wanted to negotiate with me anyway. My bare foot in the general's grasp, I kick back at him as the rest of the guards move to detain me. The motion leaves me unbalanced and clinging to the edge of the bars of the cage I just escaped to keep him from pulling me further.

This really sucks.

I thought I was going to escape.

The Necromancer would probably make some kind of cruel comment about my inability to do anything without causing a scene. He would be correct, and I would flip him off, and most everything would be right with the world. Unfortunately, he isn't here, and I only have myself to depend on as the guards paw at my shoulders and arms and continue to cling to my foot.

I'm not going back into that cell. That's not an option.

Which leaves me only one way out of this.

Pink glitter mars the ground, my body thrumming with the power that's been returned to it since removing the shackles. I just need one word; a plea wrapped in a sense of security. I need to utter it with focused intent, just like Gemma taught me and the Necromancer tried to refine.

Nobody else is coming to save me. I won't leave this dungeon alive if I give up now. Throwing the rest of my draining energy into a single command, I turn to magic as my saving grace.

"Freeze!"

My chest warms, and then fire races down my arms, gathering in my palms and then out into the cold dungeon. The guards closest to me let out a unified, surprised yell before the spell hits them. Scream or shriek as they do, there's not a word to stop what I've started. Within seconds, the six men and one general around me have taken on a pale hue.

They're not stuck in space. They're frozen like ice across a meadow in the dead heart of winter. Preserved. Trapped. Buried alive without the touch of sunlight to save them.

Shoot.

That was more powerful than I meant. There's a crunch as I wriggle out of their holds, and I keep my eyes forward instead of looking back to see if I damaged their reaching hands. I whisper an apology as I retrieve my stolen boot and shove my foot back into it. It's only seconds before I'm on my feet and racing for the exit.

The stone steps leading to the upper floor are covered in a thin layer of ice by the time I extricate myself from the scene in front of the cell. It's nearly impossible to walk up. Gripping the handrail, I slip and slide and make my way upwards as the storm continues to grow.

Sparks of pink swirl through the snow now falling from the ceiling as I look back from the relative safety of the stairs. Wind composed of my desperation howls through the hall. It rattles the open door to my cell and plucks at the armor of the guards in a deafening crescendo. I didn't just freeze my opponents. I unleashed a blizzard indoors.

The castle walls groan under the pressure of the storm. A regular batch of wind and snow couldn't overtake this place, but one made with magic and set in its basement could very well be its downfall. I'm no longer just escaping the clutches of a group of guards. If I can't get it to stop, the deaths of a hundred people could be on my head.

A wicked thought takes up residence in the front of my mind. King Anerald Charming is somewhere in this building. He wanted to bring about my demise with a vicious finality that brokered no arguments. It would help the rebellion more than anything else I've done if I let this place crumble to its foundation and take down everyone who has aligned themselves with the charade of a fair monarchy we've been leashed to for generations.

It would help the rebels, but it would hurt the kingdom.

Not everyone here believes in Anerald's decision to limit magic or to target different groups of people on the basis of their natural talent for magic. As a member of the Guild of Fairy Godmothers, Gemma used to work here. She'd still be working here if she had been able to replace her wand. As much as she's created chaos in my life, Gemma's a pretty good example of someone willing to do the right thing despite the harsh realities of the rest of the world. Other people like her have to be up there, whether it's a rare nobleman who actually wants to advocate and help those in need, or a cook just trying to make enough money to support her family, or a guard who is unable to quit serving the kingdom that raised him. I have to believe there are good people here who don't deserve such an end.

For all I know, there's a prince somewhere above me in desperate need of saving since he wasn't able to get down here to help me.

I can't just let this place fall because it would be easy to do nothing now.

Irrevocably responsible for my own magic, I hold my hands out in front of me and lean against the handrail to support myself. It only takes one command to initiate the catalyst for a spell. Stop doesn't seem like a strong enough word. Halt has its own connotations. Warmth would relieve the cold that has seeped through everyone down here, but it wouldn't necessarily fix the storm. I'd probably just end up turning it into a hurricane and really tearing down the whole building on top of myself.

Skin sticking to the iron railing where my shirt pulled up, I peel myself back and take a deep breath. I settle on my word. Pink glitter coats my skin. It lines my chest and itches in my hairline. No longer a hive of wasps trying to escape me, but, rather, a flurry of fireflies caged and awaiting my command to release them. I square my stance the best I can on the icy stairs and shout into the blizzard.

"Calm!"

Pink flecks coat the walls. They run down the steps, not melting the ice nearest me, but encumbering the making of any more. The wind rages away from me, running from my magic in an attempt to keep its freedom like a wild stallion given a chance to be rid of its reins. It's not faster than my command. Soon, the pink swirls through the blizzard, marking the snowflakes like paint splattered over a canvas. Pink and white war down the hall. The guards are struck by one and then the other. Some movement shifts through the group, the little more than half dozen men released from the initial spell and left to survive this next one.

The wind continues to howl and rage and scream its resistance. "Come on. Calm down!" I snap, my arms shaking and knees threatening to give out beneath me.

For the first time, I wonder about the depths of my stolen magic. Gemma mentioned that the wand came with an innate amount of magic, and everything else was carefully controlled by the administering powers in charge of fairy godmothers. It shouldn't feel like a lake has opened up inside me, should it?

I wobble and fall to one knee, ice cracking from my weight in a shattering rush. The wind hurls itself in every direction, a wild thing refusing to be contained by the pink sparks. I was already exhausted. I'm spent, my vision blacking out at the edges, and my arms too heavy to hold up. I brace my hands on the iron rail and grit my teeth.

It's a terrible thing to realize I need more magic.

I have no idea where to get it from.

That wasn't exactly covered in one of my quick lessons.

The king employs his own magic wielders and wizened advisors. One of them could help me, but I can't leave the scene here. The door is ripped off my cell and narrowly avoids any of the guards huddled on the floor together before it's tossed down the hall into that unknown abyss of darkness.

It's too dangerous to turn my back on them.

Why do I have to have a conscience?

An idea builds in the back of my mind as the wind begins to celebrate its success, whipping the wet hair of the guards one way and then the other before storming back towards me in an icy rush. One man isn't enough to stop an element. I'll remember that the next time I decide to play with magic unattended.

For now, I focus on every magical item in the hall. The portable magic light. The dim light that hung in my cell. The boots on my feet.

If I can siphon magic from them, I should be able to stop the wind.

Maybe.

It's worth a shot.

Gemma would probably scream that this isn't how magic works. It's dangerous. I might not make it out alive, I'd rather die from overextending myself through my use of magic than by the sword of the king.

With a grunt, I move my left hand to my ankle, wrapping my fingers around the enchanted boots the Necromancer left for me. It's going to be a whole lot harder to get out of here without invisibility on my side, but it's a worthy sacrifice in the face of what I've done. There isn't a word on my mind. The pink that signifies my magic is already moving, though, in the same way that I've been able to communicate with Skelly without giving him direct commands.

A swarm of butterflies taking flight in spring, it attaches to the lights, thin wings layering together over the objects until we're drenched in darkness. All that remains is the occasional shimmer of pink. It glitters over my feet and stains my hands. I take a deep breath and imagine those pink butterflies eating the magic items, consuming them in nibbles that add up to a big bite and distended bellies. The lake that is floating somewhere between my brain and my heart begins to fill. Magic. Warm, beautiful magic. It returns to me in a trickle and then sweeps through me all at once until I can breathe without worrying that I'll fall over from the lack of resources to keep myself up.

I tell the storm one last time to calm, to dissipate, to leave this place. It listens. Subdued, it sinks. No longer a flurry of wind bustling one way and then the other, it forms into a stiff fog that curls into a comfortable spot on the ground. The storm sleeps.

Days of lying in the dungeon here have done little for me by way of strength training or renewed levels of endurance. I'm too heavy. Undoing the laces on my one tied shoe, I wriggle my feet out of the Necromancer's boots. There's no way I can wear them out of here. My legs threaten to revolt completely when I stretch back up to my full height, the presence of the handrail and nearby wall a steady guide the rest of the way up the stairs. I can't handle one more thing. Hopefully, the Necromancer can forgive me for losing his shoes.

If I see Gemma again, I'll have to admit to losing another pair. She'll think it's funny. I miss the way she laughed in my face.

My bare feet slipping on ice as snowflakes that coated my eyelashes and made a nest in my hair begin to melt, I make it to the top of the stairway and through the door nobody bothered to lock on their way down here. I'd be surprised that nobody else is waiting in the halls if the king hadn't made such a big deal about wanting me far, far from him in a place people would forget me. As is, there's nobody to tell about the blizzard in the lower levels of the castle, and I limp along, breaths gushing from me in haggard pulls of oxygen that fight to return to my lungs each and every time.

I make it up another flight of stairs, tipping left and then overcorrecting back to the right. My muscles seize as I fall into the closest walls. I make no attempt to ascend the castle levels with a shred of dignity. I crawl. I pull myself forward one trembling step at a time. I do not stop.

Still, nobody sees me. I'm not asked to stop my sluggish pursuit of freedom. I'm allowed to claw my way out of the dungeons until I feel the heat of a kitchen and nearly sob at the way the warmth coaxes the quivering mess of my muscles further on.

If I survive, I'll have to drop an offering at the altar of one of the gods who watch over luck. They're not recognized as they once were, their spontaneous and random acts of magic not as useful as those organized by fairy godmothers, but I feel they must still be out there, surrounding me now as I manage to sneak away from the dungeons without any real repercussions. Maybe there was a reason people used to throw themselves to their knees and pray to the invisible forces around them. Maybe being on my knees forces me to have a different perspective. There's plenty I would worship from down here if given the opportunity to do so, not wet and shivering and moments from a sleep that promises to leave me dead to this world. I make a point of not thinking about the Necromancer in that kind of situation and trudge on.

The first person who sees me, slinking like a worm across the floor, lets out a scream that they clap a hand over. She calls for help. Two pairs of hands lift me from the ground and into a chair, and they set it to the side of a pile of flour bags. Out of sight behind the curtain that guards the pantry area, I can barely keep track of what's happening, but I'm bundled in a thin blanket and given a cup of soup, and the two servants lean down to ask me questions.

I don't know if it's kindness that loosens my lips, their gentle murmuring keeping me in this moment as they put magic herbs in me via my soup. It could be that I missed human contact in my days down below. I think I recognize the curve of their noses in a customer who used to come to the tavern.

Familiarity is all it takes to make everything feel okay for just a fleeting moment.

The brother and sister get me to eat a shortbread cookie and then several sips of soup, my insides warming from their quiet care. I tell them the truth when they ask.

Yes, I'm the one who was in the dungeon. Yes, it's because I used magic on the prince. It seems they don't know the full extent of what happened in the city center, but enough rumors have worked their way through the castle staff to keep them aware of me and my crimes.

More questions.

More nods and bursts of words through my dry throat.

When they finally settle down, the brother with freckles speckled over his face and a smile that softens my soul, allows me a moment to ask my own question. "Why would you help me?"

The sister touches my knee, then catches the soup cup when it wobbles in my grip. "Why? Why not? You've gone out of your way to help people like us, and everyone is demanding your release. There's been picketing for three days now."

In rapid sentences that overlap one another, the siblings fill me in on everything that has been happening outside of the castle walls. The king didn't choose to send only a few men down to the cells; he had a few men not working a patrol in front of the castle gates to deter the protesters there. Hope has flourished in my absence. I didn't just fall into a bad deal with a witch. I made a choice to go to the city center, to accidentally shoot the prince with a golden arrow, and then to look at these people and tell them it's okay to ask for change, to believe in dragons, and to rage against the world until there are better days.

For the first time, I'm struck by the impact my existence has on the greater world. Nobody pays attention to a tavern keep. I didn't mean to become a revolutionary activist, but if that's what I am now due to magic mishaps and circumstantial actions, then I need to start being a better role model.

"What happened with the prince was an accident," I try to explain in halting breaths as I begin to feel my fingertips and toes once more. "He's good for the kingdom. I don't want you guys supporting any attacks against him, okay?"

The sister scrunches her nose. "We know that. That's why you didn't actually injure him."

Oh. Right. The siblings rattle off examples of the prince being kind to them, but my mind is swirling around what they've said. They weren't worried that the prince would be hurt. Wynnifred meant for him to be impaled with an arrow, though. At least, she insinuated as much when she sent me on an assassination errand. She was sure he would be the downfall of the king. Yet, King Anerald Charming spared me one glance in the interrogation room. He was hardly concerned about his son's health when they got into an argument in front of me.

Wynnifred wants the Charming monarchy to fall. She doesn't really care how it happens, so long as magic is returned to the land and the laws are changed. It's hard to be a witch in most circumstances and impossible right now. I know from Gemma that the witch already lost a love interest over all of this, let alone family or other people and places, in an attempt to stay alive while the full force of Briargild's hate poured onto her simply for being herself. In order to stop living in the forest and hiding who she is, Wynnifred might have bent her morals to get straight to the point of removing the king from the throne.

Was there ever a client for the potion that became a golden rune embedded in my hand? Could the king have been her customer? Would removing the son he hid from the kingdom for almost thirty years via a staged, magical assassination help him keep his power?

A dark ball of doubt forms in my stomach, nearly forcing me to lose soup in a hot rush of vomit. I have no idea what I've gotten myself into. The plots around the kingdom are far more than any I've been tangled in before, but there's no turning back.

My story no longer ends behind the tavern bar. I don't get to quietly grow old and pretend that the world's problems don't affect me. I'm a person fully entrenched in the revolution, and it's time I stop sitting around.

Pressing the soup cup in the brother's hands, I clear my throat. "I need to get out of here. Which way is best?"

Arguments spill from both brother and sister for me to stay put a while longer, but I've made up my mind. I've spent enough time here. The longer I linger, the more trouble they'll be in if anyone finds us. Reluctantly, they admit that the castle has fallen into as close to a slumber as it ever does.

I'm safer waiting out in the gardens for several hours than I am staying in here.

Pushing out of the chair and leaving behind my blanket, I thank them profusely and then, much stronger than I was when I got here, start down the next hall. Their directions flee my mind the moment I'm out of sight. Was it left and then right or right and then two lefts?

It doesn't truly matter. If I stick close to the walls, still leaning on them for more stability than I would like to admit, I should make my way to a door leading outside eventually. According to my saviors in the kitchen, more and more guards have been patrolling the streets at night instead of the castle. Between that and my efforts in the dungeon and the line to stop the protestors, there isn't a huge amount of them left to discover me as I stagger through the halls.

Several servants pass me as I wander. All are in a rush to some task or another. None stop to talk to me. I don't blame them. I'm several stages past disheveled. Wet and leaving a trail of footprints behind me, my clothes are torn, and I must look to be a problem they don't want to have to solve.

They could be more supporters of the revolution.

Not stopping me is almost support of my actions, isn't it?

A bell starts ringing in several halls into my aimless wander. It seems someone has found the mess I made of the isolated dungeon hall, or the original guards finally managed to disentangle themselves and get word out about my escape. Either way, I have less time to explore than I thought. Picking up my pace, I keep my head ducked and scamper through the halls like the vermin I feel like, clinging to pockets of shadows and keeping entirely to myself in a new prison decked out in red and gold.

I keep up this pace until I find myself creeping through a dining area, another kitchen, past a storage room, and finally wind up at a dead end of a very long hall with no alternate pathways. Once again, I feel like I'm traversing a space purposefully put far from King Anerald's life. A large, metal door looms ahead. There's noise behind me.

The handle for the door is near the ground. Bending, I pull it upwards, the whole thing squealing with the movement. I stare at the confined space behind it. An elevator. It clearly isn't the way out. It's bigger than the ones I've seen around the middle city. A whole ox and wagon could be pulled into here.

Maybe it's meant to move supplies quietly from floor to floor of the castle.

It could be a hiding spot if nothing else, right?

I'm out of time to waste. Stepping in and shutting the door, I grab the rope off to the side and give it a tug. The steel box moves. Up.

Up is my only option, then.

Weak from the past few days, tired from the magic use, jumpy and paranoid, I pull the rope again and again. The box shifts under my feet. I go up what seems to be several meters at a time, orange light peeking through slits in the top of the odd elevator.

Plans try to form in my mind as I work the pulley system. If this leads to another storage area, I might be able to duck somewhere small and stay inconspicuous for the rest of the evening, biding my time before my grand escape. Even better, if there's a window up here, I could try to sneak out that way and creep across the castle roof until I can drop down near the gardens. As long as this path doesn't dump me at the king's feet, my decision to climb into this steel box might be the best thing I've done all night.

I pull the rope and lift the box until it won't go any further, the ceiling of it gently thunking against a hard surface. There's a knob for me to secure the rope to, and I do so, checking it twice before I'm sure it won't give way under me when I try to leave. Once more, I bend low and grab the handle. I scoot the door open only a hand's width and then squint out into the dim room beyond the metal box.

It's not a storage room. There's definitely a bed.

I don't slam the door closed in time to avoid drawing attention to myself.

Prince Alexander Charming is next to a small stove, brewing what must be tea and looking right at me. "Well, come on in."

14

It was remiss to state that the prince is making tea without mentioning that he's doing so without a shirt on. I'm caught like a fish on a line, hunched down looking between the door and the floor, and unable to escape from the way he's glancing at me over his shoulder. There's a bright bandage wrapped around his middle and up over the opposite shoulder. I spent more than a few moments wishing I hadn't shot him with an arrow while I lay in the dungeons.

I spent quite a few thinking I should have punctured him a second time when he let me rot down there.

All of the anger I felt down in the depths of the castle seems to be forgotten now when the prince smiles over at me, amusement softening the corners of his mouth. "Come on. I promise not to get any revenge on you."

I try and fail to fit this image of the prince into the rest of the times I've seen him. It's less than a handful. Out on the street on the winter solstice, cheeks red from the cold and at the mercy of guards who clearly didn't recognize him. Up on the stage in the city center, a calm presence speaking out for those who can't defend themselves and then ensuring I didn't meet an untimely demise with a quivering command as blood covered his front. In the interrogation room, desperate for information, desperate enough to tell me something truly unfathomable.

Now, he looks calm, seated in front of a small kitchenette that has been built to the right height for his position in his wheelchair. His hair is wet and pulled into a bun at the back of his head with loose pieces left to curl around his ears. He must have gotten out of a bath before I came in and began to settle down for the night.

It is getting late.

Hours out from midnight, but late nonetheless.

I let my gaze slip over that eyepatch covering his right eye and then think about what he said. "Did you just tease me?"

His smile is a devastatingly sincere thing. "If you want answers to any questions, you're going to have to come in."

Men and their irritating ability to withhold answers at my expense. I clearly have a type.

I can feel my heartbeat in my fingertips. This is one of those decisions that could change my life. I'm on the brink of something, whether it be good or great or a fate worse than what I was destined in to in the dungeon. Prince Alexander Charming, the way he's looking at me now as though we're conspirators in a grand scheme, would be all that haunts my daydreams if that pesky Necromancer didn't exist.

"You'll be harboring a fugitive," I hesitate, still hovering in the partially cracked doorway at a hunching, downward angle that is far from flattering.

My blood is hot, pumping loud enough to drown out the steady stream of anxious thoughts pounding at the front of my mind. I want to step in. To stand in front of him. I want to run. I want…

I've never wanted anything more than what may unfold in the next few moments, and that thought scares me more than the full might of the king's men or every minute I faced down in the dungeons.

Still, I don't move. Now is the perfect time for the prince to reconsider. He could send me away and keep himself safe. I know his secret, and I have no intention of sharing it, but my presence alone would be enough to convict him as a rebel and give the king a reason to have the prince removed from the castle. Perhaps worse. The castle is a dangerous place, but it's important that some rebels live within it to try to change things from the hideous inner workings of it. Caution should be our first choice.

Still, he doesn't look unsure. My fingers are hooked around the bottom edge of the odd door, cool metal pressing into my palms as I blink out at a man who should be steering clear of failed assassins and escaped prisoners if only to save himself. I am trapped. I'm barely breathing. My wants war with logic. He has to tell me to leave right now because I don't have the strength to turn away from someone who continues to look at me with so much hope.

"You think people often sneak into the isolation hall with keys to release prisoners?"

It's not an admission of guilt. He's not telling me he hired the Necromancer to come to my aid. He's also not *not* saying that.

Gods, the two of them do know each other.

I wish I could have been a fly on the wall of that conversation. There has definitely never been another time when two very attractive men needed to have a secret meeting to discuss the matter of me. I wonder…

I shake my head. I'm definitely romanticizing this far more than it deserves. The prince gave me a secret to gain my trust. He may be using my escape and subsequent stagger here as a fortunate addition to his plans without having been the great mind behind them. There isn't a ton of evidence here to prove that he's been looking out for me.

I could choose to go back down there. There's someone planning to meet me at midnight. I could turn my back on the prince and accept my odds at running from the guards until I find the perfect hiding spot in the gardens.

I could, but I won't.

Besides, I have no idea if the Necromancer made it out of the dungeons. If he ran into trouble, if he got stuck in the blizzard I conjured, I could be freezing in the greenery all alone and without much of a plan to do more for myself.

More prepared to find solutions to cooking disasters or drink mix-ups, I stall. My mind works, but I'm barely conscious of processing anything. I'm stuck in the garden of possibility that is a warm room and an open invitation from a prince with a kind gaze. There has to be a right answer. I should choose to be careful after being a pawn in the witch's deal and spending days in the dungeon. I just can't decide if careful is the calm room of a prince or the risky escape plan with the Necromancer.

Why can't it be both?

I have a few hours to waste. The alarms aren't blaring up here. It's highly unlikely the guards would come up here to check for the escaped prisoner, right?

Almost without my consent, my arms lift the door the rest of the way. My frozen feet are on the fine rugs, leaving splotchy patches of moisture from the still-melting ice on my form. The door groans as I ease it shut behind myself. For better or worse, I'm sealed in a room with Prince Alexander Charming.

My heart is beating far too fast.

"I'm sorry about the…"

Mess. Not just the water, but my general presence. Me. I don't know why, but I have an intense desire to be anyone else right now.

He's quick to shake his head, the tea steeping in two cups now as he turns his chair to face me. "I'll clean it. It's just fabric. You look pretty cold. Why don't I run you a bath?"

The heir to the throne of Briargild did not just offer to make up a bath for me. My stunned opinions must be etched on my features. His laugh is a sweet rhythm I could spend whole afternoons listening to as he moves his chair from the kitchenette to around the bed, passing close enough I could reach out to touch him and make sure all of this is real and not simply some bizarre hallucination imagined up while I'm still lying on the ground in the dungeon. Prince Alexander Charming is through a doorway to my left with the rushing noise of running water starting up a moment later.

He's serious.

The man offered me a dangerous secret and is now taking care of me.

As much as I want this to be real, I'm prepared to notice when things seem too good to be true.

I haven't forgotten the prince is the entire reason my life has been uprooted from its regular chaos. Not for the first time, I miss the tavern. The smell of fresh mead and a home-cooked meal was dealt out to our customers. I miss the pockmarked bar I polished every four months. My plants, the lush green things my father insisted shouldn't be able to live inside the warm exterior of the tavern, all of them turned to rubble and ash in the subsequent fallout from my wish. I even miss cleaning the cobwebs out of the rafters and having to promise my father three hundred times that I wouldn't fall to my demise.

I haven't really had someone since he left to tell me to be careful.

Gemma had her own reasons for helping me. Trauma has bonded us together in ways that couldn't be easily replicated, and I was prepared to die at the king's hand with her identity as a secret because our friendship means that much, but she also had little say over my care and well-being. We were both struggling through circumstances together.

Here, now, with a hot bath running, the steam peeking at me from the doorway in curling wisps, I'm stricken into a stupor. This isn't just a man above my station going out of his way to be kind to me. This is intimate. It's far more than would ever be allowed by societal standards.

The water stops, and I still haven't moved. The puddle at my feet has stopped spreading at least. Prince Alexander pops his head out of the bathroom.

"I already ran the water. It'll go to waste if you don't get in."

I'm running out of excuses, but my hand flaps in front of myself. "I've been in the dungeon for four days. I don't think you want me to clog your fancy tub or-."

"Five," he cuts me off, his previously sparkling expression dimming. "It's been five days, and that's partially my fault, so I would appreciate it if you let me help you be comfortable."

The fight leaves me. I can't make him ask me again. There's a pleading edge to his words that cuts me to my core. Head tipped to the side, he studies me as though there's nothing else in the world worthy of being his sole focus so long as I'm here.

Mouth dry, every imperfection a prickle along my skin, I glance away.

People don't look at me like that.

Princes definitely shouldn't.

And yet...

I squash wherever that line of thought was headed. He moves out of the doorway, sliding his chair close to the bed as he gives me quick instructions on how to add more hot water if I need it and where to get the soaps from. It's a pity and a blessing when I click the door shut between us.

My back to it, I struggle to pull in a whole breath. Half an hour ago, I fought tooth and nail to get out of the dungeons. I used too much magic and had to be saved by kind strangers before staggering here half alive and clearly far too foolish for my own good. If I had any sense, I would make a quick exit, forget about the Necromancer, too, and go find my fairy godmother.

My goals in life used to be so freaking simple.

Now, my fingers remove my sweat-ridden, bloodied shirt from my shoulders as if they belong to someone else, distant as my mind continues to whirl. I'm not sure what I'm doing. Everything used to be about the tavern and helping my father. Without him as an anchor in my day-to-day life, I've gotten mixed up in almost every kind of inopportune scenario afforded to me. I didn't use to be a criminal easily detained by the royal guards. I wasn't a magic wielder or a revolutionary advocate. I made cocktails and poured ales; I was the least of anybody's concern, and far from interesting to a prince.

Would he have spent a moment lingering over me if that's all I still was?

I don't know. I don't really want to know. I've been preening under Prince Alexander's gaze for too long now to go back on it. Besides, I'll never be just a tavern keep again. Wynnifred was clear that she wouldn't be able to remove Gemma's wand from my palms, and I'm very sure it has only become more infused with my own being. Even if my wish is reversed, some things will be different.

I flex my fingers, the standard pink glitter denoting my magic few and far between now. It still sparkles occasionally as I drop my pants on the pile of dirty clothes by the door and move to the tub. Two weeks ago, I didn't have the imagination to conjure up half the things I've done since breaking Gemma's wand. Now, I don't want to think about going back to a life without it.

I created a blizzard. With my hands and mind and the stolen power in my veins. Who else does that? I stopped it, too. Given time to learn more about it, there's no limit to the kinds of acts I could accomplish with magic.

Before I can succumb to the excitement that line of thought brings me, I step into the bath. Near scalding water devours my right leg and then left. I wriggle my toes, getting used to the biting temperature I could never achieve in my own apartment. There's running water in the farthest reaches of Briargild, but heat is still secured by boiling pots of it before adding to the bath, and most of us are too exhausted to go about doing that after a long work day, so we settle for cold wash-offs. This is the full meaning of luxury, though. A bath run by someone else, hot enough to leech the trials of the past several days from my bones, and complete privacy to do as I please. Soon enough, I'm submerged in the enormous tub, soaking up to my shoulders in soap that smells like roses.

The tub is brown by the time I'm done, slipping out of the cooled water to wrap myself in the softest, red towel imaginable. I dry off as I watch the mess of the last few days slip down the drain. No more blood or dirt or sweat or grime on me, I accept a loose pair of black, lounge pants the prince laid out on the vanity, but forego the plush robe emblazoned with the crest of Briargild. I do not believe in slaying dragons surrounded by roses and won't don any more of the colors of King Anerald than absolutely necessary.

I swipe a hand over the mirror, bending over the sink to look at myself. Same face, same dark eyes, my mother's eyes. A prickly line of stubble along my jaw. No obvious other differences. It's odd to see no injuries or scars to mark the last few days. The magic herbs they keep around the castle work quickly to right the worries of the world, pulling bruises back from my eyes and covering blemishes in moments. There are some nasty marks on my back and arms that sting from my transition from a hot bath to the warm air, but my face is just my own. It tells nothing about adventures in the forest, crafting dragons, and sneaking into the room of a prince. I look like myself, and I can't decide if that's disappointing.

It's not that I want to be someone else. I'm just struggling to see who I've become in the lines of who I was.

I smear toothpaste on my index finger and scrub at my teeth, doing everything in my power to fully clean up before I go back to face Prince Alexander Charming. Several minutes pass as I take my time opening up every bottle on the low shelf beside the sink to smell the different contents in their floral and musky glory. I apply lotion to my cracked knuckles and liberally everywhere else I feel like, basking in a scent that's not roses and yet something I can't quite name. The prince's rebellion lives fully here in a place where he strays from traditional roses to be only himself as much as possible.

Not yet ready to return to the other room, I glance around the still steamy bathroom. The area behind the tub is packed full of shelves with plants. Some are similar to the leafy things I kept back at the tavern. So many, though, are completely unknown to me. I lean into the furthest corner of the bathroom to run my fingers over variegated leaves I've only seen in illustrations or to smell the pristine petals of flowers that are wild and lush and not any kind of relative to a rose. It must be sheer determination to have them thriving through the winter months here. The entire room is white tiles held together by grout, painted or infused with gold, and then broken up by the prince's greenery obsession.

I might be able to eventually enjoy gold if it's always displayed like this. Not the center of attention. Not even a warning to those perceiving it. Just a color that glimmers on the edge of so many shades of green, highlighting the beautiful foliage and rare flowers. Green and gold without a trace of the standard red of Briargild.

Maybe that really is the man waiting for me in the other room.

A rare flower grows in a harsh environment and does everything in his power to flourish.

Muscles rubbery from the heat of the bath, I step away from the plants and reach for the doorknob.

I'm really doing this. I'm having tea with a prince.

Like I'm some gent in a proper fairytale.

Snorting at myself, I swing the door open with all the confidence I can muster and step back into the prince's chamber. "Oh," Prince Alexander says from the small dining area, his pianist fingers fiddling with cutlery as he lays it out on either side of the single table. "I thought you would be longer. I'm almost done setting up dinner."

He drew me a bath and cooked.

This is starting to feel like a dream come true, and it takes all of my self-control to simply walk across the room and sit down in his offered seat instead of bolting for the door. I don't do this kind of thing. I shouldn't be doing it now. I have no idea why the prince decided to confide in me. The Necromancer coming back made sense; he felt guilty when he learned of Wynnifred's part in everything. The prince, though, is a puzzle I can't decipher, and I'm too tired from the last few days to put up much of a fight against his kindness.

Prince Alexander Charming becomes very interested in the kitchenette. He dishes servings of heavily seasoned poultry onto a bed of chopped vegetables, drizzling it all in a sauce I think he whipped up while I was in the bath. Those scarred hands dazzle me with knife work and preparation as he continues in the pursuit of culinary excellence. Somebody who lived in a castle shouldn't be so proficient at these tasks, should they?

I can make dinner. It's often leaning towards burnt, but edible, and that's been enough to get me by when we didn't have leftovers from the dinner rush at the tavern. This is a level all its own, a show of dedication to an art form that should be beneath someone who wears a crown.

Maybe I've been jumping to unnecessary conclusions about him.

Maybe I'm being pampered and led to my own downfall.

Guess I'll have to keep playing along to find out.

The prince brings over the teacups, pulling the ornate saucers from what looks to be a heating pad, and sets them down. "I hope everything is to your liking. There's sugar here," his movements are so fluid as he instructs me around his living space and then turns back to the kitchenette, loading up a tray on his lap with our food to leave his hands free to roll back to the table. "It's been a long time since I got to cook for anyone."

Well, I was right about something then. Princes aren't supposed to go around being culinary geniuses. I murmur something that probably made no sense by the time it got across the table and then immediately scooped two heaps of sugar into my teacup. I stir in milk from a little carafe and then press it to my lips, the solid edge as hot as the bath I just enjoyed. The tea is almost too sweet. My fault. I should have tested it before going crazy with the sweetener, but the prince was looking at me, and I forgot how to act like a rational human being. Beneath the sharp sweetness that coats my tongue, citrus notes burst at the back of my palate. It's the essence of late summer in a cup. The last ray of sunset was wrapped in a cloth and saved from the coldest months of the year. I don't think I've ever tasted something so filled with longing.

He didn't have to share something this special with me.

The prince sips his own drink, adding nothing to it. I'm an unsophisticated oaf slopping sugar into his priceless tea. Hoping I didn't just ruin my chances with him, even though I shouldn't have any chance to begin with, I clear my throat and try to dig in. The prince lets me moan and groan and audibly appreciate his cooking for several moments before he breaks our relative quiet, a sincere grin curling his lips around his words.

"So, do you make a point of dealing with witches?"

I set my fork down and take another sip of tea. My cheeks are warm. I'm almost too hot sitting here half-naked in his company. It hasn't escaped me that I made a point of dressing equal to him; this moment, the last we will ever truly be equals, hiding away from the responsibilities of the world. Chest tingling from either the tea or the way the prince attempts to look at me from under his eyelashes, I bite back any snarky reply and settle on honesty.

"She's the first."

I hope he doesn't think I would sell out Wynnifred for a bath and a good meal. Even though he claims to be a rebel, I'm not going to blow everyone else's identity. Their secrets are their own and I've no right to out them after being a part of the magical world for mere days. I shift in my seat as the heat from the tea spreads out of my chest. It flits from my abdomen and into my limbs like moon spiders along the tavern beams in search of the best nook for a new web.

"Any reason you chose her?" His fork never scrapes the plate the way mine does.

"Convenience."

I'm battling myself with every question he passes my way. My tongue is a disloyal lieutenant permitting all sorts of words past my teeth. If it were up to me, I would blabber the entirety of my life's story. I would give up all my secrets. If it meant I could stay here, in this too warm moment with company far too good for the likes of me, I would tell Prince Alexander Charming everything.

"I assume that wasn't the first magic you conjured then. The witch's spell?"

While I can't quite meet his focused gaze, I do notice the curve of his eyebrow, how it implores me to answer him as he chews and waits. "Almost. Magic seems to go wrong around me. I haven't quite figured it out."

Gods, I'm sweating— a lot. I take a bigger sip of my tea than is polite and try to keep my hands from trembling. I glance around the space to find a window or a bucket of ice or anything to help me cool down. When I don't find anything reasonable, I add more milk to my tea and take another gulp of sunshine.

"You might want to slow down on that."

The teacup is still in my hand. It's warm and pressed against my knuckles where I curl my fingers around the handle. Prince Alexander looks concerned.

I drop it, and milky bits of liquid splatter across the table before dripping onto the floor. "Did you poison me?"

Of course, this would happen to me. I knew this was a bad idea, and I simply went with it anyway. I swear there isn't one decent person in the entirety of the magical world. Obviously, there wouldn't be one in the noble realm, either. It just makes sense that witches send me on assassination attempts and princes with the prettiest eyes try to send me to an early grave.

This is great. I shouldn't have come in here. I need to get out before I lose the ability to move.

My legs twitch, the spreading warmth having seized them. I'm too heavy. Dandelions have nested in my knees, and their roots are connected to the chair. At least, that's how I feel. There are no physical marks or spouting plants, but I'm stuck here nonetheless.

"No. Not poison. It's a sedative to help rest your magic that may have some side effects of truthfulness from the person who takes it." He's holding his hands up like I'm a caged bear ready to slash a paw across this table before he gently gestures to himself, being sure to remind me of his wheelchair with a half-hearted shrug. "It won't hurt you or have lingering effects, but I did have to make some calculated decisions for my safety. The sedative will wear off before long. I just need to ask you some questions to make sure we're on the same page."

We aren't in the same storybook. I want to spit the words at him, but I lock my jaw instead. That's what he wants. He needs the magic to influence my speech, to draw the truth out of me, and I have no intention of helping the insidious grasp of magic do that.

Sensing that I'm not going to willingly answer him, he clears his throat. "I don't like having to be mistrustful in my own bedchamber, either. Please, don't turn me into a villain because I'm cautious. Besides, I didn't lace your cup."

And then his uncovered eye flicks to the sugar jar.

He's talking about how this will be easy. I can work with him.

We'll be done in a couple of hours, and then I can go wherever I want.

I arch my own imperial eyebrow at him. If he wants my consent now, he's not getting it. If I had access to my arms, I might be willing to show him the same finger I flashed to the Necromancer before I raced off the field in front of our conjured dragon.

Gods, I wonder where he is right now. I don't believe he got caught in my blizzard. The fool would have come back to show me up in a magical lesson that was completely ill-timed and unnecessary. The Necromancer is probably stalking through the castle grounds like he owns them in his black clothes and sweeping coat. With the news of my departure definitely having spread through the whole castle, he's probably hunkered down in the garden in the perfect place to wait for me. The Necromancer, who has far more secrets than I, wouldn't waltz into a prince's chamber, and he certainly wouldn't fall for poison in his drink.

He probably doesn't even like sweetened tea.

"You really only attacked me because of a bad deal with the witch?"

The magic wheedles its way into my jaw. It sprouts budding lavender just below the surface of my skin. Under the direct questioning, I'm helpless to hold out.

"Of course, I told you the truth," I snarl, fighting the tendrils of magic that try to choose kinder words.

While he looks mildly put out by my fierce declaration, I note the way his shoulders relax. Prince Alexander Charming was actually worried. Tense, at the very least.

I let out a slow sigh. I hate that I can understand where he's coming from. There's no doubt that I would be tipping every scale in my favor if I had to meet privately with Wynnifred again. As much as I don't appreciate his methods, I understand them.

Instead of simmering with pent-up rage about another situation overwhelming me, I clear my throat. "Every time I answer a question truthfully," I emphasize that word, and he has the good sense to appear bashful. "You have to answer a question I have. I won't make you eat the sugar. I'll believe you at your word, but it's only fair since you tricked me."

The corner of his lips twists upwards immediately. He doesn't have to agree. I literally have no power in this situation, but he nods enthusiastically to me anyway.

"Deal. Ask me anything."

There's something that's been on my mind while I was down in the dungeon, and I figure it's as good a starting place as anything else. "Do a lot of people want you dead?"

He shrugs. "Define a lot."

I roll my eyes at him, but stay quiet as I wait for him to come up with a real answer. Feeling returns to my fingertips as my mood lightens, the magic sedative only holding me hostage if I'm overly excited. I push the teacup far from me and spend a couple of moments nibbling at the vegetables on my plate before Prince Alexander breathes out his own sigh.

"If I were to die, there would be no heir apparent for Briargild. There has been speculation for years that my father's tampering with magic has made him barren and, since he only managed to make one fucked up son despite a number of mistresses since my mother's passing, it seems to be true, so my death would bring in a flurry of neighboring royalty who have been vying for a foothold in Briargild for a long time. Or," he steeples his fingers in front of himself, focused on his hands rather than me, "there's a consensus that magical folk would be able to take back the kingdom without a reigning power to stop them. The lands could be divided between the people, and they would have the best chance in generations to take care of one another without threat of prejudice or overtaxation or the policing of their magic. Either way, it's a fantasy people have been toying with for a long time, but I have been seemingly difficult to kill, so we haven't had to explore it yet."

Wow. Yeah. Makes sense. I have questions, but Prince Alexander is already pushing his own objectives before I can ask for clarification.

"Will you tell me your name? I can't keep thinking of you as the handsome stranger who shot me."

Handsome? Me? I would forget how to use my mouth entirely if the magic in the shape of blooming daisies didn't put me on the right path to forming the syllables of my own name. It comes out as a question more than a confident response, but it doesn't matter. Prince Alexander grins and repeats my name in his own, warm tone.

It's the best thing I've ever heard.

I want him to say my name again. And again. And…

I am here for more than obvious infatuation with a prince, and I'm supposed to at least be irritated about him tampering with my tea. "About a week ago now, you were in the outer city. You probably don't remember, but I got in between you and some guards who were destroying a book you had."

My mouth is almost too dry. I haven't asked a question. It feels trivial in the face of a prince who lives his life knowing there are people out there just betting on his demise. Still, I wouldn't be here today if I hadn't stepped in to help him, and I need to know it was worth it.

I lost my father because of that stupid fight.

I need it to mean something.

Recognition dawns in his gaze. It's a star sparking in the dark galaxy of his eye. I'm a stranger one moment, and the next I'm still a stranger but with far more substance.

"I knew I had to know you from somewhere," he whispers, the words secretive and hesitant as though he has more to say but isn't quite ready to share.

I work through the flush of violets in my chest at the way his attention shifts to awe and adoration in the same way the Necromancer's did when he proclaimed I was the one in charge of fulfilling the dragon prophecy and spit out a question. "What did you need that book for so bad that you couldn't tell the guards who you were?"

For the first time in our conversation, his expression shutters. I'm more cut off than I would be if I just stared into his eyepatch. I've hit some kind of nerve.

"There have been rumors around the court that a dragon would return to Briargild, bringing with it great change, and I wanted to know more about the supposed prophecy before I got fully mixed up in it."

That sounds very made up. There's more to the story. He's countering with his own inquisition before I can call him out for not being entirely honest with me.

"Where did you get the dragon from the city center?"

Skelly. My chest tightens. I have to believe he's as safe with Gemma as she is with him. They escaped the inner city and the kingdom edge and made it far, far from the danger I've been dancing a little too close to for days now.

"From the forest," is enough of a truthful answer to appease the sugary truth serum in my system.

Prince Alexander presses his lips together. He wants to say more. He waits patiently, though, for me to take my turn, our plates now empty.

"You had some big ideas in your speech. Assuming you survive any more assassination attempts, are you really going to change the kingdom? Isn't it a bit late to get people to start listening to you?"

His single eye bounces between both of mine. "That's two questions. You'll be indebted to me."

It's a teasing jab. I shake my head at him and pluck the plates off of the table, carrying them to the sink to wash as he talks to me. The truth serum has given up its tenacious hold on me, and I want a chance to stretch my limbs after their temporary captivity. It doesn't escape my notice how natural, how easy, how comfortable things feel between the two of us.

"I'm trying, Cinderfella. It's hard to get anything done when everyone just stares at me with pity." He lets out a choked laugh. "My father wouldn't let me be in the public eye for the first thirty years of my life, sure he would find a solution to my condition and fix me, and now I'm working against every obstacle possible to build resolve in people."

I nod, only daring to look at him from the corner of my eye as I wash and dry the dishes and then slip them back into his cupboards as if I've been here for longer than an hour. Maybe I've spent too long with my head in the metaphorical sand. Obviously, I'm not the only one who has had a heaping helping of grief and trauma decorate the beginning of my tale. The prince lost his mother, too, and it sounds like he became an experiment in the wake of his father's grief, left to grow up in the shadow of things he could never hope to overcome and watch how circumstances not only festered but completely changed a man who might have once been responsible with his power over the kingdom and shifted him into a monster instead.

I hate to admit that a crown doesn't make the prince's life any easier than my own. In fact, I'm beginning to realize my anonymity and low-stakes life procured by my father was a blessing in its own right. If I hadn't made a bad wish and lost everything, I wouldn't be out here thinking about other people or trying to see how I fit into a revolutionary scheme. It's not that I lacked care for the greater world, but because the definition of my world had become so small in the scheme of grander things. I loved a person and a place so much that there wasn't a single distraction from it. The prince, though, has been watching the state of the world and putting his life at risk, even as it means he continues to be in danger.

I don't regret the way I lived my life before now. My eyes are open, though. The world is on fire, magic is a weapon that has been smothered and is now writhing and lashing out, and it's going to take all of us working together to make things better than they are now. There's still time to do right by my community, my fairy godmother, the Necromancer, and even the Prince.

When I've settled back across from him, a glass of cool tap water in front of me instead of my laced tea, Prince Alexander continues the conversation. "What is it you want?"

I open my mouth. Words don't come out. I close it.

This should have been the easiest answer all evening.

I want my father back. I want the tavern. I want…

"I want time to figure out my options. I want to help those I care about and those I haven't met but understand and empathize with. I want some of my old life back, but I wiggle my fingers to display the glitter that seems to always be on them and marvel at the way Prince Alexander Charming keeps smiling at me even as I continue to be an oddball. "I think I want to figure out why I started to do this and what it could mean in the future."

The magic coaxes the words out of me without resistance. It's the truth. It shouldn't be. A couple of weeks ago, I wanted nothing more than to take over the tavern from my father and continue life as we always have, bringing in new clients and taking care of our regulars regardless of seasonal changes. Now, though, I've been shown that there's more than the four walls of our tavern. Magic has given me power and motivation that I previously lacked. It's gone and mixed up my mind. I should be upset, but I'm not.

Maybe I do want some time to figure out what I want in life. I would still help at the tavern, after we rebuild it, of course, but there's more to my world than pouring drinks and mopping floors. If I took a night off now and then, I could even make time to see certain men with dark eyes and darker intentions.

Not that there's any reason I should be thinking about the Necromancer or the prince or both of them. I'm blaming the sugar for muddling my mind. Romance should be far from my thoughts.

The prince reaches across the table, gently touching my fingers with his own, watching as the fine glitter sparkles on his own skin from the brief contact. "Would you consider taking a position closer to the castle? Should the revolution win, that is. I would need a personal advisor who could give me insight into parts of the world I've yet to immerse myself in."

The sugar must also be affecting my ears. "You're offering me a job?"

He nods, firm, gaze locked on the glitter I'm leaving on the tabletop as my magic flourishes from my general rest. "They say to keep your enemies closer than your friends, but I would like to have someone next to me I could truly trust, maybe," he stalls, chewing the corner of his lip as blush overtakes his cheeks until they're nearly the same color as the duvet over his bed. "Well, I don't have very many friends, and I would like someone who can remind me what to do when things are difficult. It takes more than one person to rebuild a kingdom into something worth dreaming about."

The hand touching. The words. The way he whispers them like a promise just between the two of us. Prince Alexander Charming, the crown prince of Briargild, is hitting on me. Me? Me. The man who accidentally shot him and then rotted in the dungeons and staggered half-dead into his bedchamber.

I thought I had terrible taste in men.

Even so, my whole body is warm and tingling from his words. For half a second, I let myself bask in the fantasy. I'm still clinging to my ideas of bringing back the tavern and saving my father, but it wouldn't hurt me to add to that life, to take on a paramour, to revel in things that aren't just alcohol and grubby cleaning tasks.

Half a second is already too long.

Reality is there, waiting for me, pummeling me with the impossibility of such a thing. Even if I wanted to be his, my body and soul, we couldn't marry. I would never be more than a prop at his elbow in the eyes of the kingdom, a dishonorable distraction for the new king. We could keep it a secret, but my heart stutters at that option. I don't want to be something that simmers in the day to only burn bright at night. If I am going to let myself fall in love, I want to do it loud and proud and, if we're completely honest, probably a bit messily.

Even if the disabled prince was the most productive king when it came to pushing progressive ideas in the history of this kingdom, there's not a shot he would be allowed to trot me out in front of the masses and introduce me as anything more than an advisor. A friend. A man who stands slightly behind and several feet off to the side to keep people from thinking we would ever dare to be more.

It's a ridiculous dream to want to ask for more.

He asked me to be his friend. Maybe I'm imagining more to it.

People like him don't settle for men like me. Princes don't marry paupers. Princes don't marry men. That story has been signed and sealed for a very long time.

Before I can wrap my mind around the implications of the prince's proposition and the way my heart has started down a wayward path with it, a bell chimes near the elevator. The prince jerks backwards, his hands finding his wheels and angling himself towards the door to his room. He lets out a curse when the bell chimes again.

"I need you to hide right now."

Sure that there isn't a single person I want to risk seeing come through that door, I'm quick to get to my feet. I am not quick to find a solution. My eyes flit around the room, taking in a dozen more plants of varying sizes and shapes. He must love them a lot to keep them in his personal chambers. It's a fairly open floor plan with empty space to allow him a range of motion in his chair. There aren't a lot of hiding places in here. I could go back to the bathroom and shut the door, but that feels like I'm asking to be found standing in the tub with a towel over my head. He has a wardrobe, but I have no idea if I would fit inside. Hopeless, I stand in the center of the room like a deer in front of a careening carriage. The bell rings again, faster and longer. Someone is demanding to come up.

"Just. Under the bed or something," the prince, so in control of the situation just moments before, is now fumbling as he rolls across the room and opens the door, giving him the access he needs to untie the rope I knotted on my way up here.

I'm not about to ask twice when a handsome man tells me to crawl under his bed. Scrambling, I flip up the red bedskirt and shimmy underneath the frame. I press myself close to the wall with my cheek on the floor.

The prince doesn't speak to me again. His breathing has picked up as the elevator is delivered to the bottom and quickly begins to ascend back to us. Prince Alexander doesn't move to put on anything to cover his midriff or the wound there, so he must be comfortable with whoever has demanded access to his bedchamber.

Except he's breathing hard like he's on the brink of a panic attack.

Who is coming up in the metal box to disturb the prince at a time like this?

While my own perverse fantasies would love to see the Necromancer stroll out of the elevator, I should have expected the man who finally steps into the room. I squint to see under the bedskirt and past the wheel of Prince Alexander's chair.

His panic makes sense.

My own heart has stilled as I hold my breath and pray that nobody looks down.

The king is here.

15

King Anerald Charming sweeps into Prince Alexander's chambers in his full military gear. A red cape that nearly touches the floor, the same shade as fresh blood dripping across a battlefield. Gold-plated armor is attached to his thighs by leather straps, and I assume he has a matching chest piece above where I can see. The whole thing is rather ornamental, the king having been far from war or violence for twenty years as he reigned within this castle and used his guards for brutal efficiency. I try not to make eye contact with the insignia of the pierced dragon that dangles from a medal attached to his belt, the same symbol carried by every member of Briargild's illustrious court and military.

I hold my breath as my heart kicks back to life with a thunderous start. It's a miracle that the king doesn't immediately realize I'm pressed to the floor with the way my traitorous organ taps out a plea to leave, to move, to do anything besides hide like a mouse from a cat.

There's nothing I can do, though.

This isn't just the King of Briargild. He isn't just the father of the rebellious prince. He isn't even just the man pushing dangerous laws and limitations against people of the kingdom, people in my community, and outright exterminating the free use of magic anywhere within our borders. This is the person who took my mother's life and forbade her from having a place in my world as anything besides a ghost that haunts it or the character in a fairytale my father continued to tell.

If I weren't half-naked and weak from my days in the dungeon, I might be stupider about my actions. My heart screams a war cry for revenge and revolution. I would be seen as a hero if I struck down the king now. As much pleasure as it would bring me to crawl out from under this bed and deck the tyrant now looming over Prince Alexander, I'm aware that it would be my last act. Every muscle tense, I do the one thing my father always begged of me: I hold my tongue and refuse to act recklessly.

My mind is moving fast, too fast as it tries to outrun the bloodthirsty beat of my heart. I have to be rational. The prince just offered me a job. Whether or not it could be more than that, Prince Alexander is already scheming to replace our current king and wants to bring me into a better world with him. I want to live to see the world become a better place. Which means I have to stay still, stay silent, stay hidden even as the king begins to speak.

"I assume you've heard there's been a dungeon breach?"

No hello. No, how are you? Nothing but a cold question as he looms over the prince.

I can just make out the tips of Prince Alexander's fingers and the way they quiver over the spokes on his wheel, but that's the end of his nervous energy. There isn't a tremor in his voice as he answers, "I was not made aware of the details. I was instructed to stay in here until it was handled. I assumed you had everything under control."

Bravery isn't the only word I could use to describe Prince Alexander, but it swells to the forefront of my opinions on the man now. I've stood up to my fair share of bullies. The prince sits firm in the face of the man who created him and then cast him aside for his imperfections. He doesn't flinch when the king stomps closer, his very presence shrinking the already cramped space.

When it seems his intimidation alone, punctuated by a swelling silence between them, isn't enough to get the prince to say more, King Anerald switches the subject. "Were you expecting company?"

I can't see Prince Alexander's upper body, but I assume they're both looking at the several cups on the table. "I spilled my first tea. You know how I am."

He says it so simply. He doesn't hesitate. It's just a fact of the matter.

My lungs seize. Fury whips through me for a man I've yet to get to know fully, but already think the entire world of. The king doesn't know a single gods damned thing about his son. He isn't some helpless, careless klutz. He's brilliant. Far brighter than me to say the very least. And kind. I don't know how to he came out so kind when his father is hard edges and a harsher demeanor.

Not all heroes are forged in battles that the history books collect. Some are crafted in homes where love has walked out the door.

The king's polished boot is a single centimeter from the dripping puddle I left near the table, and I curse myself for being dramatic during dinner. He makes a loud, disdainful sniff. All of his actions are prolonged for the sheer torture he knows they're causing his son, and I writhe with newfound hatred for him.

"We should increase your lessons if you think it's appropriate to be leaving these kinds of messes around your bedchamber."

I have no idea what exactly he's threatening, but I hold my breath as he stomps around the room. If he's looking for imperfections, how long do I have before he stoops to check under the bed?

Actually, that's not the only sign of me.

Shit. Fuck.

I left clothes on the floor of the bathroom.

The steady, confident thud of King Anerald's boots continues to travel around the space. I grit my teeth to keep from saying anything about that, but my muscles are tense as I try to think through my options in this moment. There aren't many. I can stay quiet, or I can act, and I know for a fact that I will crawl out from under this bed and put myself between the prince and the king if he dares to attack his son for something I've done. Prince Alexander has been an exemplary host. I should have agreed to everything he asked when I had the chance and the pleasure of his undivided attention. I wish he knew he wasn't so alone in this moment.

His knuckles are white as he grips the edge of his wheel. "I'll do as you see fit."

It's a canned response. Something he must say a lot, the syllables leaping from his tongue without any of the respectful inflection I'm sure they're meant to hold.

"We're weeks away from the ball, Alexander. You will not screw up this betrothal. Do you understand me?"

Talk about my heart beating too loud. I want to shush it. I want to slither out of here and pretend that I didn't just hear those words. Prince Alexander Charming cannot be betrothed to someone else. He just offered to make me a part of his world.

"I can't screw it up. Everything has been so perfectly organized. All you need is to roll me out onto whatever stage you see fit."

I should have been less worried about the king finding me. He doesn't even search the bathroom. It seems his son has gotten under his skin with his dry, sarcastic responses.

Everything happens so quickly. I'm watching the edge of the king's cape swish around the room, and then he storms back towards the prince like a seasonal storm given a second burst of energy. A gurgled choke escapes the smaller man. I squirm forward to see what's happening, pushing a pile of rumpled dark clothes out of my way. King Anerald has the prince in his grip, grabbing his jaw and jerking him up to dangle out of his chair.

Is it better for me to reveal myself now and create a momentary distraction that will cause the king to still punish Prince Alexander for hiding me, or should I stay here and let a lifetime's worth of tragedy unfold in front of me?

There isn't a right answer here. There isn't a wish I can utter that will turn back time and restore the woman whose death left Prince Alexander without a mother and turned the king into this shade of a monster. There's no version of the universe that makes it okay for Alexander to be treated like this, and I refuse to watch.

I have the power of surprise and a somewhat unpredictable magic on my side. Regardless of his mistreatment of the prince, this is likely the only time I will see King Anerald without his advisors and guards. He must have come up here without company to commit his dark deeds without anyone to answer to. Not everybody in this court can be okay with this obvious abuse.

I'm certainly not.

I'm going to do this. I'm going to reveal myself and be more foolish than I was any time I punched a debt collector or overzealous guard. I'm going to change the whole damn kingdom in one fate-filled moment.

I'm…

The bedskirt closest to me wriggles. I stop my quiet attempt to slide out from under the bed to look at the plant curling a vine around my wrist. A plant. One of the many things the prince had decorating his room. It wraps around my wrist and then rubs a lush leaf against the side of my thumb. The flexible stem gives me a gentle squeeze when I move, stilling me once more.

Apparently, everyone is better at magic than I, including the prince who should definitely not be weaving a spell to hold me captive while his anti-magic father screams down at him for insubordination.

I watch his fingers curl in my direction, the plant responding by stroking my wrist. This is his choice. I wait. I watch. I do not barrel into the scene like the hero I want to be.

It takes every bit of self-control in my body to swallow the bile in my throat and simply stay lying on the dusty floor.

The plant gently, ever so gently, brushes its leaves against my cheek. I try not to notice the drop of water slipping down it. There's an explosive tirade happening mere steps away from me, and yet I'm being treated like the most important thing in this room.

My heart breaks for a thousand tiny reasons, all of them leading me to the man who slumps back in his chair when he's released. He keeps a straight face, refusing to touch the red splotches on his jaw and cheeks. I can see from my odd angle now that I'm almost to the edge of the bed. Shoulders straight, he offers no argument to Anerald, daring him with his eyes alone to do something else, something more, something worse.

The entire time, the plant keeps a firm hold on my wrist, twisting and caressing me in turn. Prince Alexander Charming has nerves of steel and the magic to show for it. He probably wouldn't have panicked if he had created a man-eating plant instead of a carriage.

"You will be at the ball. You will marry that queen and you will fill your role in this kingdom as necessary. Don't get any ideas about messing this up, Alexander."

I want to ask how many times the prince has managed to scheme and derail his father's plans while also being deemed as inferior to the entirety of the Briargild court. Enough, it seems, to merit worry from the crown. Whatever he's set up, whoever he has promised to marry the prince off to, there's too much depending on it.

What is he trying to achieve?

The man already has an entire kingdom of people fearing him. He's passed laws to obstruct most uses of magic, gifting it back to the kingdom only through the power of the fairy godmothers. There isn't a lack of wealth and power for him.

The closest kingdom I know of, the one my father often traded with to get specialty wines shipped in, is across the sea. It takes two months to get between our port and theirs, with an additional three days of carriage riding to make it back to the tavern. There once was a kingdom closer to Briargild. It was one of fairytale novelty and magic living in the roots of every tree. My father once made a comment that it was somewhere my mother loved on his inspection of a map he thought was printed incorrectly.

Realization washes over me slower than I appreciate. The prince. The distance. He's trying to get rid of his son.

If there's no prince here to speak out for the people of the kingdom, if the only rebel from the royal lineage suddenly leaves, how well can the revolution fight back against King Anerald's wicked ways?

I just started to get to know a guy. Of course, his father would send him away. I can't have one good thing going for me these days.

"If you hear news of the prisoner," the king begins, his voice gruff as he cuts through my thoughts.

"I'll let the nearest guard know where he went. I don't think he's going to be much of a problem. It's not like my tower is the best place for him to hide."

The audacity. The blatant lie. The way his voice still doesn't tremble.

Prince Alexander Charming is a work of art wrapped in a web of misdirection and good intentions.

Fortunately, the king doesn't find it necessary to punish his insolence again. Instead, he strides from the room, a natural disaster now directed elsewhere with a lingering threat to return should any detail of the prince's existence change. The door to the elevator slams shut.

I wait only long enough for the plant around my wrist to unwind before I crawl out from under the bed. The small vine wraps back into its pot as I move around the bed to stand next to the prince. He doesn't meet my eyes.

"Prince Alexander..."

I don't know what to say. I'm not sure there is any combination of words fitting for a circumstance like this. We definitely were not raised the same. The last conversation with my father was probably the worst we had ever fought with each other, and I gave far more than he did in the way of cruel words. I wouldn't have hit him, and he wouldn't have put his hands on me. Lost without a guide for this interaction, I stand by the prince, taking in the red marks that will surely be bruises by morning.

"I'd prefer if we didn't use titles," he finally says, pulling himself back together again with a meticulous breath and a turn of his wheels.

He bids me to sit on the edge of the bed, and I do, mouth dry, palms spread on the red cover as I watch him move around the kitchen. A long moment stretches between us. Not the threatening silence Anerald tried to use for his own benefit. This is an easy quiet. It doesn't grow or pressure or sow ill intent, it simply exists with us in this room as the prince goes about figuring out how to continue the night. I owe him time if that is all I can offer. When he turns back to me with a couple of water glasses and a chocolate in a golden wrapper on the tray between them, he looks more himself, more sure and comfortable at least. "I like sweets when I'm stressed. Would you like to share with me?"

How could I ever tell him no?

I accept a square of chocolate when he returns to my side, trying not to think about the way fireworks seem to work through my knuckles at the brief contact between our fingertips. "So, I should call you Alexander, then?"

"I would prefer just Xander."

I bite my chocolate in half, relish in the smooth experience of it melting on my tongue, and then forcibly remind myself how to swallow when he eagerly looks to me for a reply. "Do you let all your stowaway prisoners call you that?"

His nose scrunches as he shakes his head at me. "How did you know this was a pattern for me?"

I laugh and accept more chocolate. The tension of the king's visit leaves the room faster than the man himself. For a brief moment, I forget that there are bigger problems beyond these walls. Right now, it's just me and the friend I've made, the one who has shared a cruel truth about himself and wants a moment of comfort. I would stay here eating chocolate for the rest of my days if that was an option.

He had offered to make me an advisor.

Which can't happen if he's married to someone else in a kingdom far away from here.

"So," I say slowly, sure that I'm about to dampen the entire mood by pushing the subject, but incapable of letting it go. "You're betrothed?"

With a sigh, he sets down the chocolate square he was working on and licks the edge of his finger. I suppose it's a normal action. My entire focus has narrowed to the flash of pink tongue on flesh.

The things I would like to see that particular tongue do…

No. Not appropriate. I've been single too long, and my thoughts are wandering into ridiculous territory. I need to pull myself together.

"It is a plan my father has been working on. I haven't agreed to anything beyond showing up for the big day," he shrugs, his brown eye searching my face as he answers as though my opinion means anything. "I'm not in love with her if that's something you're interested in knowing."

"Should I be interested?"

Chocolate coats my tongue and throat. I'm smothered in sweetness. None of it compares to the way he's looking at me.

"Eli…"

My name. Gods, my name from his throat, soft and beckoning in a way nobody else has ever uttered it.

He doesn't continue where that thought was going, though. Instead, he gives a stiff shake of his head. "You ought to rest. It'll be best to sneak out of the castle around midnight. There's a guard change, and you'll need all the help you can get since they'll be on high alert from your escape from the dungeon."

He looks around the room. Then, back at me. Something weighs on his mind; the only sign of it is the way he chews the corner of his lip.

"I have some business to attend. You can take anything you need when it's time to leave."

Xander means to leave. I don't know what it means that a pit opens up in my stomach at that realization. I don't want this moment to end. We were already rudely interrupted. I thought we would at least have a couple of hours before I'm off to my next leg of this escape.

I no longer want to run away from him. Not in the way I had considered when I first entered this room. For the first time since losing the tavern, I feel like there is somewhere new I would want to put down roots. Not the castle necessarily. But…

I shake that thought from my mind.

Because it's stupid.

Foolish.

Impossible.

Instead of offering an argument, I nod. The prince, because he is a prince and not an option for me to be anything else with, hands me a small, sugared leaf from a jar with the promise that it'll help my magic rebuild while I nap. He's kind enough not to drug me twice in one night without my consent. Peppermint bursts on my tongue as he bids me to crawl under the covers.

I fight the urge to shut my eyes the entire time he gathers himself, takes a bag that was tucked in a chest by his wardrobe, and slips into the elevator he pulled back to our landing. Prince Alexander Charming hesitates to shut the door while I lie on the softest pillow in existence. He looks me over and offers a smile that seems almost as sad as I feel.

"I'll see you again," he vows.

I don't say anything. The magic leaf has me in its grip. All of the drowsiness and exhaustion I'd been fighting off since leaving my dungeon cell seems to swim up to meet me at once.

Dreams don't compare to the moments I shared with a prince I can't have, but I say his name in my sleep and let myself pretend that he could ever be just Xander with me.

16

The world pulls at my sleeve. It pokes my nose. It creeps along my hairline and whispers something unintelligible into my ear. I snap out of my sedative-induced slumber with a groan.

My muscles feel much better. It takes no effort at all to sit up. The red blanket the prince let me borrow slips to the floor with my motion. My head doesn't pound or swim, and there are no more black spots inhibiting my vision.

Xander is nowhere to be seen. I wish I could have gone with him on his errands. If they were rebel meetings, I might have had a chance to meet up with the Necromancer even earlier than midnight. I don't regret the rest, though. I feel more like myself than I have since uttering the worst wish in history.

The slitted windows positioned too high up to properly see out of show the dim light of the waning moon. Midnight is almost here. I do have another man to meet.

The prince said I could take anything I needed, so dressed in lounge pants and definitely not prepared for whatever sneaking out of a castle entails, I crossed his chambers to the large wardrobe I spotted during our chat. Xander and I are a similar build. I'm sure he has something else in my size I could borrow until we see each other again. He's the one who said we'd see each other again, wasn't he? Not all of this was some fever dream.

We're not following any normal attempt at flirtation. I should definitely be worried that the prince is attracted to someone who shot him with an arrow. Yet, it's hard not to bond quickly when the world is on fire and our options are so limited.

He's desperate. He's looking for a way out of his father's plans. I'm not against being a scapegoat.

Or, worse, it's all in my head and he's just being polite in a tense situation because to be kind is its own act of rebellion, and he's made rebelling his entire life.

Shaking that thought from my mind, I look around his room now that I'm alone to do so. There are more plants situated on the top of the wardrobe. Greenery with large leaves, most with trailing vines like the one that touched my wrist while I was under the bed. I wonder how nobody else has figured out the has prince magic. It seems like a very difficult secret to keep when the entirety of the castle is bent to the king's will and his anti-magic propaganda. The spots of green interspersed through the red and gold of the kingdom's colors pulse their own rebellious cry as I look over them and think of all the plants I lost in the tavern's devastation.

Throwing open the heavy doors of the wardrobe, I take in the plethora of clothes awaiting the prince. Sorted from left to right by order of most ornate to nearly normal clothing, I flip through my options. I don't want anything that will make me stand out from those I might end up walking past in the castle halls, and also nothing that will be too expensive if I get caught in my attempt to escape. I can't exactly afford to die more than once for my growing list of crimes.

I finger the plainest clothes, wondering why the prince has so much black in his wardrobe, and then figuring that mourning clothes never go out of style. Maybe I don't need to dress like a thief or a Necromancer. I do only get one chance to do this. I may as well do it with a little style. Everybody downstairs will be looking for a prisoner with my description. Maybe it'll confuse them that I dressed up for the occasion. Maybe it will inspire those hidden rebels to see me alive and well and masquerading in our enemies' colors.

Pulling a soft, white tunic from a hanger, I dress in Xander's clothes. The hem, collar, and sleeve cuffs are heavily embroidered with roses in sharp, abrupt stitches. Where I once lived in blue, I'm now dripping in red as I slide on trousers in a matching color and tie them at my waist. The soft fabric rests against my skin, carrying a scent of pine needles and lilacs. For a man supposedly confined to his rooms in the castle, he smells a lot like the forest. Again, I wonder how nobody has figured out that he's part of the rebel cause. He's not doing a great job covering up his antics.

I curse under my breath as I paw through the rest of the wardrobe. Even his socks are softer than anything I've ever owned. I reach towards the back when my fingers hit something that isn't fabric.

The prince is allowed to have secrets. I should leave the stack of letters where they are. I definitely shouldn't pull the twine off and read the first one.

I'm not particularly good at doing anything that I should.

The letter is on crisp, expensive parchment with a swirling script that glides across the page, which is annoying. I never learned to read anything besides standard font. I squint and tilt the page, trying to pick out any letters I recognize. There's a spattering of vowels I see, but none of it means anything to me besides the last line.

Whoever is writing letters to the prince signs them: Yours.

His. I can't make out the signature accompanied by the wax seal of a flowering tree.

Royals. He probably has a bunch of people he's worked to string along as potential suitors should he survive the betrothal his father set up. More interestingly, there's a bundle of raised dots in the corner of the page. Too patterned to be a mistake. I run my thumb over them several times, but can't glean much meaning from them. If the prince is passing secrets in his letters, this is a pretty good way to do it. I tuck the letters back where I found them without giving them another thought.

I don't feel bad about snagging a particularly nice pair of boots and sliding them onto my feet. Black dyed leather. Long laces that haven't even been finished being pulled through the perfect holes. A gold buckle rests on the toe of either shoe in the shape of a rose to symbolize the kingdom I'll never escape. Fancier than I deserve, I marvel at the cushioned feel of the shoes as I slip my feet into them.

Finally dressed to more-or-less impress, I refrain from going through the rest of the prince's belongings. I don't need to look for a weapon. My magic is writhing under my skin once more, awake and ready to be called upon. Ready to do this, I pull up the elevator and transport myself to the bottom floor.

It happens too quickly.

My fingers quiver as I tie the elevator rope to the knob on the right. I have to start pretending that I'm stealthy.

Those magic boots would have been really helpful right now.

Taking several deep breaths to calm my nerves, I slowly open the door and peer out into the adjoining hall. It's quiet. It's empty. It's almost too dark to see; the late hour is a great time to conserve the magic used to light the orbs that dangle from the ceiling, since there's no point in lighting rooms nobody will be in.

I should have asked the prince for the best way out of here. As is, I creep out of the elevator, back down the abandoned hall that definitely shouldn't lead to the prince's private rooms, and simply pick a direction. Wallpapered walls filled from floor to ceiling in swirling, gold depictions of roses lead me from one hall to another. The motif of roses covers most things, their thorns a sparkling accent in dripping gold in paintings, in marble busts of past monarchs, and pressed into floor tiles, revealed by the absence of rugs in general walking areas. Every time I hit the junction of two halls meeting, creating three alternate paths I could take, I look up at the ornate chandeliers that hang above, a twisting bush of threatening florals.

The artistry around me is impressive to say the very least. I press forward, passing portraits by artists forgotten in the crushing turn of time, even as their work lives on here in a castle where it isn't truly appreciated. I'm sure King Anerald hardly walks these parts of the castle; the back end of the building is still beautiful but lacks some of the expense put into the front, where they constantly house guests and throw parties.

Disgust curls through me as I cling to pockets of shadows and frown at the blatant waste of so much space. Nobody needs a castle to be filled and not used. There are people starving on the streets of the kingdom, people who could easily be warm and housed and fed if some of these resources were reallocated. I note the hard work that must have gone into creating this place and the work that must continue to go into it to keep it clean and in relatively good repair. Artists and architects and cooks and cleaners. Good people. All who deserve more than a measly penance for their time and efforts.

If I were in charge…

I shake that thought away immediately. I don't want to be in charge of any of this. I want my father and our tavern back, and it will be more than enough to keep our social circle fed and cared for in the trying months. If the prince doesn't beat his father, things are going to get worse for the people of Brairgild.

But if Xander can lead the rebellion and remove Anerald from the throne…

There's hope. Not a sprinkle of it. A heap is now lifting the weight from my shoulders and removing some of my anxiety about my current situation. If Xander succeeds in what he's been working towards all of his life, then everything could truly be different.

My inadvertent wish could come true.

If Gemma were here, I'd ask her if there was a grand plan for me. If I were sent on this path via one misplaced wish and an awful night, and if it all really could help the kingdom for the better. She'd remind me that magic doesn't work like that, except when it comes to me.

I have to get out of the castle before I can think more about that.

My steps echo down every hall. I'm a walking commotion. Cringing at my apparent lack of ability to step quietly, I change tactics from stealth to speed. One of these halls will eventually lead outside. If I can get there fast enough, maybe I can slip outside during the guard switch before anyone is alerted by my presence via the oxen stampede that is my footwork.

It's not a solid plan.

None of my plans seem to be.

It's better than nothing.

My steps continue to pound too loudly. In response, my heart crawls closer to my throat. Someone has to have heard me by now. There's no way the servants and nobles who live within these walls are used to the heavy sounds I'm making as I jog through the space in search of a way out. At any moment, someone is going to come out from behind these closed doors and find me: a servant bid to give up my position even if they agree with my escape, a nobleman with expensive face creams smeared over his features and not yet soaked in during his sleep, or maybe a guard with enough common sense to realize I'm masquerading as someone I'm not in these bright clothes.

I'll be okay as long as I can get outside. I repeat the sentiment over and over again in my mind. It has little to do with my own belief in myself and a lot to do with the fact that I know the Necromancer is somewhere beyond the castle walls waiting for me.

Is it inappropriate to be excited to see a different man after being so intimately hosted by a literal prince?

Maybe. The Necromancer is his own breed of devious, but he hasn't dosed my tea yet, so that's a point in his direction. He also doesn't have a handful of letters from someone else hidden in his sock drawer, as far as I know. Not that I'm comparing them for my own needs. I'm merely collecting fascinating facts about the men I would have never met behind the bar of our tavern.

I manage to finally make my way into a hallway that leads to a door and not another hall. No guards currently stalk this area. It isn't oversized like those that lead to the throne room, all of my previous clients making a big deal about the dragons carved in wood with golden swords thrust through their chests in an overzealous display of Briargild's pride in ridding the magical creature from the world. There's a seal pressed into the wood. Gold letters swirled together.

My heart, already overworked by my anxiety to get this far, threatens to collapse in on itself.

I know what this is. Gemma mentioned it to me. It's a rumored occupation that would never be an option for someone living in the lower city. This is the office for the Guild of Fairy Godmothers.

This is where wishes are determined.

This is where they go after someone utters them over birthday candles or under the serene moon of the winter solstice or, even, when it's said in an angry rush. My fingers are on the golden knob. I could go in there and fix my wish all by myself.

No more deals with witches. No, depending on men with more advantageous political footholds in the world. Not even Gemma to tell me the right way to do things. Just me and the room beyond: the sole destination, determination, and deliverance of wishes. If anyone can fix it, it's whoever runs this department.

Hope lurches through my system. I could make a detour. The gardens and the Necromancer will still be there even if I sneak into the Guild of Fairy Godmothers. My wish could be reversed. I could be minutes from seeing my father again.

Gods, I don't know how I'm going to explain all of this to him. The tavern collapsed, and the way he turned to gold dust in my hands. My days of running. My arrest. The two men who have been present in my mind. The fact that we'll have to rebuild the tavern and then make it big enough for my dragon to come inside, because magic may have ruined my life, but it's not something I'm willing to give up now.

I stare down at my pink-stained palms as glitter trickles from my general excitement. Everything I've been trying to achieve is right here, just behind one more door.

Flashing signs of danger couldn't keep me from turning the handle. A snake could bite my wrist now, and I would still plunge ahead. This is a loophole in Wynnifred's deal. It's how I save my father before I doom myself completely with the revolutionary acts I can't turn my back on now.

I'm inside with my back to the door in half a breath. Gold light filters through the air here in semi-circles of glittering brilliance. The room is nearly as large as the meadow used by the revolutionaries on the winter solstice, a jarring difference from the slim halls I've been slinking through since leaving the prince's room. Along the walls, there are diagrams of wands and the golden handles they're all assembled with. Instructions are crammed into the edges in an illegible script. Secrets to being a fairy godmother, or, at least, behind the magic of the wands. Deciphering it is the least of my worries, so I turn my focus to the middle of the room.

An enormous globe rests there. Clear crystal outer edge, there's a thousand golden strings tangled within it. All vibrating. The tiny movements flutter through the entire sphere, the golden web given a heartbeat no different than the stammering rhythm that fills my own chest.

Wishes given substance. I leave the firm presence of the door to creep closer to the globe that could have fit our entire bar inside its glass edges. Taller than me and more than several steps to either side, I move towards it and raise a hand.

Once my fingers hover over the globe's edge, the golden strings begin to oscillate more vigorously. The entire golden center pulls towards the side I'm standing on, each strand personally demanding my attention. It's entrancing. I forget about my reason for sneaking in here and place my palm on the glass.

The wishes whoosh towards me, brushing the other side of the glass with erratic, ribbon-like fingers. I can hear them. Tiny voices calling out to me in muffled shrieks.

I wish…

I wish for a better home.

I wish my brother would make it here for my wedding.

I wish to have enough to feed the children tomorrow.

I wish for…

Treasures. Luxuries. Necessities. The list could be written into a novel with ten thousand pages, and still it would go on, repeating similar themes but never the same wish twice. The voices start as individual strands of personal inflections before building into an indecipherable crescendo of chorusing wishes. The entirety of Briargild is screaming from within this globe.

And then I hear a voice that's familiar.

Too familiar.

My own.

I wish for everything to be different.

It's not a golden strand. It's vibrant pink and dipping in and out of the shifting mass of wishes from the rest of the kingdom. It's trapped in there, knotted on one end and flailing on the other. I stare at the frayed edge as it whips towards the spot I'm touching on the globe.

This has to be what went wrong. A rogue mistake with my wish. If I can get it out of there, then the magic can finish what it was supposed to do in the first place, right?

Gemma would know so much more. I wish she were here now. At my elbow, pestering me and telling me what to do in that matter-of-fact way of hers. With her yellow hair and bright eyes and unwavering faith that she's on the right path in life, I could really use her help.

Instead, firmly on my own, I pace the outer perimeter of the glass globe. The whole thing seems to shiver under my perusal. It waits, the threads of wishes smoothing into a less convoluted entity for a moment while I try to think. There has to be a way for the fairy godmothers to get the wishes out, right? Gemma mentioned the wands coming with their own magic, but needing the wishes to do the rest of the work, so clearly the web of desire can't stay stuck in there forever.

There has to be a door. A window. A tiny lever that pulls back a piece of the glass big enough for a wand to slip into it.

It's here somewhere.

I make it around the globe two full times. Nothing stands out to me. The quivering mess of wishes slinks along the interior of the globe in pace with me, but it offers no solutions. I watch my malignant wish swish and sway and seriously make no effort to atone for its crimes. It pulses pink like Skelly's heart. It's pink like the glitter that is almost constantly coated on my hands. It's pink and seemingly innocent, and I'm not sure if it's really the root cause of all of my problems, but I'm too invested to simply walk away.

I turn my attention to the walls filled with diagrams and take a step closer to one with a clear illustration of the globe in the middle of the room when voices interrupt my focus. Two people. One I recognize with dread dripping down my spine.

King Anerald Charming is in the hall.

He's coming in here.

I search the space for somewhere to hide, but there's nothing. Smooth wood paneled walls, smothered in parchment, aren't great camouflage. The one desk here has boxes shoved under it, the caretaker of the guild's space clearly as good at organizing as I am. There are no windows with draped curtains for a stranger to slip behind. There isn't even another door for me to escape through as the knob behind me turns.

I hit the floor. My knees crack on the cool tile, and I press myself to the edge of the globe, hoping nobody is going to look straight through the glass and see me. It's a terrible hiding spot, but the best I've got because the door is open and the king is shoving a woman into the room ahead of him.

My heart skips at the flash of blonde hair. It's not Gemma, though. Somebody is in charge. A woman who sniffs and smooths out her skirts and grovels as King Anerald snaps questions.

"We had him in custody, and you still haven't fixed this!"

The king's voice explodes through the room on the clipped heels of the slammed door. My hands ball into fists at my side, and I take in a sharp breath to steady myself and hold still. Twice in one day is too many times to be accidentally confined in a room with him. I try to be smaller, to be invisible, as I squint through the glass and the way it distorts the muddy reflection of the people on the other side of it.

"I've never seen anything like it, Sir. Any attempts to remove the strand have been near catastrophic. If that magic is released, there could be serious consequences for the kingdom."

Her voice is thin. This woman, presumably the person in charge of the Guild of Fairy Godmothers, is used to being in a position of power and fighting every inclination to raise her voice back to the man screaming at her. She doesn't shrink back from King Anerald as he looms over her like an omen given life.

"He's escaped. There's about to be severe consequences for you and everyone else who failed me if this isn't fixed."

Well, it's nice to know I've been a general annoyance for his royal highness. I stay kneeling behind the globe. The strands of magic behind the glass swell and dip to be near me. While I appreciate that the golden strands give me a little more privacy, I'm sure the woman on the other side of the room will instantly know they aren't behaving as usual.

The conversation has her captivated for now. "I set up the trap for him as you asked, Sir. He made a wish. I don't know what went wrong with the fairy godmother I sent out into the field, but she's missing, and now magic is reacting strangely. It's going to take time to figure this out."

Gemma. My wish. I'm learning too much and not enough. King Anerald doesn't grab the woman, but he looms closer, stepping into her space so she's forced to either let him be on top of her or back up.

Which means I have to move.

Crawling opposite to them, I try to stay right across the globe with the swirling strands, hopefully distorting any piece of my reflection from their view. Every scuffed scrape of my knee on the floor sends my heart into a hummingbird's rhythm. The rapid pounding fills my ears. I barely hear the king's next snarled words.

"The magic of the Alcinder throne only passes between bloodlines. As long as an heir continues to exist, this marriage will not matter. None of this will matter!" He flings his arms out to encompass not merely the office but the entirety of Briargild.

His knuckles rap against the glass surface of the globe, and the magic threads within recoil from him. Whether it's from him or the magic-nullifying gold rings on his hands, I can't be sure, but I know that magic is a near living thing with an ability to act wild and free, and it wants nothing to do with King Anerald Charming.

All of the excitement moves the threads up and away from the king. He's staring straight through the unobstructed globe. I hold my breath.

We make disturbingly direct eye contact.

I guess it was only a matter of time before I was caught sneaking in places I wasn't meant to be. King Anerald is snapping commands to the woman in charge of fairy godmothers, sending her to the door to get the guards while moving straight for me with those leaden footsteps that echo through the space.

There's no use in staying on the floor. I push up, my hands resting on the globe in front of me as I waver on my feet. All of the swimming threads are back by me, writhing within the glass. They squirm and slither and slam themselves against the glass to get to me, to get to the pink sparkles staining my palms, to get to freedom.

Which gives me an idea.

I'm going to need a little bit of magic and a whole lot of luck.

Keeping my hands on the glass, I skim through all of the magic lessons I've had up until this point. Gemma with an acorn squash, telling me to visualize and project my magic out through my fingertips. The Necromancer shouting at me to conjure shields while throwing projectiles at me that I took down with explosive precision. Magic is wild and real. It's right here in this room and begging to be released.

I need a distraction to stop the king from strangling me himself, so I refuse to answer his shouts and curses and demands for me to turn myself in as guards stomp in the nearby halls and instead turn all of my attention on the glass under my hands as I raise my voice to just above a whisper. "Crack!"

I imagine a soft sound as the pieces of glass slip away from each other. I expect it to be clean and quick. A burst of pink, and my will is done.

Magic, though, has never been complicit in my plans.

The crack that appears is about the length of my arm. Sharp

and sudden. The globe seems to have taken an impact from my still hands, spraying glass shards into the fray of swirling wishes. Glitter keeps pouring from my palms.

It tingles in my wrists and leaves my elbows feeling scraped raw along the bones. Magic festers below my skin and needs the barest permission to leave, falling from me now in a waterfall I can't stop. Glitter slides through the impressive crack in the side of the globe. It spills and seeps and showers down into the sphere until the whole contraption is brimming with raging, trapped wishes and my uncontrollable magic like a malignant snow globe waiting to be shaken.

To my right and coming closer, the king has his hands outstretched for me. Seconds pull into the longest moments of my life. Longer than all the nights in the dungeon felt. Longer than the early morning hours in which the tavern collapsed before I was sent to trudge through the forest. Longer even than the time stretched taut between me and the prince and the cup laced with truth serum back in that tower bedroom I should have never left.

Red-faced, his maroon cape flitting in the air behind him like the twisted tail of an angry cat, King Anerald charges for me. Even royalty is not enough to stop magic. The glitter crawls up the sides of the globe. Between specks of spreading pink, I watch the ribbons dart around the remaining space in the glass enclosure, prodding at the crack and searching for further weakness.

King Anerald is on me in the next moment. His hands on my shoulders, he shoves me back from the globe. "I will not be usurped by someone like you!"

Until I made that bad wish that apparently landed me in a carefully laid trap, I was just a regular person. King Anerald Charming was terrible and wouldn't have gotten my vote if we had that kind of government, but he seemed to be a world away, and I had plenty to busy myself with around the tavern. We could have gone our entire lives without being in the same room.

Now, he bears down on me. Thick-fingered hands paw at my throat. It takes me a moment to realize that I need to fight back. This is surreal. Magic has pushed the trajectory of my life into some strange places, and this may just be the worst.

I wrestled a fairy godmother to get here, and now I might not survive if I don't brawl with a mad king.

He's bigger than me. Rounder. Stiff at the shoulders. Baring down on me with a couple decades of malice I haven't had a chance to collect.

The stiff scent of garlic leaks from his mouth as he berates me. Curses. Slurs. A dedicated speech on how penniless peasants won't take everything from him.

"I should have found you when I killed your mother," he fumes, my vision blurry from the lack of oxygen as my ears ring with his open confession.

This isn't random, then. It's not merely me stepping into the wrong circumstances and fumbling to get myself out of them. For my entire life, my father skipped around the subject of my mother. He told me fairy tales with ambiguous endings instead of telling me the truth. I know Adira Cinderfella deserved a better end, and I have tried to honor what I remembered of her, but I couldn't have guessed my actions would have dumped me here.

King Anerald Charming barely looked at me the last time we were in the same room. I was merely a pest. Now, his features scrunched into a mask of ire, his hands clenched around my throat so hard that the chain from my locket digs in, Anerald gazes down at me like I alone could be the undoing of his kingdom, and he can't settle for such a thing.

If it's going to be me or him, I can't just lie down and accept my fate.

Squirming gets me nowhere. I can't knee him through the gold-plated armor encasing his torso and thighs. Grabbing his hands leaves us both smeared in pink glitter, but me still strangling while he shoves me down onto the ground.

I might have stood a chance on my feet, but Anerald clearly has the upper hand. Guards have entered the room. There's an audience gathered for my murder. None of them speak up. Nobody is going to step in.

Anerald is on top of me. The tiles are harsh and unyielding as he crushes my windpipe. There's no air making it past my teeth. My mouth is dry, and I cough and wheeze and choke on the fury of a King I do not claim as my own.

Glitter sticks to his beard. I don't manage to punch him in the face as much as I try.

Blinking past black spots, I think of all of the glitter in that cracked globe just behind the king. My magic is right there. It's waiting for a command.

I rasp the word out through clenched teeth. "Explode!"

And so, I set off a glitter bomb in the office of the Guild of Fairy Godmothers.

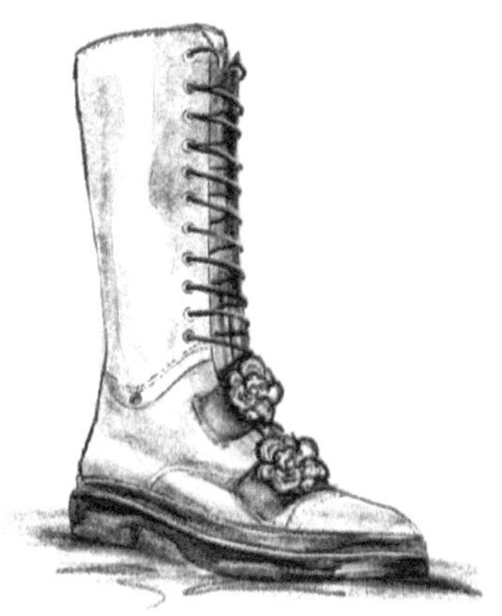

17

The explosion rocks the castle to its core. Pink glitter and glass, and the sinewy, fragmented wish ribbons scatter through the room. Shouts are barely audible in the aftermath as glitter wedges itself up my nose— every part of me itches and aches.

I rub my hands over my eyes, sitting up without the weight of the king on me. Glitter cuts at my eyelids. It scrapes my corneas. The thin flecks of magic wriggle and dig into my skin, burying themselves in me once more as I cough up dust and debris from the initial explosion.

There isn't time to gather myself.

I need to get up. I need to get out.

"Grab him!"

"Halt!"

It seems everyone else has already regained their senses. The guards from the halls are on their feet and coming towards me through the haze of glitter as I spit pink onto the floor. To the side, the king hasn't moved.

His cape is entirely stained by the soft shade of my magic. Cuts mar his exposed skin, the glass having raked along his knuckles and cheeks, and a particularly bad gash at the back of his head. He lies flat on his stomach, unmoving as I stagger up to my full height.

Stepping by his pronc form, I glance back around the room. The diagrams on the walls are completely shredded or made useless by the thick layer of pink covering everything like a burst can of paint. The threads of wishes are flung around the place, smattering the floor and walls in thick, lifeless globs. I'm not sure what happens to wishes when they're not cared for properly, but that feels like a problem for someone else. Everything is coated in glass shards, making it a slow process to actually cross the space and stop me.

Past the king, the wall nearest the globe is completely gone. Bricks have been dusted into smithereens, and I can see outside. I was one wall away from finding my way to the outside world. This looks like my best choice, so, knees full of cotton as I wobble from one leg to the other, I jog as quickly as I can to the hole in the office wall.

Fresh air sweeps into the room, flicking the glitter that lingers nearest the impromptu exit. I suck in a deep breath, and it burns all the way down into my glitter-infested lungs. More guards yell for me to stop. Instead, I lean into the open space and stare at the ground that is a little further away than I would prefer.

We must be on a second level of the castle.

There's a good chance I could survive a jump, right?

At least, it has to be a better chance than choosing to stay.

When I jump, it's in a tripping, jerking motion that leads me from firm flooring to open air. The wind touches my face. It kisses the cuts on my hands and laps at blood on my forehead. There is no protection from inevitability in the arms of the wind.

I meet the gravel-covered ground in a jarring conclusion that puts me on my knees once again. Coughing, wheezing, still living. I push to my feet as shouts gather in a crescendo above me.

King Anerald's voice booms out of that broken office. "Stop him!"

Guards gather at the break in the castle wall, willing themselves to follow me down the desperate drop. I don't wait to see how many follow. Curses snap at my heels as I make my way to the left towards the first hints of greenery.

I'm basically a free man.

Worse for wear and leaving a glittering trail behind me, but free.

I am so freaking close to escape.

Which is not nearly close enough.

A second shudder tears through the night air. I glance over my shoulder to see the side of the castle collapse. Apparently, my magical blizzard wasn't the only danger this place faced. The vibrations may have been felt in the city center from the way the castle shudders and shakes. Out there beyond the dangers of soldiers and rose gardens, Gemma is probably somewhere safe and feels this rumble, too. I hope she knows I'm up to no good with magic once more.

When the ground stops shaking from the unnatural force of my magic and a good quarter of the castle is gone, the yells are renewed. Louder. More vehement. They're all strangled by Anerald's threats to kill me before I can make my way into the rest of the kingdom. I'm a weed pushed through fruitful soil and too dangerous to allow to live. I'm no longer a nobody from the lower city. I'm a villain marked so by my refusal to bow to a king who wants my death in order to keep his power. I'm Eli Cinderfella, and I don't yet understand the prophecy or my place in these plans, but I know I'm out of chances here in Brairgild.

It no longer matters if the prince thinks he can help. It wouldn't change anything if all of the citizens of the lower city showed up at my beheading to mourn and say that this shouldn't happen. Anerald has shown his hand. My death is the only thing waiting for me now in Briargild.

Well, Death and perhaps a Necromancer.

With the guards dazed and figuring out their next move, I push forward. My ears ring. I let out my own rasping coughs and spit pink specks onto the ground. Dirt and glitter cover my borrowed clothes. I could probably bathe six times and still find glitter in the water.

I suppose that's the price of power.

Glitter is innocuous in small amounts and lethal now as it hangs thick enough in the air to block out the stars. Sluggish, I lean to one side as I make my way towards the pink-smeared garden. Green leaves slump under the weight of my magic, the twinkling specks gathering like aphids in their centers. Roses glimmer in the orbs of light that mark the beginning of the garden, smooth red with pink edges. It appears that nothing has been spared from my desperate spell.

I have a head start on the guards, but I need to get myself out of here fast. At the very least, I need to put as much space between them and me as I possibly can, but my bones feel scorched and itchy from my release of magic, and I don't think there's enough hours I could possibly sleep to stop feeling exhausted. I really wish someone had explained the limits of magic to me before I found myself once again tiptoeing along the boundary between alive and consumed by the very magic I wield. I should have stolen more of those herbs from the prince before I staggered down here to make a scene.

All that currently matters is that I'm alive and moving. Blinking past the spots refusing to clear from my vision and the glitter that clouds the air, I stagger onto the main path of the rose garden, only to realize it's not a normal garden. It's a maze. The castle isn't just boasting its namesake in florals. It's laid out an entire swath of land absolutely crawling with the damn things. Thorns prick me whenever I slip to the side, nipping at my hands and pulling at my clothes, and altogether reminding me that there isn't an option to stop and lie down as much as my body is yearning for twelve days of undisturbed sleep.

I have to move.

I have to escape.

I'm in the gardens, *so where the fuck is the Necromancer?*

I made a pretty big scene back there. If he was waiting for a signal that I've arrived, he definitely saw it. I hope he's weaving his own way through the glitter-stained rose petals because I don't have time to search for him. Already, the vibrant, red petals and the gold markers designating the paths through the aisles of thriving flowers are too much for my sore eyes. I rub at them. Glitter bites at my palms and scrapes across my retina. I don't think I'll ever be able to rinse the damned substance from my eyes.

Why does my magic show up as glitter? Why couldn't it be something soft and less bothersome? Like puffs of pink fluff? Cotton candy? Nobody complains about having too much cotton candy.

The image of crawling through a mountain of spun sugar is incredibly amusing until I hear the first shout of oncoming guards. Crap. I thought I would have more time. It sounds like the first lookouts got a second battalion to join their attempt to catch me. There are at least twenty men shouting to each other and stomping into the gardens behind me from an actual doorway instead of the one I blasted through the castle wall. I bet they know the layout of the maze better than I do.

There's no time for mistakes. I can't waste any more of my energy on trying to wipe my eyes free of glitter. I have to move, and I have to do it now, and I can't turn the wrong way because I'll be forced to surrender or cast more magic to save myself. My heart stutters at that thought, even as my singed veins fill with more potent magic, looking for a way out. I think I would rather burn up from the inside than go back to the dungeons, but I don't want to test that theory.

Right. Left. Staggering, stumbling, leaning into bushes that don't catch me but bite my fingers and wrists and tear at the clothes I borrowed from Xander. I keep moving as pink-washed greenery closes behind me, obstructing the view of the oncoming guards.

I'm so distracted by the confusing layout of my surroundings and the impending doom at my heels that I completely miss the arrival of my anticipated company. The Necromancer sneaks up on me, lunging out from a bushy area and grabbing my elbow before I can wander past him. Once again dressed from head to toe in black, complete with a mask covering half his face while leaving those mismatched eyes out for me to admire.

"What part of the plan said to create a bomb, Cinderfella?"

This man did not show up in my moment of need to lecture me. Clearly, I wasted too much time in the dungeon and on my way here, admiring him. It shouldn't even be a competition between who has my affections between him and the prince I left back in the castle, who I hope is safe from all of my meddling. I had forgotten the Necromancer's a brusque ass.

"You should have made a better plan," I gripe as he pulls me to him.

He claps a hand over my mouth and steps back into the bushes. "Quiet," he hisses and then snaps a command under his breath in a language I don't speak.

The roses seem to understand, though. They swivel floral heads towards us and then sweep their leaves back to reveal a hiding spot. The Necromancer in black and me in red and white and a brilliant coat of pink, we're entirely engulfed by the garden as if it's the only place we've ever been expected.

I hold my breath, my back pressed to the Necromancer's front as the hedge made of viney rose bushes curls back around us, sealing us together in an embrace. This is… Well, intimate seems too intense a word to use, but I can't think of another way to describe it. All of him is pressed into the back of all of me. We're so very close to each other, his gloved hand gentle even as it continues to cover my mouth. His other arm is wrapped around my middle, supporting my weight back against him as his hand lingers near my hip.

This is almost more scandalous than some of the things I've done in the quiet corners of a barn with a willing partner.

Almost.

Encased in roses, quivering between the effort to stay perfectly still and give into the urge to lean further back into him, I focus on how his breath trickles through his mask to tickle the back of my neck. His heart is beating hard enough for me to feel it reverberating through my own chest. The Necromancer must have been running towards me from the end of the maze before I met him here. That, or he's more worried than he ever lets on.

The guards finally catch up to us, far closer than I ever realized they were from the distorted way their yells chased me through the maze. I had minutes before I would have been captured if the Necromancer hadn't found me first. Gold armor clanks by us, all of them streaked with the pink glitter that still brands the air. The guards stomp through the gardens, swinging swords and hacking away any vines that get in their way. The sheer number of men sent to detain me would be unnerving if I hadn't been informed by the king himself that I'm the biggest enemy of his empire. We watch them run by, and I lose track of the number of weapons they're each carrying. Nobody in the garden is here to detain me. The king wants me dead, and they're going to do it in his honor if they find me.

I'm shaking without realizing it and trying to be still, trying not to shift back on the Necromancer or out in any way that leaves me pricked by the gnarly bushes entwined around us.

I was moments from being hacked to bits, and I'm too gods damned exhausted to hide the terror filling me now.

The Necromancer brushes his thumb over my cheek. It's an unprompted response. He must feel me shaking. We're too close not to. Still, a small piece of my heart melts at the smallest show of kindness.

Seconds stretch mercilessly into minutes as the guards advance through the gardens, their steps nearly as deafening as my glitter bomb. We stay together, hidden in the roses, well after they pass us, listening between panted breaths to the sound of them leaving the gardens and then circling around the castle to continue the very important search for me.

Me. The criminal. The magic wielder with no care for the world around himself.

They called me all sorts of things in their walk past us. Curses. Slurs. The story King Anerald spun about me is already becoming something bigger, nastier, and incredibly malevolent. These people will follow his lead and twist his words to fit their own agenda as needed. Nobody wants to hear my side.

I had my head in the clouds in the tavern. My father had created a safe environment, and I'd let myself forget reality in order to spend more time thinking about fairytales and improvements to our very small corner of the world. Fairytales don't get to be true if we don't fight for them. Grief flashes through me, a flood for what should have been and what was taken from me, but it evaporates quickly to be replaced with a rage that has been festering my entire life.

The world isn't fair, but it could be.

My mother was taken, and I now have a target on my back, but this story doesn't have to end with me following her steps to a carefully curated demise.

I get to decide the shape of my story.

It takes me three slow breaths to calm the boiling in my veins. The Necromancer lets my face go, giving me the space he can for me to breathe and consider my options. A week ago, I would have flung myself out of these rose bushes and figured out my emotions with my fists without care for repercussions to myself. Now, I sit and wait and bide my time.

They can call me whatever they want. They can get sick drinking down the lies of a tyrant. I'm still going to win this particular excursion. As superior or right-minded as they think they are, none of them realized I was sweating a hands-width away from them, tucked against someone even more powerful than myself.

"Do you think it's safe?" I dare to whisper when I'm feeling calmed and more ready to deal with the next stage of our escape.

The flowers press closer to me, perhaps more curious than I am about his answer. It's foolish to think they're jealous of his proximity to me, but the thought crosses my mind as more thorns press into my exposed skin while the greenest leaves caress his wrist next to my face.

"You stopped being safe the moment you met me."

I roll my eyes at him, aware that only the contaminated night air and the roses will know I've done so. He can play the part of the tortured hero, but I know the decisions I've made up until this point. It was my own fault that I cast a bad wish into the universe and lost my father. I'm the one who couldn't give my newly acquired fairy godmother two minutes of my time before trouncing into the forest to fix my problem. I lost her in a hole in the ground and then entered a party to satiate my own curiosity in the guise of saving her. Not to mention the entire chase with the dragon that has become somewhat of a personal pet, the accidental assassination attempt on the prince, and an escape from a literal army of guards hellbent on taking me dead instead of alive. Safety was never my top priority.

I wriggle in his hold, turning around to face him even as the blanket of roses tries to keep me in place, and force him to meet my gaze with that mismatched tone of brown and gray. "We can't just stay here all night. Is it safe enough to make a run for it?"

"Where are we going to go?"

"I thought you had a plan."

He responds with a chuckle that has my heart twirling. "I gave you magical boots that you seem to have lost. Why would I trust you with my plans?"

I let my lips pull into a smile. "So, you admit you have a plan."

One of his hands still lingers on my hip, the other caresses my jaw. "With you involved, I have to have several plans."

Whatever words I had lined up next flee me entirely. I'm more than distracted. He's staring at me, his gaze catching on the curve of my lips. Crowned in roses, the Necromancer takes up the sole focus of my world.

Yes, there's a king who wants me dead.

Yes, there's an army of men who are searching for me in pursuit of that very purpose.

Yes, I should be running and sprinting and altogether getting the heck out of this kingdom.

But he's here and his hands are on me and for a moment I want to be crazy enough to believe he's under the same spell I feel unraveling in my veins. It's not magic I cast all on my own. There's been a taut string pulled between the two of us since he swaggered into the rebellion meeting and called me out on my bluff.

"I wish I could see the rest of your face," I blurt without thinking about it.

He visibly swallows. Then, hesitates. The fingers on my hips tremble. I almost think he's going to give in, but he responds in a low voice that deters any argument.

"Close your eyes."

I'm out of things to lose and clinging to a moment I know will have to end, so I let my eyelids fall. There's a rustle. Rose petals brush my cheek, my throat, my bloodied knuckles. The Necromancer leans into me, his body heat the only warmth in this winter night.

"My identity is a secret that protects more people than just me, Cinderfella, so I can't share it just yet." We linger in a maze of roses, too close to be just allies and yet not close enough to slow the fire burning through my veins. "But if you want…"

Want cannot cover the depths of my desire. Need isn't a strong enough word, either. I craved him in my fantasies while trapped in the dungeons. I let him traipse through my thoughts every other moment of my day. The Necromancer is here and he's offering, and I would be a fool to stop now.

So, my hands reach up to cup the back of his head even as my eyes remain closed and I gently tug him down to me. The Necromancer isn't complacent. He meets me halfway with more passion than I could have assumed. Soft lips quickly followed by his tongue and teeth on my bottom lip as he pushes for as much as I want to give. This isn't a boy fumbling with the unknown in a secret meeting. This is a man who knows what he's doing, what he wants, and, more than anything, it seems he wants me.

Safe in a hedge, he magicked around us; he doesn't pull away from the rough edge of the beard I haven't had a chance to trim. He kisses me gently at first and then deeper, breathing in a sudden chuckling growl when I change the rhythm. The Necromancer kisses me again and again. He kisses me on purpose as though he's been thinking about this as much as I have.

When he pulls away, lingering in darkness and roses, I wait until he has his mask back in place to clear my throat and open my eyes. "Well, that was…" My face has to be pinker than all of the glitter that exploded in the castle. "Where are we going after this?"

All playfulness leaves his expression. "You're going back to the forest. Wynnifred should be waiting for your arrival to make amends."

That's over a three hour walk from here with no distractions or altercations with the guards and a whole lot of cutting through personal property to avoid the main roads. Impossible. Besides, I spent all night trying to track this man down. I'm not leaving him now. Not even the Necromancer gets to kiss me and then leave.

"If you want to regroup in the forest, that's fine, but I'm going where you go."

I can't see the bottom half of his face, but I think he chews on his bottom lip before letting out a sigh. "I can't be expected to babysit you all night, Cinderfella."

"I'm not leaving your side until we have Gemma back," I insist, ignoring the patronizing twist of his words and keeping my grin to a minimum as I take in the way the glitter covering my body has transferred to him in pink patches everywhere we were pressed against each other.

His gaze flicks upwards, to the slim edge of the moon, and then back down to me. "Things are about to get really bad here, not like anything you've ever seen. The crown is scared of that act of magic you committed in the city center, and this glitter bomb isn't going to make anything easier. They want to make an example out of you," he lets that last bit linger for a breath before pushing once more for me to go to the forest with a terse tilt of his chin. "Leaving now is probably your only chance to get away from all of this."

I could argue with him all night. I'd rather be kissing him. Instead, I look at the gardens, at the flowers that still lean towards his broad shoulders, and shrug. "Are you just trying to get out of telling me the truth about yourself? I'm making a vow now that I won't keep kissing men who can't tell me their real name."

For the first time since meeting him, the Necromancer looks as caught off guard as I always feel around him, concern and mirth sparring in his eyes. "You really want to stay and deal with things that don't concern you, Cinderfella?"

Maybe I'm reading too much into this. Maybe I'm delusional. I can't tell anymore. Magic has warped my sense of reality. It feels only natural to reach out and lay a hand on his chest, his steady heartbeat a soft anchor keeping me grounded in this moment while his eyes flare with thoughts I wish I could glimpse.

"My fairy godmother told me that we would have to be a little more extraordinary than we originally anticipated to survive these times. I think this kingdom deserves to see people who fight back against the wrongs of their tyrants, especially people who don't look or act the way society deems proper. I'm done running," I add quickly, his eyes unwavering in their devoted hold of my gaze. "I want to be where you are, teaching people and helping people and doing whatever needs to be done to make the world a better place. You've made me believe that's still possible, so I don't want to leave you, okay?"

Carefully, almost reverently, he clasps a hand over mine, holding me securely to his chest. "I can't decide if you're simply brilliant or a brilliant fool."

"Let's stay together and find out."

I've made my proposal. I've thrown down a metaphorical gauntlet, and I'm waiting for him to pick it up. He has to. The man broke into the castle dungeon to persuade me off the floor and back out into this chaotic mess of an attempted revolution. He hid me in roses. He kissed me like I would be the last person to ever matter to him. He has to accept the fact that I'm his problem now.

As much as I liked talking with the prince, as much as I want to pretend there's something that can flourish there, I've made my decision. The Necromancer is still way out of my league. He's a looming power that makes my knees weak for several reasons. He's someone who is also no one and yet takes it upon himself to try to make the world a better place.

I think he and Gemma would be good friends if they could meet.

My own father pointed him out to me on our last night together.

If that's not fate nudging me in this direction, then I don't know what else to believe in.

Tapping my fingers with one of his own, he finally nods. "Fine, but I don't want any complaints when I make you work on your magic."

My insides are fireworks on a holiday, they're as warm as all the stars in the sky, and I'm aflame in front of him. "Deal."

I don't know if it's the same feeling alight in his chest, but he doesn't let my hand go. Maybe he holds onto me because he's sure I'll be lost on my own and can't afford yet another distraction from me. Whatever the reason, I flee the castle gardens hand in hand with the Necromancer.

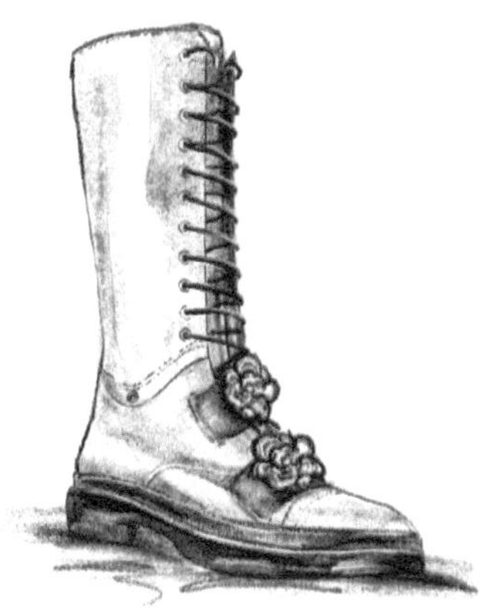

18

The cloud of pink glitter extends far from the reaches of the castle. Carried by the wind, it sticks to roofs and carriages and coats the ground in a fairytale shade that the king will hate having to look at when it's lit up by the morning sun.

I hope the prince sees it and thinks of me. Maybe it'll bring him solace in the morning. Not all rebellions get a standard color code, but I think pink is a pretty good one.

The paths directly outside of the castle had the most guards, all of them bleary-eyed from their exposure to my glitter bomb and not expecting to stop two people leaving the castle grounds. Servants milled around with rags to wipe at glitter from their patrons, the entirety of the castle seemingly evacuated. Heads bowed, fingers interlocked, we walked right by the guards as an overwhelming amount of nobility crowded around the lawns in embroidered robes and hair curlers and odd contraptions I couldn't name for the sake of retaining their beauty. Everyone was too busy asking questions about what happened to worry about us moving past them.

"Looks like my plan paid off," I whisper at the Necromancer's back as he pulls me from the castle and into the surrounding city.

"It's not a plan if you just cause chaos, Cinderfella."

I laugh. A real sound. A tired one. Emotions bubble close to the surface, making my nose tingle and my already irritated eyes prickle. Gods, we're free of the castle and on our way to the forest, and I think everything might be okay after all.

I'm so much closer to finding Gemma again.

To seeing Wynnifred and finding out what she can do to help me reverse my wish because I did deliver her spell and paid far too many consequences for it and I kind of blew up my only other option to fixing it myself.

My life, wrecked from a single wish, is back on track.

Hope is a blanket over my shoulders as we brace ourselves in the frigid temperatures of winter. I barely notice the cold with the Necromaner's warm, gloved hand keeping hold of mine. He, however, seems to notice it quite a bit, throwing looks over his shoulder at me as my teeth chatter.

Racing us past a string of upper-class shops showing off brilliant gowns that cost more than I could make in five years, the Necromancer tucks us into an alley and grabs the collar of his coat, unbuttoning it.

"I don't think undressing makes us more stealthy."

"The castle is going to try to keep this quiet for as long as they can, but we can't escape if you wake up the neighboring towns with your shivering."

Oh. He's worried about me. Because I would mess up his plan to escape by simply being myself, that fact doesn't seem to matter, though, as he pulls his arms out of the sleeves and holds them out for me.

The long, black coat is slightly too big on me and incredibly warm. Far too warm for someone who wants people to believe that he works exclusively with the dead. I turn back towards him, buttoning the middle two buttons to secure myself into his clothes, and grin at him.

"How do I look?"

I wish he weren't wearing that gods damned mask. As is, I think he smiles at me. Without the hood up to cover the top of his head, I can finally see that he has brown hair that looks soft to the touch. It's pulled into a secure knot at the back of his neck. I've never known myself to be a hair-puller, but I think that'll be worked into my fantasies shortly.

"Like you won't freeze," he murmurs, reaching forward to fix the collar, his hands lingering a little bit longer on my shoulders than necessary because he pretends to be cool and composed, but he feels just as riled as I do and can't do anything about it since I've made sure we won't kiss again until he feels comfortable telling me the truth.

He goes to pull away, and I reach up, our hands brushing as I stare at him. Dressed in all black from his mask to his sleeved shirt to his pants and boots, the scrap of white at his shoulder is stark in comparison. Too slow to pull away, I hold him as I reach forward to pull back his sleeve.

"Are you hurt?"

His free hand clamps down on my wrist before I can reveal more of the bandage. "Some asshole got in a good shot. I'll be fine."

All the handsome men in my life can't seem to avoid injuries to their shoulders.

Which seems too coincidental.

But that doesn't make sense.

The prince…

I open my mouth to ask a question, to push, to pester, to see if the details add up to what I think they will, but he speaks first. "Why don't you just focus on trying to keep up?"

I would take some offense to that if he didn't follow it up by interlocking our fingers once more and tugging me back out into the city streets. Our quick steps echo as we briskly move through the upper quarters. I've never spent much time up here. There seems to be a bakery on every corner. There are more places to buy just beverages than there are actual eateries down by my home. The frivolity and uselessness of the noble cities bother me more than I can say.

Some of us starve and barely pay our bills, and these people are out having tea parties every afternoon for the sake of not having enough work to fill their days.

It's a broken system.

I wonder if the prince has a solution for that, too, or if he has been distracted by playing dress up.

It's probably a problem that all the people I'm attracted to currently are political leaders looking to destroy the foundation of the place that has been my home for almost thirty years. I've made my choice, though. Briargild will change with me regardless of the identity of the man at my side.

My mind is turning on details that shouldn't matter so much in the middle of my run away from the kingdom, but I can't seem to stop it. "You're going to have to let me call you something besides the Necromancer if we're going to be hanging out together like this."

We're outside a butcher's shop. A single lantern burns somewhere behind the polished glass. Someone is awake in there, working late and probably watching us linger on the steps outside of his shop.

The Necromancer pulls me with him away. "I wouldn't exactly call this hanging out."

The crisp, clean lines of the upper city bleed into the unrefined squalor of pretty much everywhere else. We pass through the city center, a ghost town at this late hour, without the crowds or vendors from the other day. The walls of the surrounding buildings are still spattered with pink. There are lingering, glittering footprints from Skelly on the ground that we follow for a few minutes before they dip into a direction that the Necromancer isn't using for our exit.

"You do have a name, though, right?"

Windows boasting well-kept flower boxes have been exchanged for boarded-up spaces. Cracks appear in the streets, and then the pavement is completely lost, replaced with the kind of dirt roads I've spent my entire life walking down. Gold no longer tracks its way into the impoverished lower city, but my glitter has landed in the empty streets and nested on top of mailboxes and is tucked into door hinges.

"My name isn't important."

Pink flecks hang in the air here, too, the wind having found fascination with my magic and taken it on a whim. Decades may pass before the last of the pink glitter is washed away from the window sills and cleaned from gutters and scooped out of drains. Maybe it'll never be gone. Perhaps it'll be like that first spell I cast, the carnivorous plant turned beautiful flower, and the entirety of the kingdom will bear the lingering mark of my existence.

With how likely it is that I'll die sooner rather than later, painted a martyr for the people or a criminal against the crown, it is nice to momentarily think I'll last here in the kingdom where my heart was born.

Alarms rip through the silent streets. It seems the king and his guards have figured out I escaped their clutches. They're letting the rest of the kingdom know that I'm a fugitive who should be stopped at all costs. I grit my teeth against the sharp ringing as the Necromancer lets out a curse. He's been huffing and puffing for the better part of the last three streets. We're both exhausted and sweaty, and I'd had a fleeting belief we would get out of the kingdom quietly before it came to this.

Already, lights flicker to life in the windows around us. Candles are held by sleepy neighbors. Doors crack open as we move past, far too many eyes taking in our retreat.

"We can slow down if you need," I tell my companion even as my ears pound with my overzealous pulse.

The Necromancer was dragging me at first. Now, I could easily overtake him. His steps are faltering. I'm not sure we'll make it back to the forest before the guards can catch up to us in this condition.

"I don't need special treatment," he grumbles back at me, pushing me into yet another alley. "We need to get off the main roads."

The two of us stagger through the mud and trash-covered space, his breath pluming in front of him in jagged clouds through his thin mask. Around, the brown walls seem to tip in closer. We scrape through them and out into a row of tiny backyards.

"We have a head start on them. There's no way any of them will be out this way yet, and I need you in fighting condition if we're going to survive the forest," I insist, pulling on his hand to slow him down.

If the man who is better at magic drops dead from exhaustion, we'll be screwed in a brand new, totally avoidable way. He lets out a frustrated groan, his steps faltering for only a moment. Glancing one way and then the other to check for potential hazards like he's done a hundred times before now, he whirls towards me.

"We're not racing men, Cinderfella. We're trying to get beyond the barrier."

Barrier. The towers erected around the kingdom's limit that held the golden walls I shattered on my return.

"I broke it."

"You caused an inconvenience, Cinderfella," he jerks my arm, pulling me off balance, but keeping me out of a very deep puddle of mud as he takes three more steps into the yard, cramped with what could be weeds or perhaps herbs waiting out the cold season to flourish once more. "You were in a dungeon for days, and the city mages have been hard at work strengthening it. If we're not beyond the barrier before the runes are activated…"

His voice trails off, and he pulls me again, walking forward regardless of my resistance. We're almost back to the streets, I recognize, about twenty more minutes from the forest's edge. Two streets over from Harold's tailor shop, we're on the fastest route back to the witch's cottage. There's no way we won't make it.

"I've walked through the barrier twice now, you know?" I grumble at his back, and then, because I'm petty and tired and not in the mood to be ignored, I add, "The prince talked to me a lot nicer than you. I'm sure he could have explained the intricacies of the barrier and why you're so worried about it."

All of my tugging and resistance was unnecessary. The Necromancer stops and turns back towards me, dropping my hand with an irritated flick. His eyes are wild as he speaks.

"The manacles that blocked your magic in the dungeon, Cinderfella? There's a series of runes etched into the guard towers all around Briargild. It takes one signal to the guards there to activate their post, and then it'll form a circle that stops magic inside Briargild. This isn't just about us. It's now going to affect everyone trapped here. It's the king's safeguard against any magical rebellion, and it hasn't been tested, so I have no idea what kind of effects it'll have on Briargild."

Oh. Well, that does make sense, and it sounds bad. I open and close my mouth without answering.

"Do you think the prince could have done better than that?"

Wow. Is that jealousy coating his words?

I want to say something, to press him to tell me more, but he grabs my hand and turns to leave. And then he drops his hold on me like I'm made of fire and he is only ice.

The Necromancer isn't moving. As though his legs are frozen in the mud he saved me from, he stands like a pillar in the middle of the yard while his shoulders shake and panted puffs of air bubble out from the edges of his mask.

I look around for the danger he must have seen. It's far too late for regular people to be awake. They have just a few hours to rest before it's once more time to wake up and go about the exhausting cycle of daily chores and responsibilities. There isn't the luxury of a servant to warm their houses or fetch their morning meal. Out here, there's only self-reliance or the need to care for one another that drives them through their days. If they haven't woken from the alarms, I hope not to disturb them with my conversations in their backyards.

There isn't anything out here besides the two of us.

"What's wrong?"

He shakes his head, wavering on his feet. "Can't you feel the absence of magic?"

Ummmm no. I feel as good as I have since he threw me the key to release my shackles in the dungeon. Actually, better, the prince's medicinal herbs are helping me recover faster than I should have. I'm tired, but my muscles are fine and my magic is very much alive, a secondary pulse to my own heart. Before absorbing Gemma's wand, I spent every single day as a magicless citizen. I should at least feel like that, right?

"I feel fine. We need to get to the forest."

He offers me one curt nod as a response, but remains frozen. This is the man who came to bail me out of the dungeons, the one prepared with speeches and magical artifacts designed to assist me. This is the man who didn't hesitate to throw bone shards at me or send a dragon to literally eat me. This is the Necromancer. He doesn't freeze or stumble or ever stop knowing what to do.

"Eli," his voice is a low whisper, a lure pulling me back to reality. "I can't get to the forest like this. You need to leave me."

I reach out, holding his hand again, even as he tries to push me away. "That's ridiculous. We'll go together. I told you I wouldn't leave your side until I got Gemma back."

He shakes his head, still struggling to shake me off, his pupils blown open as if they can find a better solution to his problem if only they can be wide enough. "Wynnifred will assist you. You enter the forest and keep walking until she finds you. She wants to bring back the fairy godmother just as much as you do, but I can't help you anymore."

I don't understand why he's being so stubborn. We're not being closely trailed by the guards. There's no audience to our conversation. It's just him and me and the stars blinking above.

"We're going together," I insist again, tugging harder.

The Necromancer collapses with a pained exultation. Covered in mud as well as glitter, he makes no move to push himself up from the ground. He doesn't meet my gaze when I drop down next to him, apologies rushing over my lips like water over a cliff.

"I won't leave you here," I say again, hesitant to touch him as he glares off into the darkness around us.

Distantly, there's another alarm bell. One more shrill than the last. Everyone who slept through the first sounds is about to wake up to this one. We can't stay here.

"Tell me why you can't go now," I press him, my words inflicting a different kind of wound as he flinches and continues to look away.

"Eli," he says, clearly unaware of the way his tone makes my heart beat faster even as I wish he would go back to using the teasing syllables of my surname. "You are the kingdom's hope. I will be fine here. It's you who has to leave right now."

I don't have any idea what that means, so I stay focused on my argument. "I'm not leaving you in the dirt after you risked everything to save me."

He lets out a desperate sound, something between an exasperated cough and a strangled laugh. "You have no idea what I risked. It's time for you to go."

His hand on my chest is firm, pressing me backwards as lights begin to ignite around the city. The people are awake. We'll have a mob trying to cage us before long. Without knowing what's happening, they'll be all too reckless with telling the guards there are two men on the ground between lettuce scraps and carrot greens. I'm incredibly conspicuous in my clothes from the prince.

I'll be hanged. Beheaded. Dragged through the streets and made an example of. The same will come of the Necromancer.

And, so long as he isn't willing to take off that mask, there isn't a damn prince to save us now.

So, it has to be me.

Wiping a hand over my face, I take a deep breath to steady my voice and to keep my frustration and panic at bay. "Without magic, you feel weak and scared. I understand. This isn't the time to give up, though. We have to push forward into the forest. Please. Let me help you."

His jaw tenses. I think he's going to yell at me. He isn't given the chance before curious strangers peek their heads around to our terrible hiding spot.

"I think we've got something here."

"Is someone hurt?"

"What the heck is happening back there?"

"Guards!"

I want to believe that if Gemma's magic hadn't erased my identity, these people would be quiet. They would recognize the kind face from behind the tavern bar, and they would hold their tongues in sympathetic regard for the man who once poured their drinks on their hardest days. I want to believe the people here wouldn't turn on us immediately.

Believing means nothing right now.

The people from the edge of the kingdom aren't coming to stop us, but they're alerting officials. They've hammered down the nail in our shared coffin. The Necromancer and I have no hope of a stealthy escape.

He still hasn't tried to get off the ground.

"We didn't escape the castle dungeon to give up here in the mud," I lecture him, my words sneaking past clenched teeth as I place my arms under his knees and behind his shoulders.

The Necromancer argues. He tells me to stop. He struggles, his arms flailing in opposite directions as if he has a chance to slow me down.

I've made up my mind.

We're going to make it past the barrier.

Somehow, I get to my feet despite his actions to the contrary. A crowd has gathered, but none move to stop us as I stagger out of the garden and back towards the forest. Now would be a great time to attempt magic, to conjure up something to help me, but I don't dare slow down. If the Necromancer is stranded without his magic, I probably just haven't been affected due to my limited experience and the cocktail of healing herbs I've taken in the last few hours. I know plenty about working hard and persevering, though.

Each step is weighed down by the man in my arms, the one who is no longer fighting me, but has turned his gaze away from me as if he is still expecting me to drop him and save myself. He didn't leave me to get caught in the castle's rose garden. I'm just returning the favor.

For whatever reason, I have the means to get us to safety, and I'm going to do it.

Shouts chase us down the last streets. The metallic clang of armor vibrates the air. We're far from alone now. I don't dare look back.

My lungs ablaze and my head spinning from the lack of oxygen, I cling tighter to the Necromancer and plunge ever forward. I don't pay attention to the snow that begins to fall or to the uneven dirt paths. I have a single line of thought. We will survive.

Arrows appear as I near the edge of the kingdom. The golden wall is erect and shimmering against the dark night. The Necromancer was right. Of course, he was. He's been planning on stopping King Anerald for a long time now and has uncovered some of the underhanded planning of the crooked king. It makes sense that the rebels met in the forest for privacy, but they also needed to stay connected to their magic.

"Hold on, we're going to be okay," I huff out to him, nearing the shimmering wall threatening to keep us in.

Last time I walked right through. When I came back with Gemma and Skelly, it broke. I don't know what effect it'll have this time, but staying here isn't an option.

In response, the Necromancer buries his fingers into the front of my shirt, but keeps his face on the coming wall. He wants to know what'll happen, too. If anything, it'll be a better way to go out than serving as kindling for the king's next pyre. Behind us, guards demand we stop. Shouts tear through the night's air. The smoky scent of torches chases us, the guards having to rely on sticks and flames like the rest of us, without their access to magical light sources in the current state of the kingdom. Everything is a blur of stone and gold, and I can't slow down.

I charge straight into the barrier with the Necromancer clutched as tightly to my body as possible. It singes me from my fingertips to my hairline, but, again, I'm allowed to pass through it. The Necromancer lets out a cry of pain in my arms and no other complaint. It wasn't fun, but the zap wasn't enough to deter us in our desperate state.

Now, it's just us and the forest. The trees are right there. Danger doesn't stop following. Calls are sent out between the guards, and those on the top of the towers release a volley of arrows. Around me, the trees offer all the protection they can, bleeding sap as the sharpened points plunge into their meaty torsos. Weapons meant for me, to slow me, to stay my step, to finish me and drag me off the face of this earth, attack everything else. They pierce the ground and the trees, and one whizzes terribly close to us. I hear the Necromancer gasp as I stumble further forward, his palm steady on my chest.

Reaching the forest wasn't nearly enough.

The guards continue to chase us as I find paths that resemble the same ones that led Gemma to a hole in the ground and that Skelly scaled in his wild attempt to attack me. More arrows let out muffled thwacks as they hit stones and ricochet from the impact. Splinters cling to my clothes. There are pine needles in my hair. None of it matters.

I am nothing but a will to move and live.

"Cinderfella," the Necromancer snaps, pulling at my collar to bring my attention to him. "My magic is back!"

Great. Fantastic. I don't have a spell at the ready to hurl backwards at the approaching flanks of the castle guard, but I know that I won't be alone with the Necromancer, capable of casting his own magic once again. We just need to be able to set him down, so the two of us can face the hordes of armored men together.

I stagger into a clearing. Maybe it's the same spot I first set eyes on the Necromancer, without the magic to make it appear as spring. Maybe I'll think of him every time I walk into a grassy circle with the trees as a curious audience around me. Either way, there's grass underfoot and space to spread our magic, and likely a thousand bones beneath us for him to unearth; this man is my greatest ally, even as he remains a mystery who proclaimed that he isn't a necromancer.

I set him down on weak legs, and he tilts down to his knees. "I'm fine. Pay attention. They aren't far behind." He commands when I try to help him back up.

Of course. There's a league of guards looking for my general demise. I should be a little more concerned about it, shouldn't I? Instead, my gaze lingers on his knees, the way the grass bends for him like a crowd of devotees curling to the ground to give him the greatest show of affection. I have to tear my head away from the scene before I become too enraptured by it and fall to the ground as well.

"Any plans?"

He scoffs. "I can't be doing all the thinking for you, Cinderfella."

Apparently, he's extra grouchy when he's momentarily lost his connection to magic. I huff and puff and make no actual complaints about the trembling in my forearms or the way my lungs still want to jump out of my body and leave me to wither alone. One of us has been really pulling all the weight of this team, and I might be bold enough to say it's me.

I'd like to see him pull out some bones or roses that fix the problem at hand.

That would be much better than simply snapping at me.

As is, our company has arrived. "Hands up or we fire!"

"Go away, and we won't make you regret chasing us out here," I shout back, cupping my hands around my mouth while the Necromancer pulls at my pant leg like he can make me stop speaking out of turn.

He can't. Nobody can.

I've worked so hard to get here. I'm not going back to the dungeons. I'm not going to be quiet and surrender. I'm going…

I'm going to do some magic and make them wish they had never left their homes.

Inspiration strikes me as I glare up at the wispy clouds in the sky. The snow falling on Briargild hasn't quite reached us here. There are a few ways to make a guard truly unhappy. Bad weather is definitely up there as one of the worst things they have to deal with when not chasing after criminals against the crown.

"Last chance!"

Vaguely, I see them raise their weapons. Some have changed to close distance options like swords and daggers, and a mace or two. Others are still holding onto bows with sharpened arrows already notched and pointed towards us. Off to my left, I see a couple of figures in robes. Not armor. It seems they've brought their own magic to the forefront of this battle.

I don't need any chances from them. Bracing myself in front of the Necromancer to hopefully shield him should things go wrong, I reach my hands up towards the air and utter a single word. "Rain!"

Honestly, I expected it to take a moment. I thought more clouds would roll in. Instead, buckets-worth of water are dumped onto the field. We're ankle deep in mud in seconds, and I can hardly hear the complaints of the guards through the hammering insistence of raindrops all around us.

The snow that had already fallen turns into slush, and people start slipping all around me. There are curses and shouts. Someone exclaims that this isn't possible, but they don't know me. I crafted a blizzard indoors. I helped build a gods damned dragon. A little rain is nothing for me.

That being said, I hear the Necromancer curse at me for my spontaneous and messy spell before muttering his own to pull magic from the ground. Tree roots emerge, grabbing people and tossing them aside as if they weigh no more than a bag of flour. There are bone shards pelting guards in their exposed bits. We're making a noticeable stand.

But it is just the two of us against an army.

The guards who are not immediately deterred by the rain and the initial onslaught are coming closer. They have us surrounded. Even if I had the strength to pick the Necromancer back up, my limbs trembling from the exertion of running this far and casting magic far beyond my physical prowess, there's nowhere to go. We don't have a safe place to hide from this.

I'm just choosing not to go down without a fight.

"Eli!"

The Necromancer is next to me, smeared with mud, his clothes obviously drenched as his sleeves cling to his muscled shoulders in a way that is incredibly distracting. There isn't really time to speak to him. It's nice to know he'll be the last one to say my name.

To the side, the crown-officiated magic wielders are pushing out fire in blooming streaks of orange that chew through my rain. The wet grass is crisped and crunches underfoot as they come nearer, trapping us in a circle of fire almost more deadly than the armed men coming for our heads. We are caught between a ring of fire and imminent death. I guess we gave them a good run.

The Necromancer reaches up to pull me down by the back of his coat. Mud squelches under my knees. The prince is never getting these clothes back.

"Close your eyes."

No. I laid in the dungeon and thought over the concept of my death. This isn't what I wanted, but it is a bit of an homage to my mother. She, too, cast too much magic and found herself burned for it. Maybe this is where my life was always headed.

Maybe there isn't a way to escape the generational story.

I should have spent more time pestering my father about the things he remembered about her. We didn't want to spend our time together being sad, and she was a bleeding wound that never closed up. It would have been nice to know about the kingdom she traveled from, the way they treated magic, the way she was seen and respected, and how she rebelled against every person in the place that became my hometown when she married a poor man who made her his entire world. I wish I had been braver. I hope there's a chance to see her in whatever comes next.

The flames are so close. They lick over my hands and my hair, and one stray spark singes my collar. I'm not going to shut my eyes and give them the benefit of turning me into something less than human.

They're going to look at me and know the crimes they committed, and I hope to haunt them the way my mother's absence has followed me for my entire lifetime.

"Trust me and shut your eyes, Cinderfella."

My last name. The man kneeling beside me has a plan. Pride blooms in my chest and my heart nudges me to listen to him, but I shake my head.

"Whatever you're going to do, do it now."

Rain drips from his brow. There's grass stuck in his hair. Mud dirties his mask as the thing clings helplessly to his jaw. Still, he's unbothered by everything except for me.

"I don't want you to see me like this."

The heat of the flames is making me sweat despite the chilling rain turning to a drizzle, my magic faltering in the face of this dilemma. I'm out of last second plans and single words that dazzle those who would dare harm me. If he's going to do something, I'm going to be here to watch and appreciate him for whatever his heroics entail.

"I'm not going to see you again if you don't save us right now," I gush, wincing as a flame licks at my knuckles and my sleeve catches on fire.

With a curse, the Necromancer remains kneeling but straightens his shoulders and looks out to the nearing circle of danger. His shout rings out next to me, the word lost to the roar of flames and the general commotion of the oncoming guards. His intonation strikes me in the heart nonetheless. This is the voice of a man made into a god.

Magic is the sword that slices through his enemies. Even kneeling in the dirt, he is a being for whom all else must bow.

The screams rip through the air before the thud of bodies. Around us, the forest vibrates from the pain and unlocked horror. I squint against the wall of flames to see streaks of red roses and the gold armor they effortlessly throw away from the bodies of guards.

Next to me, the Necromancer pants out another command and then reaches up to his face to tug off his mask. Blood drips from his nose. His brown eye slips into a shade close to the gray of his left.

I barely notice that the fire fades with the crushing fall of the magic wielders as I gape at the man capable of such carnage.

I suspected, and I can't believe it.

More bodies thud, and I tear my gaze from the kneeling man beside me to look at our surroundings. We're no longer in a clearing of grass. We're in a scorched garden. The Necromancer didn't just use objects in the forest at his disposal; he seems to have turned the guards' insides against them.

The Necromancer…

The…

I know his real name, and yet I can't bring myself to comprehend this reality, and so I continue to stare around us. Red roses burst from the chests of the men who followed us. Maroon bleeds across the ground, threatening to taint every last blade of grass and haunt this place forevermore. From a fight to a graveyard, I turn my eyes away before my revulsion can cause me to lose what little food I still have in my stomach.

The Necromancer wobbles next to me. I reach out to catch him before he can crash to the ground.

I'm only beginning to understand the kind of power magic steals from a person, the effort it takes to cast spells, and the limits a body can take. The Necromancer is barely breathing. He looks too small. This man, who has been raised on a pedestal in my mind, is now limp among the bodies he subdued in order to save my life.

Cradling him in my lap, I look around at his sacrifice. Over two dozen men lay reduced to plant nutrients for the sake of my life, and the rest, if they survived, have fled. Nobody has ever done something so dramatic for me.

Yet, I know I would have done the same for him.

Exhausted, shocked, perhaps a mixture of several other things I can't find the words for at this exact moment, I'm only a bundle of exposed nerve endings. I thought my view of the world had been upended when I learned the Necromancer was not truly a man in charge of weaving magic over the dead. That was a far easier thing to understand than this.

Prince Alexander Charming lulls in an unconscious fit in my hold.

The prince that I shot, the one who revealed he was a rebel and then made me tea. That prince. He's the same man who wrapped us in the garden's embrace and followed me out here.

Not just a prince.

Xander.

I'm too tired to stand. The danger is currently subdued. I shrug out of the jacket he let me borrow and lay it over him before pressing my hand to his chest, depending on my fingertips to tell me he's alive, he's breathing, and he's still right here with me.

I just need a few minutes to recover.

I'll get us somewhere safer soon enough.

And then we're going to have a very serious conversation about the secrets between the two of us.

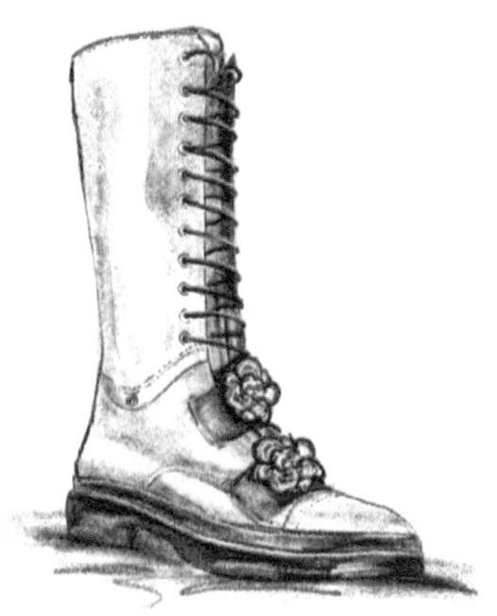

19

Time continues to move whether or not I understand the world around me. The stars have dimmed. The moon, barely visible as she was, turned away from me and dipped beyond the tree line. Sunlight rakes cautious fingertips over the forest floor, flinching as more blood and gore are revealed, the violence something I never needed to see.

In my lap, Xander still doesn't stir.

Half-frozen, clinging to the slowed heartbeat in his chest, I hold him tighter. What else am I supposed to do?

My fairy godmother is gone, along with Skelly.

My father is lost. My home is gone. My kingdom has turned its back on me.

I have no plans to continue forward.

I am so very alone besides the half-dead man in my grasp.

If I believed a wish could save me, I would wish for him to wake up. I would yell it at the trees and kick the blood-stained terrain. Instead, I sit in the icy runoff from our last stand against the Briargild guards and wait.

Which is the absolute worst.

I'm not sure what else I'm supposed to do, though.

I was raised in a tavern. I know how to lighten a bad day with the right cocktail. Hot meals stave off the worst of seasonal depression. Besides the few nicks and scrapes and colds I've survived,

I had no reason to learn anything about medicine. I certainly don't know anything about medical cures from overexposure to magic use.

I just have to wait.

And hope.

No. Actually, no. I'm not that kind of man.

Lurching to my feet, my limbs full of needles that prick with every movement, I stand over the man who saved my life, gently laying him flat on the ground. Twice. He has saved me twice from my own imminent demise. I'm not going to let him freeze out here. I know one person who should be haunting these woods.

Her name is ripped from my throat more from a desire to do something for him than anything else. I don't want to see the witch again. I don't even want to collect on our deal. The spell she had delivered through me didn't kill the prince, and I won't be dipping my hands in any cauldrons to try again. My father wouldn't want to come back because I spilled the blood of someone else.

Even a nobleman.

Even the prince.

Especially the prince, because he's gone out of his way to take care of me, and it's only led to him being exhausted in a dead zone. I think my father would have liked him a lot if they had gotten the chance to meet. I would have liked that scenario. Not access to the crown or riches or anything besides a chance to be closer to Xander.

I'll find another way to fix my bad wish and bring back the tavern.

But I still need the witch of the woods.

"Wynnifred!"

I only dare to creep around the edges of the clearing. Rose vines tug at my shoes and prick my ankles as I move in a steady circle, hands cupped around my mouth to propel my voice into the dense forest beyond. There's no sound of birds or squirrels or the buzz of a firefly. Xander told me over and over again that she would find me if I could just make it to the forest. She has to be able to hear me if I make enough noise.

Keeping Xander always at the corner of my vision, I steadily progress around the battlefield twice, shouting out into an abyss of apologetic trees. There's no backup plan to this action. My lungs are bruised internally from all the running, yelling, and struggling to breathe last night. It takes too much effort to walk slowly, my arms trembling from the act of holding my hands up to my face. Only the sunrise cares to supervise my struggle.

Tears streak my cheeks when I return to his still form in the center of his rosy carnage. Sitting next to him, I lay my hand once more on his chest, check for his breath even as I can see it pluming out of him in small, soft clouds, and try to accept that all of our sacrifices were for nothing. I'm too exhausted to take him, and I refuse to leave him here. Without help, we're screwed.

Leaves crunch somewhere off to my right. I sit up and twist to see what it is. Maybe I was wrong. Maybe there are critters out here. It did sound much larger than the red-furred squirrels that linger in the trees near the kingdom's edge.

There's no way any of these men would wake up, right? Screaming. Writhing. Trapped by thorny roses put there by the man I'm devoted to protecting now. Bile rises to the back of my throat again. I don't think I could handle that.

Thankfully, a slim shape moves at the edge of the clearing, so I'm at least not dealing with a zombie. "If you don't be quiet, Cinderfella, you're going to draw the whole army to my backyard."

Wynn. Wynnifred. I've never been more excited to see her.

She doesn't enter the clearing, her amber eyes too wide as she takes in the mess we made. "Please tell me he's alive."

My words spill over each other faster than I can actually make them coherent, but the message gets across anyhow, Wynn waving a hand to quiet me. I have my hand on his chest. He's still breathing. We're going to be okay because she's here, and she has to be obligated to help after all the crap she already put me through with her cauldron spell. She's the reason he was shot in the first place, so she owes him.

She turns away. Flicking her braided hair over her shoulder, she scoops up her skirt in one hand and starts to trek back through the forest. That's not what's supposed to be happening.

I lurch to my feet, the entirety of the world spinning around me in a blur of green and brown and so much red. "Wait. You have to—"

Her hand is back up, silencing me. "You won't make it very far, and I'm not coming in there. Just let me grab my house."

I don't know what that's supposed to mean. I'm not sure I'm comprehending most of what is happening around me right now. The earth welcomes me as I plop back down next to the Necromancer, to the prince, to Xander, and I lay my hand on his chest once more, assuming my position as his guardian whether he wants me to or not.

My eyelids are terribly heavy. It's taking me too much effort to squint out into the distance and hope I see a cottage wandering about on two legs. I snort. How silly would that be.

Cool pressure weighs my hand down onto Xander's chest, and I turn to see him, his hand holding mine like we did in the garden. His eyes aren't open. His breaths are still so shallow. Yet, I hope he knows in whatever dreamland he's trapped that I'm right here waiting for him to come back.

Unlike the fairytale depictions of witches with cabins on leg-like stilts, Wynn reappears at the edge of the clearing with a dark door behind her. I can almost make out the rest of the structure if I squeeze my eyelids closed, the house shimmering on another plane of existence. Maybe it's fully there, and I'm too riddled with exhaustion to understand it. Whatever the reason, there's a witch in front of a door waiting for me to come closer.

"I cannot step where blood is spilled," she declares, holding her arms across her chest as if the sight alone dissuades her from helping me. "You need to get him inside. I can help him."

Of course. Just one more thing. My life is one long story of Eli and the great endeavor to do all the small tasks in between the great things of those around me.

"I don't want to drag him," I confess when I'm on my feet once more, woozy and blinking away the urging demands from my body to simply lie down and rest for the next century.

"I don't care how you do it, you bring that man here. He alone determines the fate of magical beings. Our kind will not continue if we lose him now."

That's all great and dramatic, but it doesn't give me a way to move him through this field of roses and gruesome evidence. "You asked me to shoot him. I don't think you get to be high and mighty about all of this."

"I obviously didn't know that, Cinderfella! Now, get him in here or his death is on your hands."

Her words spur me in a way I hadn't expected. Maybe I'm the kind of guy who can get more done when yelled at. Maybe I'm just putting aside my needs to make sure Xander is taken care of. Unwilling to give her any credit for the burst of adrenaline coursing through me, I reach down and hook my arms under his body. The tendons in my legs snap and protest, but ultimately, I stand at my full height with his weight firmly in my grasp.

It takes everything in me to walk him the thirteen steps to the edge of the clearing. All of my focus. Several breaths that threaten to ravage the rest of my lungs. Straining muscles in my arms and the push against knees that want to do nothing more than collapse. Rose vines line my pathway, red petals licking at my ankles and reminding me of the chaos caused by the man in my arms.

I never think twice about getting him to safety.

My body gives out when I make it to the edge of the clearing. Holding him tight to my chest, I let my knees crack against the frosted forest floor. Frozen blades of grass crunch and crumple beneath me. All of it stops mattering.

The world is no longer spinning around me. It's fading. The colors are dimming, and I can't see even a few inches from my nose. Distantly, Wynn speaks, but her words are little more than an incessant ringing in my ear like the buzzing of a begrudging bee.

I don't know if I fall forward or backward. Maybe it's to the side. What I vaguely remember is that I fall and Xander, the man who is so impossibly Xander, remains in my arms.

We're safe. At least, as safe as I can promise.

The world curls around me like steam from a hot cup of tea, the next time I'm conscious enough to be aware of it. Sage and mint tangle in the air around me. I'm too warm, my skin slick with sweat as I try to hold onto the vivid blur of impossible dreams.

They hold secrets I can't seem to comprehend.

My heart stutters at the whispers of things I've forgotten in my sleep. Questions rattle against the forefront of my mind. I want to stay here. I want to go back to sleep. I want…

Nothing can come from me staying like this.

Wasn't there something I was taking care of?

Not something. Someone.

My eyes snap open. Above me, dried herbs dangle from the ceiling. Everything comes back to me in a crushing blow. Wynn. The symbolism behind the roses that I'd heard so many rumors about around the tavern: rain and slush and so much red. The Necromancer isn't just some guy in black. He's…

Where's Xander?

I fling out my arms, every muscle in them screaming from the movement. Nobody is nearby. I'm lying on the floor. If I remember the details from my trip with Gemma, I'm lying on the floor of the witch's kitchen.

Lovely.

Groaning, I sit up and rub at my face with shaking hands. My entire life couldn't have prepared me for the past twenty-four hours. I'm still not completely comprehending everything that happened. We ran from the guards. I set off a glitter bomb that is probably going to irritate the kingdom's lungs for the next several years. Roses. My stomach roils at the thought of roses.

And then the impossibility that the prince I can't have is the Necromancer I wanted.

There goes my attempts to date someone closer to my own league.

I'll just go back to being a single tavern keep. The rest of the world has proved to be far more complicated than I can handle. Princes. Magic. Chaos and destruction amid a glitter of bright pink.

I don't think I was made for this kind of story. If it were my choice, I'd be the casual hero in a cozy romance. Here, now, I don't know where exactly I stand. The horrors of the forest aren't the thing of normal fairytales. The things Xander can do…

I have to see him. I need to talk to him.

I lurch to my feet and then look down at myself for the first time. Large, wet leaves cover my arms and torso in shades of muted yellow— my bare arms and midriff. Wynnifred took my shirt. More leaves coated in sticky paste are pressed to my throat. I can't pluck them off myself fast enough, shredding the pieces into a pile that gathers at my feet.

What is this? Who hosts like this? Obviously, I know the witch is much smaller than either me or Xander, and she had to pull us into her home all by herself, which I'm grateful for, but I didn't ask to wake up sticky on top of all of my other qualms. I try to blame my tumultuous emotions on the unfamiliar surroundings and odd circumstances of waking up, but there's an underlying current to all of my actions. It's a shimmering flame like that of a candlewick in a dark cave. The heat of it keeps me going.

I need to know where Xander is before my worry eats me alive.

My feet bare, I stumble along the worn, hardwood floors. I have other things on my mind besides wondering where my shoes have gone. That's the fourth pair. I'd argue that the invisibility boots shouldn't count since I know what happened to them. Three have definitely been lost. I shouldn't be trusted with boots ever again. Xander probably wouldn't have wanted them back anyway after all the running that led to mud and blood and glitter smeared onto them.

He does owe me for dragging him all the way out here instead of letting the King's guards discover him.

His father's guards.

It really wouldn't have been good for the rebellion if its leader had been apprehended before they could truly begin to make changes.

Slower than I would like, still picking at the leaves glued to me until their fragments are buried deep into my fingernails, I walk out of the kitchen and pass the cauldron seating area, where I met with Wynn when she set me up with the terrible deal. There's currently nothing brewing in the oversized bowl. No purple goop designed to ensnare unsuspecting tavern keeps. Everything is empty and quiet and more than a little unnerving.

None of that is enough to deter me from my search for Xander. I told him I would stay with him until we got Gemma back, and I meant it. I think I still mean it, even knowing what he can do with magic under duress.

Soft voices waft towards me from a hidden alcove in the darkened expanse of the back of the witch's cottage. I brush aside the sentient plants that bristle at my proximity. Fear doesn't halt my steps like it did the first time. I'm on a mission.

I'm going to find the man who has both filled my dreams and now lingers in my nightmares as something I risk losing.

I hadn't realized he had become so important.

Breathing through my mouth to somewhat escape the cloying scent of lavender, I plunge into the far end of Wynnifred's living space. A curtain hangs over the only other doorway. Living alone, she probably doesn't need it covered often. Covered in yellow flowers that remind me of the first dress I saw Gemma in, I gently pull it to the side to reveal the other two members of my current group. Wynn is between me and the bed. I can just make out the impression of legs under a thin blanket on the other side of her.

He's here. Obviously, he deserves the bed. The floor creaks as I step in, and the witch whirls to meet me with a hand raised up.

"Hold it, Cinderfella."

No. Not an option. I sweep into the room regardless of her protests, and she's only stopped from trying to drag me back out by Xander clearing his throat.

"It's okay, Wynn. Clearly, he knows who I am."

"I have enough of my own secrets to keep to worry about yours," she waves at him, grabbing a bucket of soapy water and sending me back out of the room after I've only had a moment to stare into Xander's mottled, gray eyes. "You're going to clean up before you come in here and leave a mess."

Right. Of course. I refuse her offers to fill a bath as she herds me through a small doorway into her personal bathroom. A bucket, a sponge, and the sink are fine. I scrub at my chest and throat and arms and stomach until I'm more bubbles than leaves. The layer of sticky residue scrapes off with little effort, contorting the shape of my sponge until I wring it out. It takes me a few more minutes to get it out from under my nails, and then I look up at the mirror.

At myself.

The man who looks the way I feel.

Glitter touches my cheekbones. There's a ring of pink around my pupils that would be startlingly unnatural on anyone else. My eyes haven't gone a completely different color like Xander's, but I'm finally showing evidence that I've been touched by magic.

More than touched. Consumed. Changed.

I think my father was right. I look like my mother. I hope she's proud of me, wherever her ghost has been taken by the wind.

Wynn taps on the door and shoves a bundle of clothes at me. A soft linen top in blue and brown pants. It's almost too abrasive on my sensitive skin.

"Stop overdoing it on the magic, Eli," she lectures when I come out and she sees me pulling the fabric away from my chest. "There won't always be someone around to patch you back up."

"Thanks," I manage instead of starting an argument.

She rolls her amber gaze and crosses her arms over her chest, firmly blocking my path back to Xander. "Look, about the deal, I didn't know who he was when I sent you out to save the kingdom. I wanted to take from Anerald the way he has torn all of us apart from our families and friends, and altogether hurt us, and I thought removing the one royal he seemed to be hiding from us would be the answer. Magic is mischievous, though. I wanted to force change more than anything, and I think the magic took that as a challenge. You weren't just the arrow from me, Cinderfella; you are the first real change this kingdom has seen in decades.

"I just need you to know it wasn't my intent to hurt him. As much as we didn't see eye to eye on things, he has been the best thing to happen for outcasts and magic wielders. I apologize for putting you through the extra trouble."

Since she's the one who brought it up, I let my desire to get back to Xander falter. This is important, too.

"I'm glad I didn't deliver that spell the way you wanted, but I still carried it out. I did my end of the deal. Is there anything you can do to help me with undoing my original wish?"

Her lips pull down at the edges, and she holds out her palm, no longer marred with the golden rune that matched me. "The parameters of our deal were not met. The magic won't stand."

Yeah. Makes sense. I figured it from the moment I watched that golden arrow pierce the prince's shoulder. Still, I didn't ever want to be in a position in which I chose which life to save: the man who raised me or the man who might hold some part of my future. I wanted to have a hope that I could fix everything.

"Don't go getting sad on me," Wynnifred admonishes without giving me a chance to cope with the news. "Magic is special because it's fickle. There isn't just one way to solve a problem. We have plenty more we can try to do. Besides, you're headed to the magic capital of the world to rescue my Gem, so we'll figure out something when you're back."

Her Gem. My fairy godmother. "You know where she is?"

Wynn nods quickly. "The kingdom of Apricity. They're a paranoid bunch. Your magic, combined with his inside that dragon, would have been enough to grant them entry, but they won't let anyone leave their borders once they've entered."

Kingdom. I don't understand. Apricity. That's not a name I've seen on any map, but it's one I heard over and over again in fairytales my father told.

A single ivy vine enters the small hall we've been in and taps Wynnifred on the shoulder. She waves it off and then scoffs at me.

"You should talk with Xander while I set up lunch. The two of you have quite a journey ahead of you still."

I follow that trailing vine as Wynnifred stalks off. It leads me back to the man who is not only a prince but has never been a necromancer. The vine loops itself back around a curtain rod over the one window, and he looks at me with something akin to hope.

I let myself fall into the chair set next to the bed. "You have a lot to explain."

And yet, I feel myself looking him over. Checking him. For injury. For something worse than magic exhaustion. The only obvious change to him is that his eyes match each other in that silver shade.

We shouldn't have survived the fires and arrows and entire force of Briargild's prepared guards. We only did because of him. And he's okay.

My heart patters out an unhelpful rhythm as Xander wets his lips with a nod. "I want you to really listen, okay? You should be mad. I understand if you hate me or can't find a way to forgive me for the way I kept my identity a secret, but there were so many times I wanted more than anything else just to tell you.

"You were the only person who made me second-guess having to do this thing by myself, Eli Cinderfella. I had a handful of bad options, and I refused to drag you down with me, and I'm so sorry that I ended up doing so anyway."

He's right. I am mad. I'm confused, curious, and captivated by him. Mad is far from my biggest emotion.

I can't believe we're talking.

Without a mask between us. Without a crown on his head or guards literally scouring the building for me. We're having a conversation as best as we can as equals.

When I don't speak, he lets out a shaky breath and continues. "My father believes I'm cursed. I was born wrong. I could never live up to his expectations of a man who could lead the kingdom after his time ended."

Carefully, Xander pulls off the blankets to reveal his bare legs. Well, where they should be. Covered in shorts from hip to mid-thigh, his legs end at his knees. I look further down to see where his flesh connects to a carved, wooden leg in place of where his real ones should be. Green leaves wrap around the wooden pieces, melding together the spot where his knee becomes pale flesh instead of dark wood. It's the leaves that respond to his movements as though they crave his touch more than I ever could.

"He might have eventually been able to forgive me for my deformities, but he couldn't accept the magic." Xander sniffs, his fingers absently moving and causing the leaves to twirl for his attention. "My mother was a kind woman. Forgiving. She never cared that I was different, but she wanted to find a way to make my life easier, and so, on her deathbed, knowing that sickness would take her long before she was ready to go, she begged a woman from the outskirts of the kingdom to bring me the gift of magic."

He pauses. Silver gaze flicks to me. He's making sure that I'm following, but I couldn't stop listening now if I wanted.

I know where this is headed.

"Our stories have been intertwined for a very long time, it seems," he starts again, voice gruff with an emotion I can't name. "It was your mother who braved trials I don't know or understand and brought me the gift of magic. I'm sorry she paid the ultimate price for it. I would give up all my magic if I could undo the grief I've caused you."

My stomach has turned into a rock and is attempting to fall through the seat. I thought that's what he would say. Not only did his father kill my mother, make her an example of what would happen to magic wielders in the boundaries of Briargild, but it was because she helped him.

Of course she did, though.

My mom was known for going door to door in the sick season to hand out bowls of soup. She made medicines at night after all the kitchens were done being used for food. There are a hundred customers who continued coming to the tavern long after she was no longer there to keep repaying their respects to her husband in her wake. Her kindness shifted the culture of our corner of the kingdom.

Her kind heart created the man in front of me.

Two men, so very different from what society begs us to be, we're equally haunted and crafted by the mothers we lost too soon.

My chest tightens. I would have given a lot of things to have my mother in my life. It almost feels like an ironic twist of fate that she and I have worked to save the same man. Her magic is the reason he can play with plants with only half a thought.

My father and I managed in the years after our loss of her. Xander might not have survived his father's grief and wrath after losing a family member if not for the magic that coated his veins. Even though it became a weapon for the kingdom, one he has tried to rebel against, that magic is a piece of hope from a woman who believed the world could be better.

"Obviously, I was young, so I don't remember it clearly, but it's said your mother stole the last breath from mine and crafted it along with some spare magic from her time in another kingdom. It took me years to realize I had that magic, that I could use it to move and pretend to be normal, even though I never truly will be. It took me longer to come to the understanding that stolen magic will always carry consequences." He blinks those dazzling, silver eyes at me. "The castle has impressive rose gardens for that exact reason."

"You've killed a lot of people, then?"

With a shrug, he answers, "Accidentally. The first time changed my eye forever, marking me as someone who took more magic than I ever gave back. That's why I needed someone to help me with the revolution. Small magics are within my grasp, but I wouldn't be able to make any grand displays to get my father to step down from the throne without the magic lashing out and taking everyone within a certain vicinity down with me." Xander's voice cracks. "I can't keep watching his laws hurt and kill people from blatant discrimination, so I was getting ready to do something stupid, something that would kill him and me both if it meant that the rest of the kingdom would have a chance to rebuild, but then you walked into my life."

Warmth blooms along my rib cage. It's daisies pushing through the frost on the first day of spring. I can't give in to it, though, my heart is a hopeless romantic still willing to leap from unnecessary heights for the rebellion leader bedridden in front of me.

I have to be rational. More than my life hangs in the balance.

"You could have told me the truth. I wouldn't have turned you in," I whisper, which hurts the only one still lingering.

I had to find out the truth after he collapsed. In a muddy field. Surrounded by corpses and more gore than I thought ever possible.

I talked to him about the prince. I made comments, and he just waved them on as though we were talking about someone else entirely. It doesn't matter that I understand. I would have understood, and I would have helped him without all of the secrecy.

He sniffs. "How could I have known that?"

I don't have an argument for that. He just should *have*.

I'm an upstanding guy. I certainly didn't send a dragon chasing him through the woods or mean to impale him with a magical arrow. I've been a pawn in this world for too long, and it would have meant everything if he had treated me as special, as an equal, before we got to the point of imminent demise via the entirety of the King's personal battalion.

"If I had trusted you and you turned me in to the king, to my father, to a man who would have been willing to pay any price to learn the identity of the cloaked figure foiling his plans, it would have cost more lives than just my own. You only know a couple of people connected to me. You can't imagine the number of people hoping we'll overturn the government. The amount of executions," he swallows hard again, slowing down his rambling explanation with another sniffle. "He would make me kill them, Eli. He wouldn't have me killed. Do you understand that?"

Tears coat his cheeks before I realize he's holding back his sobs. I'm out of the chair in half a breath. I was being petty. Of course, I forgive him. Of course, I understand. Now, I sit on the edge of the bed and rub a small circle on his upper back as he leans his head onto my shoulder.

Xander cries with dignity. He doesn't wipe away his tears. There's no attempt to hide the sparkling bits of grief that streak his face with all the finality of a rainstorm moving over the gray landscape. He sniffs and pulls away with a sigh.

"If it were only my life on the line, I would've told you when I came down to the dungeon, Eli," Xander whispers those words with a sense of awe as though the truth surprises him as much as it does me. "I'm not asking you to simply forget my indiscretions, but I need you to know that I'm more than my circumstances. I do care about you. The way you think and the crazy stuff you do with magic. I don't want to presume anything about you, but Wynn told me how she found us and…"

The roses. The bodies. The sacrifice he made to ensure my survival. Of course, I wasn't going to abandon him, and I was prepared to fistfight a witch if she didn't help me take care of him.

But I liked him well before manslaughter came into our lives.

"There were plants in the bones you threw at me in the forest, weren't there?"

He tilts his head back with a wry smile at the fact that I'm finally included in his personal joke, so effortlessly still leaning into my hold as though he belongs there. "Nobody takes plants seriously. Dark magic. Death magic. That's what makes people think twice about backstabbing you, so I created a story and ran with it."

I nod. The bed squeaks as I shift back to really look at him. The soft light of day caresses his jaw in a way I crave to do the same. I keep my one arm looped around him and my other at my side, fighting every urge to simply console him.

"So, the entire beginning of our relationship has pretty much been a lie?"

"Eli…" his voice wavers, a knife's edge threatening to sever whatever bonds we may have started to create between us. "Not all of it was a lie. Not to me. I was handing off pieces of myself to you long before I realized I wanted you to hold them."

While I'm still trying to figure out what to say to such a declaration, Xander continues like this is the last time he'll ever have me alone to himself. "You were gorgeous in the revolutionary meeting, Eli. Stupid and proud and beautiful. I know you think you ran away from the fight, but I was there with everyone after the dragon took off. You inspired them. You gave them the kind of hope I hadn't been able to fully instill in them on my own. I don't even remember what I said to them, but the meeting ended, and I ran after you.

"I had never seen magic come to life. I had no idea how I was going to save you or stop the dragon, but I wasn't about to lose the most interesting man I had ever met or let him get eaten alive over a misunderstanding. So, I ran through those woods, tackled you just to be close, and when you got away from me again, I followed. By the time I caught up, you were making it help you out of that hole. It was the bravest thing I had ever seen. Brave and impossible. Magic didn't work the way it did when you used it. Had I known Wynnifred meant to send you after the," a subtle blush overtakes his cheeks, and he lets out a chuckling cough. "Well, the prince, in a way to spark the revolution faster than my own methods, I would have intervened right then, but I'm not upset you shot me or that we had to meet under such strained circumstances, only that I couldn't be honest from the beginning."

That's quite the announcement.

I feel heat in my cheeks. I'm flushed from my forehead to my navel. Xander definitely notices, turning in my hold and gently pressing his fingers to my shoulder.

"I made you a promise in the gardens," I whisper, trying to keep the thought of roses off my mind and imagine him wreathed in only greenery.

His lips curl with a hopeful smile as I lean in. No more secrets. No more masks. I kiss Xander for the first time. It's just him and me here in a witch's bedroom, and I let him know without words that I truly needed him to not only escape the kingdom with me but that I wanted him. I still want him. Sharp breaths and fingers clutching at hair and clothes and gods, there is so much fabric between us. I kiss Xander until I'm dizzy with it and then lean back breathless to stare at him once more.

He doesn't push me to say anything. He doesn't force me to have an answer to his previous statements. He waits with moon-toned eyes focused on me and every emotion I might express, prepared to accept a punishment for his actions or a full rebuke of his intentions, even as a sliver of hope shines through that I might feel some of those same things.

"I'm glad you're okay," I say gently, looking him over again to really make sure he's fine and here, solidly in my arms. "I wasn't sure what I would do if you weren't okay."

That's all I can figure out how to say. My heart was living on a pike when we were out in that field, openly bleeding from my anxieties about losing him. Him. The prince. The Necromancer. Xander.

"You don't have to be okay with what happened. I could stay here, and you could go on to find Gemma."

Wait. That's not what I was trying to say. I reach up, my fingers cupping his own on my shoulder and, when that's not enough, trailing up to stroke the hard line of his jaw.

"I said I would stay with you until I had her back, and I haven't changed my mind, so you have to keep your end of the deal to help me."

His expression falls, reality squashing the fluttering hopes of fantasy. "It was already going to be dangerous to find her, but we're in trouble if my magic is acting up outside the bounds of the kingdom."

"This is all because we're on the other side of the barrier?"

Xander shakes his head, his hair unbound and so soft where it runs across my arm. "I will always be dangerous if I have access to magic. You can't be safe if you're with me."

"You know," I start, letting my tone lift into something playful, so he knows I'm not trying to lecture him or metaphorically kick him while he's down on himself. "That all sounds very melodramatic. I think you just saved my life and I returned the favor when I dragged you off that field, so we're even, we're both dangerous since I'm reckless with my own magic, and we're going to learn to deal with each other until this kingdom isn't just done picking on the little people, but a better, safer place altogether."

"Nobody told me he was a speech maker," Wynnifred calls from the doorway, a tray held in her hands.

I never heard the tea kettle whistle. Wariness settles on my shoulders like the frost that coated the trees outside. There's no way I'm eating or drinking magical food before someone has the decency to tell me what the effects will be.

"I wouldn't have picked a leader for my people that didn't know the importance of a good speech," Xander pipes back, gently accepting a steaming glass of something that smells like sweet dreams and clementines.

I slip back into the chair and let my own cup rest on my thigh as I think about what he just said. This isn't a secret conversation. The two of them know I'm sitting right here. I don't remember agreeing to be a leader of anything.

"I still intend to fix my mistakes, save my father, and eventually run our tavern. I'm not exactly the leading type."

Wynn doesn't hide her disbelieving snort, and Xander arches an eyebrow at her before fixing his attention back on me. "You're the sort of person people notice and want to hear from, Cinderfella. You shouldn't hide from that kind of talent. It takes more than one person to run a revolution, and I'm giving you the job if you want to stick around for it."

I'm not that impressive a person. I can't even seem to keep track of my shoes these days. And yet, he's sincere. Quietly, he and Wynnifred sip their tea as they watch me.

This is another one of those big life choices I thought I wouldn't be making at almost thirty. My path in life was supposed to be sealed. I knew what the future looked like. Now, though, everything is a dizzying blur of possibility.

Instead of outright agreeing to the leadership role, I changed the subject. "I've never been away from Briargild. I'd never been to the castle before going to the dungeon. There's so much about the world I don't know. What can you tell me about where Gemma is?"

"Did you live under a rock before coming into the forest, Cinderfella?"

My mouth dangles open without a response tumbling through. I should expect such questions from Wynnifred. Still, she's frozen me in place, her eyebrows arched towards her hairline with an expression that's a tangled mixture of disbelief and disappointment.

Xander bids her to calm down and give me a break, waiting for her to sit on the edge of the bed before he speaks. "The history books have been burned, Wynn. People on the outskirts of the kingdom wouldn't know what happened several generations ago."

"Yes, well, not all of us have the luxury of living in ignorance."

Her scathing remark is successful in cutting me open. I've come to understand more in the days since I was arrested, since I learned that I could control magic, since I lost my father, that I had been given a safe and secure life with the option to pretend the rest of the world wasn't my concern. It took me years to learn about my mother. Time and several sources from which I gained information through less than morally advantageous means. I mourned one life while Wynnifred and Xander hinted at knowing the tragedy of so many that never crossed my mind.

"I can't do better if you don't tell me anything," I try, my voice coming out in a whisper, and, for the first time, I wish that Xander hadn't dosed my via tea back in his royal room so I could take a much-needed gulp of the liquid in my lap.

"It mustn't be the responsibility of those suffering to teach you to be a better person, Cinderfella."

"But," Xander cuts in again, rubbing Wynn's shoulder as if to silently convey his sympathy for her, "the world doesn't get better unless we work together, so what do you want to know exactly?"

How am I supposed to know? If I don't know what secrets are being kept from me, what history has been erased, how do I know where to start my line of questioning? I take a slow breath. The air past my lips pulls over my teeth and fills my lungs until they're near bursting. Then, out. Again. I breathe as if it's the only thing I know and understand and can do.

"Tell me about the kingdom we're headed to because I only know Apricity as a place from stories."

A shimmering start to where we need to get in this conversation, Xander obliges without hesitation. "Apricity. It was once the ruling kingdom of this continent. Beautiful beyond compare, it was a place of near constant sunlight, flourishing gardens with flowers long lost to time, and more magic than anywhere else in the world. Being the greatest place in the world typically comes at a cost, though.

"Someone who could be traced back as a very old grandfather of mine stumbled upon Apricity on a hunting expedition. He and a handful of men were welcomed into this magical kingdom, they were given a tour and a place to stay within the castle that was more art installation than powerful fortress, and they were shown wonders they had never known. Fires that could be lit with the flick of a wrist. Abundant food supplies and clean water nourished by systems the travelers never could have created alone. Everywhere the air felt clean and positive, and the sun shone on the glittering expanse of a kingdom with unlimited possibilities."

The Necromancer stalls in his storytelling. I know where this is going. As much as the details are fuzzy, I understand that Briargild didn't grow directly from the land. It stole the space it now holds, uprooting families without regard for their lives or homes. The colonization of this land led to the place I now call my own home, and I can't decide if it's a worthy cause to be drowned by guilt due to the creation of a kingdom nursed by bloodshed, when it's the only place that has ever brought me joy and warmth.

The world is a complicated place. There's room for both grief and wonder, anger and awe. I can't undo the wrongs of the past, so I need to do what I can to lessen the damage caused in the future.

"What kind of place is it now?" I ask, pushing him ahead without needing to revel in the history of dark acts that caused the kingdom to fall and leave Briargild to rise as the most powerful place in the world.

Wynn answers me, her lips turned towards a frown. "It's dark. Magic is still present, but it's not the wild abundance of old times. Briargild siphons the power it uses from Apricity, leaving barely enough for the other kingdom to survive, let alone try to thrive. They use candles to guide their way, sure, someday they'll see the sun again as they tell stories of the man they believe will come to save them," she shrugs, downing the rest of her tea in a quick motion. "They're willing to wait and hope. I wasn't, so I left, and I've lived in this dangerous border of forest between the two kingdoms for over a decade now."

"You're from there?"

It's almost a kind gesture for her to share personal information with me. Almost. She is still glaring and talking in just short of a snarl, but it's the best, most open communication we've ever shared up until now.

"Your mother was, too. She wasn't killed merely for magic. If that were the case, the King would have rid the city of every satyr and centaur regardless of their useful work skills." Wynn clicks her nails along the edge of her cup. "Your mother had connections with the ruling class of people in Apricity. She saw the potential to rebel and become their own land once more. It was her hope to move them to rebellion, but the King succeeded in making her death a spectacle nobody would forget. Adira Alcinder was a brave and noble woman. You had better be working to make her proud."

I tilt my head at that, my throat tight. "I've never heard her name said out loud. She…" It's becoming increasingly difficult to find the right words, but I need to ask this next question. "Her last name was already Cinder before meeting my father?"

At that, Wynn's face crinkles with something like a real smile. "Your father was a very poor man. He came with no surname to protect or send to his children. I remember stories told of him admitting to Adira that he had always been a tavern fellow, and she responded that from the time they were married, for the rest of his days, he would be known as a Cinderfella. It was her gift to him and then you. Your name and her blood in your veins should be enough to give you access to Apricity."

It's impossible to tell if this news is more astounding than learning I can somewhat wield magic. It's definitely a lot. My father and I barely spoke of her outside of the context of fairytales.

My next question pops out before I can think of something more important. "Do they have dragons?"

Wynn's gaze softens. "They did once. I suppose they do have one right now."

Skelly. My heart skips a beat. They have Skelly and Gemma.

"We're going to get them back. No matter what."

It's a futile promise thrust into the universe. I barely understand the grandiosity of the world, the places we'll be headed, or the people there, but I know that I will do everything in my power to save those two.

If the scene in the clearing meant anything, I would do everything I could or I would die trying.

At least, for the people I care about.

My eyes linger on Xander as he and Wynn continue to pepper me with short stories on their time away from Briargild and the hopes they have for the future. I follow along, memorizing what they say as well as living with them in the moment, laughing at the good stuff and nodding solemnly to the bad. I even find the courage to drink my now cold tea. For the first time in what feels like an eternity, I have hope, too.

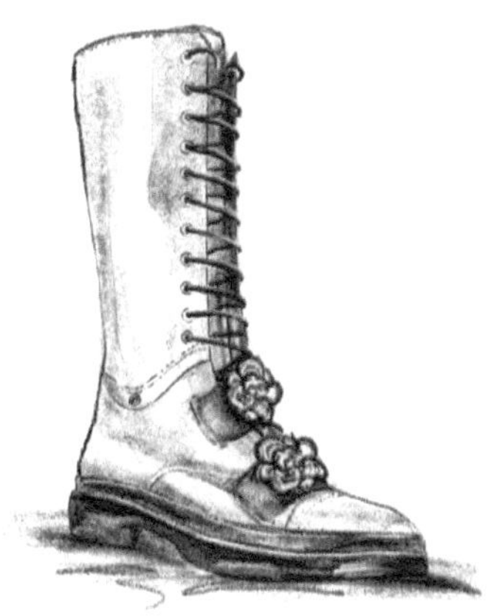

20

"You're not coming with us?"

Wynnifred was kind enough to pack us a bag that I take before Xander can try to do the same.

The man is still in a weaker condition than I am, even though he's the one insisting we leave sooner rather than later. "Someone has to slow the King and his army down. They'll be descending on Apricity sooner than expected after your theatrics in the forest. He'll know it was the prince that left, and," she pauses, trailing off with a shake of her head, none of us need to repeat what exactly Xander did in the forest. "You two will make it to the other kingdom, rescue Gemma and your beast, and plead your case to a group of people who have spent their entire lives kneeling to the power of King Anerald and Briargild's might. If you do this right, we may just turn the tide of war."

Stopping again, she reaches out to squeeze my arm. We're not the type of people to hug it out on the stoop of her cottage. Still, this is the most we can do; put our trust in an unlikely person, and then keep our word. She isn't asking me to try to assassinate anyone else, so I'm happy to go out into the world and do my best.

"You bring back Gemma or you'll have more than an evil king to worry about, do you understand me, Eli Cinderfella?"

I nod immediately, my vow already tripping over the curve of my bottom lip. "I won't come back without her."

Whether or not my words give her any solace, she nods and lets me go, tilting towards Xander and whispering a few words I can't hear. The two of them share some kind of knowing look. She does move to embrace him, apologizing for his wince of pain when she squeezes the shoulder that's still healing from her errant spell. I shift between my feet, putting the oversized supply bag on my shoulder, all too sure I'm interrupting a personal moment between them with my general presence. Soon enough, they move away from each other, utter a more general farewell, and then Xander opens the door for me, pushing me onwards to our future with the chivalrous gesture.

We wave to the witch of the woods before she shuts us out, the entire cottage shimmering and then disappearing completely from view. "Do you think I'll ever be that good at magic?"

Xander, dressed in shades of brown and green to better stay camouflaged in the forest and also because the color red seems to make him uncomfortable, even though he wouldn't admit that out loud, shakes his head at me. "If you pay attention, you might be even better."

And so our journey begins.

After the callous loss of life in the field, Xander doesn't trust his own magic, and I'm quick to give him a rundown of what happened with my first attempt at building a carriage, so we move on without a vehicle, trekking by foot in a general southerly direction. Besides, walking through a forest is what got me into most of my trouble; maybe doing so again will get me back out.

Winter still has the forest in a chokehold. Most of the footpaths have melted under the watchful gaze of the overhanging sun, but our breath still plumes in front of our faces as I follow Xander onward. My attention is split between the glistening snow in the branches of trees overhead, the inspection of flowers I've never seen before, and, more often than not, the curl of hair at the back of Xander's head.

Xander. I can't believe I'm walking in broad daylight with a man who is currently not a prince and not pretending to be a necromancer. He's just himself, at one with the surrounding forest as though it's the first place he's ever been able to breathe. It's too bad this can't be something he has forever.

"So," I start, a few steps behind him as the two of us trek towards a kingdom that shouldn't exist, "if all goes well, we'll have an army to fight your father?"

I watch his shoulders tense. "I wish you wouldn't refer to him that way."

"It's what he is, though, isn't it?"

Xander stops and turns to look at me, his jaw tight. "He stopped being my father when he used me to kill his political adversaries, Cinderfella. He is the king. He needs to be stopped. If we get to Apricity and they aren't willing to help us, I will take him down myself."

Pine needles fall around us, the shuffling of birds somewhere higher the only noise interrupting the tense quiet that's taken me hostage. The trees sway with the curious wind, the elements circling us as power blazes in Xander's eyes. "I will not continue to watch Briargild and Apricity suffer for his crimes. There is no future in which Anerald continues to rule. This is my final stand, Cinderfella. You can be with me or not, but this is it."

I grab his wrist before he can pull away, my grip gentle as his nostrils flare. "I'm here to support you, Xander. I just don't know if you have to be the person to kill him. You have enough haunting you."

He chews on that for a moment, tense, but not trying to pull out of my grasp, his skin once cold now warming under my fingertips. "You didn't say that you wanted to be a leader for the people back at Wynnifred's. I figured you were going to leave as soon as you had your fairy godmother back."

Oh. Well, they had dropped a lot of information on my lap right after I woke up from a magical burnout. Of course, I wasn't ready to make educated decisions. I'm still not sure that I want to be the front command of an army against King Anerald, but I certainly don't want to go on living life in fear of the crown. I never thought about leaving him.

"You said a lot back at the cottage," I argue. "I'm not sure how I can actually help you, but I think you're pretty great, too, and I'm not leaving anytime soon. I'd like a chance to get to know you outside of war and grief and the launch of rebellions."

He flattens a palm to my chest. His other hand is on my shoulder. We're eye to silver-streaked eye.

"How about this, Cinderfella? You can help me by strengthening your magic."

"My fairy godmother was sure I was a lost cause," I murmur, enjoying his attempt to lighten the mood even as I take on a more serious tone. "Are you certain you can stop me if things go wrong? Your magic is already-."

He pushes me back. "I'm standing. My magic is fine. Stop making excuses unless you want to admit you're too scared to better yourself as a magic wielder."

"Scared is what I should be. You didn't see the teeth on the carriage I created."

He wrinkles his nose at me, and I realize what a delight it is to see all of his face at once, to finally know what was happening behind the Necromancer's mask. "Well, I saw the teeth on our dragon, so I can imagine, but I'll teach you to stop it yourself. You can't rely on safeguards from other people. What would you do if we ever got separated in a fight?"

Yeah. Okay. Whatever. He seems to be making a very good point.

"If I do this, I want you to tell me something real about yourself."

His smirk is a glorious thing to be gifted, and I force myself to look away from it as my toes curl in yet another pair of boots I'm destined to lose. A nod is all his agreement to my demands. Fingers outstretched, I can make out the spiderweb of scars along his knuckles that reach just past his wrists. A once bloody mark from the terrible power of his magic, or maybe the shredded remnants of an attempt to save someone from his accidental roses. It shouldn't thrill me to see his hands outside of gloves, but it does.

I would very much like to see his hands other places, too.

Which is not a conducive thought for this moment. No magic will be had if I can't figure out how to focus.

"So," I have my own hands at my sides, not sure when the magic lesson is supposed to begin. "What do you want from me?"

I swear his eyes flick across my lips before settling back onto my gaze. "Should be more careful with how you phrase things to me, Cinderfella."

This is a dangerous line I could press. I only have to shift slightly forward. His eyes rake over me again.

This is the man who called me beautiful. He complimented my magic and the way I treat people around me. We haven't had very much time alone together, but he's been watching me and admiring me as much as I have him.

I have a small idea of what he's thinking because it's a pulsing desire in my blood.

But he's a prince. Even though he's Xander now. He will still be a prince after all of this is over. If we succeed, he'll be a king. There's no story out there that tells of a king marrying a tavern keep.

I'm certainly not interesting enough to make Xander break that many rules.

Yet…

I almost wish I were. I might even want to step forward, close all the space he's made between us, and take something he looks willing to give.

I've stalled long enough. Xander clears his throat and picks up a rock from the ground. "What is it you want me to do?" I manage to ask, hoping that neither he nor the surrounding trees notices that I'm unraveling at the edges.

It's been a hard week. I'm tired. I've been running around, casting magic and pretending that the world isn't out to get me, even though it clearly is. It's not a crime to lust after princes. That's literally what they're there for, right?

To see but not touch.

To want but not have.

To dream about well into the future because I'm going to do everything in my power to make sure he survives whatever King Anerald is planning to do next.

I'll always have the memories of his lips on mine, and that will have to be enough to get me through the rest of my life.

"You're going to make a shield, Cinderfella. A real one. No more explosive theatrics."

"To be fair, that was my very first day doing magic."

"Sounds like an excuse to me." He tosses the rock in the air, catching it as he gives instructions to me. "Widen your stance. Raise your hands to chest level and imagine your shield."

He doesn't have to tell me twice to spread my legs.

Nope. Inappropriate. Not where my mind has to be to get through this shield nonsense.

I do as he says, though, stepping into a stance I've seen royal guards use when preparing to attack. This is stable. I don't have a sword, but I won't need one with magic at my beck and call.

Almost every other attempt I've made to create magic that resembles a common shape has quite literally blown up in my face. First, the carriage. Then, these shields. The skeleton worked for a moment before the Necromancer turned the magic back on me. I started a blizzard indoors for Gods' sake. Magic is not my general forte, and I think I won't be able to do it the way everyone else has up until now. Even my last attempt grew into a glitter bomb that has overtaken the entire kingdom of Briargild.

"Give me a second. I want to try something."

While Gemma would have insisted I do as she says, Xander gives me a nod and waits patiently. I've been trying to make something bloom in my mind's eye that just doesn't work. When I view the world, I'm not truly paying attention to the forms and colors of everyday objects. Instead, I'm noting the way a substance feels in my hands, the texture it leaves on my fingertips, and the emotional impact it imparts on me. I relish in the feel of a wine glass against my lips differently from how I note that of a warmed teacup. I don't just see the sun set and rise, I feel it in my chest and hover in the knowledge I've managed one more day in a world that more often than not tries to remove me from its premises. My creation of magic can't follow someone else's form because I'm not like the rest of the people who have done magic, or, at least, not like those doing magic in Briargild.

I'm my mother's son.

Her magic, awakened by a fairy godmother's wand, lives on in me.

I'm going to do this my way.

Instead of pushing the thought of a shield from my mind, to my arms, and out of my fingers in that way that causes the glittering magic to bite at my skin and often ends in an epic failure, I take a slow breath. A shield offers protection. It needs to make me feel safe and secure. It needs to cover me with the kind of warm embrace a hug does from a father who would move the world to care for his son.

My throat tightens, my hands raised, pink glitter sparks to life between the two of us. It doesn't bite at my veins and sear its glittery presence into my joints. Instead, it listens, a brief swell of warmth that follows the gentle nudging of my mind. Not necessarily a circle. Not even a complete shape. Pink exists as the essence of something, though, and I nod to the Necromancer that I'm ready.

His own hesitation is gone. Reeling his arm back, he throws the rock at me hard and fast. I don't flinch or move. I believe in the magic flickering between us.

The rock sparks in a dazzling display of glitter, and pieces of it clatter to the ground. "Yes!"

I let my hands fall. I did it. I really, really did it all on my own, with my own terms.

I think both of my parents could be proud of that.

A second rock flies through the air and nicks me in the shoulder, where I'm definitely going to have a coin-sized bruise tomorrow. "That was the easy part. Put your shield back on. Wars aren't ended with one blast of magic."

Chuckling, I bring my hands up and the shield buzzes to life again, faster this time. Xander circles me. Both of his pockets are full of rocks. I'm sure this is not how Wynn meant for us to use the clothes she lent us. Even so, Xander picks his way through the underbrush, small patches of snow crunching under his boots, and begins testing my shields.

No more rocks get through my defense.

"Now, turn the dust at your feet back into rocks and toss them back."

Sweat drips from my brow. Muscles trembling, I feel the same as I would after a particularly busy dinner rush at the tavern. Pink-lined rocks are formed and fly through the air. My magic flourishes. A bit exhausted and woozy on my feet from the general exertion, but, oh, so alive.

"You have to answer my question."

Another rock flies my way. I block it without raising a hand, my magic leaping to my thoughts in the same way that I could give commands to Skelly without enforcing them the way magic had been taught to me.

Xander nods. Impressed, I hope. He clears his throat and then starts to walk away from me. "What could you want to know about me?"

Everything. Favorite foods, colors, and stories. If he has any hobbies outside of running covert rebellions. Without the insistence of secrets hanging between us, I feel there's an entire lifetime of facts

I could know about Prince Alexander Charming and not be full of it.

And so, I stick to something easy. "You control plants. Do you have a favorite?"

Stopping, he looks over his shoulder at me and holds out a bottle of water he'd stolen from the pack during his rock onslaught. "Do you care about flowers, Cinderfella?"

"I used to keep plants in our tavern. Mostly greenery, but I've always been fond of flowers."

Snorting at that, he waits while I tip my head back for the warm rush of water and then shrugs. "Anything but roses. Daffodils make me feel hopeful, but they never last long enough. The yellow always gets snuffed out by the rest of the world."

Yellow. This man, who dressed in all black to complete his necromancer facade, is drawn to the color yellow.

"I've always been fond of lilacs and honeysuckle," I confide, the path widening so we can walk side by side as I tell him about the gardens my neighbors had when I was younger and how the plants always snuck over the fence between us to say good morning every spring.

"Am I permitted to ask questions about you, too?" He asks, noticeably elated by my very slim and common knowledge of plants. "I'd like to know your favorite drink."

I smile at the way he skips forward without waiting for me to reply to his original question. Xander, without the crown or his dark clothes, is a ball of energy. He's curious and easily excited. It's impossible not to find him endearing.

"Anything you haven't touched first," I tease, earning myself a wide-jawed guffaw and a shoulder pat.

"It was for your own good, Cinderfella."

Yeah, yeah. He needed me to be in working condition to escape the castle, too. My magic was a major reason we evaded the king.

"Depends on the season, I guess."

Xander rolls his eyes. This man, raised to be the heir to the throne, has the indecency to roll his eyes at me and demand a better answer. I admonish him for asking for the truth after how often he skirted it with me while pretending to be two separate people, but that doesn't deter him from his mission to learn something about me that wasn't earned through blood and sweat and running for our lives.

So, I tell him about the blue cocktail we make every winter solstice. The one our patrons hold and ask for seconds of as wishes fly through the air. It glitters and slips easily past the tongue, and we only have it the one night of the year.

I pull my father's locket out from under my shirt, the one thing that has lasted the entirety of this journey away from the tavern. "It was her favorite," I tell Xander, showing off the small portrait of a woman I never got to know before she was taken away forever by the man we're no longer referring to as his father. "So, my dad made it every year on the night we missed her the most, and the whole community came out to celebrate and drown out their own griefs, too."

Xander reaches out, his fingertips brushing mine. I swear sparks burst from the slight contact. A combination of the wriggling magic under my own skin and that which lives in him. Pink glitter sparkles to the ground between us as he looks into the locket.

"I'm sorry my life costed hers. If I had had a choice in it-."

Gods, I know he didn't ask for this any more than I did. I shut the locket and tuck it back into my collar, where it can rest against my chest.

"Just make it worth it," I whisper more to the expanse of the forest than to him as I start walking in order to avoid looking at him.

All of this has to be worth it, doesn't it?

He may be a large part of the reason I lost one parent, but I'm the sole reason for losing the other. The entire magical world seems to be at stake. At least, those lives affected by the borders of Briargild are still under attack, and our efforts have to influence change, or we're no better than where we began before I went around uttering bad wishes.

All of this has to be worth something. I'm hoping it'll taste as sweet as a cocktail at one a.m. just before I make a poor decision. I'd like it to end surrounded by people I care about. Gemma and Skelly. My father, brought back from the twisting ties of magic and fate. Xander.

Our knuckles brush as he sidles up next to me. I'm dropping glitter like a frazzled bird losing feathers. Hopefully, he thinks it's just my inability to fully control my magic and not a very clear sign that he creates emotional unrest in me.

"It's your turn," he prompts, suddenly not so fond of quiet stretches of time in the forest with me.

Maybe he likes my voice.

Maybe he's astute enough to realize that I'm more than a little upset.

Maybe, maybe, maybe.

None of those things changes what he is. It doesn't matter if his favorite color is mine or whether our star charts align. After everything is over, our lives will go separate ways.

I'm setting myself up for a bigger heartbreak the more I play into the fantasy that Xander could be a lasting figure in my life.

Well…

He'll last. I will probably turn into one of those odd fellows who collects snippets out of newspapers and tacks them to a secret board in my room, taping together visages of the man I let slip through my fingers so he could become the king without being weighed down by whatever I am.

I might spend the rest of my life looking for the pieces of Xander that I wished I had fought to hold.

"How do you know Gemma?" I ask, skating away from anything that will make me want to cling to him more than I want to do now.

Branches snap under my boot. The forest has gone oddly quiet. I don't notice the call of birds in the trees anymore. I haven't seen a squirrel in some time now. Not sure if deer come out this far, I squint at the ground to see if I can catch sight of a reptile or fluffy side of the winter bunnies that migrate near the edge of Briargild every year.

Nothing seems to be here besides Xander and me.

His voice is soft and warm and far too easy to lose myself in. "I've always appreciated people who push the limits of our system. She thinks she's a bad fairy godmother, but I think she's a little like you." his elbow bumps mine. "You both can't follow the rules, and that's okay because you do amazing things with your talents."

There he goes, complimenting me again. I shake my head, my skin not as cold as it should be in the middle of this winter expanse. The sun hides behind a cloud, giving me a moment to gather myself in some relative privacy besides the man at my side.

"When you're king," I start, confident I can't survive in a world where that doesn't happen, "will you change the laws so women can exist without so many boundaries? She told me she only became a fairy godmother to avoid having to marry a husband."

Xander looks at something in front of us, squinting into the darkness of a fog settling over us. The weather is odd here. It feels heavier than it did twenty steps ago.

"I will always do what's in my power to help people," he answers from beside me, his silhouette turning hazy as we push forward. "I hope she and Wynn have a chance to reconcile in the future."

Ah. So he knows, too. That makes sense. I'm sure he and the witch hashed out a lot of secrets when he confronted her about the arrow I put in his shoulder.

Instinctively, I reach out for him as the scenery darkens further. He meets me halfway, our fingers lacing as though they've always been meant to do so. I try not to let my heart beat out a sonnet on the way I feel about him reaching for me. I try, but I'm sure he can hear the way it pounds as the color seeps from our surroundings until we stand in a land of gray nothingness.

There are fewer trees. The ground seems far from us, puddles of fog shifting around our feet in a dizzying display. Nothing besides the crunch of our steps disturbs the land here.

I squeeze Xander's hand. "Is it always like this?"

"The blight on the land has been getting worse. This is far darker than I remember."

"But we'll be okay?"

Xander stalls then, facing me and stepping in close enough that we can see each other clearly without the disturbance of the fog, his nose nearly brushing my own. It's been so long since we stood in those roses together, but his breath warming my cheeks now is a welcome distraction from the ocean of darkness moving in waves around us. It's a reminder we've done something terrifying before and we'll survive doing it again.

I can almost feel his lips brush my own as he speaks. "As long as I'm with you, Cinderfella, I'm pretty sure we'll be okay."

Which is the swooniest thing he could have said.

I'm almost foolish enough to lean forward and close the rest of the space between us. Almost. It's a good thing I hesitate, wobbling back on my heels, because we're not alone.

A dagger flashes between us, promptly pressing into Xander's throat as he's dragged back from me by thick, green vines. I think I yell. I definitely say his name, the syllables ripped from my throat as I'm jerked back and pushed to my knees, a similar blade held to my throat.

We're not left to struggle for long against the overgrown plants, Xander holding up his hands as a being in a blue dress steps through the fog, the dense cloud cutting around her like some odd doorway only she can open. "Well, well, well, it's about time my betrothed showed up."

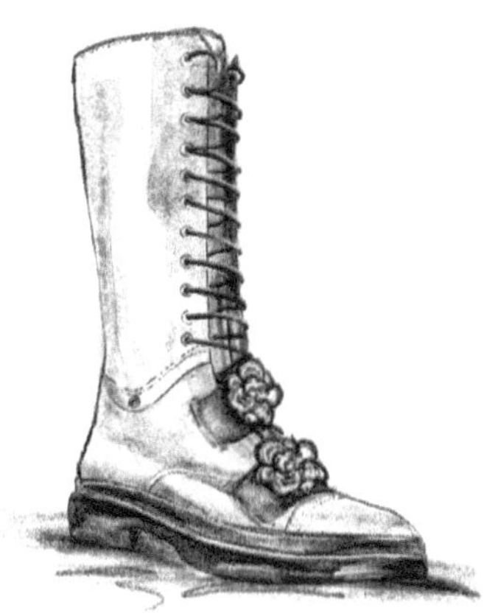

21

I can't decide if I'm more surprised by the fact that humanoid pumpkins are wielding knives and taking us hostage or that someone just referred to Xander as their betrothed. Definitely the latter. Plant magic is almost part of the status quo these days.

Of course, I'd seen the letters. I had forgotten about them. With Anerald coming after me so aggressively, it had slipped my mind that there were already other plans in motion, that the prince was being married off in the King's grand schemes to keep him from ruining the plans for the kingdom. We escaped, we kissed, and, still, we're trapped by the machinations of a plan far outside of our grasp. Betrothed seems like a curse. It's a crushing reminder that I again had no chance of ending up with a prince.

"Cam, I don't think out here is the best way to make introductions. Why don't we put down the blades and go inside?"

The woman leans in closer, the fog draping around her shoulders like a cape to go with her gown. Her hair is a wide crown of curls. I've never seen anyone with hair so large or perfectly wild. I would find it beautiful if she weren't looming over me.

In a mask.

Because everyone in this gods damned forest needs to have a mask.

Instead of covering the bottom half of her face like Xander's did when he was the Necromancer, this woman has blue fabric wrapped around her eyes. It doesn't look conducive for seeing out of, but she seems to have no problem finding me in the dirt, the plants under her control running green tendrils over my chin and plucking at my clothes in distasteful flicks of foliage.

She smiles, a harsh slash of revealed teeth. "You're the man he's been telling me about, aren't you?"

Why would Xander be telling the woman he's supposed to marry about me?

When I stare at her with a dumbfounded inability to voice any questions, she chuckles and glances at Xander, who has found a way to wriggle free of his pumpkin assassin. "Are you sure this is really him?"

"He's the only choice, Cam. Let's take this inside now."

She clucks her tongue at him. "You don't rule these lands yet, Charming. We'll go inside when I'm ready."

Even as she argues, she flicks her fingers to the pumpkin at my side, and it relinquishes me from its vines. The dagger disappears into its vine-laden body as the thing straightens. Standing on two thick vines with matching green appendages for arms, it tilts its head to look at me through carved eyes that glow orange in the fog.

Skelly can do that, too. Magic seems to make up for silly things like having no eyeballs.

Rubbing my throat, I push back to my feet and look between the two people in front of me now, a prince and his betrothed. "You're the queen of Apricity?"

The woman, Cam, pinches the wide bridge of her nose and breaths out a more disappointed sigh than Gemma has ever pitched my way. "Why don't I show you my castle, and then you can decide?"

Without waiting for a response, she spins on her bare feet and starts walking back the way she came. The pumpkins sidle up to either side of Xander and me. We're boxed in and left to move forward.

Vegetables were never on my list of possible assailants.

The magicked creations beside us lope along with steps far too wide. I don't think there's any way that the vines should be enough to keep the enlarged gourds up and moving, but they seem to manage regardless of my opinions. Almost ridiculously, our party of animated pumpkins and magic-wielding humans moves forward in the fog.

It's amazing that more people don't know about Apricity. It would only be a couple of hours' carriage ride from the border of Briargild to here. We walked it in a little over half a day. Maybe people have stumbled here, unsure of its existence as I was, and been murdered by the pumpkins that clearly guard it.

"So, you're still betrothed?"

Xander hisses between his teeth. "Cinderfella, it's not like that."

Yeah. Okay. I'll believe him when his crazy fiancée isn't leading us along with her pumpkin minions.

When he tries to say more, she shushes him. "Let him see Apricity."

Turning away from Xander, I look ahead as the fog thins. It still lingers, blocking the sun above us from ever caressing the grass that could grow here. There are no trees around. No plants. Not a single bush.

I wanted the other kingdom to be something magical and new and different and worthy of detailed notice, but that's not what it is here. Magic doesn't glimmer in the air like I thought it might. Instead, there's the constant, overcast atmosphere hanging over us and blurring the edges of the first buildings.

We are near the gates of the neighboring kingdom, a rusted compilation of snaking vines once cast in what must have been an endearing shape to welcome guests and citizens alike home to this once wonderful place. Now, it's crooked and snapped beyond repair. I don't question that the kings of Briargild did that, and it has stood, broken, as a visual statement to the world of what was lost when the people of Apricity met their fate against greedy rulers.

Where Briargild is rose gardens and white walled buildings in a competition to be the best, the richest, the cleanest on any given street, everything in Apricity has a touch of darkness. The roofs of the small houses are thatched with molding wheat. The cobblestones beneath my feet are cracked and muddied from years of lack of care. Looking up from the street and the shifting fog still settled around my ankles that the Queen confidently moves through, I stare at the sparse buildings, each one looking eerily the same with muddied walls and windows covered with frayed curtains in shades ranging from a sickly yellow to muted blues that look brown if only one tips their head away from the rare bits of sunlight that dare filter through to here.

I thought my side of town in Briargild was bad. Untidy and falling to pieces. It's nothing like this, though.

Swallowing hard, I stagger onward, my knees threatening to give out once more as a few faces appear in the windows of what looks to be a clothing shop and a smokehouse further up the street. We're not alone. The people themselves are eclectic. Some have skin several shades darker than my own, while others are pale enough to be ghosts out of the corner of my eye. There's a wild display of hairstyles: a few are braided like Wynnifred, others keep it shaved close to their temples, and more still have it piled on top of their heads with colored beads twined through it. Nobody here is trying to conform to a single, societal idea of beauty. Each of them looks different, dressed in clothes far more resplendent than the state of this town dictates, bright oranges and yellows, and a shade of lightest green that would complement the viney components of the pumpkin man leading me along.

The juxtaposition of a fallen kingdom left to rot and the appearance of its people still dressed in colors of life and love and survival is one that makes my throat too tight. That, and I've never been somewhere with so many people who look the way my mother does in that picture that hung in the tavern. She's in the locket pressed to my chest. I've carried her everywhere for this tumultuous journey. Now, I've finally brought her home.

Ahead, Cam keeps walking. She never looks back at us. Occasionally, she raises a hand as though to ask those in the buildings to refrain from running out to her. All the while, her bare feet make no sound as we move through the rubble of a once-powerful kingdom.

Another gate, this one in better repair than the last, with twining vines of metal headed by spring flowers, marks the beginning of the castle. It's only forty-three steps from there to the front door. All of it is marked by barren gardens resting through the winter in a slumber only spring can break. It's probably really beautiful. Right now, though, it looks more like a plot of land hiding centuries of secrets, a possible resting place for my bones if there's anything left of me after this coming meeting with the queen.

Xander whispers my name. He's still trying to explain things to me. I refuse to look at him, anxiety warring for my attention more so than any misplaced jealousy or loss of a man I knew I couldn't have for long. The prince doesn't try to get my attention again as wooden doors are pulled open from the inside and we're welcomed into an enormous entry room made almost entirely of stained windows, the geometrical shapes colliding together to form pumpkins of all shapes and sizes.

Maybe in another life I could appreciate such things.

Now, I stagger forward once more at the behest of a vegetable as we cross through the grand foyer to the rest of the castle, the ceilings larger than any other I've stood beneath, the grandiosity nearly an insult to the kingdom I've left behind. Another larger door swings open, all of this being done by curling vines presumably controlled by the woman in front of me. We're alive in a nest of plants and uncertainty, pests prepared to be caught in a sticky web we'll never escape.

Magic in the shape of soft white glitter, muffled by time or cruelty, filters through the air, making the hair on my arms quiver as I try to hold in any feelings to release my own magic activated by the wand I'll never give back. I let out a gasp as we seem to run right into a cloud of it. It wriggles along my forearms. The thread of something living inside me, other than my own blood and bones, vibrates up past my elbow, over my shoulders, and then coils itself through my ribs. It is ready and waiting.

Leaving behind the beauty and grandeur of the entrance hall, the pumpkin guards guide us into a smaller door and into the throne room. At least, I assume so much as I look across the small room devoid of anything else besides a chair that might have once been fancy upon its creation. Now, tufts of stuffing are falling out of the blue seat and backrest. What may have once been six buttons sewn into the backrest, one remains like an eternally open eye glaring out into the room. The wood along the top is weathered from dozens of hands grabbing it over the years. The pumpkins close the door behind us, and a lock clicks.

The Queen turns and takes her seat. Light filters in behind her, catching on the silver jewelry that adorns her ears, neck, and wrists, but it's not enough ornamentation to stop me from noticing the dirt on her fingertips. I spot more dirt on her dress as she crosses one leg over the other. Maybe she doesn't really care for royal manners. Maybe there are different rules here. Either way, she sits with her hands curled over the armrests and stares down at us with that gaze

I can't penetrate through the blue fabric.

Every time I've been near the King of Briargild, my throat has tightened and my heart has gone still, as though my body instinctively understands I'm nothing more than prey to be disposed of. Here, in front of a queen, my chest expands. I suck in a breath. I didn't mean to be so loud. A shiver of something besides fear shoots down my spine.

I'm not exactly terrified. I'm not even focused on my anger or confusion or jealousy anymore. I'm excited.

Because she looks so much like my mother.

Dark skin, fuller body proportions than would ever be allowed in polite society back in Briargild, she holds our attention without ever needing to speak. A force all her own, she runs a finger over her thick hair and then fiddles with a green leaf that definitely looks like it's whispering in her ear.

Now plants have the ability to move and share secrets.

What else will the world of magic reveal?

"You're early, Xander."

Of course the both of them are on shortened name circumstances. I don't dare look over at him. It's fine that he shared his secret identity with someone else. It's my fault for forgetting there was someone else in this very complicated picture of his life.

Maybe they would be happy together.

If the rebellion is successful, they can have two whole kingdoms full of secrets all to themselves, and I will rebuild my father's tavern somewhere far, far from it all. I'll save him. I'll get my life back together, and I'll stop running around pretending that there was ever anything else out in the world for me.

Not even men with silver eyes.

"Things progressed faster than I anticipated. We can't really go back now, so I hope you'll allow us to stay."

Her lips twitch. I can't tell if she thinks Xander is amusing or a bug she needs to squash.

It's so odd to have someone present themselves opposite to how Xander did as the Necromancer. His eyes told me all sorts of stories and gave me glimpses of emotions I couldn't see reflected in the lower half of his face. They were brown and gray and beautiful, and I was fully okay with just staring into them forever, clearly distracted by the view and easily lied to because of it.

The Queen of Apricity is the opposite; her eyes and the uppermost curves of her cheeks are concealed, so I only have the treachery of a tongue to depend on as we continue this conversation. “It would do me no good to send my cousin out into the woods, would it?”

Oh. Well, it makes sense that they’re kind to each other if they’re related. Royal families are always allowing odd marriages to keep their blood pure or whatever. It must be some very twisted family tree that spat out both of these people.

Except they’re now looking at me.

Right.

I’ve been a little preoccupied with my thoughts. Clearing my throat as cautiously as I can, I trust myself to pose a question to the room. “Are you suggesting we’re related?”

She nods. “I’m glad to see you’re incredibly bright despite your savage upbringing.”

That sounds like an insult. I glance at Xander. I don’t know why. Probably because I have been trained over the last several days to see him as the beginning and end of my major moments. If she’s going to be a different kind of cruel than King Anerald, I’ll just leave now.

I don’t need to keep putting up with powerful people who think it’s okay to mistreat everyone else.

Her lips turn down at the edges. “My apologies. Xander appreciates it when I’m a tad bit mean to him. He lives a very posh life trapped in his castle of brick and blood. You, though, may not feel the same.”

“He and I aren’t the same person. I don’t know who you think you are to me, but I don’t have to care, either,” I snap in response. “I came to collect my fairy godmother. Once you hand her over, I’ll be happy to leave you to figure out how to stop King Anerald while someone tries to help the poor savages at the borders of Briargild. Not everyone was raised in a gods damned palace, and they deserve our help more than anyone else.”

There’s a flash of white as she chews the corner of her bottom lip. Plants that once dangled from the ceiling now lazily creep along the floor, filling up the already small room. If her emotions are making them grow, we’re about to be drowning in greenery.

"I knew your mom. Aunt Adira. She was a very interesting woman who cared about everyone around her."

Oh. Of course. I hadn't considered that. I have a withering collection of memories of my mother: a hearty laugh here that haunts my dreams, a warm hand on my cheek there, a glimpse at happiness before grief became the main color in my creative palette. For me, my mother is the picture in my locket and decades of shared stories, a tradition to keep the best parts of her alive with us, as my father and I did all we could for ourselves and the tavern each day.

She was a real person for this queen, though.

An aunt.

A lost loved one.

I suppose I can't let my anger dictate my every action here. Not my lingering frustration and hurt from Xander's identity reveal, even after I've forgiven him. Not my anger at the events of the last few days and my nights in the dungeon. Not even my panic that I'll not find Gemma after coming all the way here.

I need to think about this as a man in need of help standing in front of a ruler who might be able to do just that.

I don't really want to go live in the woods. Isolation isn't a real answer. I'll never figure out enough magic on my own to bring back my father. This place, this woman who has claimed me as distant family, is my best hope at reaching my own goals.

Pride and emotions aside, I need to make this work.

"I didn't really know her. I wish I had gotten a chance before she…" Well, I think everyone in this room is aware of the last woman burned at the stake. "There's nothing I can do to bring her back, but I can fix other things, and I would appreciate your help in doing something good with the crappy world we've been given."

When she smiles, the plants loop themselves over one another in twining embraces. "That's a pretty good proposal. Should we start over then with proper introductions?

I step closer to her throne and hold out a hand. "I'm Eli Cinderfella."

She hesitates before closing the space between us, standing as equals with me in the middle of the slithering sea of green. "Queen Camellia Alcinder, but you can call me Cam. It's good to have you home, Eli." Vines drape over my shoulders, their soft leaves brushing over my skin where my sleeves end and nuzzling my neck until I'm standing in a coat composed of ivy. "The plants seem to respond well to you, too."

I give a noncommittal shrug. I'm not a naturally talented magic wielder, and I've probably killed more plants over the years than saved. Still, I feel a surge of pride streaking through my chest, a warm glow that paints my ribs several shades of yellow, at being accepted by the foliage in the throne room.

"And I'm Xander to you both."

Ruefully, I glance over at the man who was once the Necromancer and always the prince. The vines are playing with his collar. He looks so young here, lit by weak, dappled sun in front of a thousand different shades of green. Regardless of his betrothal, I wish I could know who exactly Xander is without the weight of every other title he's carried.

"You promised to bring me back the most interesting man who caught your eye, and I think you fully delivered," Queen Camellia says.

I glare over at Xander, more playful than serious as I cross my arms over my chest. "Is there a single person I'm going to meet who you didn't make deals and promises with that have come to affect me?"

"Hey, you made a deal with a witch to have me shot, so I think we're pretty damn even."

Fine. Touché. I can't be that mad. I even find it in me to laugh, which sends a trembling shiver through the vines all around me.

"You two seem a bit tired from your travels. Why don't I show you to your rooms where you can wash and rest before dinner, and we'll discuss the return of your fairy godmother then?"

I am tired. I'm not taking a delay on seeing Gemma, though.

"Do you have her in a dungeon? I want her released. I want to see her. I-."

The Queen, Cam, pushes out of her chair and gently loops her arm through mine. "No, no. Don't go jumping to the worst case. She wasn't allowed to leave because I can't trust that she wouldn't tell someone else about Apricity, but she has been very well cared for. If you wish to see her first, then that's what we'll do."

I was prepared to put up much more of a fight. I mean, that's been all of my previous experience dealing with castles and royalty. I fought to get out of a dungeon, filling it with a blizzard big enough to be recorded in the history books. The glitter of my bomb is still coating the walls and lingering in the air from my escape. I'm not sure I would win depending on magic alone here in a place with a ruler very prepared to retaliate with her own sparkling spells, but I'm surprised enough to stammer out my next words.

"Really? I'd appreciate that."

"Anything for family," she pats my arm and begins to lead us away, out of a door behind the makeshift throne, curtained by ivy vines.

Family. My heart stumbles over that word, so casually used to refer to me. She's serious. I'm somebody she sees as kin by blood, no secondary questions asked. Once we confirmed that my mother was her lost aunt, it fully sealed the deal for her. Xander follows along behind us as we enter a warm greenhouse, swatting at plants that pull his hair and clothes and altogether go out of their way to hinder him while gently moving out of the way of Queen Camellia and me. It's almost enough to make me laugh, the way she pokes fun at him with her magic without seeming to try. Almost. I'm still shocked and bewildered and overall too overwhelmed to be making too many jokes.

My entire world has narrowed down to finding Gemma. If I can get to my fairy godmother, I will have completed one part of my insane goal to fix my life. She's a detour I need to make for my general sanity.

Unlike the castle I just left behind, this one in Apricity is not looming halls and awaiting sentries. The throne room barely existed. All of the life of this crumbling structure is in the plants climbing up its sides and the people who occasionally peek through patches in faded bricks. We make it through the greenhouse and then pass into a space large enough to be a ballroom. More plants sit in pots in the corners and hang from planters draped between large columns that reach towards the open sky, the room devoid of a roof to let in the diluted, natural light of this land. There are no jewels, but the paint used on the walls is bright and charming and far more beautiful than anything I ever saw in my run through Briargild.

Green just may be my new favorite color. I need something to replace the shades of brown and gray that currently haunt me.

Open airways blocked out by arches woven over by vines lead to a kitchen busy with making food for the castle that we pass through.

Queen Camellia is happy to introduce me to a few people who look up from their work. I don't see anyone dressed as a servant or staff. All of the people we pass seem to be draped in the same bold colors as those I saw out in the main city streets. It's far more difficult to spot the hierarchical structure of this kingdom from looks alone.

I'm not convinced that this is some paradise of equality. I don't think I'm naive enough to believe something like that exists. Of course, I'm the same fool who thought himself an interesting person to a prince and fantasized about a rebellion leader, so I am naive when given just cause.

Continuing on, we leave the scent of smoking meats to step once more into a fairytale setting. The sky is above. Mostly gray and reflecting on the round area with voluminous clouds checking in on us from their lofty spots. There's a pond in the center of the wide expanse with benches around it. I lean in to see orange fish flit through the flowers that rest at its surface.

"If the King of Briargild has his way, all of this will be demolished," Cam says, close to me, her face tilted forward as I admire the beauty of a ravaged community still trying to survive. "It means that much that you've made it here."

And then we're beyond the pond. We're standing at the top of a tall hill. Stairs lead down to a dozen rows of small, painted homes.

"The castle is a show for Anerald. We have to let him and his advisors believe we're moments away from collapse. They never come past the throne room without complaints about the plants and humidity of the greenhouse, so they don't know all of this is down here. It's your secret now, too."

We step together, the blind queen never needing me to direct her as vines slither along the steps with us to direct her movements. Just as magic has assisted Xander without removing his limitations, Cam uses her magic to live alongside her people as much as the foliage of her kingdom. Already, people step out of their painted abodes to wave and call to her. Niceties. Shouts of innocuous news on sheep, crops, and other trivial things that she takes with a wide smile. Plenty of questions are shouted up the stairs about her guests, but she tells them to be patient and not to scare us off.

The crowd thins slightly by the time we're at the bottom of the long stairway carved into the side of the hill that balances the castle of Apricity. "This is a very big secret," I whisper to her as we step into the thin streets to walk by one row of the small houses composed of muddy outer walls touched with paint and windows that sport bright yellow curtains as well as hanging containers of even more plants.

She stops at the end, another steep incline ahead of us as we linger outside an empty house with a flower sketched onto its door. "This will be yours when you're done exploring and visiting. Please, be comfortable and ask the plants for anything you may need. I'll have someone send for you when it's time for dinner. Until then, I do have some business to take care of, but I will be very excited to return to our time together and speak more freely now that you'll have been reunited with your fairy godmother."

Camellia points at the inclined path that leads to what looks like a park with different structures for kids to enjoy. Apparently, Gemma didn't want to sleep in the castle. She's made herself a home beyond the general confines of Camellia's care and is only a few more steps away.

"You're just going to let me go. No guards?"

My cousin, this unbelievably solid and real person, a few years older than me, shakes her head, the gray air a stark contrast to the tight spirals of her Afro. "Are you plotting treason already?"

"Wait. No. That's not-."

When she throws her head back, I find the comfort to laugh, too. "I know. Just teasing. Besides, the plants work for me. I'll know if you plan to do something you shouldn't."

Oh. The plants don't just share secrets; they can collect them. Weaving, writhing vines hang from rooftops and linger on benches. We're surrounded by a network of spies for the Queen.

I don't know if it's a concept I love, but I accept it. Vines are a little better than armed guards. Camellia pats my shoulder and urges me on down the path.

I don't need any more encouragement.

Gemma is down there.

As soon as my cousin's hand leaves my arm, I'm jogging down the steep path. I would run there even if it was a trap. This is Gemma. My fairy godmother. Love and relationships hardly have anything on this chaotic woman who changed my fate with a flick of her wand.

I've missed her so damn much.

We have what feels like a lifetime to discuss from the moment I sent her running from the city center til now.

Dirt pounds under my feet, it plumes up around me. Tree trunks, crooked from time spent withering, bend down to watch me run. I don't even care about the exhaustion that has haunted me since I became a magic wielder. This is so much more than learning secret identities and the hidden histories of kingdoms that shouldn't exist. I am alive, and Gemma is here, and I feel like everything might be possible if only we're together again.

She's the best friend I've ever had.

Which may be sad. I've led a very secluded life, even though I was surrounded by so many people all the time. I don't care about the past I can't change. Gemma is everything I want to return to now.

The path takes a steep slope down towards the park, and I skitter onward, catching myself from almost falling more than once as rocks tumble around me. Eventually, I hit the beginning of the park, sprinting past benches and tables that don't match the hand-carved chairs pushed around them. Craft tables circle the play area for the kids Camellia mentioned. All sorts of half-managed projects lay strewn across every surface as though the citizens of Apricity were all born with a creative spirit that refused to die regardless of the terrible state of modern affairs. Paint flecks mar the ground. Scraps of fabric and thread littered everywhere else, a tangled web of frustration lay out for the peeking sun to glimpse at. In the center of it all is my fairy godmother.

"I didn't know you could wear pants," I blurted because that statement is far more important than the standard hello.

Gemma whirls around, wearing blue overalls on top of a yellow shirt with dirt smears on her knees and all sorts of thread colors caught in the curling hair captured in her ponytail. "I have legs, Eli Cinderfella."

We stare at each other, eyes wide, and then both burst out into laughter. Gods, she's really here. Completely whole and looking as mischievous as ever. Her cheeks pink from staying out in the cool winter afternoon, she meets me halfway when I stagger forward to pull her into a hug.

Gemma crushes me back just as hard. "Do you know how much I

worried about you?"

I do. I worried about her, too. On the floor of a dungeon. Running for my life. Sure, I would die in the forest. I worried about my fairy godmother, and I feel that same care in the quivering, happy sobs she tries to conceal as she buries her face in my shoulder.

A rattle of bones interrupts our hug. Skelly inserts himself, that cool, hard snout pressing to the side of my face as he makes his odd, purring sound I've truly missed.

"What have you done to my dragon?"

Skelly hops from one foot to the other, stretching out his wings for me to get a better look. Quilted bits of fabric have been attached to the bony appendages that acted as his wings. No longer naked, still wearing his bow from the clothing shop back in Briargild, he hoists his chin up and wags his tail as I take in the scene sewn across his wings.

Gemma stands back, her arms crossed over her chest. "Our dragon," she corrects me with a haughty sniff before smiling. "I'm also not done. If you hate it, we can change it. I don't even know if it'll work to help him fly yet; he's been falling during our trial tests, but I thought about you a lot while we were away, and I clearly had time on my hands."

My history of magic is displayed on Skelly's wings. Bright fabrics clash together, challenging each other for dominance over my attention. In one corner, there's an acorn squash. A carriage. The flower that came after and likely still lives in the middle of the street outside the place that once was our tavern. On the other wing, she's created all manner of roses interspersed with bones and grass to resemble the being gathered in front of me in all of his magical pride. The main portion of both wings is empty as though waiting to find out where my story is headed.

I should be out of tears at this point. I should be better at holding them in than my fairy godmother. Still, I feel hot, happy water streaks my cheeks. My throat is so tight. Emotion tingles behind my nose. I reach forward, and Skelly holds still as I stroke the embroidered edges.

"How did you do this?"

"I don't need magic for everything," she jokes. "Tell me you like it already."

"Gemma," I can barely push the syllables through my mouth. "I love it so much. Even if he doesn't fly. We can keep working on it together if that's something he wants to be able to do."

Skelly leaps away from me, flapping his wings while Gemma screeches for him not to pop a stitch. It seems he would love to learn to fly. I would love to be there to watch him do it, to see the first dragon in well over a century take to the skies where he belongs.

Xander steps up beside me, face red and breaths a little harsher than usual. He must have run the rest of the distance to catch up to us. For just a moment, the intricacies of our relationship cease to matter.

We're together. The people I care about, along with the dragon crafted from our magic.

He holds up a hand and then lets it fall, looking to me for permission. My world spins to a slow stop. The prince is looking to me for instruction. Not because he's hurt or lost or out of his depth, but because he trusts me to tell him how to approach Skelly. Obviously, I don't let the way his eyelashes lowered in deference to me matter. I can't. I haven't forgotten that I'll only ever have these few stolen moments with him, before we learn whether or not our revolution is successful, and then we return to our regularly scheduled existences.

Maybe they won't be what we had before, but Xander will have a kingdom to run, and I will only ever grasp at the tenuous control I had on my father's tavern. We have different places to go, I suppose. Life can't possibly align for royalty and a pauper even in the wake of changes. So, I don't look at the way he nervously wets his lips or memorize the scars on his hands as he waits for me to show him how to approach the dragon.

"Skelly loves people. You don't have to be scared of him," I hold out my hand, calling over the creature of bone and magic and a thousand colored threads.

Of course, the dragon doesn't act like a well-behaved beast. He charges at Xander. Paws up, he slams into the other man, and they fall to the ground, Skelly nuzzling his face as Xander coos at him.

They're best of friends in seconds.

My heart can hardly stand it. No matter what happens next, this moment with these people will forever be engraved at the forefront of my mind. I want to never forget reuniting with them and watching the man I've fallen for also fall for my dragon.

"Do you think we need to rescue him?" Gemma asks next to me, hands on her hips.

"He helped create Skelly. It's his turn to be in charge of babysitting. Why don't you tell me where we can get something to eat, and I'll tell you everything that has happened since I last saw you?"

My fairy godmother loops her arm through mine with the widest grin. "You're going to love this, Eli."

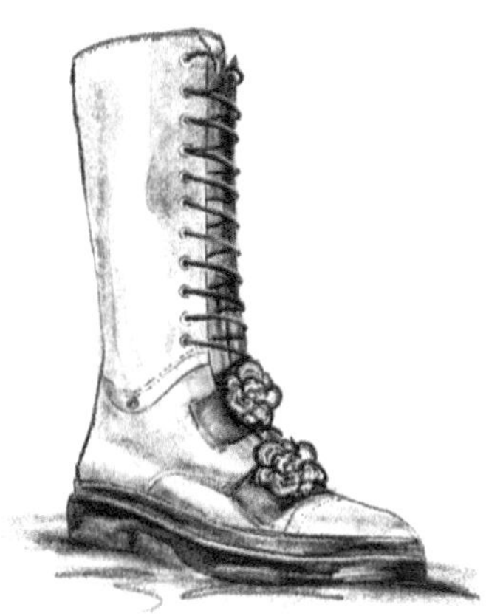

22

Camellia wasn't kidding. The plants really do offer up their assistance for everything. It's as simple as requesting a drink, and a moment passes before a green vine hands it out. Magic is pretty cool when it's not trying to outright destroy me.

"So you told me what happened, but you didn't tell me what happened between you and the prince?"

Gemma has phrased this question three times in three different ways. The first two, I ignored her, changed the subject, and made small talk about how good the honeyed mead is that the ivy keeps delivering to me. It seems I'm not going to escape her perceptive attention.

"What do you think happened?"

Her hands are cupped under her chin. "Please tell me you kissed him."

I feel my cheeks warm up, and the lie presses itself to my teeth before I can admit to the truth. "No. I didn't kiss him. How could I? We were running for our lives most of the time."

"You were alone in the woods with him, Eli Cinderfella. He complimented you like a dozen times. Told you to be a leader for his cause. What more can a guy do to get your attention?"

I shake my head. "You weren't there, Gem. There's no way that it's real. Besides—"

She holds up a hand to quiet me, always so good at making sure her points are heard before I can lay out an entire argument. "I saw the way he looks at you. It's real."

"Even if it is—"

"It is," she rebuffs me.

I roll my eyes. "He is royalty, and I am just some commoner. He's not going to change the world enough just for me. I don't want to have him for right now. If we're going to do more, I would want to have him forever, and I don't think either of us is ready to be making those commitments."

"You're making this too complicated," Gemma scoffs, swiping the last thumbprint cookie from our shared plate.

Two can play this game. I slump onto my elbows on the table and meet her gaze as she puts the sweet in her mouth.

"Wynnifred was worried about you."

Crumbs explode from my fairy godmother's mouth. They're all over our table and probably in my eyebrows from the force of it. She coughs and pounds on her own chest before taking a gulp of water offered by a plant hovering nearby. Face red, her breath hard and fast, she shakes her head at me.

"Don't even go there, Eli. That's not the same."

"How come?" I press because I don't know when to stop, and seeing Gemma flustered instead of me brings me a sick satisfaction. "You guys clearly both care for each other. If it's worth it to be with someone you like, then why can't you two figure it out? Because I don't want to be like you guys, meaning in person and yearning the rest of the time. Xander is too important to me to ruin our relationship like that."

Gemma looks past me to the prince, who has taken to telling stories to the kids playing around him and Skelly. He looks right at home in the center of the chaos. Eyes wide, his hands quick to demonstrate the details of his stories, he looks over at us every so often with a soft smile, and it's enough to make my heart melt into my boots, so I pretend not to see it while I keep my argument with Gemma quieter than he could ever manage to hear.

"That," she tells me, poking me in the arm to get me to look at her rather than the prince. "The way you look back at him. Blame your bonding on shared trauma, but you two care a lot, and you should take advantage of the time you get."

My deepest fears jerk up from where they live in my intestines. "Do you think the revolution will fail?"

She shrugs. "Change is coming, Eli Cinderfella. Are you brave enough to lead it?"

I wrinkle my nose at her. "You should've been a fortune teller instead of a fairy godmother."

Throwing her head back, she laughs at me. The day creeps towards night. We spend the evening together, happy as we can be under the circumstances, pleased to be together in a place where magic really does still exist.

Our bubble of time pops as the sun sinks and the gray fog begins to thicken, bells chiming from somewhere up the hill. "It seems the Queen is calling you back to her council."

"What if it's just dinner?"

"If you're going to be there, is it ever just dinner?"

She's not wrong. I breathe out a sigh of defeat. My presence isn't always chaotic. Just more recently, since magic wormed its way into my life.

I walk away from her and pat myself down. We didn't decide to go to our rooms and wash up, so I hope Camellia doesn't take offense to that. A little dirt has done far less damage to me than the handfuls of sparkling glitter I seem to always have on me. Stepping away from the tables, I rejoin the kids in the play area, several of them swarming my dragon. They walk through his bones and play with them like a xylophone. They grab his tail and pet his head, and all of them hand him handfuls of greenery to add to his nest just behind the play area, giggling when the dragon bounds off to lovingly place his tufts of grass and discarded leaves. Nobody fears the first dragon to return to Apricity.

With the kids distracted, I walk up to Xander and hold out my hand. "Would you like to attend dinner with me?"

His smile makes it so bright that there's no need for sunlight here. There's no hesitation in slipping his palm into mine. "You would go to dinner with me, Cinderfella?"

Together like this, I could be persuaded to go most places. Gemma's teasing lingers in my thoughts. It would be nice to assume we have some chance of a future together, but I'm still not sure.

Is it worth breaking my own heart?

I haven't been with anyone else who makes me feel the way Xander does. It's not his secrets and prestige that make the difference. He's smart and funny and challenges me in a way nobody has. I trust him. With my life. This isn't some quick kiss and romp in a barn, and then we pretend not to know each other when out in public.

If Xander offered to brand me as his own, I would want it. I'd agree. Probably far faster than I could think through the consequences. I would want the world to know that he turned me into a sappy romantic. I'd want them to look at us and believe such trivial things like love really exist.

He makes me feel like love is more than what they write in fairy-tales.

I thought it was just that I didn't want him to die. His hand in mine, running from the guards. I thought it was just security in having someone who understood a portion of my story in a way nobody else can. Gemma is proof, though, that this isn't just the way I feel about my friends. I want Xander, and it feels impossible, and I think I might allocate myself to loving him from afar if nothing else.

There isn't time to consider every angle of every option right now. It's enough to admit that I care, that, if I were alone in the dark and knew the end was imminent, I would openly say those three little words out loud for him. I'd like to have a life in which we get to choose peace instead of all of this. Maybe we met accidentally, bumped into each other on the street while he was researching ancient magic, or caught each other's gaze across a table at a party I was invited to because my father's tavern got the recognition it deserved, and had a chance to grow from there without the stress of life and death and revolution on our souls.

This is the life we have, though.

I squeeze his fingers and shake my head at him, leading him back the way we came while Gemma tells Skelly to behave himself while she's away. "If it makes a difference," Xander says when we're halfway up the hill and the backside of the castle is back in view, "I'm glad you're here with me."

Gods, he must realize that I'm wavering on my stance to stay strong in the face of kneeling in devotion to him instead of being a rational human being. "A compliment from a prince?" I try to tease him, my voice whisker thin, and I clear it before continuing, "My ego might be too much to take to dinner."

"Your ego was too much when I met you."

It's not a golden arrow, but he has pierced me nonetheless. I play at being hurt by his words, and he laughs while Gemma joins the attack on my personality.

We're loud, boisterous, and making a scene when we make it up to where Camellia left me. Gemma herds us away from the castle we came through and down yet another sloping staircase that takes us further from the city and fully underground, with the promise that dinner always happens here.

I take in the new scenery. Firm walls are erected all around us as we slip below the earth. Etchings cover them. A history proclaimed in chisel and hammer of people on their knees, a people begging to survive, and the compromises they made to get to where they are today.

Apparently, that's underground.

"There are quite a few secrets here in Apricity. Over the last two hundred and fifty-three years, they have learned how to stretch the bounds of their enslavement to Briargild." Xander says to me, his tone hushed and reverent. "Everything you've seen up until now is a carefully kept illusion. They can't be seen by my father as people getting their lives together or advancing technologically, whether by natural means or with the help of magic. Down here, away from the sun and hidden from the eyes of their neighboring kingdom, is the true soul of Apricity."

My eyes can barely take it all in. The colors they can't display on the surface are blooming down here like a garden that won't be contained. The brightest blues and sharpest yellow. A shade of green that I've never seen in nature, but seems completely at home here. Splashes of red and peach and sprigs of white. The home of the people of Apricity is a cavernous underground space with smashed pieces of tiles pressed into malleable walls to create shapes of creatures long lost to the tales of time. So many of them are dragons with flared wings, beings that make me think of the skeletal nuisance we just left in the park. Others are deer with too many limbs, their horns multi-colored and reaching far into the skies. A few take the shape of birds, their feathers given a flair for the dramatics as they're overtaken with elemental decoration; fire on one, water flowing off another, and still a third made of leaves that seem to coalesce over a pink heart. The artistic depictions show a world before Briargild, a people dressed in beautifully bright garments who lived side by side with these figments of today's imagination. Magic wasn't just real; it was a visceral part of living in this kingdom, and a way of life for so many people, erased or overtaken by the founders of Briargild.

That history is reflected everywhere as we continue down the enormous underground shafts. Here, the murals focus on the past and flickering hopes for the future with depictions of women with hair pulled back in colorful bandanas working diligently to repair a forest with rows and rows of saplings growing for them. Men are shown not with weapons and armor as so many paintings are done back home, but surrounded by those they love, feeding them from heaping platters, and offering them gifts wrapped in long ribbons. This isn't a state built on an army. It's one that has managed not to be snuffed out because of love.

My throat is too tight to answer Xander's next musing. I think my mother would have loved showing me this place. I know she taught my father everything he knew about unconditional love and showing up for each other. It's because a place like this existed that I was raised knowing the world had hope.

I wasn't a prince in a castle, but I had everything I needed.

I squeeze Xander's arm when he looks over at me. "We have to help them. These people deserve to live without fear of a neighboring government."

He bumps his shoulder into me. "Weren't you trying to convince me once that you aren't a leader?"

"I'm not," I argue, ignoring the way his eyebrow arches in obvious disbelief. "It doesn't take a leader to see that people are suffering and should be treated better. Everyone should feel this way."

"Not everyone is willing to take the steps to make the world a better place, Eli."

There's more to be said in that conversation. I let it go, though. I'd rather go back to thinking about how Xander is still holding my hand. Nobody gawks at us for the action. Not like they would back in Briargild.

I let myself slip into a fantasy in which there's a day that Xander and I can still be like this without fear of reproach or arrest or beheadings. It's nothing strange or odd; holding onto him is the easiest thing I've ever done. Back in Brairgild, openness like this would be seen as an outright sign of revolt, but I think that this option should exist for everyone. Regardless of their place of origin or their appearance, or if the person they're willing to lay down their life for happens to be of the same gender. Love should be allowed to exist in every form.

Since Xander has clammed up again, I look around at the bright cavern, the home beneath the bones of a fallen kingdom, and clear my throat. "My father would have liked you."

He shakes his head. "You barely admit to liking me."

It's a tease. A joke. The way it slides past his teeth, though, with bitter hesitation, tells me that it's more than a throwaway line. We're at the start of something I would like to consider to be a blooming romance, a relationship that doesn't just last, but exceeds the tests of time, but this thing between us is tenuous regardless of what Gemma thinks about the way we look at each other. I might not be brave enough to kiss him again, but I think this is as good a time as any to confront known hardships in our pasts and offer a reminder that I'm here even when the story isn't pretty.

"I saw how your father treated you," I start slowly, my voice low just for him as a couple of children stride over with hands full of citrus they wish to share. "I'm telling you that mine wouldn't. He would have loved having another person to dote on and to see that I was taken care of by something that wasn't our tavern. He was always trying to get me to have bigger dreams or to throw myself outside for reasons I couldn't understand at that time.

"I thought I would be happy hiding behind a bar my entire life, but, whatever happens next, this has all been worth it to have met you, and I want you to know you would've immediately been a part of my family whether you were ready for it or not."

Xander opens his mouth. Shuts it. His bottom lip puffs out as though he's working carefully to hold in his most intimate thoughts. I see a glint of his smile from the corner of my eye as he accepts a fruit that looks like an orange but with a glistening red skin that he deftly peels with his bare hands.

He breaks open the skin, red droplets staining his fingertips as floral notes fill the air, and holds out a sliver of the fruit to me. Together, in a strange and beautiful place, I stick the piece of fruit in my mouth and relish the hint of hibiscus that overtakes the citrus, tingling along the tip of my tongue and burying itself in the crevices of my gums.

"You barely tolerate me, Cinderfella."

That's it. My mouth is full of foreign flavors, and juice dribbles on my chin. I'm overstimulated and exhilarated and feeling rather rambunctious. If he wants to compliment me and get away with it, he's going to have to deal with the same treatment from me.

"Nobody infuriates and challenges me the way you have in the past couple of weeks, Xander. Nobody has made me smile or laugh or forget my tragedies the way you have, either. I'd really like to get to know you more, to know thirteen renditions of whoever you think you are, and watch you become who you're meant to be, alright?"

He swallows hard, his lips stained red along with his fingers and his eyes so damn wide. "Promise to remember you said that?"

"Gosh, you guys are so adorable. Either kiss or pick up the pace!"

Gemma crosses her arms over her chest and taps out a steady beat with her foot. I hadn't realized we'd come to a stop. Maybe I was too busy looking in Xander's eyes to remember what my feet were doing.

I hold up a hand to stall her. "If we're making promises, will you promise to just keep being honest with me even if I tell you you're stupid?"

"Why are you assuming I'll be the stupid one?" Xander asks, his fingers finding my waist.

I roll my eyes at him, my fingers almost curling in his collar. The fabric is right there at my fingertips. "You tried to lead a rebellion, knowing the use of magic alone could kill you and that any person who gave up your identity would face grave consequences. I think you're incredibly brave, Prince Charming, but also so very stupid."

"I did what I had to do, I don't think you would have made much better choices in my place," he chuckles, his warm breath on my face.

We are standing so close. I could tilt my chin. He could lean in.

Gemma's right.

I want to kiss the freaking prince.

She clears her throat, and I move away from him, still holding his hand but at a safer distance as we continue into the place built below the land's surface. Magic balls of light persuade chandeliers made of pieces of shell and broken glass to throw rainbows across the walls and floor. I'd only ever seen the yellow magic orbs in Briargild, the magic there trapped by golden vessels and forced into submission. Here, they're in any shade an artist can imagine: brilliant whites, glowing oranges, a pink fuzzy ball immersed inside a chandelier that makes the whole place shimmer as though we're looking through fashionable, heart-shaped glasses.

It's beautiful and amazing and far more incredible than any depiction of functioning magic in fairytales. This is what magic could be if unrestrained by the laws and obligations of the King of Briargild. I smile at the dazzling display, overtaken by it, and then glance to the man at my side.

Maybe I just feel hopeful because Xander is still next to me.

Whatever the reason for my mood, we're led into an impressive dining hall with more murals of lost beasts and long ago royalty pressed into the walls. There isn't a single long table in here. Instead, groups of three, round tables are pressed together like unique flowers with chairs lining their petals. There isn't a throne here, either. More ivy is clinging to the corners of the room and draped over wooden beams that extend across the entirety of the ceiling. It seems the Queen could be everywhere all at once, no matter the table she chooses to seat herself.

Xander and I are given a table, prompted to sit across from each other to leave space for my cousin to be between us, and Gemma fills the spot next to me without waiting for anyone to tell her where to go. My fairy godmother isn't leaving my side again anytime soon. That settled, we sit back as the dining hall thrums with nervous energy. Glittering cups of juice are set in front of us. Water pitchers are left on the table. Food is pushed around on wooden carts, the people offering it to us doing so with smiles as they heap far more than I could dare to try to eat onto our plates. When they're done serving us and leaving offerings on a plate for Queen Camellia, they serve themselves, lining the carts along the walls and scooping food onto their own plates before seating themselves around the room. The tables nearest us fill up the fastest, nobody speaking directly to us, but all of them doing nothing to hide the way they stare.

To say I feel mildly interesting and important would be a grand understatement.

The rest of the room murmurs between themselves in a crescendo of noise that threatens to be louder than the winds of a storm, wrapping around Xander, Gemma, and my bubble of solitude as we grin at each other over our goblets of pale juice. It isn't long before the Queen is announced. Horn-shaped flowers let out puffs of sound that weave with the stroking spines of another type of vegetation, the plants making music lovelier than anything played by a bard back home.

And when Queen Camellia makes her appearance, well, she looks just like herself.

No puffy gown or something grand as that of royalty back in Brairgild. She's lost her bright colors of before. Her dress is simple, a white shift with thin straps at the shoulder that drips down to her ankles. A plain white cloth is folded into thirds and wrapped around her eyes. Her hair is left wild and free with white flowers pressed into the curls. She alone is a presence to be noticed and doesn't need to carry on the gaudy traditions of her enemies.

"I'm happy to see you again," I confide, stepping out of my chair to help her into her seat as ivy strands pat me for my actions.

"I've some announcements to make and then you can decide whether or not you're truly happy to see me, cousin."

That seems more threatening than I believe she meant it. There are so many looming issues, though, so I understand the sentiment. King Anerald has to be on the road here by now. Even with Wynnifred slowing him down, they were expected to show up to collect Cam for the ball that would have Xander and Camellia marry each other in an effort to unite the kingdoms in a way that best suited Briargild's plans.

She sets off to eat, and I follow her lead, my attention caught on the man across from me picking at his food as blushing bits of light cling to his collar. It's too soon to accuse him of holding onto another secret. I see it, though, the weight of keeping something to himself pushing him deeper into his chair as he curtly welcomes Camellia to our table.

Something is going on between the two of them.

What else could there be besides a betrothal?

Camellia speaks before anyone else, tipping her head in Gemma's general direction. "How are you feeling now that you've reunited with your fairy godmother?"

"The best I can," I answer immediately. "Thank you for keeping her safe for me."

Camellia cuts through a piece of pork, chews it delicately, and then swallows, the motion easy to follow as her throat is unadorned. "Since I did you a favor, I think it's only fair you do one for me, too, cousin."

Ah. There it is. My stomach plunges towards the floor. I give up trying to eat. My silverware clatters to the table, and I lift my chin to her challenge.

"What do you want?"

She clears her distinguished throat and swivels her head towards Xander, some of her vines reaching up to pat him on the shoulder. "Did you not mention anything to him? I left you alone for a few hours."

Xander actually looks sheepish. He shakes his head. Then, remembers she can't see him and stutters out a reply.

"It didn't come up, and I figured if he hadn't guessed by now that maybe his family should be the one to tell him. Besides, he was happy to see Gemma and me let them have the afternoon."

She tuts her tongue at him. "Don't pretend you weren't carried away playing with the dragon."

"Skelly is a real dragon," he counters. "Of course, I got carried away."

Before he can sputter and argue anymore, she waves a hand at him and turns back towards me, her elbows planted on the table. "Well, I understand that you're not exactly prepped for this question, but my favor remains the same. I have no desire to marry. Not a man. Not a woman. I would like to be left alone with my plants, and you, Eli Cinderfella, are the only person who can take my place. I would appreciate it if you agreed to unify our kingdoms with Prince Alexander Charming here in my stead."

That was a lot of words. I understand those words. At least, alone, I can pick out their definitions. Yet, it sounds a lot like a queen just asked me to take on her kingdom.

She asked me to take on her kingdom and marry Xander.

I look across the table at the man I've been unable to shake from my thoughts. This man, the one who isn't wearing a crown but sits with shoulders molded to carry the weight of the world. He fiddles with his fork, fingers flexing so that his scars shine in the magic light from above us. This man I held hands with as we ran from one kingdom to another. The only man I've had eyes for in a long time.

This one.

Not just a prince. Not a necromancer. But Xander.

I don't know what part of this I'm supposed to believe. Xander looks equal parts hopeful and mortified, his cheeks flushed in a crimson that dips below his collar. The entirety of the dining hall has gone quiet.

"Did you…" I'm pointing at Camellia even though I can't rip my eyes off of Xander, his throat bobbing from the same effort. "Did you just propose to me for him?"

I like Xander very much. I dare to say I love him. Just to myself. It's not something I would say to him yet. It's far too soon, right?

Even so, I didn't think we would skip right from meeting, surviving death-defying circumstances, untangle his lies about his identity, and then race right for the altar.

This has to be a joke.

Right?

Twenty minutes ago, I was staring at him, wanting to do what Gemma teased me about, and holding back because it would never be possible between the two of us long-term. I can't seem to wrap my mind around what Camellia is suggesting. I'm thinking over the phrasing of her words since nobody is offering to explain what's happening to me. The only way for me to unify the kingdoms by marrying Xander would be if I were…

Anerald had made a similar comment, and I hadn't thought about it because I was worried about escaping. Besides, it couldn't be real. It was the least of my worries.

Now, though… I shake my head.

I'm a tavern keep.

I can't even say the other title.

"I can't take your position."

It's not a question. I'm not asking for any more clarification. Xander's fingers cover his mouth, shock sparkling in his gaze. I'm glad I'm not alone in my feelings.

Queen Camellia doesn't seem to care that I've declined on her blatant offer. "And why not?"

Because…

I have no idea how to run a kingdom. I can barely keep myself alive. I'm not responsible enough to have people looking to me for their lives and problems, all of it laid at my feet like the tyrants I've grown up fearing.

That's not what I am.

"Gemma, dear, did you not talk to him, either?"

Blonde curls bob next to me. "I don't know how much I can sway Eli. I told them to kiss."

Camellia laughs at that, her next question moving back to me. "Did you?"

"No, I-."

"Yes," Xander whispers in complete opposition to my scrambling words.

We stop, breathless, and stare at each other. The women on both sides of me have smug expressions. After a moment, Cam clears her throat.

"Did it ever occur to you that it was Xander's idea to throw together a marriage proposal?"

Ummm no. Why would it? I learned he was in an arranged marriage while lying under his mattress and hoping the King of Briargild wouldn't find and exterminate me. Everything seemed straightforward. The King wanted this to happen, and Xander was out of options.

When I'm too bogged down in thought to answer her, she nudges Xander with her elbow. "Are you going to tell him or are you going to make me do it?"

Xander leans back in his chair, those silver eyes begging for me to keep my promise from before. I brace myself for whatever secret is about to be revealed. This can't be more of a revelation than finding out he had been two-timing me as a prince and a necromancer at the same time.

"Look, my father threatened violence that would completely wipe out the remainder of Apricity. He doesn't want to save their culture or uphold the treaty. With the rise in magic wielders and growing tension from those in the working class being targeted by his laws, he wanted to wipe out this place in order to send a very clear message that no more rebellion would be tolerated." Nervously, he taps his fingers on the table top, speaking faster as if he can get to the truth without slowing down for me to process it. "I couldn't let that happen, so I countered with a marriage proposal. Cam and I are supposed to marry each other at the next ball, uniting our kingdoms and stopping the complete destruction of Apricity for the time being."

When I glance to the queen, to my cousin, her frown only confirms the truth. I slump in my own chair. Xander has been gambling with several lives more than his own.

I might need some fresh air. Actually, I probably need ten years to figure out my feelings and then some fresh air. This is all way too much.

The revolution isn't a fleeting attempt at stopping King Anerald anymore. It's the only thing standing between this place, these people seated around me, and total devastation. If it doesn't work, no marriage is ever going to get Anerald to stop his tyrannical ways. He'll squash wild magic before it has a chance to fully come back to life here, only caring to have all the power to himself.

Camellia reaches towards me, aware of my hesitation and tense disposition as her plants wind around my arms and pat at my head. "I never wanted to be in charge," she confides, voice low while I watch a single ivy leaf reach up to caress her cheek as though it wishes to stop her from crying. "I don't want to marry anyone, ever, Eli. Romance was not something I've worked into the equation, and it has never flourished between me and your prince, okay?"

Again, my heart flip-flops in my chest. To hear that there is one more woman in my life who has had to give up all the plans for herself to the greater good of a failing society is almost enough to crush me. Gemma did that, too. My mom sacrificed everything for the sake of doing something good. The entire system of my life has been touched by women, with only some of the rights I have by being born a man. None of them could pretend to be aloof for thirty years.

My birthday is coming up.

I could be married before then if I said yes to Camellia right now.

Which is insane.

Xander is out of his chair. He walks around the table, standing an arm's length away from Camellia and me. Pushing his hair back from his eyes, he hovers there, unsure if he's welcome closer.

"I'm not mad at you," I finally whisper, holding out my hand to him. "But I would really appreciate it if you would stop being so complicated."

His palm is warm where he meets me, pulling my wrist upwards to press a kiss to the back of my hand. My heart explodes. I don't know how it stays in my body. There should be a mess on the table and stains on Camellia's dress. His chivalrous brush of lips to my hand is about to be my complete undoing.

"You don't have to marry me," he insists, pressing on before I can try to figure out how to say words that make any sense in this scenario. "Cam really does want to leave her position, though, and she's already petitioned the people to see if they would welcome back the true heir to the throne."

Almost in unison, every head turns towards me. The people are listening. Some smile. Others are wide, dark eyes and furrowed brows. I take a good, long look at them. These aren't just a couple of people peeking at me from around the decrepit city up on the surface. This is a group of people nearly as eclectic as those who used to visit me and my father at our tavern.

Around the edges, there are several centaurs and satyrs, the likes of which I never saw in my near proximity to the castle of Briargild, outfitted in the same bright garments of this hopeful community. A few, lithe figures clothed in what looks to be a complete dress of grasses, leaves, and flowers flit between them, sipping from their cups with pinkies upraised and avoiding my eye contact. I've never seen beings like them before. Perhaps they're nymphs who have stopped worrying about trying to fit in within a kingdom that holds so much disdain for their general existence. Tilting my head back, I note smaller tables near the vine-covered ceilings and the bobbing bodies of fairies not yet seated. Near me, there's a range of people with all sorts of hairstyles and skin tones, people who have been changed over the course of time that desperately hold onto their traditions and cultures even as circumstances demand they evolve to survive the coming world. Every single one of them, magical beings and regular humans alike, stares at me with hope.

The same hope Prince Alexander directed to me back in his bedroom.

The hope that Gemma saw in me after we had overcome our differences, and the one Wynnifred nurtured before sending me back out here to retrieve our fairy godmother.

It's a hope reflected in Xander's gaze now as he squeezes my hand and drops to his knees. "Say something, Eli."

How are there any words to answer this?

I open my mouth and then shut it. Speechless doesn't begin to cover the way I feel. Overwhelmed, undeserving, incompetent. I'm literally just a guy good at serving drinks in a tavern. Everything else I've fumbled and messed up in chaotic ways nobody else could have ever predicted.

They're all watching me, holding their breath as my own chest tightens and I grapple with the fact that a man I was sure I couldn't have is still kneeling in front of me. "What if I'm not who you think I am?"

I can't focus on the whole room. I can't even look at Camellia and her bustling plants. Gemma is a hand on my shoulder, but she remains quiet as I look ahead. Dark spots cloud the edges of my vision as my mind races and air struggles to force itself past my teeth. Xander is holding onto me still, though, a single tether in the storm of panic threatening to wipe me out.

"Eli Cinderfella," his voice is low, just for me. "You are incredible. I've known since the first time we met that you were meant for amazing things, and I know that this is your destiny. You can turn it down, but that won't stop Briargild from showing up, it won't help these people, and it won't bring your father back. If you don't feel like you can believe in yourself, then know I believe in you, and I'll be here to help you every step of the way."

A startled hiccup escapes me. He's serious. Those silver eyes haven't flinched away from my gaze. He's so warm in all the places he's touching me, dutifully keeping me here with him in the present moment, even though I want to run screaming from the room.

"My whole life, it was just me and my father," I whisper, craning my head to meet the anxious looks from those nearest us.

"The world has to be more than one person, Eli." His thumb caresses my hand. "Community, building something good and strong despite the bad in the world, that's how we get closer to a happily ever after."

I shake my head. There are so many arguments I have against this. My thoughts are whizzing through my skull like fireflies on a rampage. All of it stops when a new hand presses on my shoulder.

I look up at the much older woman, one with short hair and a kind smile. She says something in a language I don't understand, but Camellia translates softly, reaching out to hold my free hand.

"She says it's okay to be scared. You hold magic, and sometimes that responsibility can be a lot, but you are also very loved, and she has waited her entire life to meet the person destined to help us shed our despair."

I look at the older woman, her hair ink black but streaked through with handfuls of gray, as I reply. "I don't know if I can live up to everything you all need."

Camellia translates again, this time for the older woman, but we're no longer alone for her to reply. Others have left their seats. They crowd closer.

"You can't be everything for all of us, but you can be yourself and keep your promises and make this world a little better than it is now," a man in a yellow shift proclaims.

"Adira's child wouldn't fear a little public speaking. You are more than this, young man."

"It is time for you to come home and help us achieve freedom!"

The responses keep coming until it seems like everyone around me has gotten to say their piece. Some are grand one-liners proclaiming I'm a prophetic son coming home to my destiny. Others are gentle reminders that greatness isn't one moment, one achievement, but a life built on doing good every single day. A young girl with a doll cradled in her arms whispers close to me that she thinks I would look good in a crown, and that's important to being a king. A centaur near the edge of the room yells that he remembers me from the tavern, from somewhere I thought magic had been completely erased, and he knows that I can do this, that both of my parents would have believed in my ability to lead people towards a better life.

I gave up trying to hold in my tears several minutes ago. My cheeks wet, my throat clogged with emotion, I let myself be embraced by a kingdom in need of a king and finally give in to their enthusiastic prodding. For the first time since the tavern collapsed, I come home.

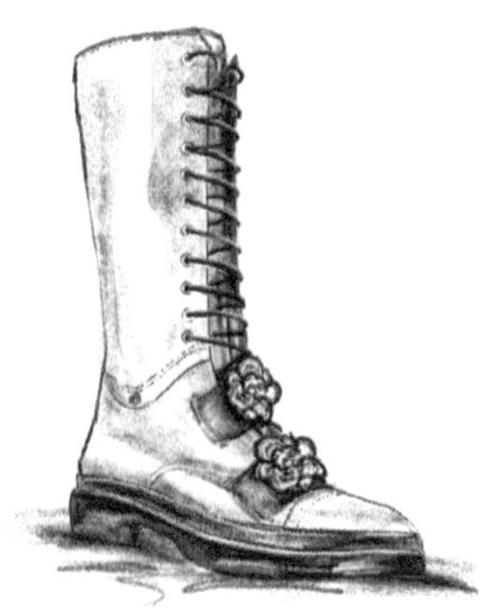

23

I stayed seated in the dining hall as every person gathered in this secret society of a still surviving kingdom bid me congratulations and promised to do their best to help my taking of the throne be a smooth transition. None of them can control King Anerald Charming or the coming of Briargild, but it's nice to know I have a devoted following determined to make sure I don't simply fall on my face within minutes of being crowned king.

King.

It doesn't feel real at all.

I don't know if the shock will ever wear off.

Of all the fairytales I've read and had told to me, none have come close to evoking the feeling I have now, an overwhelming collection of hope and optimism. I swear I'll believe happily ever afters exist if we just have a chance to beat Brairgild and spend a few years rebuilding the world out here.

The dinner comes to an end. Cheers still linger in the hall even when everyone has dispersed, besides Xander, Gemma, the soon-to-not-be-a queen, and me. "You're really sure about this?" I ask my cousin because one of us has to double-check everything before we make choices we can't take back.

She snorts at me. "Very much, Eli. I would have been free of this responsibility if the other king hadn't done away with every other heir in his attempt to gain the most control possible over Apricity."

She's quiet a second, her bare feet scuffing the ground as she thinks for a moment, swinging her legs under the table. "I believe he would have had me killed, too, if he could have figured out how to access the innate magic here. Without someone to link themselves to the magic that flourishes in this land, the plants die, and the earth tries to rebel. It wouldn't offer him a connection, though. Not after years of trying, and I was all he had left to take on the honor of Apricity's lineage."

My apology for the horrors she has survived falls flat between us. I can't begin to understand the pain of losing everyone she loves, only to be chained to a diplomatic position because of the man who caused her so much suffering. Losing my mother was a total tragedy in my world, and my father did everything in his power to shelter me from it, perhaps providing me too much comfort in our little corner of the kingdom. It was a strange blessing not to have to deal with this version of reality every single day, but I'm ready to do what I can to make up for lost time.

I want to be who they need to make things better.

"So, I'll need to bond with the kingdom through magic?"

Camellia's smile is genuine. She pats my hand. "Oh, cousin, you already did. Completely by accident. Your godmother told me about the little incident with her wand and how it easily attached itself to you. When you cast magic, you don't consume from the elements around you; you literally create life. How else do you think your dragon would have made the entire journey here?"

My mouth opens and then closes. I had no idea. I mean, I knew that Gemma had accused me of breaking her wand and casting spells incorrectly from the very first time I tried to use magic, but this is an entirely new layer to it. I swivel my head to meet Xander's gaze.

"Did you know?"

He offers a curt nod. "I suspected. Our magic felt different together. I sent a letter to Cam and told her I might finally have found the interesting man she was looking for."

"You told her I was interesting?"

The letters. With the secret messages in pressed dots on the corners. I'm breathless. Camellia lets out a laugh. Gemma teases me mercilessly, and yet, all that matters is Xander across the table, smiling at me.

Camellia clears her throat after everyone settles down. "We should call it a night. We need to get Eli prepared to take over the mantle of the kingdom. Midnight is fast approaching, and that's the best time to swap over the magic."

"We still have time before Briargild is here. What's the rush?"

"The sooner you take over, the sooner I can leave." She says, her lips tilting to let me know she's mostly joking, before her tone turns serious. "It takes more than a few days for one to understand the scope of this kingdom, Eli. You may be answering a known prophecy, the call of the return of dragons in order to usurp the Briargild crown, but you're not a god. I think we should give you all the time you need to become acquainted with being the king here before company arrives to challenge you."

That seems fair. Rational, even. I can see that Camellia wasn't just the only candidate for the position, but served as a good queen, too. She did her very best to hold things together here and is now doing everything she can to pass on the obligations of a crown I never expected. It's only fair that I follow through on the things I agreed to do.

"Okay. What do we do until midnight?"

Xander pushes back from the table and comes to my side. "I know where the guest suite is. Why don't we rest for a little bit before you go attaching to new magic?"

Gemma throws a balled-up napkin at me as Xander pulls me to my feet. "Oh yeah. Go rest lots. I'm sure you do that without clothes on, right?"

I pluck the napkin off the floor and toss it back at her without looking. "You're being a terrible fairy godmother."

When I glance over my shoulder, her grin is victorious. "Have fun, Cinderfella. We'll come retrieve you when it's time."

Out of arguments, my hand once more where it belongs in Xander's grip, I let the prince lead me from the dining hall. The chatter from Camellia and Gemma chases us out into the cavernous halls. Then, we're relatively alone. A few people amble about, drunk on punch and full of frivolous energy. It's a good moment. Easy and carefree, and warm. I want to make sure these people get to lead good lives.

And I might have my own chance at something like a good life despite the tragedies.

I mean, a prince is holding my hand and leading me to his private, guest chamber instead of the little houses Camellia pointed out earlier.

"Do I outrank you now?"

My voice echoes through the hall, it bounces off the mosaic creatures and reverberates in the air around us. "Technically, but if you keep talking like that, I don't know if they'll be able to find a crown that fits you."

I smack his arm and then laugh when he whirls back to me, catching my wrist in his hold and daring me to do it again. "Does this work better for you then? If it was just rank keeping you from kissing me…"

So, he had heard Gemma's outright confession that she didn't just support this union but had tried to get us to start without Camellia's favor. Why does the cavern feel so much smaller? My world has shrunk to just him and me and that warm spot where he has my wrist.

"Maybe I don't keep kissing every guy I'm attracted to," I counter, chin tilted up as he grins down at me from his slight height advantage.

"But you admit to thinking I'm attractive?"

He's teasing, voice dripping into a lower octave as he steps closer. My back bumps into the wall. I'm pressed into a collage of color, the art at my back an appropriate depiction of how I'm feeling. Radiant. Spewing every shade of the rainbow. I feel seen, and it is almost unbearable in the best way.

Xander doesn't crowd me, dropping his hold from my wrist to gently caress my cheek. He lingers with a step still between us, giving me the chance to push him back and turn away. "I thought you were the most gorgeous man I'd ever had the chance to duel when you challenged me."

My fingers are curled in his shirt, holding him here in this moment with me. "You challenged me," I correct, his heart thrumming so hard and fast where my knuckles brush his chest. "I probably would have forgotten how to do any magic if I were able to see your whole face that night."

The smile I earn from that comment makes my knees weak. I lean my weight back into the wall to keep from sinking into a puddle. Xander strokes my cheek again, his expression turning almost stoic as those silver eyes search my face.

"Marriage doesn't have to be a primary objective. I would be okay with unifying the kingdoms through shared diplomacy, too."

Prince Alexander Charming is giving me every chance to walk away. Not from the mantel my cousin already dropped on my shoulders. Not from the war that is coming every minute we waste, an unavoidable bit of terror that will make or break our futures. But this. Us. Right now, the spark that swirls through my chest when I look at him, whether it's my magic or my heart responding to his nearness.

"Do you not want to kiss me again?"

I know that's not the main focus of this conversation, but I like the way his eyes go wide at my question. Marriage is more than conversations and kisses. Yet, it's a good place to start. It's something I can focus on as the landscape of the life I have known up until this point continues to be a shifting thing beneath me.

His left hand gently rests on my hip. "I've wanted to kiss you since the very first day, Eli Cinderfella. I wouldn't have stopped kissing you if you hadn't pulled away from me."

"You're a fool," I whisper, pulling him towards me when he makes no move to come closer without my enthusiastic approval.

Then, he's right there. Lips brushing my own. Chaste and probing. He's kissing like a goddamn prince.

I didn't just ask for a royal gentleman.

I let my fingers roam through this hair, tugging at the strands until they're twisted around my fingers and completely mine. Xander is gentle and controlled, while I embrace him with the same wild ferocity that had our magic creating a dragon.

He tastes like the punch from dinner. Sweet and enticing. When I pull at him again, he groans and meets me.

The hard mosaic behind me is a dragon splayed for admiration. Xander, in front, admires me with mind and tongue. I am lightheaded and panting when he pulls away again.

"I do have a room here we could..."

Right. I dare to look over his shoulder at the mostly empty cavern. Nobody seems to be watching us, and yet I've never been so blatantly obvious with my affections. I should be terrified to be acting like this.

My fingers cupping Xander's jaw, I refocus on him, my prince outlined in the rainbows of a hundred broken pieces that have come together to form something exquisite and beautiful. "If we do this, I want to kiss you where people can see. I don't want to hide."

His forehead rests against mine. "You're the sun and the stars, Eli Cinderfella. Hiding you would be an impossible task I won't endure."

"Are you always so insufferably romantic?"

"Of course not," his lips press to the top of my head as my entire world spins with the crash of my fantasies becoming my reality. "I saved it all for you. Will you allow me the pleasure of being insufferable for a very long time?"

It's not a marriage proposal. Which I can handle. I let him lace his fingers into mine as I nod.

"I think I can tolerate you for a while longer, Charming."

Hand in hand with a man who is not only a prince but promising to be mine, we head to his rooms.

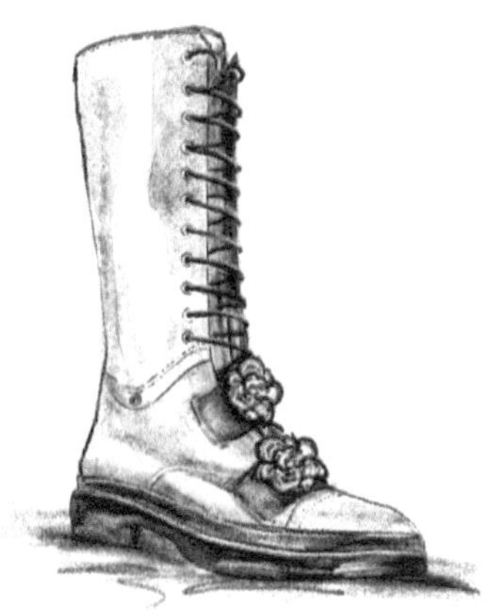

24

Xander leads me up a winding staircase, each step a carved piece of the small hill that houses the real Apricity. He tells me three times that these aren't royal suites. Not like they have in Briargild. It's cute that he's nervous, so I don't correct him or remind him that I've never seen anything as fancy as guest suites in a castle besides the one night I snuck into his personal tower chambers.

At the top of the landing, all by itself, is a room guarded by a green door. Xander doesn't have a key. He knocks twice, and the plants answer, opening it from within, the long vines as dexterous as human fingers. I remember Camellia's comments about the plants being her spies, that sometime very soon I'll be receiving the magic of the kingdom, which I still don't completely understand, and then disregard all of it because Xander is still holding my hand, and the plants are not my biggest concern.

I don't have any secrets to hide.

Right now, stepping into Xander's room, I'm exactly who I want to be.

The room is smaller than his place in the Briargild castle. There isn't a single spot of red. Instead, the walls are a muted brown interspersed with moss and greenery from all sorts of plants. A bookshelf takes up most of one wall, stuffed full with what has to be illegal texts like the one that brought our paths together so many days ago, before magic completely overturned the state of my life.

His bed is pressed against another, smaller than the impressive mattress he had in Briargild, with no space to hide beneath since there are trunks stuffed under it, but dressed in comfortable quilts stitched from the bright colors that seem to bleed through the entirety of Apricity. It's quaint and cozy and feels the way Xander does next to me, not yet a home but somewhere I could see myself wanting to be.

The door clicks shut behind us and is promptly covered by winding vines that promise to give us privacy from the way they turn their leaves away from us. Xander is still holding my hand. He looks around the space and then to me, waiting with expectation simmering in his gaze.

"It's nice," I confide, my stomach doing something acrobatic I can't seem to ignore.

I'm not infested with butterflies. The beasts that chew on my ribs and rifle through my intestines are something far more ravenous. I've been overtaken by magic and anxiety and anticipation entangled in a delicious slush that rattles me to my core.

Xander brushes his thumb over my knuckles. Pink glitter sparks at my palms in an instant response. So rough from years of labor, I consider being embarrassed about the difference between our palms, but he doesn't utter a complaint and instead pulls my hand up and presses a kiss to the back of it.

Gods, there's going to be glitter all over this room if I can't get myself under control.

Glitter. It would be a beautiful streak through his hair. He'd have memories of me from all the sparkling spots I touched him. My handprint on his chest or wrapped around his waist. Fingerprints dancing over him. A messy layout of all the ways I wanted and then had him.

My hand is lingering near Xander's mouth, his silver eyes wide as he watches me in the gentle glow of his magic lights. "I know this has all been a lot, Eli."

My first name. He's serious. I don't know how he thinks he'll have a serious conversation when he's holding me like this and looking at me like… well, like he cares so much that his emotions alone could alter our fates.

"You don't have to trust me."

I tilt my head at what looks to be a pained proclamation. "Why wouldn't I trust you?"

We've survived magical combat and running from a swarm of guards and literal pumpkins prepared to end us. If all of that wasn't enough to solidify some bond between us, I don't know what is.

"I knew you were in line for the throne here," he admits, letting my hand fall and his arms cross over his chest. "I should have told you, but Cam wanted to be the one to introduce you to everything. I've known since the rebel meeting that you were special, Eli, and I lied to you a lot, but I want you to know that I never meant to hurt you, and I intend to be fully honest from here on out."

My fingers are cold where he's no longer holding me. Glitter sparkles on the floor at my feet. My chest is aflame. A family of sparrows has taken to making a nest there, and now they're all opening their wings in a savage attempt to leave.

I may combust from the way Xander is nervously watching me.

"I do trust you," I say simply.

' He doesn't pull away when I reach up to cup his face. Instead, relief floods those eyes I've let haunt me over the course of the last couple of weeks, the eyes that I wanted to see more of when he was a prince who covered one with an eye patch and the same eyes I begged to open after our chaotic combat in the forest. His lips twitch. The first smile between two people who are more than friends or accidental allies, and agreeing to see where this may go.

"In honor of being completely honest from here on out," I continue, momentarily losing my train of thought when he bites the edge of his lip. "I did steal an entire outfit from your wardrobe at the castle and completely ruin it, and I have pretty much nothing to my name, so I will not be returning or replacing it."

His laughter flashes between us, filling the room like the glimmer of a shooting star on a clear night. "I think I know of a way you can make it up to me."

A man always prepared to verbally spar, I have a hundred accusations to throw back at him. There are at least twelve different ways he has almost cost me my life since we met; the least he can allow is for me to ruin an outfit every now and then. Words, though, abandon me when he leans in.

This is the best way to settle disputes.

I should have done it much sooner.

The scent of pine and mystery envelopes me as his free hand cradles the back of my neck, putting me in the right position for him to have his way with me. And I let him. For a moment, that is.

In every other relationship, Prince Alexander Charming of Briargild was likely the leader, the one in charge, the end-all, be-all of the night.

I've no idea if the Necromancer had a fling in his dark clothes, but I would assume he also dictated all activities of the night, a commander on the field, and a leader in the bedroom.

Xander, though, has met his match.

I see him. I understand him. I want this just as much as he does.

Plants slither out of the way when I walk him into the nearest wall, my hands on his shoulders, while his are feather-light on my hips. I kiss him until I'm dizzy with it. His hands go from ghosting touches to firm guidance, his fingers pulling the hem of my shirt up. I lay one last kiss on the salty column of his throat that has him moaning in a way far too wanton for someone who was once an uptight prince, and then step away.

"You know, we could use a bath."

He slaps my shoulder playfully as though I've offended his entire lineage. "You won't have me if I stink, Cinderfella?"

There he is. We laugh. Comfortable and without any more secrets between us.

He takes my hand and leads me through the one door other than the entrance to a bathroom that puts the washroom back in my apartment to shame. The tub is set into the floor, a porcelain bowl more than large enough for two. Beside it, there's a shelf of toiletries and soaps, enough to bathe a small army. It seems my prince has expensive taste in bathroom supplies, no matter where he is.

The plants are already running us a hot bath. "Cam wasn't serious. The plants serve the magic in this place, and they like to be overly helpful. She's not always controlling them," Xander informs me with a chuckle as I eye an especially close vine of ivy pouring bubble bath into the steaming water.

That does make me feel a little better. Cam is family by blood, but we barely know each other, and I would prefer she not get too many direct details about my time alone with this man. Besides, I'm still not sure what it means to take on the power of the magic that runs this place, but I wasn't looking forward to having a thousand viney servants constantly at my beck and call. That feels like far too much responsibility for someone who has been learning how to use magic for only a couple of weeks.

The scent of citrus bursts through the bathroom. I shut the door, and Xander arches an eyebrow at me as he collects towels from a cabinet set into the wall.

"The tub is big enough for both of us if…"

His smile flares, a sun expanding for that blinding moment before it explodes. Setting the towels on a rack by the tub, he watches me pull my shirt off over my head, hesitating six steps away from me.

"Eli, the magic helps me, but I'm not…"

The same as me. I smile gently.

"I hope someday I can make sure you know that all your differences only endear you to me, Xander," I hold that silver gaze the same way he forced me to look at him while spewing compliments I had never considered before. "If you're not ready, that's okay, but I'm not expecting someone perfect under all of that dirt and grime. I want you, however, you'll be mine."

Xander melts, tension falling out of his shoulders. His fingers are on his shirt. And then it's off.

"Where did you learn to charm someone, Eli Cinderfella?" He asks, pulling my attention back to his face before I can get lost in the rest of him that's being revealed.

I step into him because we've come so far in so short a time that any distance between us feels inconvenient. Also, so I can take a closer look, my lips quirked at his question. "I only made tips if I kept customers happy, Charming."

His jaw opens dramatically as I draw my fingers over those bandages on his shoulder. The only flaw on his entire body. The spot where I marred him for a cause I didn't understand. He doesn't give me a chance to apologize again for shooting him with that arrow before he kisses me, his fingers traveling over recently revealed skin. Pink glitter speckles the bathroom floor. It'll be in the tub, discoloring the bubbles soon enough.

Expression amused, his fingers fiddle with the tie of his pants when we separate. "So, I'm getting involved with a professional flirt?"

"We've been involved for a while now, I think," I tease him back.

He kisses me again as though I alone hold all of the hope he has in the world, and our brief connection is a breath of fresh air necessary after barely keeping his head above water for months at a time. "Take a step back before I forget to be a gentleman. We don't have enough time for all the things I've dreamed of doing, and you really should rest before Cam calls on us."

My heart does a flip. He dreamt of me, too.

Our clothes litter the floor, dusted with the pink glitter I can't seem to stop from sparkling everywhere, until we're both in our underwear. Xander sits on the floor and looks at me for just a moment, waiting, I think, to see if this is when I'll change my mind. His fingers gesticulate above his knees, and the vines that hold his carved appendages in place fall away, detaching with only the remnants of red marks on his thighs as a sign he ever had them on in the first place.

Shifting, he uses his arms to help slide himself carefully into the waiting water and then holds a hand out to me in supplicating invitation. "As long as you still want to."

I do. I want. I want a lot more than I ever thought possible.

Gods, I wanted an easy life before the last couple of weeks.

Just my little idea of family and a business that took most of our time. Our lives are intertwined with the brick and mortar as we bled out for it. I think I could have settled for being happy with that.

Now, my skin hot as I step into the bath and sit down across from Xander, I know that this is what happiness truly is. Not just a person. Not just magic and extravagant adventures. Happiness is letting myself hope for more than I'm comfortable grasping at and relishing in the moments I get to hold it close.

Rotting in a dungeon was worth this.

Knowing that a king from another kingdom is going to be hellbent on removing my head from my shoulders is worth it for every moment I linger here in a home my mother loved, in a bath with a man I love, and on the precipice of creating a life I know I will appreciate every day for the rest of my life.

I fought for this, and I'm happy to hold onto it as long as I can.

"Do you mind?"

Xander has a washcloth and soap in his hands already. "Didn't you just tell me that I need to rest?"

Lilac infuses with the blooming sense of hope in my chest as he pours out the soap and gingerly steals my left foot, propping it up on the edge of the tub as he starts to wash and then massage my sore appendages. "I think this will help you relax."

"Fine, but I'm doing you next," I threaten, leaning my head back against the tub wall and shutting my eyes.

Lost in the slice of ethereal bliss that is Alexander Charming, I relax for the first time since meeting Gemma.

I'm not fighting for my life against the intrusion of seemingly malicious magic.

I'm not running from something bound to find me delicious between its too-sharp teeth.

I'm not single-handedly facing down the bigotry of a kingdom too stuck in its roots of hate and discrimination.

I'm not pleading with gods I don't believe in to save the man now massaging me like he owes me a debt he can never repay.

I am simply happy and at peace, and Xander is so fucking good with his hands.

The hot water helps. I'm drifting. Not asleep, fighting it though as he works his way through one leg and then the other and then insists on rubbing soap on my chest, his near proximity about to be my utter undoing.

"Can I wash your hair?" I ask when he finally slows and gives me the rag to finish cleaning my more intimate areas while he retrieves another to do the same for himself.

My heart can't take many more openly sincere smiles from this man. He hasn't been treated kindly by the world. I'm gentle when I help him turn, his hips between my legs as I lean him back to wet his hair. I don't mention the scars on his back, stories we'll share on a different night, physical reminders of battles he's walked away from, and many, I'm sure, were caused by the man we're working to dethrone.

His hands cradle my knees as he relaxes into my hold, and I lather lilac shampoo through his hair. Then conditioner. Then more soaps on my hands as I massage his neck and shoulders, and feel my insecurities about starting a relationship in the middle of a war fall away as he rests back against me, the water cooling around us.

He snores before long, my prince having used all of his energy to survive up until this point and also finally finding a soft moment to relax. Quietly, I ask the plants to rewarm the bath and lean my head back, holding Xander close as I shut my own eyes for just a minute or two.

Alarms bring me back from the depths of sleep. Muffled, but erratic ringing of bells from somewhere else in the cavern system. Around me, the plants tremble and pat my shoulders to wake me. It's all of that and Xander shouting my name that brings me out of the comfort of sleep and back into reality. Xander. Not in the water. He's sitting on the edge of the tub, a towel in his hands for me as he works magic to reattach his carved prosthetics.

"What's-?"

I catch the towel as I lurch to my feet, patting water from my form in quick swipes. "Briargild made it past Wynnifred. We're running out of time to get you officially on the throne. If you don't take over for Cam, then he'll stop us and have us married and do away with you, and I can't accept that, so we need to move."

I'm also pretty attached to the idea of being alive, but it's nice to know I have someone else fighting for me. I watch in quiet astonishment as he rebinds himself with magic and makes it back to his feet, stiffly stretching his legs as he re-establishes the connection between flesh and wood and bristling greenery. Stepping out of the tub, I finish drying and start pulling on clothes that Xander tosses to me from one of the chests under his bed.

It's a good thing we're close in size.

We're dressed to match in moments. Dark pants. Our boots are back on. Yellow tops with embroidered details of leaves around the dipping collar and hems.

I want to tell him he's so handsome.

I want to stay here.

The plants are already unwinding from the door, and Xander is moving. This is the man who planned to overtake the throne from his father, whether or not it would be the same as signing his own death warrant. This is the man who led a rebellion by creating rumors that he could raise the dead. This is who he has been forced to become due to the troubles of our world, and, for just a second, I wish none of that had happened.

We probably wouldn't have met, though, and I'm pretty happy with who we are together right now.

I grab his wrist before he's all the way out of the door. "Xander?"

Silver flicks over my face, fear and tension suspended in my hold. "We need to go."

I know. I know that there's no making this stop now that Briargild is nearly here. I'm going to take on the power of royalty in Apricity. I'm going to become a king, and there's really no going back.

I will be a different man very soon.

But I want to be his right now.

"No matter what happens, I'm so glad I got to do this with you. Only you," I tell him, quickly, as though the words will not leave me before he does. "If something happens or goes wrong or-."

"I'm going to be there. Everything will be okay."

I know. I know he believes that. My heart is pounding in my ears. It's a thudding presence behind my eyes. Doom is the only thing it promises to foresee, and I need to say this before we run out of time.

"I just want to say that I don't really believe in wishes, but if I could make one more, then I would wish we had all the time to properly fall in love because I think you're it for me, Xander."

He pauses, usually so quick to banter and argue. For once, I've struck him silent. He swallows so hard. Around us, the plants quiver and nudge us, but I get to fight for one more moment with Xander, and so I ignore them. Then, fingers trembling as he grabs my waist, he pulls me closer, until we're both in the doorway, one step from our fates.

"You're it for me, too, Eli Cinderfella. You're not allowed to give up on me. We're going to be fine, okay? Promise you believe me."

I want to. Gods, do I want to.

Instead, I kiss him.

He doesn't see the tears burning my eyelids. I don't let him know that fear pounds through me almost faster than the magic that has overtaken my bloodstream. Words can no longer alter our fates. He can't comment on anything besides the hot and rushed press of what might be our last kiss. Briargild is coming, and I wish I could have taken longer, I wish I could have lingered, I risk wishing anything and everything for this man, but I break away with a groan and push him onwards.

Hand in hand, we run down the stairs and back into the main caverns, where Gemma and Camellia are already racing for us. My fairy godmother has her hands over her ears to muffle the much louder alarm bells down here. She's in a yellow nightgown and looks as tired as I feel, her curly hair pulled back from her face in a messy tie. Cam is the only one of us who looks prepared. Dressed in the same outfit from dinner, her hand outstretched, she takes me from Xander and starts jogging deeper into the hidden parts of Apricity.

Surrounded by the family I found in the absence of all the family I lost, I run with Camellia. We pass the cavern that hosted the dining hall. Deeper, we hurry down steps, plants guiding us with slithering touches as they reveal doorways I would have never found on my own. Camellia never falters. She's faster even than Skelly, racing me through the halls of her home in an effort to give me the metaphorical keys to the kingdom before King Anerald gets here to end our rebellious plans.

The earth beckons us further in. Away from the coming presence of a brutal king, further still from the sunlight, into a place where hope quietly flourishes with greenery and pockets of violet flowers. The alarms cease ringing this far down. Cam remains urgent, pulling me ahead into the chamber she refers to as the Heart of Apricity.

Breaths ragged, she gushes through a history lesson. "Before Briargild stole from us, this place was above ground. It was the center of the kingdom. People would come to pay respects to the tree that governed the land, the tree that glowed no matter the season. Apricity was once a special place because of it and now harbors it as a secret."

Xander is right behind me. He squeezes my shoulder as Camellia steps out of the way of the open doorway to reveal, not a fully grown tree, but a single, drooping sapling with no leaves at all. Its thin branches reach out, unable to move in the wind so far underground. It doesn't glow. Instead, it leans to the right as if the entirety of the weight of the world is balanced on its thin trunk, and it has decided that life would be better served snapping here instead of working to make its way back to the grandeur of the time long past that my cousin was trying to describe to me on the way in here.

"What happened?"

Camellia shrugs. "What didn't? Men from another kingdom learned that this tree gave us our magic, made us stronger, and they couldn't let us keep it, even though they had no right to what had been ours for centuries. They didn't care to preserve it. They sought to steal its power and only that.

"The first king, over two hundred years ago, chopped it down and turned it into a series of wands."

Gemma gasps. My palms tingle. The magic I absorbed when I broke her wand seems to be responding to information it should have already known. It flares in my wrists and travels to my elbows, past my shoulders, and buries itself like a molten sword into an icy lake, embedding itself to the metaphorical hilt into my chest.

"In all of that time, this is as big as it has grown, its power severed and separated to serve another kingdom altogether. It no longer flowers in the spring or whispers secrets in the winter. Our songs do not seem to reach it, our dances cannot revive it, and so, the Heart of Apricity suffers here waiting to be saved by someone destined to become its new companion, its savior, and its king."

Me.

Again.

It's almost disturbing how much all of this has lined up for me. I wonder if there's a different timeline in which my mother didn't leave her kingdom, but instead convinced the man she loved to open a tavern in this land and told me stories under the leaves of a tree I would someday revive. Would I still have been the prophesied savior, the entire hope of a kingdom, if I had been here all along? Most likely, I would have been dead like the rest of Camellia's family. Like my family. My mother. To grow up somewhere else without the magic of this place, safe and sheltered and somewhat unaware of the darkness of the world, not only shaped who I am, but made my return inevitable.

"Anerald knows it's me. I heard him talking about a trap he set for me. I'm dead whether we get this done or not." I say quietly, my eyes never leaving the pitiful tree.

Camellia nods immediately. "They have been searching for you for a very long time, Eli. I just don't think they would have suspected you of living with them after everything they had done here.

Anerald, knowing your identity doesn't change anything. We can't hide you, but we can move the magic." Cam bumps my elbow with hers. "Don't be so glum. You're not dead yet."

I manage a shaky grin for her. Midnight creeps closer. There are no clocks down here, no sun or moonlight, but Camellia pulls some budding flowers out of her pocket and explains that they help her keep time. The pale midnight blooms unfurl slightly more with every passing second.

I'm so close to becoming whatever it is I'm supposed to be.

"You two should stand back," Camellia instructs both Gemma and Xander, stepping down into the pit that holds the magic tree and waving me towards her. "Eli, it'll be a few minutes. You need to join me, introduce yourself, and hope to win the favor of the Heart."

Gemma squeezes my hand and lets me go. "You can do this, Cinderfella. I've never seen magic as extraordinary as yours."

My heart is a fist in my chest, clenched tight around this moment in an attempt to keep it from slipping away. We're out of time, chances, and sheer luck. I stare at my fairy godmother, memorizing the rounded lines of her face and recalling that she did not use to describe me in such a way. I distinctly remember her accusing me of breaking magic. There was so much yelling in the beginning, wasn't there? Throat too tight to release any words for her, I let her hug me and then fall into the goodbyes of my prince.

I can't believe we're here again. So soon. Just after I figured out that there was a chance for us to see the possibility of a hundred uninterrupted tomorrows.

Distantly, the ground rumbles. Along the walls, plants tremble and quake in defiance. Briargild is close and getting closer.

But I'm here.

For just a moment more.

Xander is slower at releasing me when he steps past Gemma. His embrace is hard and fast and then lingers, his fingers entangled with mine when he finally steps back. For just a moment, the rest of the room doesn't matter. The threat of Briargild's approach ceases. I look at him, and he stares at me with that beautiful gaze of simmering silver. If we get a chance to live a long life, I want to never forget this, him, a quickly vanishing time in which I am still a mere mortal without much to my name besides the remains of a tavern and a lineage I miss dearly, standing in front of a man who sees me as everything I am meant to be.

"I will be here no matter what happens next," he promises, his free hand reaching up to caress my cheek. "If we have to beat Briargild a different way and then try every night to coax the Heart back to life, I will be here and I will be here with you if it takes a lifetime to restore it to what it once was. I cannot express enough to you how much you made me want to be a better person, how much you have changed me from a mere idealist with a plan of revolution to a man who truly believes that there's not just a chance for us to succeed, but a true path towards it. You are magic, Eli Cinderfella, and, as long as you are in my life, I will believe that there is still time for the world to be good once more."

I shake my head at him. "Where were all of these kind words when we met, Prince Charming?"

He leans in, our foreheads pressed together even as Camellia clears her throat to announce the unfurling of her midnight blooms. "You weren't a linguist yourself, Cinderfella. I believe you're the first person to openly curse in front of royalty."

I laugh and then I kiss him, quickly, because I'm out of time even as I want to leave pieces of myself behind with this man who smiles despite the odds weighing against us. Our joy, fleeting as it may be, is a palpable substance overtaking the seriousness of the room. We've come a very long way in such a short amount of time, but I wouldn't have asked for a different story. For all of this to happen, I had to lose everything in order to find what truly matters.

I squeeze Xander's fingers one more time and then turn away before I can let my nerves slow me down, joining Camellia in the circular ditch containing the Heart of Apricity. Gently, she holds out her hand, inviting her helper vines to take the midnight blooms from her palm before she grabs hold of me.

"We stay linked. We touch the Heart. We make a wish for a better start," she murmurs, words that seem ingrained in her mind as though she has repeated them since her own takeover of the kingdom.

I glance back at the people who support me. Those two individuals and the dragon waiting outside, who wouldn't exist if I hadn't done all of this by making a terrible wish. Everything is different now. Gemma didn't get that wrong when she flicked her wand in our tavern. Everything is different and not all of it is bad, and maybe, just maybe, this next wish can be the beginning of putting together the rest of my life, finding my father wherever he's hidden in the mists of magic, and starting this kingdom towards a better tomorrow.

Together, palms clasped, we reach for the Heart.

And then a scream tears through the cavern.

Faint. But definitely there.

More rumbling spreads through the floor. Dirt shifts uncertainly at our feet. The plants around the perimeter of the room rattle and wave and try to distract from the reality of everything outside of this sacred place.

Our palms hovering over the sapling, I share a look with Camellia. We're out of time.

Briargild didn't just pass Wynnifred. They're here.

King Anerald is here.

If I can hear screams…

He's far too close.

Camellia reaches forward anyway. "We have to do this," she insists as Gemma yells that she's going to go see what's wrong.

Every bone in my body wants to chase after the fairy godmother I just got back, but there is somebody in distress, and Gemma has never been one to shy away from a hero's moment. Her footsteps disappear the moment she's out of this small cavern. I hold my breath and wait for any sign of her or a clue as to what she meets, but I can't hear anything besides the screaming. As the seconds pass, it seems to be more than one person, shrieks echoing through the distant halls of the underground passageways. The kingdom of Apricity is under attack, and I'm touching a gods damned tree as if I have time to waste.

Camellia's grip on my hand is painful, the blind woman doing everything in her power to keep me here as vines wrap around my legs and her plants wriggle with her rising tension. The midnight blooms are fully open. Glowing a soft white with purple highlights, the flowers become the only thing that can hold my attention.

If I do this, if I take on the magic of a kingdom, if I can heal the Heart of Apricity now, we might have a better chance of surviving whatever attack is already here.

Xander's proclamation was sweet, but we don't have more than one chance to make this work. It's tonight, right now, or never.

Focus.

I hold my breath, squeeze my eyes shut, and make a wish as I touch the cool trunk of the tree.

I wish for everything to be different.

For Apricity to shake off the tragedies of its past. For Xander to live a life full of love. For Gemma to be able to be herself, whether or not that person settles down with the witch of the woods.

I wish to fix a broken heart.

Beneath me, the ground rumbles. I open my eyes, but nothing seems to have changed.

The tree remains slumped off to one side. Camellia lets out a groan. For the first time since the dining hall, I doubt that I'm meant to be the person to save the kingdom. Maybe it was all just a crazy coincidence. Sure, my mom was from here, but I'm not a special person from a different kingdom to save them and take over as king.

This is what I get for believing in wishes after all the trouble they've given me.

"Just, try again," Cam commands in a manic murmur.

I'm not allowed to look back. I can't leave. I have to ignore the screams, the rumbling, the coming machinations of war, and breathe life back into a tree that seems even more stubborn than I am.

I wish I could be what everyone needs.

I wish that this act would be enough.

I wish…

"Eli!"

Xander. His distress tears through me. I try to spin to face him, but Cam holds me tighter, making sure I don't sever the connection to the tree as I jerk my head to see over my shoulder. Shock rains down on me, a spring shower that came out of the blue and now refuses to leave. My shoulders go rigid. Cam takes a deep breath, needing no words from me to detail the danger.

It's no longer just the three of us in the cavern.

Gemma didn't come back.

Horror burrowing into my intestines like a mole in a garden, I watch King Anerald place a hand on Xander's shoulder, a guard already pinning the prince's hands behind his back into those magic-stifling shackles. Without his connection to magic, his legs buckle. He collapses, and Anerald tips his chin back with the tip of a dagger.

Every fiber of my being demands to be taken from this tree, to turn my stained palms on a man who deserves my wrath and to unleash more magic than ever before, but Cam has her plants wound around both of us, lush tendrils shackling me to a looming responsibility. As is, my skin crawls. The sharp edges of the glitter scrape against my tendons. It demands to be released.

I stare across the space between us, at the seven steps that have turned into a chasm between Xander and me as his chin is kept tilted upwards. Trapped, I want to yell, to threaten, to scream questions and insults alike, but Cam is trembling next to me. My mind is working both too fast and too slow.

I'm too slow to figure out how to save Xander.

If Wynnifred fell, it was ages ago.

We're too gods damned late to stop anything.

"So, the rumors are true," King Anerald begins, his husky drawl the kind meant to haunt nightmares. "If you really wanted to resign, you didn't have to find a peasant to take up your position."

Camellia jolts as though she's been slapped. Her hands are shaking when she touches me, but otherwise, she keeps her shoulders squared. "Your Majesty," she begins, her tone kept light despite our circumstances, chin tilted up in the direction of the chamber's entrance. "I was trying to surprise you for the ball. It's a delight you're here early."

I know she's trying to talk us out of trouble, but we're literally caught with our hands in the cookie jar, or, more literally, pressed to the magic tree that governs this land. Even the King of Briargild isn't that stupid.

"Go ahead and surprise me, Camellia. I won't have a reason to keep you alive if you give your power to this boy."

Finally, her grip loosens. She may not want to be queen, but my cousin wants to live. All she has ever wanted is to live, for herself and her plants and for the sake of life. Around us, the plants slither and scheme as though they can take down a king.

"We're going to march out of here together and discuss the

plans for the ball. I think you'll be excited to know it's the last one Apricity will be throwing," that dagger presses into Xander's throat. "Once you two are married, the entirety of this land will belong to Briargild, and anyone who tries to stop that will find out what it looks like when our prince is pushed to his limits."

The roses around the castle. Those briar bushes we left over corpses in the forest. Xander's magic turned malice. The panic that flared to life in his gaze the night I learned his identity is back full force. His worst fear is not only revealed, but made inevitable.

Cam is beside me. Bartering. Talking. Doing everything she can to gain a sliver of control in a situation that is broken, with brambles all around us. Hope has shriveled to a useless seed planted into uninhabitable soil. Anerald is answering. They're taken up with each other, a man in charge always needing to have the last word over a woman raising concerns.

I don't pay them attention. I don't need to because my entire focus is on the man who hasn't moved his gaze from me. Silver with regret. Silver with sorrow and panic and shifting wildly between my own eyes and the lack of options currently left for us. Silver, with an apology he mouths even though the syllables never make it past his lips.

Prince Alexander Charming isn't going back to Briargild. He didn't become a rebellion leader to give up now. Dressed in the soft greens of a kingdom meant to come back to life rather than necromancer black, he makes his choice.

Even without his magic, he still has a choice.

Even forced to his knees, he knows what he has to do.

As the only heir from Briargild who could carry on the legacy of magic because it was gifted to him decades ago, he is the most important piece on the metaphorical game board. My prince is a strategist. His heart and his mind were always more important than his disabilities or control over plants. Without him, there's no chance for Anerald to force the final takeover of Apricity.

All of the promises he made in the stairway…

We both knew it might be our last moment together.

His name is ripped from my throat as I watch the inevitable choice shift into action.

Xander lunges towards the blade.

Chin up, he pulls the guard forward with him as he aims to impale himself quickly on the angled blade. His resolve remains unwavering. There are no other options. As far as he's concerned, he's ending this on his own terms, those gray eyes that have haunted me all this time going cold and distant.

My breath turns to stone in my lungs. Heavy and settled and refusing to let me pull in any more air. I don't shut my eyes as his body tips forward. I can't. I can't leave him alone to this fate, so I stare ahead at the man who has become the tentative home for my heart and hope that it's quick and painless and worth it.

If one of us isn't meant to survive tonight, if it has to be him who pays the ultimate price for saving more than ourselves— but two kingdoms' worth of people, then I only need it to be worth it.

A single drop of blood dangles on the edge of the dagger when the king pulls it away.

Xander's sacrifice is stopped prematurely.

I stare at it, glad the man I love isn't dead and horrified that the king is smiling down at that red drop. He tuts his tongue. Head tilted back, he lets go of his hold on Xander and ignores the prince as he struggles and snarls and spits, but ultimately is unable to do anything in his pinned position, a second and third guard coming to make sure he's secure.

"How terribly dramatic," he drawls out in a rumble of disapproval.

Xander curses. Forced to kneel, he keeps fighting. He's fighting so hard, he doesn't realize what King Anerald has planned next.

It should have been noted earlier in the story that those who can't wrestle magic for their own nefarious needs find other ways to commit their vile crimes. Anerald has always had a penchant for swords and daggers and sharp objects that leave his supposedly treacherous revolutionaries screaming in the dungeons under the Briargild castle. Once I heard it whispered that Anerald had a sliver of kindness in his heart whilst his wife lived and breathed, but that piece left him like dandelion fluff on a windy day. It hollowed him out. Violence became his favorite method to garner results in his favor. The man doesn't even announce his next move.

It's an afterthought. It's a means to an end. It's the right decision to get all of his plans back on the correct path.

I numbly watch the dagger leave Anerald's hand, celebrating that it's further from Xander's throat and the stripe of red that I can see bleeding towards his collar.

The blade flies through the air. End over end. Silver flashing in the light of magic, swelling almost too large for its round containers in the corners of the room.

Everything then happens all at once.

Xander, first, screaming. I think it's my name. It could be anything, and I would listen, but I'm not quite able to make out what he says as shock dissolves like poison in my bloodstream.

Camellia throws her arms up, urging her plants to slow down or stop that dagger with its shining, gold hilt. She's smart enough to move away from such a dangerous weapon. She is, however, not fast.

There's a stunning lack of pink glitter as panic roots me to my spot.

And I, well, I stare down at the knife as it embeds itself in my chest.

25

The dirt floor catches me. Its rough hands cradle my body as I continue to blink down at the golden hilt sticking out from my chest. My heart is beating. A bird in a cage with no way to escape.

Distantly, I stare at the spreading red. I've ruined another one of his shirts. The orange of a sunset dyed into fabric decays under the steady flow of blood, turning rusted and then sopping too dark to be the burgundy of spilled wine. I'll never be trusted with borrowing from his closet.

I won't live long enough to get that chance again anyway.

Around me, panic ensues.

Vaguely, I note warm palms on my face. Maybe Camellia. Not Xander. I can't see the prince.

King Anerald put a knife in my chest, and all I want is to see Xander one more time.

Gods, I'm a fool. A love-struck, magic-wielding fool. A brilliant fool.

I try to say something. His name. To call back to him, but there's corroded coins in my throat and I only let out a gurgle, a cough, a gasp of pain.

Somebody tells me to relax. They tell me everything will be alright. My eyes are open, but I can't see Cam or squeeze her hand back when she fumbles with the blade in my chest. It's tugged from my chest in a staggered movement, my body not yet prepared to relinquish the brutal metal as it lets out a slurping, gasping complaint at the sudden removal. The blood won't stop.

Not when hands are pressed to the wound. Not when plants wrap around me to staunch the flow. Not even when magic pulses pink from my palms and chest in sputtering attempts to make everything better.

There isn't a word to fix this. A spell to stop it. I can't turn back time and reach out for Xander before trouble sauntered into the cavern.

Xander again.

He's on my mind, refusing to leave me alone as the world dims and sound fades and a creeping cold begins at my toes. I would shiver if I had the energy; a chilled blanket seemingly lay across me, pinning me to the floor. But Xander is here.

Xander, who was once a necromancer and always a prince, and whom I told I cared about, but didn't phrase it in that all-important way.

I didn't tell him I loved him.

I really thought we would have more time. There weren't guarantees for the future, but I would have loved to see him grow older, to brush my fingers through strands of gray in his dark hair and tease him mercilessly over the years. I would have loved to share a dance with him at a ball, just once, had a chance to hold him close in front of the kingdom we had changed. I would have loved…

I would have loved every moment I got to have with him because we fought for everything to be together.

The cold is at my waist now. It licks an icy tongue over my skin. Winter has never touched me the way this cold does now. I can't move my arms, my legs, and my chest stops expanding.

Somewhere, midnight slips away as blood turns the dirt muddy beneath me.

Xander is still there. Not in the room. I don't know what's happening out there anymore. In my mind.

The pain is a dull tie to reality, the last one binding me to the world, but I don't pay it attention as I feel warm fingers on my cheek. His fingers. Scarred and trembling and sure of only one thing. That he'll stay.

Gemma must be nearby, too. I swear I can hear laughing. Yelling. A demand for me to do the right thing and to stop breaking everything.

She tells me not to leave her.

I touch those fingers on my face. Brace myself to see Xander, but all I get is shifting swirls of gray against the blackness that has taken me.

I don't want to leave.

I want to stay. To fight. To get the happily ever after we all imagined.

The cold is at my throat. Magic rattles in my gums. It wriggles along my tongue and covers my teeth. It's trying to leave before I'm no longer here.

I wonder if my death will be beautiful. Pink, at the very least. There will be two kingdoms of people who see the color and know that it once belonged to me. If nothing else, I'm a stain on Briargild and a streak of hope for Apricity.

It has to be enough.

Because I'm cold and my mind is conjuring up fantasies I never got a chance to explore. Xander is here. He's warm and beckoning, telling me it'll be safer if I step across the threshold to somewhere better. I'm sure there was something else I was supposed to do, but he's here and I want to see where he's leading me.

Make a wish.

The command is a whisper that I don't hear, but one I feel. It slips across my shoulders like a familiar cardigan. It sinks into my bones. It's the last thing to do before I can cross over.

It's the last thing I can do for this world.

So, I remember. Warmer places than this. Taverns and crowded holidays. Embraces. A promise to fix everything I broke.

With all that is left of me, I wish I could have saved my father and saved our corner of the world from the spreading wickedness of Anerald.

Distantly, I hear my name, but I'm no longer present in the chamber that holds the Heart of Apricity. I'm dying. I'm bleeding out for the cause, Prince Alexander Charming began, and it is an honor even as the pain tears a final involuntary lurch through my person. My name sounds again, and I stand in darkness without even the figment of Xander to keep me company.

Eli.

Eli.

Eli Cinderfella.

It's a chant of syllables joined by more and more voices. Cool hands touch me. Cold. Not warm. Not Xander. I'm alone except for the hands on my wrists. On my shoulders. Some on my forehead and cheeks. Others pat my legs. These must be the souls on the other side in charge of ferrying the newly dead to whatever awaits them beyond the land of the living.

Magic lives here, too, a swirling, swelling mass that distracts me from the fact that everything that hurts too much has stopped.

It pops. It sparkles. Pink glitter rains down on me.

In that small way, a gift from that wand I absorbed so many nights ago, I'm glad I get to take Gemma and my magical life with me. I hope the others will be able to see it. Maybe they'll look up to the stars and see a flutter of pink sparkles and know that I'm where I'm meant to be.

I hope Skelly is able to outlive me.

The absence of pain and oblivion and the sparkling sense of something more stretches out infinitely beyond me. I suppose this isn't so bad. There was so much I was meant to do, so many lives I was still supposed to touch and improve, but, if my death can warrant anything, I hope it at least gives the others a little more time. I hope they remember me and the fact that we must continue to fight despite the overwhelming odds of failure that the other side wants us to believe.

They never needed me to win their freedom; they just had to know it was possible.

Maybe someday, when we're all colored bits of sparkling dust, we'll meet again.

They'll tell me that they won, they were free, and, despite my absence, they learned to be happy.

Gods, more than anything, I wish that to be true.

I wish for the world to be given a chance to be a better place.

Time means nothing in the abyss of the afterlife. There are no meetings to run late for or drinks to push across slick counters. There's no one to speak to, but I never truly feel alone. More sparkles have joined my pink colors. Bursts of blue and a dazzling gold. There's purple that reminds me of Wynnifred and a swirling vat of gray that takes me back to the way Xander's eyes changed when he used magic. Pink glitter eclipses it all, a swirling mass doing something I can't understand.

I am too tired to truly care.

There isn't anything else for me to do besides lie here and wait.

❦

My first breath back in the land of the living is a burning, suffocating imposition on my current state. I writhe and groan and, more than anything, try to slip back to where peace equates to the end. Voices swarm around me like the buzzing of an aggravated hornet's nest. None of them are loud enough for me to focus on. Instead, I'm stuck drifting, half-alive in the glowing aura of overwhelming light that I can't quite open my eyes to as those voices shift up in panicked volume.

Gentle hands cradle my cheek. Someone is holding my hand. I'm anchored here in the land of the living, even though I've made my amends with the gods who rule the afterlife.

I reluctantly agreed to go.

I took a gods damned dagger to the heart.

Somehow, I'm still here.

My next breath is grating across my teeth. It pulls at the dry edges of my throat. With more effort than I can truly expend, it fills my lungs. A hot air balloon resistant to lifting off from the ground, I breathe.

And then I do it again.

Once more.

Someone whispers my name.

It's not the ghostly tone of those spirits I could never see on the other side. This is something I recognize. My heart beats to syllables I can't name.

The dead want me, but not as much as the living.

The last clawed fingers of the other side release me, and I open my eyes to look up at the tear-streaked cheeks of my fairy godmother. "Eli Cinderfella!" She screams at me, her hands shaking where she's touching my cheeks. "You don't get to scare me like that ever again!"

I feel so heavy after being nothing more than a drifting consciousness for who knows how long, and cough up at least a pound of stale air as Gemma helps me sit up to drink some water. She's not alone. Wynnifred rubs my back and doesn't let go of my hand. I've been guarded by the women who stepped in to guide me when my mother could not.

I would cry if I didn't feel like a skeleton shaking off the dirt of its grave.

Downing the cup of water, trickles of liquid dribbling down my chin, I stare at the two of them, at the worry that lives there, and how it's focused completely on me. Beyond Wynn's shoulder, I can see the tree that represents the heart of Apricity. Rather, I can see the charred remains of what King Anerald left.

My clothes are covered in blood and soot. The walls of the cave are filled with cracks and scorch marks. There's a clear stain spreading out from my body, but Wynnifred and Gemma look okay. What the heck happened?

"Where..."

The kingdom matters to me. The magic that has gone dormant, and I was supposed to save, is still important. All of it matters, but I need to know something first.

I can't even get his name out before Gemma lets out a moan. "Oh, Eli. He and Cam are back in Briargild. They're supposed to be getting married today."

Today.

How long was I gone?

Wynn is watching me with those amber eyes, an amazed grin pulling at her lips. "Four days. I've never seen a soul return after more than a few hours, but Gemma had a lot of hope we could bring you back."

I swivel my gaze to my fairy godmother, and then she points to a pile of polished sticks. No. Wands. They're laid at the foot of my spot on the ground as though everyone who visited me was terrified to actually touch me.

"I called everyone in the council. I told them what Anerald had done. They knew about this place, but not how terrible the people were treated or that there was a true heir trying to return to make it better." Her voice is thick with emotion. "I begged them, Eli, and I don't know what changed their minds, but yesterday they showed up and donated their wands to your cause. The magic..."

She can't seem to finish her story. Wynn reaches across me to squeeze her shoulder while I stare at the discarded pile of wands. The night she and I met, I had absorbed her wand. It was a gift that apparently repeated itself now, letting me take on the magic of these relics.

"How?"

Gemma shakes her head, throwing her arms up in absolute confusion. "How does anything work with you, you incredible man? I don't know and I don't care because you're back and there's something you need to see right now."

The witch murmurs for my fairy godmother to take a breath and give me a moment. I had a long journey back from the other side. Looking more closely at my clothes, I note specks of sparkling glitter. The magic I was seeing while I was drifting towards death was here all along.

It was my magic, gifted to me by a community trying to help me live.

A rainbow glitters across me and stains my skin where dried blood should be. I pull the edge of my shirt down to look at the jagged mark left by the king's dagger, only to find a scar filled in with dazzling color. Magic. Fucking magic. After all of this, I truly appreciate it.

"The tree..."

I'm alive, but I failed where I was meant to help others. Xander is gone. Cam is trapped in her version of a nightmare. Apricity has fallen. Where joy should be, I only find a crippling sense of guilt and sorrow.

I don't know if I can get up to see whatever it is Gemma wants to show me.

I don't know if I can live in a world where bad still happens.

I don't know...

Wynn stands up and plucks something off the ground behind her. She holds it out. I stare at the glittering seed.

"A heart is a resilient thing," she tells me, gently pressing the seed into my hand and urging me to hold onto it until things settle down enough for us to give it a good home.

The true Heart of Apricity fits folded in my palm. A seed for tomorrow. A sliver of hope wrapped in an organic casing. Smooth and small and surreal. We have a chance to start over. To make things better. To make a kingdom the best it can ever be.

And yet…

Gemma tuts her tongue. "Look, we've wasted enough time. If you don't come see your surprise right now, there won't be time to get you on the road to Briargild, Eli Cinderfella. We do have a wedding to stop today."

I blink up at her, her head of curly hair tangled through with all sorts of glittering specks from me and her hard work to bring me back to the world of the living. Hope hits me like the flap of a dragon's wings, unable to be ignored and threatening to knock me flat on the floor once more. It spreads between my ribs, stretching out from the scar on my chest. It winds around my bones and stiffens my spine. Gemma stares back at me with bright blue eyes and the same emotion twinkling there.

"We can stop the wedding?"

"Have you never read a romance novel, Cinderfella? It's basically the most romantic thing a guy can do for his true love."

Chuckling, I let the two of them take each of my hands and help tug me off the ground. My feet feel as though they're clay bricks attached to a foundation beneath the soil, with the sole instruction to pull me down under the ground. Heavy, sluggish, tilting to the right, so I slump onto Gemma, but I stay on my feet. Taking steps is a different problem. My body is a limp willow trying to bend one way and then the other as my spine relearns how to hold itself up. Wynn tells me it'll be fine, it'll pass, but I'm too distracted by what else is happening to really pay her any attention.

Glitter sparks at my fingertips. Pink and green and blue and flashes of blazing silver that sparkle a burning white when I tilt my head one way and then the other. My heart thuds against the cage of my ribs, and I suck in a painful breath as the magic tears through my bloodstream. My veins swell with it. It digs sharp edges into my organs and sticks to my bones. I am no longer just myself. I am full of magic that rages to be used.

"Just breathe through it," Wynn instructs, her shoulder under my arm to support me as I tremble and quiver and altogether do what I can to simply stop myself from exploding outward with the weight of the added magic. "Again, this is unheard of, but the entirety of two kingdoms have come together to make sure you live, so we're going to go show them what their compassion has created."

Two kingdoms. My father's home and my mother's are being brought together by the likes of me. I swallow that thought along with the magic that erratically swirls through my chest. As much as I would like to ask a million questions or spend another four days lying down until I understand the weight of the magic in my body, there are people who need me and a wedding to stall.

Gemma and Wynnifred walk me out. Out of the caverns with the cracks in the walls. Away from the fire that clearly started in the chamber that held the Heart of Apricity, but left me untouched by some blessing of magic I may never understand. We pass charred plants and crisped rose vines. Xander. He must have gotten out of his shackles and fought the entire way out, the caverns almost too dangerous to walk through now. He fought, and his magic seared itself in me as a final testament to our feelings for each other.

"Xander…"

I can't bring myself to say it. I can picture it in my mind's eye. The prince broken and dragged out of here when his magic was blocked once again.

Silver flares at my fingertips. Did they force him to his knees again? Did he push his magic out of his fingertips and beg it to find me? Did he…?

Gemma pats my hand. "That's why they stalled the wedding. The king wanted him to be presentable, but he did a lot before he was defeated."

Oh, Xander. I stagger through the remains of the cavern, huffing out panted breaths and averting my eyes from the one-man fight that ensued here. The death that he wrought for my spent life. Roses mar a once peaceful kingdom. Jagged thorns pierce more corpses here than they did in the forest clearing. The gardens of Briargild don't hold this many flowering bushes. Love as a desperate plea turned violent, the evidence of Xander's fight is the only thing to survive

King Anerald's siege.

Every other piece of Apricity I reveled over and appreciated and loved is gone. The murals are all crushed. Bludgeoned with sword hilts or hammers or something else as vicious. Broken bits of colored tiles litter the floor, all charred and cracked from the fire that tore through these once beautiful halls. The reminders of the past are gone and erased. No depictions of dragons survived the assault. The solid hopes for the future of a kingdom to bloom in peace have been dismantled. It's enough to make my knees go out from under me.

Wynnifred never loosens her hold on me. She doesn't let me sink back to the gray ground. Not when we pass the destroyed murals or the scorched plants. The witch who once got me thrown in the dungeon now pulls me from the depths of the earth. It is her sheer determination that guides us past the devastation of Apricity, while Gemma openly cries next to me, and I do everything in my power to move one shaking step at a time.

We break through the entrance, and I suck in my first breath of fresh air, the sensation both wonderful and excruciating in equal measure. The gray fog that covered Apricity has cleared out. I step from the charred, brittle bones of a kingdom crushed into the blinding gaze of the sun.

A hiccup skips over my lips.

It has to be a good sign that the sun is shining, right?

There are a few people at the mouth of the cave system who call out my name and wave, and then sprint to the stairs to meet us. By the time Gemma and Wynnifred get me, panting and dizzy, up those steps, a small crowd has formed. At the forefront is my dragon.

Skelly bends down, pressing his cool forehead against mine and purring almost louder than the cheering crowd behind him, his wings spread to show off that tapestry in the bright light of fading day. I remember the quilted squash and other symbols that decorated the edge of his wings. There's been some changes, though. The main portion of both wings has crude depictions of two figures. Two men. Both wearing a crown. Their heads are tipped back as though they mean to lean in for a kiss or simply to share a laugh. My darker frame displayed against dazzling blues. Xander's pale silhouette shrouded by reds and pinks. Two men who came together to create a dragon and maybe, just maybe, change their worlds.

I should be out of tears at this point. My throat is so tight. I reach forward, and Skelly holds still as I stroke the face of the man representing Xander. It's so beautiful.

"How did you…?"

"I believed you were coming back," Gemma says vehemently. "And I needed to keep busy in case I started to doubt that."

This is too much. I love it. Gods, I love him, don't I?

"I'm so glad you're alive, buddy," I murmur just for Skelly, Gemma sniffling and patting him with me.

The dragon then takes over for the witch and my fairy godmother, lending his shoulder for me to lean on as I walk towards the gathered people. I keep one hand on him, my breathing slowing as I look out at the crowd. There are at least a hundred people. Some are clear citizens of Apricity, their clothes bright and smiles wide and heads tilted towards me as though they still see me as their king, regardless of my inconvenient demise.

Then, there are the others. The people dressed in the muted colors of Briargild. Already, we've managed to unite the kingdoms.

Skelly clacks his jaw together, adding his own kind of applause to the mix as we step past the first rows of people. Some reach out to me, touching my arm, shaking my hand, and patting me on the back. All of them say my name in a wave of chants that promise to overtake me.

Eli Cinderfella. Once nothing more than a tavern keep and now a king. It's a terribly impossible story and, yet, here I am, living it.

We move further, Gemma lecturing a few overly enthusiastic people to give me space as we meet the line of people who are clearly from Briargild, their clothes functional and in neutral colors without any of the gold pins of the wicked king. Harold is there, beaming for the skies like he's the last star left to keep it lit. He crushes me in a hug regardless of Gemma's lecture, and I don't even care that it hurts, rainbow glitter sparking from my form as my toes leave the ground.

"You came to me even when magic made me forget you," he says, patting Skelly with friendly recognition as well. "I'm very proud of how you've held up, Eli."

I blink once, twice, making sure that I heard that correctly. "Wait.

The spell lifted? You remember me?"

Answers ring out among the crowd. I stare out at them in undisclosed wonder. This isn't just any collection of Briargild citizens. These are my patrons, the people who watched me grow inside those four walls of the tavern. Recognition glows in each of their gazes.

And then Harold has me by my shoulders, and he's saying words I can't believe. "Your father is back, Eli."

I blink at the satyr with his fuzzy horns and glitter-coated beard. My father. I look around him, and then Gemma is back at my side with a hand on my elbow.

"He couldn't wait anymore, Eli. He and the rebellion are already on their way to Briargild."

I was gone in that other realm for too long. My mind isn't moving fast enough to keep up with this shift in my story. Mouth opening and closing, I can't get questions past my stiff tongue.

Hector understands. "He said he didn't do enough when we lost Adira. He couldn't lose you silently."

"But how?" I croak around emotions that have followed me my entire life, all of the grief and tragedy twisted with shining threads of hope.

"You made wishes, Eli, and they came true. We heard it all the way in Brairgild and came here to find you."

Skelly nudges my face with his snout. The bone is wet when he pulls away. Glitter and an excess of tears seem to be all I am now.

The rest of the crowd has moved in while we talked, and they're all looking at me. Gemma wants me to hurry up, to go, to get a move on, but Wynn sets a hand on her elbow and murmurs to me.

The people have been waiting for me, and I should say something.

My people have been waiting, and I have to say something.

Anything.

Throat tight, chest full, I gaze out at faces that are both a mix of familiar and new. People spread between the two eras of my life. My first home and my new one. Bright clothes and brighter eyes, muted shades of the rainbow, and people who still peek around the shoulders of their neighbors with the same shimmering hope in their expression, and they're all waiting for me.

My father was always the one making speeches. Xander is good at speeches. I swallow hard.

"Thank you," I start, because it seems like the right thing to do as rainbow glitter continues to spark at my fingertips. "Thank you for waiting for me to find my way back here and for still believing I can help change things."

Skelly stretches his neck up as high as it goes. He stands as an icon above our gathered crowd. The dragon has returned, and now the rest of the prophecy has to be completed.

"I don't know what all the future holds, but I know this," I continue, my voice strengthening as I stare out at faces that are braced for promises and blazing with the same need I feel settled in my bones. "Anerald falls today."

The cheer that rips through this group sails across scorched ground. It lingers in the nearest trees. It is a cry that echoes deep into the forest.

"Tomorrow will be for rebuilding and change and fostering peace, but today I will finish what he started. The crown of Briargild will fall. The hold they've had for hundreds of years on magic will be relinquished." My words are punctuated by flaring glitter at my shoulders that sparks and falls to the ground, the magic shoved to capacity within my own form, escaping in excited zaps. "Today, we fight for Apricity!"

If the first cheer was an echo that tangled in the limbs of trees, this one is a wave that floods the forest. The people scream. They cheer. They gather themselves for the next part of our story.

Let Briargild hear us now.

The kingdom of Apricity is ready to take back all that was always its own.

I am prepared to lead them there. To stand up against Anerald. To put myself between him and these people and…

And Xander.

There's a prince in need of rescue.

Gemma leaves me for a moment and then returns with a leather saddle in her grip. "We have until sundown to get to the castle in Briargild, and I have a crazy idea to get you there." She drops a handful of those magical herbs into my hand along with a water flask. "Eat all of that. You need your strength."

My mouth is full when I blurt my question. "He can fly?"

Gemma pats Skelly's white snout, the dragon preening under our attention and kneeling immediately for her to strap his saddle into place as she explains that the ride here was uncomfortable and the saddle should fix that for me. "We did a test run and he ended up stuck in a tree, so I think you should just move through the forest in a regular fashion, but you're hours behind the rest of the rebel group."

Well, that's far less grand than flying a dragon into battle. The magic prickling under my skin seems to agree. I have an inkling of a plan to help him. "Do you want to fly, Skelly?" With a hip and a hop, the bone dragon starts stampeding towards higher ground, immediately prepared to do what it takes to get airborne. Gemma screeches for us to focus. "One chance," I call back to her. "If he doesn't take to the air, we'll run on the ground, but this would technically be faster."

She mutters about technicalities while Wynn chuckles, and then the crowd trails us towards the highest point of the Kingdom of Apricity. In the courtyard in front of the castle, they wait. Skelly and I climb the stairs and then make our way up onto the roof of the castle, flesh and bones moving between soot-stained vines from the devastation caused by King Anerald's departure.

When we're up there, his claws sinking into the vines that Camellia was able to control so easily, I put a foot on his leg and then hoist myself into the saddle, using the ends of his bow as reins to keep me upright. "You ready to try this?" I ask him, the wind seeming to pick up as if it too is excited to see us succeed.

He clacks his jaw twice and then extends his wings. The tapestry Gemma sewed for me shines under the afternoon sun. There's no doubt in my mind. We're going to fly.

Whether it's the herbs or the wands or the fact I'm bursting with too much to fit in my own body, I don't have to think too hard about the magic. We need more wind. I don't even wish for it, and the element is there, teasing me with caresses to my cheeks and a ruffling of my clothes.

When Skelly lurches forward, I believe in him, and he flaps once, twice, three times, picking us up with the help of the wind. He isn't a piece of fluff floating through the wind. The dragon and I fall. My weight combined with his aerated body isn't a great flying combination, but that's the whole point of magic, right? I lean in close to his neck and visualize the wind beneath his wings as we drop. We need to go up. We need to ride the wind like a bird returning home for the spring. Glitter in every color of the rainbow showers the spots where his wings beat against the mischievous wind. It rains down on the crowd cheering beneath us, and we propel up into the sky.

With a hoot, I look down at the people of Apricity. They gather themselves and start on foot towards the other kingdom, a small army of pumpkin soldiers appearing at the edges of Apricity to guide them forward. Gemma shouts and hollers and swings Wynn in a wild display as Skelly drives us further through the air.

In the distance, the castle of Briargild looms. I pat Skelly's neck, magic swirling around us with the gentlest nudge of my mind. There's no way to miscommunicate my desires to magic right now. I have one goal and only that goal on my mind as Skelly's quilted wings beat against the air.

We're off to make history and save the man I love.

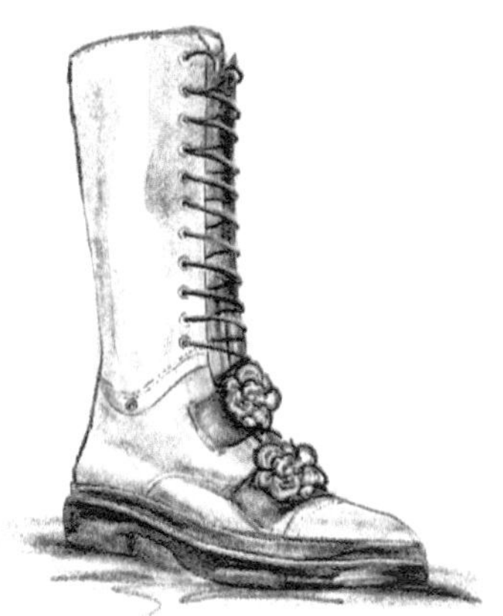

26

Skelly is not a terribly adept flyer. He has all the heart and endurance to make up for it, though. Much the way dogs will paddle helplessly out of a stream they've accidentally found themselves prisoners to, Skelly erratically flaps his wings against the wind. I try to coax it with magic, bring it under his wing strokes, and keep us level, but, more often than not, I end up hanging on for my life.

Winter is harsher here than on the ground. The atmosphere that hasn't yet decided to turn to snow whips across my face. It freezes my knuckles. A thin layer of frost gathers over Skelly's bones.

It's brutal, but also the wake-up call I needed to remind me I'm alive.

This is the cold of the living world. It's a cold that bites and cuts and tries to wriggle its way through me, piercing me to the core. I lean hard against Skelly. It's a cold I welcome as we fly onward.

We're far above the tree tops and further from the forest floor as the sun dips towards the horizon. I squint forward against the bright smear of it. The sky painted in a barrage of blinding oranges, we cross the forest onwards to Briargild.

"Careful, buddy. I'm sure they're expecting something."

Not a dragon. Obviously. There would be no reason to anticipate an attack from a dragon, but I'm sure there are some efforts in place to keep the rest of the rebellion from ruining this arranged marriage.

Skelly flaps his wings, bringing us closer to our destination. Far below my feet, I make out the charred spot where Briargild's magic wielders forced us to fight back. There are roses somewhere beyond what I can see. Another vulnerable spot of Xander's fury.

I want to make a world in which he never feels trapped into doing that again.

I'm going to make sure of that.

It's only a couple more minutes of flight before the ring of Briargild's lookout towers comes into view. A dragon flew from the forgotten kingdom to the borders of Briargild. Gemma will be excited to find out that he made it all the way here. My magic is enough to keep him in flight. Bits of sparkling rainbow linger under him with every flap of his wings. The focus on keeping Skelly in the air helps me from trying to plan ahead and anxiously overthink the way I have to face down King Anerald.

I have to get to Xander. Once we're together, I can deal with everything else.

He's down there, having spent days assuming I was dead, and I'm about to rock his entire world by saving him.

This is my hero moment.

I'm far too concerned with fantasizing about how Xander will look at me when I storm into his wedding that I don't notice the first assault before it begins. Skelly clacks his jaw twice in a clipped demand for my attention as fire flings into the air. Catapulted. I stare at the ball of fire as it just barely misses the bottom of Skelly's ribcage. I didn't even know we used those for anything besides museum relics of an ancient history. It's been so long since the kingdom has needed to protect itself from an oncoming enemy.

And now, I'm that enemy.

"Higher, Skelly. They won't be able to get us if we're higher."

It's a solid plan. I don't really have time to come up with anything else. Skelly is in the motion of flapping diligently, as I call on the wind when I hear the shout of someone who's not a guard.

The rebels.

A short flight to our left. Stopped at the golden barrier guarding the kingdom with a litany of pitchforks, short swords, and faltering hope. At the edge of change and pressing forth against the seemingly impossible, they stare up at the fiery ball being thrown at me with mouths full of warnings. Skelly rolls out of the way, and we sink below the line of the trees.

Just out of sight.

Moving towards the group calling my name.

The voice I can't believe I hear bellowing over the others.

A voice I wished for and didn't believe I'd hear again.

I'm off Skelly's back after just a few of his long strides. Dirt plumes around me. The attacks from Briargild have paused as I race forward.

"Eli!"

I don't falter. I don't slow down. The last dregs of death shaken off my shoulders, I launch myself into the man coming my way.

My father staggers back. Our arms are around each other. His beard scratches my cheek as I hunch down to hug him. I squeeze him until he gasps out a choked laugh.

The entire world slows for this. My wish has come true.

When we step back from our embrace, he holds my shoulders, his own shaking with uninhibited awe and grief and shock and the tears I rarely saw him let out over the course of our lives. "You look different."

"Same me. I wasn't sure I'd see you again, and then I found out you were leading a battalion in my honor," I whisper, the crowd of rebels joining our reunion with cheers and claps on our backs and a reminder that there is still a whole war to wage if we want to see the end of the day.

Rainbows marred his clothes everywhere I touched him. "Your fairy godmother told me about you and the prince. If he was going to be the last shred of you I could hold, I was going to get him out of there. This, though," he squeezes my shoulders. "This is better than all of my wishes coming true, Eli."

I huff in a short breath. "We still have to get through this," and then I raise my voice for the rest of the gathering since there are so many of them staring at this rather intimate and emotional moment. "You could turn back. I don't know what will happen next, but you don't all have to risk your lives. I could-."

My second speech as king is cut off without hesitation. By my father. By the centaur who recognized me from the rebel meeting on the winter solstice. By fifty people who watched me shoot a prince with a golden arrow and then escaped Briargild holding him in my arms.

This isn't a battle for one man. It's a revolution. For us all. Every human and magical being who tried to make Briargild a home and then found themselves tangled in the web of corruption woven by wicked kings. I can stand up for them, but there's a kingdom and a half at my back.

Briargild will fall today. Not only because of me. Not only for those wronged in Apricity. For every citizen of Briargild who managed to tear their head out of the metaphorical sand and saw the rampant injustice running through their home.

Together, we're here to storm the gates.

Nobody stands in the way as Skelly kneels, and I climb back into his saddle. There's a simple plan of action. I will bring down the golden magic, and we will proceed to the castle to find my prince and stop a wedding.

Even I can't mess up this plan.

Of course, though, there's already a problem.

The shouts are from the guards on top of the towers. They didn't stop shooting at us because I was having an emotional reunion. That's asking for too much. Rather, they set the forest on fire and can't seem to get it to stop.

"Access to magic has been spotty since…"

My father trails off. Me. My death. My revival. I'm filled to the brim with the magic of two kingdoms. Up on the towers, I can see court-ordained mages with their hands upheld. Their focus isn't on the fire. It's on keeping the golden barrier and the runes on the towers intact against the rebellion they can see coming from the trees, golden glitter sparking at their fingertips in erratic puffs.

Around us, the fire gnaws on trees that have stood for generations. I've walked the perimeter of Briargild my entire life and wondered what lived beyond it. It's not just trees and mystery anymore. Wynnifred's cottage is somewhere out there. Apricity is beyond. The rebels are here in a semi-circle, about to be trapped here by the fire.

As much as I ache to just move forward, to run to the man who needs me to save him, I have to put out this fire.

I'll just add it to the ever-growing list of things I already have to do today.

A new plan comes together. My father and the rebels will stay close to the golden barrier and be ready to run inside as soon as the magic falls. Skelly and I have to get ourselves back into the sky.

The gravity of the situation presses me firmly into the saddle. We're standing between a second devastation of Apricity and a whole lot of death here at the border of Brairgild if we can't get this fire put out. Holding out my hands and telling the flames to simmer down doesn't seem to have an effect. Magic isn't suddenly an innate skill I possess, even with the abundance of it in my veins. Unlike Xander and Cam, I can't just swish my hands and expect the glittering expanse of power to answer. The easy solution once again evades me.

So, back to the wind, the wind that carried us here and settled us back onto the forest floor. The wind that immediately swirls around us as I raise my right hand, grab the rainbow glitter that falls from me intermittently, and twirl it in lazy circles. The wind answers, but only seems to help the flames grow as it dances towards the widening wall of orange.

Skelly backs up. He trembles beneath me, his pink heart pulsing hard. The first dragon in over two centuries has no magic of his own to offer and nervously stands beneath me.

I pat his neck. I'm not going to let anything happen to him. Searching the forest, I let my tired mind unspool. If one word can't stop the fire, if the wind is not enough, then I have to try something else.

I'm Eli Cinderfella.

I broke magic and then brought it back, enclosed in my chest and vibrating down my appendages. I started a blizzard in the dungeons. I set off a glitter bomb and released a thousand wishes; the consequences of my actions are a stain on this kingdom for generations. If anybody can do this, it's me. I can put out a gods damned forest fire.

It's time for a little wayward magic.

The guards on the uppermost levels of the towers have notched arrows at the ready. They're aiming for the rebels, not yet threatened, but prepared should the golden wall fall. I'll deal with them in a moment.

Thighs clenched tight around the saddle, I hold my hands over my head. The sky listens. The sloping stretch of orange becoming burgundy and then black leans in. I've got a word prepared.

This isn't the time for a drizzle. I'm not asking for regular rain. Shouting a command back to the rebels to hold onto anything they can, I yell a single syllable up into the darkening heavens.

"Flood!"

Clouds don't move in. There's no need for them when magic flows through me like a river into the atmosphere. Skelly holds his ground, his claws dug into the dirt as the magic is pulled from me faster than ever before. It's out in the open. Gold and white and pink and green and blue and so many other shades of colors I've never seen mixing together into a fog that eclipses the sky here outside of Briargild.

And then my spell hits.

Water gushes from the rainbow collection of glitter. This isn't the rain I compelled to existence the night I learned the Necromancer's true identity. This is an onslaught, an unforgettable assault of water against the land. It snuffs out the fire almost immediately in a cascade of sizzles that turn to smoke and then continues, carving new paths into the land as it splashes against Briargild's golden barrier and then sluices back into the forest.

Behind me, the rebels hold onto trees that threaten to topple under the combined force of the water and the fact that the flood is taking dirt away with it, forming a moat around this part of the waiting kingdom in seconds. A centaur splashes. My father holds onto a low branch and reaches into the gathered water to pull out someone who has lost their own grasp on safety.

The water keeps coming.

Skelly has his wings tucked in and scrabbles to hold onto the shifting land every time the water pulls away from his current spot. The pink pulse of his chest lights up every splash that comes our way. I'm soaked from the waist down with my hands above my head within seconds. No word I shout into the glittery mass gets it to slow down or stop.

Once again, magic has stolen the upper hand of an already tumultuous situation.

We won't be able to hold out for much longer.

I try to remember Xander's words, his brief lessons about magic when he was no longer just the necromancer to me. Gemma got me through the basics, and then he helped me expand on my grasp of magic. I made a shield.

I could do that again.

Or, I could build a dam.

"Hey, buddy, we've got to get back in the air," I shout to Skelly over the water, his left leg slipping again.

I need to see what I'm doing, and that's not an option from inside the tempest I created. If I knock the golden barrier down, all of this excess water will flood the lower city of Brairgild. I can't do that to the people who have come to our side, those who have lived alongside me all my life, whether or not they've found the courage to stand up to Anerald. Back in the air, I'll have a better idea of what to do.

I pat Skelly's side as his wet wings spread out to the sides. They flap. Slowly. Too slow. We'll never get out of the water like this.

Instantly, glitter springs to his limbs. Not the wind this time. There's a golden cord that winds through it, spreading from one bony wing tip to the other.

A wish. One of the threads I released when I set off the glitter bomb at the castle. I stare at it in numb fascination, waiting for it to do something and then realize it's also waiting for me.

Skelly can't make his own wish, so I raise my voice over the thundering flood. "I wish my dragon could fly!"

The golden thread sinks into his bones, leaving a metallic sheen to the uppermost pieces of his wings as he begins to flap. Once. Twice. On the third flap, his feet leave the ground.

Clacking his jaw in excitement, he tries harder. We're above the water in a minute and then above the tree line in the next. I hoot back to the rebels down below who cheer at our flight, the entirety of the group clinging to one another in midriff high water and holding on as I figure out what I need to do next.

Unfortunately, revolution doesn't come with an instruction manual.

I take only a minute to look around at the damage, the still spreading water, and the weakest points of Brairgild's dwindling barrier. The two magic wielders in charge of keeping the golden sheen alive are sweating and shaking and trying desperately to do their job, and also keep an eye on what I'm up to. One of them screams for us to be shot out of the sky.

All of the guards tip their arrows towards us.

Great. Lovely. Just one more problem.

"Skelly, we're-."

My dragon doesn't give me a chance to talk him through this next part. His confidence granted by that golden thread, he pushes us further upwards, weaving one way and then the other to keep us out of the way of the arrows being shot into the sky. Gemma's quilted wings flutter as the dragon swirls and twirls and outmaneuvers the entirety of the tower guards.

I desperately try to keep my stomach from falling out of my throat and hold onto his ribbon reins with one hand while directing another to the trees closest to the flood. Inspired by the pumpkin minions Cam had working all over Apricity, I shout for the trees to uproot themselves and stand at attention. The flood water slows the second the trees break away from their rooted spots and step up onto the forest floor as if the glitter from one spell interrupts that of another.

There's still so much for me to learn about magic, but, for now, I need my rebel group to make it into Briargild and the people beyond the golden barrier to not be buried in more water than this kingdom has ever seen at one time. The trees move with minimal commands on my part, the magic running away with my idea. It guides them in sparkling steps to the edge of Briargild's entrance. Trees shake, angry branches clenched in bristling fists, and throw themselves at the golden barrier. One after another, they attack and then lie down, scooping layers of dirt and debris into their crevices until they've created an impenetrable wall where the water is most likely to slip into the kingdom.

A final tree holds out its branches to the rebels, gathering them as I turn my attention to the court-ordained mages. Already, the golden barrier is barely there. They're fighting a losing battle.

One of them realizes it.

His hands shift towards me. Golden robes whipping around his thin form, he commands the nearest guard to shoot another arrow at us. Skelly is moving before it leaves the tower. The golden barrier falls. A cheer resounds from the rebels who are carted over the dam by the last tree, and I watch the single arrow shimmer gold.

It's faster than it should be. It's not moving in a straight arc. The sharp thing glints in the final ray of sunset.

Guided by magic, it's coming straight for us.

"Skelly! Get past the tower!"

We're out of time. The rest of the rebel cause is a nuisance, but I'm the real problem. If I'm not at the castle soon, Xander will be forced into a wedding that serves his father and nothing else. He'll act out again. I saw him lunge towards that dagger that ended up in my own chest. I saw the roses he left in Apricity. If he has any choice, he'll end all of this before he and Cam are sealed together in a wicked fate.

I can't let one arrow stop us. Ignoring the irony that I am trying to run from a golden arrow after casting one myself led me to this very spot, I push Skelly on. Just past the towers with the runes that aren't glowing and the barrier that has fallen. There will be somewhere to land and hide on the other side.

With my right hand ahead of myself, I put up a shield. One that guards us against a fatal blow. Skelly pumps his wings harder, first pushing us up and then past the towers that have loomed over me my entire life. That arrow follows every maneuver.

We're past the first street. My attention catches on a white bloom, a lasting reminder of the tavern and my start on this magical journey. A flower that is a revelation that I didn't just find myself a victim of magic, but I was always meant to take this path. The Heart of Apricity is with me, and plant magic has always been in my blood.

Still, that arrow trails us.

When it catches up, it cuts right through my shield, its spell built on bitter malice that severs my own desperate magic without hesitation. It misses both of our hearts and instead tears through Skelly's left wing. It looks like a sword was drawn raggedly through the quilted fabric, the two halves flapping helplessly against the air as my dragon lets out a helpless clack of his jaw. He flails. Wishes can't save us now.

Up too high to stop anything, I watch the destroyed edges of the quilted wing flap. Gemma is going to kill me if I survive this crash. "You're doing good, buddy. Just keep us up as long as you can," I tell him, my knees holding onto the saddle as both my hands stay by my head.

I have to get that shield back up. We're plummeting now. If we hit the ground at this velocity, I don't know what will happen to Skelly. There's no telling if my original magic is strong enough to keep him from shattering into a hundred different bones and effectively eliminating the only dragon on the continent.

I need to soften a dragon's descent.

Xander's lessons on shields flutter through my mind like pages of a storybook lost to the cruel hands of a storm. Imagine. Push it out. Make the magic protect.

Eyes squeezed shut, Skelly clacking his panic, I push magic out from myself. Taking it a step further than anyone who trained me, I feel it. Safety. Protection. Hope. I make the shield inch away from my body and crawl over every bone comprising the dragon beneath me as he pulls in his good wing and we continue to fall in a haphazard heap. Imagining it like a bubble that contains both of us, I hold that intent tighter than I hold onto my dragon.

I open my eyes at the last second.

A swirling second skin of glitter covers both Skelly and me. Not just pink. Red and green and gold. A thousand different colors. Magic from all the fairy godmothers who sacrificed their wands to bring me back from the dead.

It's here now, making sure I don't cross that threshold a second time.

I cling to Skelly as the ground comes closer. It'll be okay. I repeat that promise over and over in my mind as I focus on holding the shape of our shared shield. We're going to be okay.

Skelly's claws barely miss raking the top of a building before we fall into an alley just past the city center that brought me to Prince Alexander Charming in the first place. Skelly jerks his head back, probably wishing he had eyelids to squeeze shut as he holds out his legs to stop our fall. And then the ground is there.

Skelly should shatter, my own bones should be splintered and useless, but my shield holds. We bounce. Once, twice, a faltering third time as Skelly regains his bearings. Then, my dragon is up in a heartbeat while I'm still trying to figure out where I left my lungs up in the sky. He skips from one foot to the other as though to tell me we should do this again sometime.

I won't be agreeing to such things.

"We still have to get to the castle, Skelly," I pat his shoulder and then tug on his makeshift reins. "We passed everyone else, so they'll just have to catch up. This was always our fight."

Yells follow us through the city. Apparently, everyone was too drunk or tired to see my magic collapse the tavern, but they're all awake and ready to tattle on me for crashing a dragon into the city. It should be expected of the nobility.

Skelly and I are causing traffic jams. I pull on Skelly's ribbon to try to move him out of the way of carriages, but the drivers of the vehicles are already in a panic. Several pull too hard into a sidewalk, getting stuck tilted to one side, women in frilly gowns clutching their hats and screaming to be let out of their seats. Horses whinny and shift under their riders, giving Skelly a wide berth even as my dragon tries to slither by with his wings tucked in and head down. He's doing his best, but we're not very stealthy, and everyone is in our way.

The guards are back on our trail after only a few minutes of strained maneuvering through the clustered homes and businesses of the noble class. Arrows prelude them. They plink off of buildings and spear themselves through windows, raining glass down onto the streets as we race through Briargild.

It's probably for the best we abandoned the rebel group. We wouldn't have all made it through this horrendous maze now. All of the danger is focused on Skelly and me as we race from one obstacle to another and try to remain unscathed in the face of the king's men, who want nothing more than to bring us down.

With the guards at our back, Skelly rears in my hold as a different group of men steps in front of us with several meters of rope in their hands. Their crisp, white suits with golden pins denote them as some of the richest men in Briargild, and they've clearly united to slow us down. Damn. We've been corralled here.

"Skelly," I start, my mind exhausted and magic flickering at my fingertips in glittering sparks.

I just need a minute. I can get us out of this. One minute. To think. To ponder and fiddle with the problems. There are just so many gods damned problems, aren't there?

The guards are getting even closer. One in my periphery to the left unsheathes a sword. They think they're close enough to pull me off of Skelly.

I'm sure they aren't meaning to take me as a prisoner.

Magic writhes through me, demanding a purpose until my bones are raw and my muscles sore from the jittery connection. I have so much power and no idea what to do.

I didn't fly a dragon just to fail.

The magic leaps to do as I bid when I point to the rope getting closer to us, Skelly having been on his own to rake his claws and snap his jaw in order to keep them back for us, while I tried to think of the best plan. I couldn't have asked for a better partner than the dragon with me now, his heart pumping in glittery blasts of pink beneath the saddle. Everyone has told me that my magic was different.

Things don't just come to life when magic is used on them.

But it happens when I do it.

One hand on Skelly's shoulder, I think of how he looked too much like a snake in the beginning. He was terrifying. All snout and teeth and slithering movements. Snakes were my biggest fear besides losing all the pieces of my life, and now I launch that on the noblemen.

The rope wriggles in their hold. It unwinds, stretching and stretching and stretching so much longer than it should have been. A writhing mass with too many heads and so much body and a flicking tail, the snake-inspired monstrosity rises. Collectively, the four men let it go with strained yells, but dropping it isn't enough. My rope, turned snake, entangles their legs and pulls them down. It holds them hostage the way they wanted to take my dragon, and I feel absolutely no remorse about it.

Skelly jumps over them and charges forward. We're once more on our way to the castle to face my next biggest fear: losing Xander before we have a chance to be anything more than a happenstance bundle of moments that could have been more.

We make it two more streets. The crowds are fully gathered. Alarm bells have pulled them from their homes, and they watch in mixtures of awe and horror as we run by.

The castle is in view. We're so freaking close.

There's also a battalion of guards waiting for us, lining the space in front of the castle gate shoulder to shoulder once more with a menagerie of weapons.

It's becoming clear that nobody wants us to attend this wedding.

I straighten in the saddle as Skelly slows. Magic swirls around us, my shields quickly pulling into place as I face the men in front of us. "Look, we can do this the hard way, or you can just let us in. If an entire city and catapults couldn't keep us out, what hope do you have?"

One of the guards looks ready to argue, to call for them to attack, to stand his ground, but he's cut off by the sound of running feet behind us. I dare to look back at my next problem, and then my heart clogs my throat.

That's not a problem.

Servants in their plain clothes with hair pulled back from their faces and grime from their chores still smeared on their arms, round the street behind us. They brandish farming tools and baking pins and whatever else they could get their hands on, hoisting their everyday items turned weaponry above their heads with a battle cry. Even without the rebel group, Skelly and I aren't alone.

Whether it be that I caused enough trouble to gather a crowd or that they saw a dragon and knew it was time to revolt, the lower class of Briargild rises up. Today will be the last time that they are scorned and abused and belittled. Apricity will not remain a secret. Briargild will not continue to rule unopposed.

A dragon returned, and now the crown will fall.

They charge the guards, and a call goes out to open the gates. The same guards who dragged me to the dungeon and spat on me now cower before the charge of the people. Violence flares, but it's short-lived. The gates fall open, and the guards stagger away from the onslaught, no longer willing to fight a battle they didn't start.

"Let's go, Skelly," I nudge him forward, accepting cheers from the crowd at our feet as they clear away from us.

I call my own thanks back to them, and we step past the looming golden-plated gates. Nobody decrees for us to stop now. We move through the open space, my legs sore and gelatinous from the hard journey here. To the side, I can just make out the beginning of the rose gardens and the major dusting of pink glitter across the castle from my bomb.

It almost feels like coming home.

As though King Anerald placed all of his defenses further from the castle, no more guards came to defend the place. We race through the open front doors. Skelly's claws scramble on the clean, tile floors, dirt and soot splashing around us. We leave behind the others, my dragon far faster as I direct him through the halls, picking the ones obviously decorated for the so-called wedding. It takes us almost no time at all to find the doors to the ballroom.

Xander is right there.

I'm so close to saving him and Cam and making things better.

Skelly rears back on his hind legs to kick down the doors without me having to do more than encourage him with a squeeze of my knees around the saddle. Wood splinters. It never had a chance against him.

We fall through the doors amidst a wave of gasps that compete to drown out the sound of our entry. In unison, the esteemed guests of the wedding turn to look behind themselves. I don't care. They can look all they want. My own eyes are on the front of the room. King Anerald stands between Camellia in a white gown and Xander, seated in a suit in his wheeled chair.

They look like they've been holding perfectly still for a portrait.

"My, my, my," King Anerald's voice booms over the room, breaking the stillness of my sudden entrance. "I thought you would never make it, Mister Cinderfella."

I don't have a reply as realization blooms through my mind. King Anerald was expecting me.

Gods, we're royally fucked.

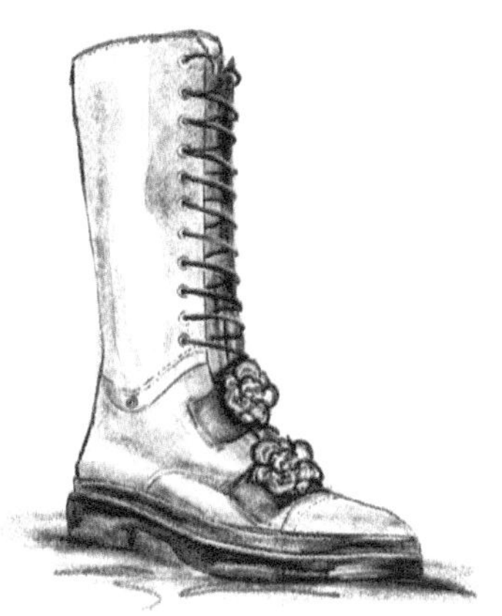

27

The entire act of rescuing Xander and Cam was a trap. King Anerald utters a command. He doesn't shout. There's no extra vehemence to the syllables. This is just a plan he's following through on.

A plan I voluntarily walked into.

It's too late to realize that the instruction was to cut the rope on a net dangling above the entrance. I try to urge Skelly forward, but there isn't time. Amid a collection of gasps from the nobility, the lot of them rising from their seats in a ridiculous blur of feathers and sparkling jewels as they run from the scene in their finest finery, the net crashes down on top of us. Gold flashes in my vision as it falls to imprison us.

Skelly shakes his head one way and the other, stretching his wings out as he fights the net. It was advantageous for him to be made of bones for his better aerodynamics and speed, but we need brute strength, and he doesn't have it. The net is on us, and no amount of thrashing seems to be able to dislodge it. My dragon throws back his head and gnashes his sharp teeth together as he crashes to his knees and then flat on the floor.

Defeated, he takes me with him, tangling me in the netting as my left foot gets trapped in the saddle. The net isn't made of rope. It's metal. Finely wound together and far too heavy for either of us to shake off. Pinned to Skelly, I dig my fingers into the holes and try to adjust it enough to get a clear view of the room.

Skelly shudders under me. If he had vocal cords, he would probably scream, growl, roar his distaste over our current position. As is, he thrashes until he's out of energy, vibrating with a quiet rage as I pat his shoulder.

I feel it. We should have known better.

We just have to get out of this, too.

At least, I can see Xander.

His hands are on the wheels of his chair. Knuckles white, expression matching the fury tearing through our dragon, he's at the edge of the makeshift dais set up for his nuptials, but held back by a guard with a hand on his shoulder. His gaze, silver and worried, cuts to his side. I can just make out Camellia swaying under sword point. They learned their lesson in the hidden caverns of Apricity to keep sharp objects from the prince and threaten his friends instead of him.

The three of us are in quite a freaking pickle.

I grit my teeth. We're going to be okay. This isn't how the story ends. I did not fly on a dragon composed of bones and magic to be defeated.

I'll use magic and get out, and Skelly can eat King Anerald for all I care.

Except…

Something's wrong. Glitter should be falling from my fingertips. The rainbow of a hundred pounds of borrowed magic should be flitting around me like it has ever since I woke from my own death. I have felt too full ever since leaving Apricity, stuffed to the brim with magic that wasn't my own. It should be easy to feel it prickling along my limbs and festering in my mind, searching for a way to be released and harnessed for a greater purpose. Yet, there's no feeling of buzzing hope under my skin.

The net.

The metal net.

Just like when I had been arrested and shackled in gold plating that could stop my magic, my connection now has been severed.

Panic latches sharp teeth on my throat. Skelly and I are both under the torturous metal.

Skelly.

He's stopped moving.

As if my realization has caused it, the bindings of magic holding his collective bones together shudder. The pink pulse of his heart glows dimly against the edge of the saddle from where I can see, my cheek pressed to the floor as I wildly try to look closer at him. It throbs lighter and lighter, pale in comparison to the nearly neon thing it has been since the moment I created him.

"Skelly. Buddy. Skells," words tumble from my mouth, his name is a whimper I'm not proud of, and I cannot hold back.

Distantly, I hear people murmur. The nobility is watching this. Watching me be trapped and my dragon be taken.

Killed.

"Skelly, come on. You have to hang on," I croak.

But he doesn't shift. There's no more shaking of his head. He doesn't clack his jaw the way I've grown accustomed to hearing and responding to. His wings do not flap, and his claws don't click against the tile flooring.

We flew all the way here. I led him into this trap.

Twisting my neck to look at Xander again, I watch the same horror dawn on his expression like a sun setting too early and distorting the horizon. There's no hiding our emotions. Our grand plan is in motion. The rebellion is in the streets. We did everything we thought we needed to, and still, Skelly is in a trap and pressed to the floor.

Cam says my name. I can't look at her. She doesn't need my attention the way my dragon does right this second. Trapped in an entirely different way across the room from me, she says his name, too.

The first dragon to return to the kingdom is dying under me.

"Skelly," I stroke a hand over his shoulder, the only place I can reach him from the way we're tangled together.

That glow, the heart I put in his chest with magic I didn't understand, slows. The pink becomes mottled, filled with holes as the metal burns through my spell. It untangles the knots my magic worked together so many nights ago, shredding the blushing tone until it is the flare of a candle not quite lit. The pink evaporates. A flare of white shines and is quickly snuffed out.

The light dies.

And so does my dragon.

Clattering fills the decorated ballroom as the final connections between his bones give out. I slump to the floor among his bits and pieces, frantically grabbing at them and trying to shove them back together even as the net presses more firmly on top of me. Skelly is no longer here among the bones.

I scream. I yell and thrash to no avail, kicking myself out of a saddle that no longer sits on top of anything besides trapped air.

This isn't happening.

It can't.

I can't lose anything else.

First, my mother. Then, my home, my culture, a chance at a normal gods damned life. All of that followed by the man I love, my cousin, and countless other people that this king has hurt with his unjust actions. Now, my dragon.

My dragon.

Skelly.

I hit the ground in frustration as I scream the name of the king who has cursed us all. "Anerald!"

My throat closes around the hard edges, grief a palpable pressure behind my eyes and nose as I feel the tears press forth. Pieces of Skelly in my hold, my magic stolen, I stare out at the scene around me. An audience of shocked nobility was watching me stain this ballroom with my antics. I am a blemish on their society, a pool of ink threatening to ruin every fine fabric they decided to wear to this false marriage. Pouts of disapproval stare back at me from the sophisticated sea of pearls, lace, and silks.

When I get out of this fucking net…

Rage tips me closer to a murderous path than I've ever welcomed before. I swivel my gaze to Xander, to the edge of Cam's shoulder that I can just make out from my pinned position, and to the guards still holding them captive. Magic exists in this room. Not mine. Trapped magic in those gold-bottomed orbs that only display the cool yellow light of a kingdom emptied of hope. No amount of staring at the lights gives me a chance to call on the magic there. As long as I'm trapped under the net, I'm useless, but fury percolates in my limbs, and the beginning of a plan forms.

Desperation has me focused on Xander again. I wish I could see him under the full might of the sun just once. Smiling. He has a beautiful smile when not covering his face with a mask or staring down authoritarian figures. My last memory of him cannot be tinged in the yellow hue of Briargild's stolen magic.

He is silver and hope bundled in a disguise.

He is right freaking there.

Our story cannot end like this.

Further still, I search the room and find the quivering gaze of servants backed into a corner. Tears leave streaks down their cheeks. These are people treated just as much like they are dirt on the bottom of a fancy slipper as I have been. Trapped, too. They look at me with trepidatious hope and a willingness to believe that this isn't how today must go.

A dragon returned. Half of the prophecy is already true. Anerald's going to lose his crown. I can promise that much to myself as I paw through Skelly's remains for a single bone I could use to my advantage.

Eyes on the crowd, I watch the shaken and shifting emotions of those in the room who have not benefited from Anerald's reign. As much as I want to save Xander, as much as I want nothing to happen to my father wherever he is in the streets of Briargild, as much as I hope Gemma is safe, I am more than my love for one person. I am more than desperation and failure. I am more than broken magic. There's no crown on my head, but I am the hope of a kingdom. I will get out of these bindings and avenge Skelly and bring the depths of my magic down on Anerald's head.

He hasn't left me any other option.

King Anerald Charming tuts at me from across the expansive room, the irritating cluck carrying despite the collected sounds of heeled shoes on the polished flooring and swishing skirts and flailing fans as the women nearest me murmur to each other about the state of this wedding as they catch a blonde-haired woman who fainted from my so-called theatrics. "Now, now, Mister Cinderfella, lost child of Adira Alcinder, I should have seen you sacrificed for the greater pursuits of power many, many years ago." He speaks slowly as though I'm not capable of keeping up with him, stepping away from the dais to join me on the ground level as he walks down the line of noble people watching this happen, watching their king humiliate a person without uttering a single syllable of rebuttal. "But it just so happens that you're exactly what I need to make the union of our kingdoms permanent."

I have no idea what he's talking about. I frankly don't care. I spare another glance at the unsettled nobility. These are people of wealth who have been raised above those considered common folk because of their loyalty to the crown. Some sneer still. Others don't look so certain, though.

That hope I saw flashing in the faces of the lower class is reflected here as fear. Fear of what is to come, of change, of the fact that it is imminent and inevitable. They're likely terrible people crafted by grief and trauma in the same way my father chose to remain kind in the face of our tragedies. Choice is the only thing that separates us. They chose to follow the given system. I won't.

King Anerald is stepping casually forward, caught up in his thoughts as though he's traversing a meadow and not openly plotting my second murder. His villain monologue sprawls between us. I'm a gift he could never have predicted. I'll be bettering my kingdom. It is for the greater good that he guts me now and lets me bleed magic into Briargild.

I can't pay too much attention. There are more important matters at hand. Trapped in this net, unwilling to wait for death like a fish on the pier, I keep searching through the pile of bones.

My dragon's bones.

The night I met Xander as the Necromancer, they weren't just bones. They were weapons. I asked a skeleton to put one through his heart. Pushing at the net, my cheek pressed to the floor and my shoulders stiff from fighting the weight of the gold-covered metal, I blindly reach my hands out to clutch at the sharpened bones.

I don't need anything fancy.

Something sharp.

Something strong.

If I can shove it into one of these metal rings, I should be able to use the bone as leverage to open it. Break it, even. With just one link in this net broken, I should be able to get my hand out, to reach for magic, and turn the tables on this interaction with Anerald.

The King steps away when I find what I'm looking for. A claw. The tip fits into the gap in one of the metal links.

"Anerald, if you touch him!"

It's not a full threat. Xander spits it anyway. His father turns back around, hands on his hips, so his cape is splayed in a way that blocks the prince from my view.

Which is okay. Xander is creating a distraction.

One I truly need.

I jab my shard of bone into the gaps in the metal links and twist. My wrists shake from the effort of holding my arms at such an odd angle, while my elbow digs into the ground, and I try not to give in to the overpowering pressure of the net on top of me.

I am so tired. The metal has drained my magic, my spirit, my will. It would be easier to give up. Back in the dungeon, I was ready to give up. Now, though, with my father returned and people depending on me and Xander yelling in the only capacity he has to try to save me, I want nothing more than to live.

"We're only doing all of this because you couldn't get the job done in the first place, Alexander."

King Anerald doesn't raise his voice. He already has a captive audience. Instead, he waits for the echo of Xander's yell to quiet down and then shoots back his reply with the same deadly precision as a snake waiting in shrubs.

"I never agreed to any of this," Xander snaps back.

There's some commotion up front. I assume he threw out his arms, and the guards shuffled closer to stop him. I'm a little busy prying at the metal link to try to crane my neck in any way to get a better view of his efforts.

This is our only chance, and I won't survive without magic. I just have to get out of this net.

It should be illegal to produce items that take away magic.

Maybe I will make that illegal when Xander and I work to change the kingdoms.

Metal scrapes against bone, the sound loud next to my face but unnoticed by anyone else as father and son stare each other down.

"It was your responsibility when I allowed you to live, Alexander."

Xander lets out a harsh laugh, a deep, throaty sound that has the nobility shuffling towards me rather than be anywhere near the prince. "I lived because mom wanted me to. She begged someone to save me, to give me a fighting chance, and she would have loved to see what I've become. I don't think the same can be said about you."

King Anerald takes two steps away from me, his hulking form easily overtaking the aisle set in the middle of the ballroom. "If magic could save you, why couldn't it just be used to save her?" Spittle gleams in the air as Anerald unsheathes a blade at his side. "I wanted her to live. I gave up on everything when she was taken from me, taken because she used magic and her last hope on you. A broken failure I couldn't truly accept as my heir. The second I'm not on the throne, you will be overtaken and tossed aside for someone competent. That's why we need this binding with Apricity. So I know you'll live because that's all she ever wanted."

This seems like it could have been a conversation between closed doors two decades ago. It might have saved much of the heartbreak now marring the ballroom. As is, both men are too far gone, aligned on opposite sides of this battle and refusing to back down.

That dagger in Anerald's hand catches the golden light from above. He's speaking, yelling, condemning his son for not being born perfect.

Which is wrong.

Xander is amazing. Different. Unique. A beautiful concoction of challenges overcome via his control of magic or general sheer will.

I wish there had been a chance for me to have fallen in love with him that first meeting on the winter solstice. Just as he is, seated with an illegal book and a plan to change the world regardless of every obstacle in his way. He was gone so quickly, I had no idea how much he was going to change my life.

We've been bound to this moment since our mothers came together to save a life. Humans made a choice, and the consequences are following through now. Without them, fate might not have brought us together. Destiny may never have been involved. I'm not sure if the stars would have aligned or if the moon agreed with the action of tying the cords of our lives together, but I would have chosen him without any of those signs.

I want to choose him now as I tear my way through this net.

King Anerald is a bully, telling his followers that Briargild will always be the best kingdom in all the land. They should disregard every insult he just threw at his own son. His villain monologue continues…

Blah. Blah. Blah.

I stop paying attention. The bone and metal combination squeals, and then the little piece of sinister gold gives out. The single link clatters to the floor next to me. There's a hold in the net. It's definitely not enough to squeeze my head and shoulders out of, but it's big enough for my purposes. I drop the bone and plunge my hand into the hole I've created during Xander's distraction.

I reach my fingers through it into a space not consumed by its lack of magic.

My lungs fill completely for the first time since falling out of the air, power surging through me more suddenly and completely than it did when I woke from the fitful sleep of the dead. Magic winds its way back into my body. It pulses from my chest. Hot. Writhing. A second entity stuffed into the compact space beneath my skin. It winds sticky fingers around the notches in my spine and tilts my head back so it can whisper in my ear.

Power.

There's so much power at my literal fingertips.

I could bring the whole castle down on us right now and end this awful scene in a swift crush.

I won't. It is tempting, though. It takes me far more effort to ignore the tense presence occupying my mind with me and make my own decision.

Focusing, I solve my first problem. The net. It has to go. Magic bounds from my fingers, and the dastardly metal dissolves into a pile of glittering, pink dust.

The net is gone. I'm alive and free to get up. The bones around me remain lifeless.

Skelly.

Hesitation has me on my knees surrounded by bones that don't wriggle or glitter or pulse to life. I wait, but my dragon is still not here. Magic doesn't flock back to him like it did me.

Throat tight, I don't have any more time to spend on him, on the lack of him, as the gathered nobility gasp and shriek and altogether warn Anerald of my presence. I push to my full height. A man in the middle of a small mountain of glitter. Untethered and unrestrained. King Anerald does his part by slowly, dramatically turning towards me. He takes in the mess I've made of his net, and then a slow smile curls his lips into a wicked expression.

"I knew you were my missing piece. Just look at how powerful you are."

Much like he did in the cavern of Apricity, he jerks his hand back and throws his dagger. It never gets close to me. The blade turns into a puff of dandelion fluff and floats away.

I barely thought about it.

More glitter falls from me than normal. Gold and orange and a fiery red. It itches under my fingernails and cuts my gums. Glitter sticks to my face where I've cried and coats my hairline where I sweat. I'm dressed in glitter like it's statement jewelry adorning my brow, throat, and wrists. It floats in the air around me, a threat lingering in a careful circle around me in case anyone in this room has forgotten who I am.

Anerald takes note of that all with a steady flick of his gaze. "Parlor tricks. All of this power is wasted on someone like you."

"Someone like me?" I grit out, that second intention residing within my brain, pounding out a death wish for the man in front of me.

"A peasant," he snarls. "A nobody. Someone like you could never aspire to rule like me."

For the first time in our brief interactions with each other, I choke on my own laugh. "Aspire to be you? No. Never."

The glitter at my feet swirls lazily back to life, sticking to my pant legs and crawling up my form as though to rejoin with the magic still trapped in my body. There's so much of it. I'm overwhelmed by the sheer amount of power pushed into myself, stored to the brim like a flour canister that someone has hammered a lid onto before it was shoved to the back of a cupboard.

"I'm very inspired by you, though," I go on, admiring the way his eyes widen at my admission. "Inspired, that is, to show people there's a better way to live."

King Anerald snorts, reaching into his belt for another blade. He truly means to make me bleed for Briargild. It's unfortunate for him that I don't share the same goal.

Instead, I glance around the room. Creativity has always been a strength of mine. I don't need to think twice about what I want to do. The mad king is entirely focused on me, but there's someone I need to help first.

The guard holding Camellia is someone I recognize. He's the same rapscallion that threatened me on the solstice. The man who trashed my father's tavern and threatened us. As much as Xander's presence in my path nudged me to my current place, this man's existence is the very reason I made the wish that changed my entire life. Whether or not he realizes his place in my story, he's about to find out I have a pretty good sense of humor.

Plus, I need to even out the battlefield here.

I don't point. There's no need for gestures when the magic is melded so closely to my mind. I merely think, and it leaps to my command.

The familiar guard yelps. His sword clatters to the ground as Camellia staggers away from him and the blinding light erupting from his chest. Glitter coats him in thirty shades of green. It swirls and stiffens around him. His armor clatters to the floor to join his weapon, and then a gasp overtakes the room.

In the place of the guard is a very pretty, very tall plant topped with a pumpkin for a head.

Thank you, plant magic.

Camellia's anxious expression shifts to one of excitement. Her hands immediately at her sides, she turns her wrists in easy circles, already influencing the plants in her nearest vicinity. Red roses stuffed into wedding bouquets spread their petals. Green stems sharpen to points out of their vases. Vines emerge and creep up the dais to my cousin. As the only other person here still with magic to use, it's her and me against the rest of the room.

We're about to turn the tide of this war.

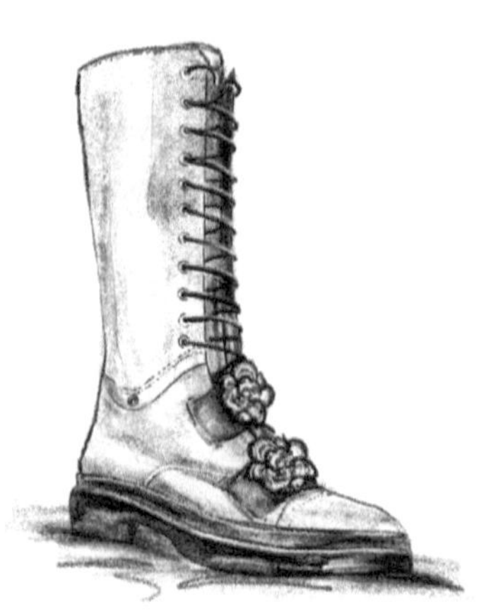

28

"This is for Apricity!"

Camellia, a flurry of motion in her ill-fitting wedding gown, jumps from the dais. Her magic unhindered by shackles or nets, she raises her hands like a magician about to do close-up magic for an audience, and then the floor rumbles. Shrieks ring through the room almost as loud as the destruction she brings.

I tilt to the left as the floor crumbles. Enormous vines shoot up from the ground like thick, green tentacles of the Earth brought to life from her will alone. Dust fills the air, and people cough and yell and curse and altogether act out in their discomfort as I watch this woman I've only just met bring the highest ring of the crooked kingdom to its knees.

She is the endurance of a nation shackled, and her rage rings through Briargild now.

Enormous green vines of unknown power respond to her beck and call, the blind queen knocking over seating and pushing back the nobility with mere flicks of her wrists. Camellia is a tempest, a flurried hurricane tinged in green. A jungle forms around her as greenery from every corner of this ballroom flocks to her side. The abrupt juxtaposition of gold against the green of her magic is a clear sign that Apricity isn't going down without a fight. She alone has control over the battle. With a snap of her fingers, she sends the pumpkin guard to the other side of the dais.

Confusion and panic warp the nobility of Briargild. None of them is prepared to fight back. The pumpkin guard reaches Xander's side. Lithe and taller than the man at the prince's side by at least a half meter, his presence is enough to intimidate Xander's guard into scrambling back off of the dais.

The three of us are free of restraints.

Xander reaches behind him. He doesn't have a sword or a dagger or anything sharp at his disposal, but he's always been good at improvising. He draws one of the crutches strapped to the back of his wheelchair and brandishes it like a sword at the guards hesitating in a circle around the dais. His silver eyes find me in the chaos. Hope glints there sharper than any blade.

Nobody moves. Trapped in indecision, the guards look to Anerald, who hasn't moved this entire time. He remains firmly in the center of the carnage as flowers burst from the ceilings and several more angry, seething vines wrap tendrils of greenery around the arms of the nearest guards.

A queen, a prince, and a tavern keep walk into a ballroom…

Gods, the scene we're creating. I want to laugh at the insanity of it all. To my right, a group of women run from daffodils on spindly legs, the flowers crafted with thorny protrusions that remind me of the carnivorous carriage I made at the beginning of all of this. To my left, men in suits marred with glitter and greenery step up onto the few tables and chairs not overturned by Cam's magic. They've abandoned their wives and mistresses to save themselves. The first cracks in Briargild's foundation are widening. Soon, it'll be broken, and they'll have to accept defeat.

King Anerald Charming, seemingly untouched by the magic turning into vengeful plants, clears his throat. Nobody actually looks at him. They're too busy trying to figure out what to do with all the rampant magic. Panic has seeded desperation in their hearts, and their loyalty to the crown has diminished. I linger behind Anerald, waiting for his next move with my hands open at my sides.

Xander rolls to the edge of the makeshift stage, a regal silhouette cut against the chaos with his chin lifted and crutch extended towards the guards, who take a half step back. "Give up now, and you can leave."

It's an ultimatum. It's not a threat. It's a promise that anyone who stays will be dealt with permanently.

My hands tremble. I try to breathe through the magic raging in my chest, the voice in my head saying to act now and not extend mercy at all. I could turn this room into a handful of grain without much of a strain on myself. There's too much power stuffed into my joints and crammed into the cage of my bones and flesh. The magic is ready and willing and pushing so hard against the confines of my body.

Xander stares past his father at me, checking on me. I'm still here. That silver gaze is filled with resentment and a cruel willingness to do hard things, but it softens just for a second when our eyes meet. He is the blinking shine of stars just before they go out. My prince, my necromancer, my Xander. I could stare at him for the rest of my life.

The room quiets as everyone waits to hear Anerald's reply. He's the only one here wearing a crown on his head. Steeped in gold and foaming at the mouth, he sets his hands on his hips, his rings glinting in the overhanging lights before being tucked under the edge of his blood-red cape.

This isn't the anticipation of greatness. Nobody is holding their breath because they actually believe Anerald is going to step down from the throne he has held onto for nearly fifty years. The hush that overtakes the ballroom is the kind of quiet that grips the community when nature takes a turn for the worse, the immediate realization that the world is moving and we're inconsequential to it. Anerald will make his choice, he'll say his piece, and the battle will continue.

Still, he has our attention as he stares back at Xander. "I only need one of you," he finally says, sweeping a hand out to the three of us separated throughout the space. "There's no reason to keep all of you alive if it's always going to be a problem."

Without weapons, it seems like a bluff. The words of a mad king, realizing that the end of his reign is nearing. Anerald doesn't huff and puff and demand order, though. He's certain of himself.

Which is when I hear the sounds from outside the ballroom.

A soft thunder cloud is working its way down the halls. The steps of far too many people. There's some muffled yelling. Then, the doors burst inward, and a hundred more guards wade into the room, kicking Skelly's bones in their haste to join us here.

The final piece of the trap Anerald set. His backup plan. If all else went wrong, he had an army coming back from the towers and the rest of the city to deal with us. He just had to bluff and blunder until they could return.

Well, we're not going down without a fight.

Xander is already shouting directions to Cam. Hands raised ahead of herself, depending on the prince to guide her since she doesn't have time for the plants to fill her in on visual cues, Cam unleashes herself on the ballroom.

The large greenery from the floor sweeps the length of the ballroom, grabbing at guards and tossing them aside as easily as dusting lint from one's shoulder. Screams take over our limited landscape once more. Glass shatters. The rest of the furniture collapses in the panic, sending men falling into the way of the green tentacles. There are a dozen head injuries in half a minute as people are swiped from the middle of the room.

Anerald is clipped by a guard and tossed backwards, his hulking form unfazed in the carnage that has once again overtaken the scene as he pushes the other man off to the side and shouts his next command. "It's just a plant. Cut it down!"

The collective swoosh of swords pulled from hip sheaths overtakes the yells of the nobility. Everywhere around us, guards chop at the plants. I lose sight of Xander as Cam continues pulling up fresh vines and sending them after the guards.

Before I can figure out what to do to help her, to help our cause, Anerald is in my face, completely blocking my view of everything else. Ire rests on his features, a comfortable expression that has shaped his image. He looms ahead of me. Red from head to toe, besides the areas with glitter gold, he faces me with a new dagger in his grip.

"This has been a cute display. Have her stop, or I will have her beheaded instead of apprehended."

I don't believe him. Giving up now isn't an option. None of us are safe to see tomorrow if we let Anerald decide to have his way with us. My entire life has been composed of rules and regulations made by a king who didn't care for his lower class, for magic wielders, or for anyone who questioned the kingdom's legal system. I spent five days rotting in the dungeon here. I spent four days in a land between this one and the final door of death. I am done letting other people decide my fate.

"Touch her and it'll be the last thing you do," I snarl back.

I leave my palms open and direct them to the scraps of vegetation being haphazardly chopped around the room. Glitter sparks. The greenery moves from its fallen spots on the white-tiled floors like leeches in a pond. It has a target. It has a lust for blood. It cannot be stopped.

Anerald swipes at the green globs when they wriggle towards him. In our corner of the ballroom, guards scream when the plant pieces crawl under their pants legs and wrap around their ankles. My magic is an infestation that overtakes Cam's efforts. It's insidious and spreading. The more parts of her original vines that are cut away, the more my glittery army has to work with. Red mixes with green and gold and white until the ballroom is an array of panic and pain.

The nobility fight each other to get out of the doors. They elbow and kick and knock one another out of the way. One woman loses her entire golden wig as she falls screaming to the ravenous expanse of my green battalion.

The guards falter. Some abandon their posts. Racing past me for the doors, only to realize the halls are filled with an entirely different group of people.

The rebels have arrived.

Anerald, swiping at my sharp-toothed greenery with one hand, shouts commands to the other side of the room. The guards that have remained come together as one. They abandon fighting separately and surge towards Camellia.

My cousin was doing well one-on-one. She had the entire room quivering and pleading for her to stop, even before I intervened with my own magic. Now, though, she falters in the face of the full force of Anerald's dwindling army. They stomp on her plants, and she winces as her magic bleeds out in sparkling bits of green all over the destroyed floor. Her eyes covered and her white dress stained green, she stands above the convening guards on the dais as a martyr ready to be painted for future generations, for them to remember and then to heed if they don't want to meet death in the same way. The blind queen, the last queen of Apricity, the woman who stood up to the tyranny of Briargild, knowing she wouldn't walk back out of this ballroom, Camellia Alcinder roars in the way my dragon could not and sends her last faltering bits of magic at the guards.

Greenery splatters against gold. Men fall. Cam staggers.

I don't want her to be remembered.

I want to give her a chance to spend time with her plants. She has sacrificed enough for me, for Xander, and for the greater good of a kingdom forced to kneel.

Behind me, the clattering of a second battle wages. The rebels shout and try to force their way into the ballroom to join us. They've sacrificed enough, too. Every person who has been moved to support this cause, to support me and the dream that the world can be free of tyrannical kings wishing to keep us segregated and struggling, they deserve a chance to live past today. I can't watch them die for a fight I joined too late.

My father is somewhere in that crowd.

Heart festering closer to my throat, I look out at the expanse of a war I brought into this castle, at the blood-spattered floors and the hole-filled walls, and make a decision. As much as I flew in here on a dragon with the sole purpose of ending this war, as much as I wanted this to be the last fight for Apricity's sake, I want these people to survive more. The rebels don't win anything if we all die today.

I wish I could see Xander, but Cam has my whole attention as Anerald repeats his threat to behead her.

Apricity may not be free today, but I will stop at nothing to make sure their queen returns.

I've already lost my dragon today.

I won't lose Camellia, too.

"Cam," I start, my voice quieter than I would like. "Camellia! Stop!"

Hands raised, greenery quivering with pent-up motives she's lost the ability to follow through on, she presses her lips into a frown, swiveling her face to where she guesses I'm standing. "Has the king surrendered?"

Sweat glistens on her brow. Her arms shake. Exhaustion drapes over her entire frame. The magic has taken its toll, and Cam is prepared to burn out completely before giving in to the guards who step in to grab her wrists and push her down to her knees. My cousin doesn't cry out. She doesn't complain. Instead, she keeps her chin tilted up towards me and trusts I'll make the right decision.

Which is not a position I ever thought I would be in.

I used to be Eli, the tavern keep. I was just a regular guy trying to get through the monotony of every regular day. Now, though, the weight of her life and those of the rebels in the halls is on my shoulders. I have one chance to talk Anerald out of killing my cousin, out of slaughtering the rebellion, and going through with his plans to fully steal the magic of Apricity.

"We need to have a civil conversation, and it's hard to focus when you're doing so amazing," I say to her, trying to keep my tone cheerful even as my throat tightens at the sight of her restrained and kneeling.

My mind is working too fast and not fast enough. I have to deal with one problem at a time. First things first, it's really hard to behead someone without any sharp objects in the room. Magic blooms at my fingertips. Glitter-streaked plants fall back to the ground as I let my magic spring to more important things. It touches every sword, axe, mace, and the gods damned forks from the banquet carts. Daisies fall to the floor where metal once was. Imminent danger removed, I let my shoulders relax slightly and direct my attention fully to Anerald.

He glares down at the flower in his grip and then tosses it to the ground. Done with this game, fists clenched almost as tightly as the muscle in his jaw, he moves towards me. His boots thud on the tiles, indiscriminately crushing bone shards and plant pieces alike. For an old man, he moves so quickly.

My head whips back. Blood blossoms across my tongue like a tree in spring. Anerald curses as he pulls back his hand.

Vision splitting, I blink at the separate layers of the ballroom wavering in front of me. Anerald appears in three different shapes. Darkness. Red. Gold. Blurry features and broad shoulders. The shadow of demise is lingering just in front of me.

If someone yells out in my defense, I don't hear it over the thundering of my own heart. I spit out a mouthful of blood and wipe the back of my hand under my nose. Every muscle in my body is tense. This is exactly the kind of altercation I used to find myself in while tending the tavern or traveling around the lower city. My first instinct is to hit him back. Hard. I want to make him bleed and writhe and beg for mercy.

Magic rattles my bones. It's a fungus spreading from my heart to my limbs. Growing, clawing at my skin for release, it pushes to retaliate, to do anything besides simmer within me as I take a deep breath.

Promises come next. That second intuition whispers directly into my mind. There are so many things I could do if only I unleashed it on the wicked king in front of me. Turning a person into a pumpkin-headed being was nothing compared to the full force of the magic in my limbs. Anerald could be incinerated before he takes another breath. I could tear the whole castle down and let the wind take his ashes out to the sea.

He deserves it.

This is a man who spent his entire life causing harm, crippling another kingdom, and planning to fully steal magic.

This is the man who abused and belittled Xander.

This is the man who took my mother.

I could end him now, but my heart and my mind can't seem to agree on a course of action.

Simply killing Anerald isn't the answer. The people gathered here, both the guards and the rebels, are fluent in violence. It's a part of life in Briargild. The powerful have been hurting people for generations.

I make no difference here if I simply cut Anerald down the way his family has been doing for the entirety of the history I can recall.

And still the magic whispers that I should.

I should stoop to his level and treat him the way he has treated the downtrodden citizens of both kingdoms.

I should give in to the call of powerful magic tumultuously twisting in my bones. For all it cares, everybody in this ballroom could be turned into mulch to line the soil of a better world.

I let out another shaky breath as Anerald glares down at his bloody knuckles. He hesitates in front of me, lost in the fact that I've had a physical effect on him. Me. Nobody from the lower city. The peasant, he threw in the dungeon. The boy who didn't realize he was meant to grow into a king, too.

A single person was never meant to bear this power. I'm shaking with the effort to hold the magic inside of myself. It's tempting me. To let go, to do the worst, to give in to the insidious power gathered in the forefront of my mind.

Instead, quietly, just for the king and me, I pose a question as a brilliant idea bursts forth from the darkness swirling through me. "Where is it that magic belongs?"

The rest of the room has taken enough of a break. The guards who have corralled Cam split into different factions again. An unnecessary number of them continue to hold her captive, while others circle Xander.

My Xander. Still trapped on that stupid stage.

His crutch is yanked out of his hold and thrown to the ground away from him. Guards openly heckle him. They've never respected him as the prince after watching the way his father treated him, and they're not going to start now.

Around the room, standing at the outskirts of the destruction, there are too many people watching this altercation with dwindling hope. The rebellion, the people who yearn for change, outnumber King Anerald's remaining cause. All of them watch as he hits me again.

I throw up a shield the third time he tries to strike, spit stringing from his lips as he screams at me to concede or watch my cousin die. Glitter bursts between us. A rainbow. A small display of magic in retaliation for the violence he offers.

For a moment, I'm lost in the rage-ridden gaze of Briargild's king. Dark brown. So much darker than what Xander's left eye used to be.

Anerald never answered my question. On my knees, my face screaming from the second punch and bleeding where his rings cut my cheek, I push myself back up in the shower of glitter.

"Do you think you can handle all of this magic?"

My taunt does exactly what I expected. Anerald roars. He throws another punch. Glitter sparks. I am untouched in the wake of his fury.

Something shifts in the watching crowd. Not quite a surge of hope. Their desperation has paused. I've changed where this story was heading.

Glowing in a swirl of every shade of the rainbow, I take a step towards Anerald. He's lost his daggers. He's lost his control of this situation. He's losing and not about to let that happen.

King Anerald Charming punches and grabs and snarls as I walk past him. His hands come away covered in glitter. I don't slow down.

My steps leave sparkling spots on the destroyed floor, a trail more permanent than breadcrumbs or flower petals.

Ahead, Cam has her head tilted. Her shoulders are being held by more guards, trying to stay strong for their failing king. The nearest plants bow their leaves and turn yellow, shrinking in the despair of their captured queen.

That second voice in my mind tells me to turn them into squashes. Not to threaten. Not even to warn. Just to make them into vegetables that will rot by the end of the cold season.

Cruelty cannot heal an already broken kingdom.

I cannot be the first king of Apricity in at least thirty years and act the same as the tyrant we're trying to break away from.

So, numbly, I let them hold her. I force my spine to stay straight. I meet the gaze of guards, nobles, servants, and rebels alike.

It seems like a good time to make a speech.

For the betterment of the world.

Anerald beats me there, though. I'm three steps from the stage. Refusing to let myself look to Xander in case I lose my carriage of thought and suddenly give in to the raging power in my veins because I cannot live another minute of him and Cam being openly abused, the other king's voice rings through the decimated ballroom.

"You think any of this makes a difference?" Anerald isn't speaking to me. His bellow passes me to pierce his son. "Magic didn't fix you, and this man won't, either. Ask him how he feels about you now that you gave up your magic and can't get out of that damned chair?"

Xander doesn't immediately respond. My eyes are on him now. He's been a pull on my focus from the moment I met him in an unlikely meadow in the woods. Now, I watch the confidence of a rebel leader, of a prince with secrets, of a man determined to change his world seep out of him. Tears sparkle in the corners of his silver eyes, his gaze permanently changed from his time with magic.

"You can't ask because you know. You have always known you lack worth without magic." Anerald, still in the center of the devastated ballroom, swings out his arms and directs his next question to the crowd. "Who here could accept Alexander as king?"

Coughs. Laughs. Sneers jump around the room. The people Anerald expected to be on his side.

There are so many more people here, though.

A young woman with red hair and a smattering of freckles steps forward from where she had been pressed back behind the overturned banquet tables, shaking off the hold of those near her to lift her chin. "I would accept him. Prince Xander has always been kind."

"Xander made sure we got food and clean water years back when your experiments with magic tainted the supply in the lower city," a centaur from the rebellion calls from the open doorway to the hall.

"That prince is the best thing you've ever done for Briargild!"

It goes on. A dam burst, a bomb going off to spill glitter into the surrounding universe, and the people raised their voices for Prince Alexander Charming. It's a crescendo of agreement. The rebels finally push the rest of the way into the ballroom. Cam manages to get back to her feet amid the scramble, her plants capturing the guards who held her down.

Anerald cannot quite control an entire kingdom.

He stands with his mouth open, his brows pinched in horrified understanding, as the battle shifts once more. Nobody openly attacks. They stand at the ready, though.

Xander has a hand over his heart. The community he fought to gather in secret is here, defending him after he dedicated his life to them. Anerald has dug his own grave, and I'm prepared to put the final nail in his metaphorical coffin.

"Your disability has never made me think less of you," I take the final steps to the stage, joining him at last.

My pumpkin guard pulls flowers from somewhere and hands them to me. Romance and rebellion have never gone together so well, but if we're going to change the world and be together, we may as well make a full statement now. A bouquet of daffodils in the dead of winter, I hold them and ignore the rest of the world to be here with him.

"I want a life in which I get to cherish you just as you are, Xander. No more secrets. No more trying to do things on our own. I see you, and I want to be there in every capacity you'll allow. If you wanted me to carry you up a mountain simply to see the sunrise, I would." My throat is fighting me, emotion suffocating me as guards nervously inch towards the exit, and Anerald scoffs behind me. "I wish I could turn back time and give you a better beginning, a family that understood your differences wouldn't define you. I wish I could undo all the pain, but I think there are a lot of people here who benefited from you turning out the exact opposite of your father." A cheer erupts in agreement, and I wait for it to fade before continuing my speech. "Since I can't take anything away, I just wish to get a tomorrow with you and, if you'll keep me, maybe the day after that, too."

Xander sits up straighter in his chair, a sniff the only punctuation between listening to me and bursting into his own statement. "You don't have to make wishes for me, Eli Cinderfella. I'm glad my magic went to you, and I would make that decision a hundred more times. If I get to choose to have a tomorrow with you, my answer will always be yes."

Gods. My heart. I would swoon if every fiber of my being wasn't shaking with the effort to hold onto magic that is prepared to leave me in insidious bursts.

Anerald has been oddly quiet.

Camellia yells.

I turn too late.

I shouldn't have dropped my shields. I was too busy looking at this man I love. Now, I can't unsee the tip of a sword sticking out of my chest.

29

I am a better pincushion than I have ever been a king. There is a sword in my chest, and so much glitter running down the front of me.

Glitter.

Not blood.

Xander is screaming my name regardless. He's trying to catch me, to cradle me, to be there when I need him most in all the ways he couldn't the last time Anerald stuck something sharp through my chest.

"Tell him again you're glad he came all the way here. Tell him you're happy to see him die," Anerald snarls, his hands releasing the sword he shoved through my back.

I'm not even sure how he got another weapon in here. Maybe I wasn't as thorough as I thought. That detail doesn't seem to matter as much as the fact that there's still no blood soaking through my shirt.

My knees do hit the ground. I am kneeling in front of my prince, and he's crying again. Gods, my heart. It's beating in my fingertips as I touch the rainbow pouring from my chest. Sound isn't quite reaching me. I'm not cold. I'm here. I'm right here in front of Xander.

He looks at me the way I must have looked at Skelly's disassembled bones.

Devastation makes a home on his brow.

"I will always be glad you came to save me," he says, voice cracking as the last of his self-control crumbles.

If he had his magic, this would be the time that roses would lash out to take down the rest of the kingdom. He would pull his father into the thorns and shred him. Xander would have stopped at nothing to dole out the pain he saw on my face.

Except, it doesn't hurt that badly.

There is still so much glitter.

Xander's hand is hot on my knuckles, pressing my palm into his thigh to steady me. I want to tell him that nothing could have kept me from him, but I'm distracted. I've already done this. I died and came back, and this is not what happened the first time.

Outside, the sun had already set. The last embers of the day saw our rebellion race in here, but it'll be the moon peeking through the wide windows of the ballroom that learns our fate. There is so much carnage in here. Plants stomped to green pulp. Chairs thrown and tables upended. Torn fabric from fancy dresses and feathers dropped on the cracked flooring as noble women fled without concern for their headpieces. Chaos overtook the ballroom, and now a soft sob fills it.

Everything is quiet besides sniffles and gentle cries, and I am lost to it all as I stare up at a man I have only begun to understand, but know that I would love in every version of life if we were allowed a chance to share it.

Prince Alexander Charming. The Necromancer. Xander. Just Xander.

We deserve more than a tragic end.

It's time we told a better story.

I'd like to believe in things like happy endings.

"Eli!"

A voice I didn't expect rings out across the devastated ballroom. Everything is silent besides heavy footsteps. My father is next to me in what feels like only two breaths, his shoes disturbing the glitter now dripping off the stage as it continues to spread and spread and spill from me.

He's not alone.

Gemma made it here, too.

And Wynnifred.

My support system surrounds me as I continue to watch in a daze of disbelief as magic soaks the stage. Anerald staggers back from it. Moving away from my father and the witch and my fairy godmother to move to Xander's side, he doesn't have any more cruel words to express.

Briargild's king has no idea what to do with so much magic.

Which gives me an idea.

One, I may not survive.

I look at each of the faces gathered around me. Gemma with rosy cheeks and snot and a croak for me to not do this to her again. Wynnifred beside me, silent and strong, her hand on my shoulder as though she can keep me from exploring further into the land of the dead this time. Xander, awash with grief and rage and horror and so much glitter spilling all over his lap. My father…

John Cinderfella. A regular guy with a dream to open a tavern who fell in love with an extraordinary woman from another kingdom. He keeps saying my name, his lips trembling and hands brushing my face.

"I need your help one more time," I whisper to him. "I need to get back to my feet."

Xander grips my hand tighter. "You can just stay. You-."

I squeeze his leg. "This ends today," I bite the words out in breathless huffs, the magic taking my thoughts with it as it continues to stream from my chest. "Anyway we can, right?"

We'd made a deal with each other. To end the suffering of the two kingdoms. No matter what it took. He's going to follow through on it now, glitter covering his hands and curling up his wrists and speckling his cheeks where it got caught in his tears.

Magic quietly returns to the forsaken prince.

"What do you think you can still do?" Anerald nears, his trepidation of the magic lessening as it spills and spreads and sifts around his arrogant steps without consequence.

My father has one of my arms looped over his shoulders. Wynn and Gemma support my other side. The sword continues to stick straight out of my chest as I step between Xander and Anerald.

There's one man I trust here to do what must be done.

I will always trust him.

I'll always love him.

Reaching into my pocket, I pull out the seed Wynnifred gave me back in the burned remains of Apricity. Round and simple. Nothing exciting. Just a regular seed holding an extraordinary secret.

Like everyone here.

The ballroom is bursting with people who care, people who have fought, and people who reminded me that love isn't the only ingredient to fixing things, but a starting point that we all need. They're each unique and extraordinary in their own ways. I plant my feet and hold the seed up for all of them to see.

The Heart of Apricity.

"Where is it that magic belongs?" I repeat, forcing myself to make eye contact with the graying king as he realizes what I'm holding and lunges forward.

"With me!"

Commotion comes from all sides of the ballroom. I don't look around. I can't. I shift the seed from up in the air to directly in front of the pointed tip of the blade, hoping Xander knows to hold me steady.

We have one shot at this.

"Magic belongs with everyone!"

Anerald tries to snatch the seed from me. Xander waits until the last moment, his grip on the hilt of the sword and the people at my sides the only thing keeping me from falling under the force of the king's assault. The blade pierces the Heart.

Through my chest, through the Heart of Apricity, and through Anerald.

Shock stalls the wicked king. We stand together, the Heart trapped between us as the slurp of the blade through his chest becomes the only noise in the ballroom. The red of his tunic darkens. Glitter sparks. Three different generations are skewered together.

It's time for the very last piece of my plan.

Squeezing my eyes shut, I ask the magic to leave. I wish it.

Magic isn't a finite source meant to be hoarded.

This power was meant to be shared and celebrated.

It should return to those who cherish it.

I honestly don't care as long as it leaves me and evades Anerald.

When it responds, when it does exactly as I wished, the stream of glitter becomes a flood. It tears out of my chest in an unstoppable flurry. Magic flees me all at once. My scream is the only sound I can hear over the torrent as the magic is ripped away from me in a thousand glittering bits.

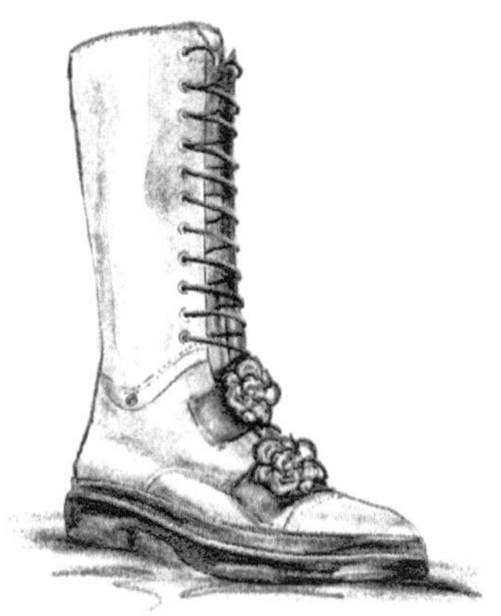

30

At this point, sacrifice should be easier, shouldn't it?

I expected it to hurt less the second time.

I thought for sure this decision to release magic back into the rest of the world would carry me back to the land of the dead, but I'm still conscious. My bones are brittle, and my muscles wither. There's too much space in my chest where magic was crammed into every crevice just moments before. I am empty and exhausted and still here.

The sword is gone.

The seed is gone.

My heart flutters in the cavernous space within my ribs.

Then, my name. Said a hundred times. Quickly. Quietly. Reverently. Hopefully. I suck in a breath that threatens to be my last. Dry and rasping. My eyes open. It takes me several confused moments to untangle the impossible sight around me.

Glitter touches every surface of the ballroom. There is no longer a roof. My body on the ground, thrown back from the release of magic collected between kingdoms, I stare up at the night sky and a thousand specks of stars to gather for this historic event. They twinkle at me as hushed voices tell each other that I'm alive, I'm awake, I'm still here with them.

Gently, so damn gently, hands cradle my face. "Hey, Cinderfella. You scared me there."

Xander. My Xander. His fingers tremble along the line of my jaw. He's on the floor with me. My head is in his lap.

"Did you grieve me so soon? You're the one who told me to always have a plan," I tease, forcing my arms to work so I can cover his shaking hands.

Here. I say silently, applying pressure between us until he believes this is real. I'm really still alive.

Somehow.

"You have never planned a day in your life," another voice joins in, my father, his arm thrown around Gemma.

It looks like they've been crying into each other for a few minutes.

I smile at him. A real smile. A happy smile. A smile that says I just perished and cannot believe he's siding with Xander instead of me.

Xander helps me sit up with a groan so I can see the rest of the mess. Glitter spilled from the flood I released coats the entirety of the oversized room. Dazzling blues are smeared on the walls and wrapped around golden light sconces that have cracked and dimmed. There's green on the floor, a gemstone shade that revived all of Cam's fallen plants into a glittering meadow. Pink shoots out from me in a jagged radius, marking the spot where I fell and staining the group that stood with me while every other color of the rainbow sticks to sleeves and collars and is brushed through the hair of the people that have remained.

"It's beautiful," Xander murmurs, his lips close to my ear.

Sore. Shaking. I stare at the mess I've made while he keeps a white-knuckled grip on me as though he alone can keep me from making stupid choices that tip my scales in favor of death.

Beautiful is definitely a word for it. Chaotic is another.

Everywhere, people test the bounds of their sudden power. The magic is spread thin. There's not enough in any one person to wish up whole gardens or dragons or create the kind of man-eating carriage disasters from my first moments as a magic wielder, but it's far more than most of them have ever known. There are giggles of astonishment and cheers as people fiddle with their fingers and watch the magic swirl through the air. Orange bursts and maroon sparks and purple puffs. A woman in the middle of a group of rebels holds up a single, yellow flower to her lover, who squeals and immediately puts it behind her ear. Small magics litter the air.

It is beautiful.

Kind Anerald is a stain in the middle of it all, though.

One hand extended, likely the one trying to grip the seed, his head tossed back in a roar of pain and surprise, his visage and that arm remain recognizable while the rest of him is blurred into the lines of a tree sprouting out of the ground. Mottled bark in dark tones with hints of color if one was curious enough to pry away the top layers. Bare branches reach up towards the open sky. A few buds of leaves to come are nestled among the twisting crown of limbs.

He is one with it. No longer a man but more a wooden carving fused to the Heart of Apricity and the tree that blooms from it. I stare for far too long before Xander clears his throat and squeezes my shoulder.

"Don't feel bad. He got what he wished for."

Right. Wishes. There's no way to predict exactly what will happen when a wish is granted, is there?

Still reeling from what I've done, refusing to move away from Xander, I'm surrounded by familiar faces. People from Apricity declared I was always the rightful king. People from the tavern agreed that I was special. A chorus of voices, and none of them are fully decipherable as I blink at the flurry of motion around me.

My ears are still not quite working. My throat is tight, and I lean into Xander for support. A lot has happened. More than I can possibly process in the seconds between people coming to speak to me.

The evening blurs around handshakes and hugs and pats on the shoulder, my legs slung over the edge of the stage so I can meet everyone without having to stand up. There are trinkets given to me. Others share stories about waiting for this day. I nod and blink and smile when it seems appropriate.

People keep calling me King Cinderfella.

Not Eli.

I'm not quite sure if I'm ready for that step, but I don't correct them. Xander's hands remain firm around me. He's caught in this hurricane of affection and attention, too. For every person I've touched in this journey, there are two more here to thank him, to tell him they're sorry, to ask what's next.

And I honestly don't know.

We didn't consider what would happen when Anerald fell. We

dreamed. We hoped. We hypothesized something like a relationship and a partnership in running these kingdoms in a more symbiotic system, but I don't think either of us truly believed we would be sitting here and having to figure out what the next step is.

I'm saved from the fourth person asking me that question by my father returning to my side. His own magic has flared the red plumage of forgotten birds. It stains his fingers, every attempt to corral the magic a quick and sudden failure that poofs into glitter that still sparkles in his beard as he approaches Xander and me.

"How are you doing, Eli?"

Nobody asked me that yet. I thought I was done crying. Blinking away the emotion, I stare at my hands and the lack of power itching just below the surface of my skin.

I died. I came back. I killed a king.

I gave up my magic for the greater good, and I feel like a chunk of my heart abandoned me.

I'm empty and confused and happy and hopeful and utterly overwhelmed.

My father crouches down and puts his hands on my shoulders. The way he met me after we'd been separated by magic. The way he held me before our fight that started this entire journey. The way he has always held me when I needed it.

"Your mother would be so proud of everything you've done. I will always be happy to see her in you."

A broken part of my heart sews itself back into place. He doesn't seem to mind anymore that I'm wild and unbidden like the magic floating in the air, like the woman whose legacy I've continued.

I don't mind, either.

My shoulders heat up under his touch. A familiar heat flares along my arms. Pink glitter gathers at my fingers. I let out a surprised hiccup.

Maybe magic hasn't completely left me.

I pull the locket out from under my shirt and open it to stare at the picture I've carried between two kingdoms. Adira Alcinder. Adira Cinderfella. The woman who started a revolution that hopefully now ends with me.

"What are we supposed to do next?"

I ask a question I wish she could answer. I wish I could hear her voice. Xander, though, is still at my side.

"We live. We do what we promised when this started, but, for now, I think we should rest. I know a guy with a room in a tower who might be willing to share with you."

My father helps me back to my feet as I blush at Xander's words. The two of us get Xander back into his wheelchair, and then the handles are in my grip, and the prince is directing me which way to go, while the rebels agree to get everything sorted in the ballroom.

Xander's right. We didn't die today. We get a chance to hold hands as the moon regales the stars with the story of how we got here. We do what we can, and we live for another night.

I'm pushing him over the grass that now fills the space when another voice screams my name over the general din of the crowded ballroom. It's a voice that has screamed at me in a tavern and yelled at me in the streets and from the depths of a hole in the forest. I would know my fairy godmother anywhere, and I turn back to see what she needs with the rest of the energy in my body.

Past my father, past the staggered groups of people playing with their fair share of magic, just past Gemma's elbow, a white shout appears. I leave Xander to fend for himself. My legs barely work. I stagger and stumble and shove past everyone in my way to get to that clacking jaw.

The dragon meets me halfway, nuzzling my face and wrapping himself around me as we fall to the floor. "Hey, Skelly," I murmur, hot tears falling on his skull as I hold him tight to me.

Once a combination of hundreds of bone pieces pulled out of a mass grave in the middle of the forest, Skelly is sturdier than ever. The places where his pieces fit together glitter with every shade of the rainbow. Much like the scar on my chest, he's been filled in with magic. Wriggling in my hold, he nips at my face and flaps his wings, the tapestry still needing to be repaired but dangling from a few strategic places by frayed threads.

I still don't know what we're going to do next, but my dragon is here, and hope filters back into my world as my fairy godmother crouches down to hug Skelly, too. The first dragon in centuries likes to be pet, scratched, and cooed over, and I let him have all of the attention he deserves. We might actually be okay after all.

It feels like hours later when I finally place my hand in Xander's and crawl off the floor to walk with him to his room, a dragon in tow and a kingdom irreversibly changed.

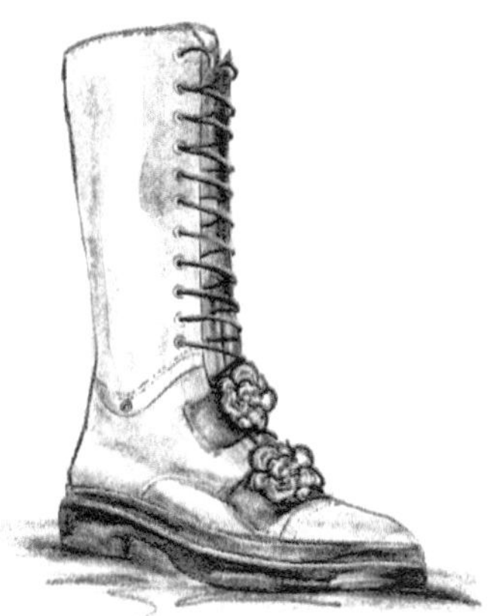

One Week Later

"You have to get out of bed if you want to make it to your own coronation, Mr. Cinderfella."

The blankets are pooled around my waist as I throw an arm over my face to hide from the already dressed man sitting at the foot of the bed. "You could come back to bed and I'll promise to put the crown on tomorrow?"

Rolling his chair to the side of the bed, he reaches out, not quite touching me as something playful dances through his silver eyes. "I'll let you wear the crown to bed while we-."

The elevator bell rings, cutting Xander off at an incredibly inopportune moment while my mind snags on what exactly he was going to promise instead of the looming responsibility on the lower floor. He pulls away before I can capture him and bring him back into the blankets, a green set that we've found to replace all the red of his previous bedspread. Laughing at what I can only assume is a frustrated and helpless expression on my own face, Xander blows me a kiss and starts to roll to the door.

"Please put on some pants, Eli."

I tease him that he's been bossier since stepping up as King of Briargild and then duck into the bathroom before he can respond, his deft fingers busy untying the elevator to let up our incessant guest. This room has become familiar. Our toothbrushes are both on the edge of the sink. I must have come in here a hundred times since that first bath after escaping my stay in the dungeon.

A week has passed, and I don't know how I lost track of all the time.

One moment, I was dead, fighting for mine and Xander's lives, making grand speeches against a tyrant, and now I've been in charge of finding new homes for the people of our joining kingdoms. There's so much destruction to fix, both physically and systematically, and I find myself stepping out of meetings early to walk the halls until I find Xander once more.

Gemma berates me for it.

I can't find the time to feel bad about wanting to be near him, with him, sharing this time with him when I was so sure it wasn't a real future for the both of us to work towards.

Both Briargild and Apricity will be there when I'm ready. Whatever the kingdoms are destined to become will wait while I take a few deep breaths. For now, I get to live.

There was a conversation the day after Anerald fell. A quick banter. A chance to give Xander and Cam their lives back, to rule as though tyranny had never bashed in the confines of their kingdoms. Without Anerald Charming, Cam could still keep her throne and…

She shut me up with a leaf to my lips. The throne was there. She retired, and the people were ready for me to take it.

I had worked hard to save them, and they wanted me to continue.

Besides, I wouldn't be King alone.

I had friends, family, and a prince becoming king to advise me on the intricacies of politics well above my skill level. I trace the memory of Xander's smile in my mind as I button myself into plain trousers and a white shirt, the sleeves rolled up to my elbows. Simple. Clean. Unembellished. Just a regular guy stepping into an incredible role.

Gemma has other ideas when I step out of the bathroom. I should have known she was the one threatening to barge into the room I share with Xander. "What do you think you're doing?"

I wave down at myself. "I'm dressed."

Blonde curls bounce around her shoulders as she mutters about me, and then Xander prompts her to hand me the box in her hands. "Harold and I worked on this for you. This is the kind of occasion you dress up for, Eli."

My life follows a circle of ribbon. I am once more standing with a wrapped gift from Harold. It's open in half a breath, and I stare down at the most beautiful ensemble.

"How did you do this in a week?"

Gemma waves me to put the vest on, the blue fabric easily sliding over my arms. "Again, we don't all need magic to do amazing things, Cinderfella. Sometimes love is enough to bridge that gap."

Throat tight, I fit the silver buttons into the holes and then run my fingers over the threads marking the entire, blue expanse. A tangle of light-blue vines weaves over the fabric. It's interrupted by leaves and flowers all in different shades of blue. It's the color I told Gemma gave me hope, and now I'm wearing it. My fingers find the single acorn squash done in cerulean tones over my heart. The beginning of my story and the expanse of how far I could still bloom.

My fairy godmother squeals when I lunge across the room to hug her. I twirl her in the soft, pink gown she's picked for the occasion. She doesn't complain when my exuberance leaves glitter trailed over her shoulders and shining in her dress.

"Come on. You're going to be late."

I let her wave us into the elevator, standing tall beside Xander in his black suit, the darkness broken by green embellishments. He's gorgeous. Gemma steals his attention, but I revel in the wink he sends my way before the door opens once again. The three of us chatter as we take the halls that have become a temporary home for me.

Change is still coming. It starts with this next step.

We don't head to the ballroom that is now a meadow holding the Heart of Apricity. We don't go to the throne room. Instead, we make our way to the library. I've learned Xander loved after an extensive tour through all the books he read about magic and happily ever afters, and the hope that he could find the same fate.

It's not the biggest room in the castle. Previous kings haven't spent as much time adoring stories as much as the one beside me now. It's enough, though. A small crowd parts as I enter the room and walk towards the front, where a silver crown sits on a writing desk.

Cam stands beside it. She shoos Xander to his spot in the front of the crowd. My father is there beside him. Our close friends and family and confidantes take up most of the rest of the space with a particular, bone dragon curled up by the fireplace on the left of the room.

The entire affair is only a few minutes. Cam says some words. She reads out of an old book. The crown is placed on my head, and I promise the people here, the people that didn't get a chance to make it to this part of the story, and those who have yet to come, that I'll do my best as the next King of Apricity.

There's applause. There's cheering. Xander is next to me, and nobody else leaves the room, all of them eagerly hushing each other.

"What's going on?"

Surrounded by good people, good books, and a good chance for our future, Xander grins up at me. "If a crown is all you wanted, I would be okay continuing our partnership for the betterment of our kingdoms, but, if you wanted more, more from me…"

Oh.

Oh my.

I know what's happening.

My heart is a fluttering thing. I shake my head at him, the weight of the crown so permanently there. "Are you about to ask what I think, or do you just fancy me in a crown?"

"You look great in a crown, Cinderfella," he laughs low and then pulls my hand to him, kissing me there in front of the room that quietly *oohs* and *aahs*, and somewhere, vaguely, I hear Gemma tell someone that she's the reason we're together. "But yes. I want to ask you the question we put off before.

"Marry me. Let's show the world that change can happen, and it starts because two people care about each other. Marry me, Eli Cinderfella, and I'll show you that fairy tales do come true. Just, please," his voice is a whisper and his hands tremble where he's holding me, "say you'll marry me?"

This is what it feels like to be happy, immeasurably so. The room around us doesn't move or shift or dare to make another noise. Everyone is waiting for my answer.

"There's not even a ring. How can I know you're serious?"

He chuckles. "Why don't we call this being even for you losing my shoes, and I'll find you a ring when the time is right? I'd like nothing more than to be bound to you, Eli Cinderfella, in life and politics and the hope for a better tomorrow."

"I love you, too," I murmur as I bend down, kissing him amid a raining cheer from the gathered remains of two kingdoms prepared to unite as one.

King Xander Charming pushes up into my embrace, one hand holding mine and the other cradling the back of my neck, and it's the stuff of magic. When we pull away to a call of congratulations and happy shouts and the very loud crying of my fairy godmother, he keeps a hold of me. I'm not sure what's next, but Xander is already two steps ahead of me, the man too good at making and keeping his plans.

"Our story is a little too big for one room, isn't it? Why don't we go outside?"

Crowned and engaged, my hands wrapped around the handles at the back of his chair, I follow Xander. We make our way through the rear end of the castle and through a door that leads to the gardens. A party has already started. There's food and music and so many people, but my attention is snagged on the actual gardens. It's not the way it looked when I set off that glitter bomb. Gemma points out a group of fairy godmothers who have lingered in the wake of Anerald's retirement and made grand changes.

The roses are gone. Every mark of Xander's rebellious magic, made cruel by his father's desire, has been wiped out of this area. Instead, there's a wave of purple and pink. Lilacs and carnations and camellias and hydrangeas. More flowers than I can name. It's a crashing display of the beauty magic can bring, of what the community can do while working together, and the change we hope to encourage in the years following this revolution.

Skelly prances in the reimagined gardens, plucking strands of greenery and flowers alike to fiddle with until some women agree to craft him a flower crown befitting the hero he's been. My father is sharing fairy wine with Harold and a group of rebels turned friends. Gemma is making her way to Wynnifred. Everything seems to be right. My heart is full as the sun sets on a full week of a changed Briargild. Befitted in the orange glow of those last rays of light, cheers call for Xander and me to join the dance floor set out just in front of the garden's entrance.

"I don't know if I have enough magic to stand right now," Xander confides when the music picks up with renewed vigor.

"I guess that means you'll have to let me lead."

Our laughter joins the chatter of the people as they move aside to let us into the middle of the dance floor. I step out from behind Xander's chair and dip into a bow like I've seen done before. He teases me for not knowing what comes next, whispering the steps of a dance I wouldn't have learned in all my time at my father's tavern, and then lets me show him some dance moves far from fitting for a king. Other couples begin to move and twirl and show off their excitement in dizzying displays.

Above, the first stars of the coming night spark and shimmer, begging for wishes to reach them. Puffs of glitter overtake the landscape as the people of our kingdoms continue to play with their connection to magic. I'm exactly where I'm meant to be. I spare the stars one last glance.

I don't think there's anything else for me to wish.

Xander is here.

My prince.

My king.

My fiancé.

I take his hand as my mind swirls with everything that has happened.

A wish gone awry has given me all of this.

A tavern keep now a king. A man no longer alone. A people freed and a future secured.

All the flowers of the garden sway with our celebrations.

We dance. We laugh. We relish the way our dream begins to look like a reality.

The End

Acknowledgements

First and foremost, thank you. You. Each and every reader who has picked up Wayward Magic and given this little story about revolution and love and hope a chance in a time when it is scary to talk about those things. Whether you were family and friends supporting this long coming dream, my initial pre-order campaigners who took a shot on a debut author, or simply a stranger stumbling upon this stunning pink cover and thought it sounded like a good time, thank you for reading. I hope Eli Cinderfella brought you as much joy as he has me.

I'd like to extend my appreciation to Jessika with Plush & Regal Press for all of the support and care and genuine enthusiasm she has poured into this project. Thank you for getting a book submission for a Cinderella retelling and not tossing it aside when I sent you a duel between some fool named Eli Cinderfella and a supposed Necromancer. You have changed my life and I will always be grateful for that.

Further, there are so many of you who have inadvertently touched this book and me over the course of my writing career, so I have to thank you, too. Thank you to those in my writing groups for listening to my bonkers ideas and telling me that I could make this story come to life and listening to that duel scene like thirteen times as I perfected it before sending it over to Jessika. Thank you to my parents for giving me an embedded love of stories and writing and not forcing me out of my room where I was scribbling fictional tales to go act like a normal person. Thank you to my counselors in both high school and college who told me to pick a more rational career because nobody was ever going to publish me, spite like hope is a secret ingredient important to success. Thank you to my friends who have let me talk their ears off about my silly characters and not treated me like a crazy person every time I referred to Eli like he was sitting right there beside me, for all of your efforts in DIYing cute things for Wayward Magic, and letting me sit in on your bookclubs.

Thank you to my beta readers. This book took a lot of drafts to get to a coherent place. I needed the comments and criticism as much as the cheerleading to get me through it.

Thank you to Stephanie for the design of this book cover, it is truly more remarkable than I ever imagined.

Thank you to A Seat at the Table Books for championing this novel and running a pre-order campaign with me. It was an absolute joy to do so.

Thank you to Bridgette for being there every step of this journey, from the moment Eli began to the moment it became a real book. You have helped me flourish as a writer more than you will ever know. I appreciate you for your steadfast belief that this could happen, for your amazing photography skills, and for simply being a beacon of hope every time I doubted myself.

Finally, thank you to my wife. A woman who not only held my hand through the ups and downs of this process, but acted as my very thorough editor and agent and social media director and (please insert everything else you did here because there are not enough end pages to this novel to give you enough credit). Fourteen years ago, you changed my life by becoming my best friend. Ten, you told me to never give up on this silly writing thing. Today, you are my inspiration and motivation for continuing and every reason I believe fairytales can come true. Thank you for doing this crazy thing with me.

about the author

A. D. Reece is a queer writer in Sacramento, California with a love of fantasy and fairytales. When she's not righting the mishaps of her protagonists, she can be found browsing local bookstores, creating fiber art, and sneaking away from her desk to see friends. She looks forward to creating more wayward stories brimming with magic and love to read to her wife.

about the publisher

Plush & Regal Press was started in 2024 by Jessika Raisor and Trent Lindsey. We are a queer-owned, micro-press nestled in Amish Country, Ohio. We are an Artist-First company— meaning we recognize there are no books without the storytellers.

If you are interested in shopping more from P&R, visit **www.plushandregal.press**

www.ingramcontent.com/pod-product-compliance
Lightning Source LLC
Chambersburg PA
CBHW020257030826
48979CB00026B/1333/J

* 9 7 9 8 9 8 8 2 0 9 6 4 5 *